A JOB TO DIE FOR

The girl was still there, virtually running on the spot. Her face was turned away from the water, and she was pounding her breast, yet hardly moving through exhaustion, her shoulders bowed and her thin chest heaving. Long locks of black hair poured from the knot on top of her head like waterweed. And the loose white shift could not disguise the emaciated outline of her body, making her seem more wraithlike than human.

Kate shut her eyes consciously for a second time, knowing that if the girl was real, she would have to do something to help . . .

Why had she felt such fear?

Also by Lis Howell and available as Coronet paperbacks

After the Break
The Director's Cut

About the author

Lis Howell was born and educated in Liverpool and has worked in television for many years. After starting at BBC radio in Leeds, she became a TV reporter, presenter and producer, then Head of News at Border TV, going on to be managing editor of Sky News. She was the first Director of Programmes for GMTV, served after that as a producer on 'Good Morning with Anne and Nick' and is now Director of Programmes for UK Living, the cable and satellite channel. *A Job to Die For* is her third novel.

A Job to Die For

Lis Howell

CORONET BOOKS
Hodder and Stoughton

Copyright © 1997 by Lis Howell

First published in Great Britain in 1997 by Hodder and Stoughton
First published in paperback in 1997 by Hodder and Stoughton
a division of Hodder Headline PLC

A Coronet paperback

British Library Cataloguing in Publication Data
Howell, Lis
A job to die for
1. English fiction – 20th century
I. Title
823.9´14[F]

ISBN 0 340 68222 1

Printed and bound in Great Britain by
Caledonian International Book Manufacturing Ltd, Glasgow

Hodder and Stoughton
A division of Hodder Headline PLC
338 Euston Road
London NW1 3BH

To all at UK Living and UK Gold

I would like to thank Martin Brown, Dr Rod Jones of Silloth Health Centre, Matthew Jones, Andrea Sullivan and Anne Manson for their help.

CHAPTER ONE

It was the beginning of April and the south of England, even at this early hour, lay stunned by a freak heatwave. The day was dawning over London in Mediterranean style, but alongside the canal, the sun bounced off the banks without penetrating the dark earth.

There was surprisingly little debris in the green water. Even at the height of summer this dark, dank stretch of water failed to attract many strollers. The light could only reach just one bank, and today the lurid colours of the few crisp packets and plastic bags on the bright towpath were muted by condensation. The other bank was as dark and cold as winter, hiding its secrets, so that the body bobbed suddenly into view in the sunshine as it floated lazily from one side of the narrow canal to the other. On the sunny side, it seemed to shine like a fat balloon, the soaked clothes taut with trapped air. In the shadows it lurked, hardly visible under the black parapet of the darkened towpath.

In the distance, a truck rattled over the bridge, intent on some early delivery. Its thoughtless noise set up a disturbance which caused the body to turn slowly round. It drifted to the dark side, where it waited, patiently, like a bloated reptile, to be discovered.

A few miles away Kate Wilkinson stood on the tree-lined suburban pavement feeling elated. The air was light and clear and Kate wanted to shout 'Good morning!' rather than tiptoe to her car. It was a long gentle road leading down to the Thames, with balconied villas, Edwardian semis and neo-Georgian town houses nestling up to stretches of renovated terraces. And at seven o'clock in the morning it was silent.

Kate was on her way to work, and had left her lover smiling in bed with the sun dappling through the makeshift curtain. She was sure she had never felt so happy in her life. There was only one more thing she hoped for, and if she was right, that too might be happening. She stopped adding up the weeks again. By the end of the day, she would be almost certain. Every hour it was more likely . . .

She braced herself to open the car door and rip up the calm with the ignition, but something stopped her. She looked up. Her lover was framed in the bedroom window flourishing something black and frilly at arm's length. Kate's eyes widened and then she started to laugh as she realised what he was holding.

The previous evening, back at her own place, Kate had rifled through some old clothes to be sorted out for when she and John moved in together. In an orgy of clearing, determined to define her new life by what she chucked away, she'd come across the basque. She had bought it sometime in the early eighties. It had a plunge neck and rigid underwired cups that puffed up her breasts like choux pastry. To prove she could still do it, she'd squeezed herself into it. By the time she'd arrived at the house she could hardly breathe, and when she'd undressed, John looked alarmed rather than aroused. He should have peeled it off her in one seductive move but he failed to find the zip, and went for the fake laces instead.

'Idiot!' Kate gasped as she undid it herself. When they'd stopped laughing, they abandoned it on the floor and forgot about it. Until now. John was expecting the builders that morning and the bedroom was an empty shell without cupboards or wardrobes, with his few clothes stored in plastic bags. Now Kate had visions of the corset thing lying on the floor for the joiner to walk around.

'Stuff it in a bag, I'll get rid of it later,' she mouthed at John, trying not to laugh out loud. Then she noticed John's eyeline flicker, and turned to see why. One of the neighbours had been out walking his dog, and was now transfixed, staring up at the window where the new vicar was waving women's underwear.

Kate laughed out loud as John disappeared from view, then she turned to give the neighbour her most engaging smile. She was rewarded by his amused nod, and felt relieved because in a few months she would be moving in as the new vicar's wife.

Still smiling, Kate started the engine and negotiated the parked vehicles clogging the road. Then she punched one digit into her carphone to connect her to the converted warehouse where her new career was based.

Until a few weeks earlier, she had been a freelance producer in cable TV. Then she'd had her first professional break in years, and was still feeling the nervousness which unexpected success can bring. But John had insisted that it wasn't just luck.

'You're good at your job,' he'd said sternly. 'Why shouldn't you be offered a great opportunity?'

'Because media isn't like that. And I'm suspicious when everything goes right. Within a few months, you get a parish in London, and I get a fantastic new job. Why should we be so fortunate?'

'Why not? After everything that's happened, Kate, perhaps you deserve it.'

Kate had wondered about that, but she wasn't arguing! The breeding frenzy in cable television had begun and everyone wanted to start new channels. As one of her colleagues had remarked, new digital TV was offering more openings than Cynthia Payne, and one of her patrons from the past was investing in the future. So Kate Wilkinson had been approached to become the General Manager for the embryonic Food and Health TV Channel, due to launch that September. She still woke up suddenly in the night sometimes, wondering how it had happened, and trying to assess whether it was a challenge or a professional suicide bid. One of their ebullient American shareholders had said with devastating objectivity, 'This is a great chance, but if we don't get it together fast, it'll be over before it starts!' His ruthlessness was tempered by good nature, but Kate felt the pressure twist like a tight waistband.

She had racked her brains over how to staff the project on the tiny budget. She needed someone at her right hand whose intelligence and drive would make up for the experience she could not afford to buy. She fervently hoped she had found the right person. Having pressed the pre-set key, Kate listened to the tinny drone of the phone ringing out at the other end until it was answered by a slightly breathless voice.

'Hello, Jenny Sims.'

'Jenny! You shouldn't be there so early, but I thought you might!'

'Oh, I'm only here because I couldn't sleep after my first

experience of late-night shopping, London-style. I had no idea just how many men you could find on one meat counter! Talking of which, what's the difference between a man and a supermarket trolley?'

'I don't know, what?'

'The trolley has a mind of its own.'

'Very funny!' Jenny was a friend whom Kate had taken on as her deputy, and for whom she had great respect. But instead of feeling amused, Kate felt uneasy. Jenny had wisecracked or snapped continuously since moving to London a fortnight earlier. It seemed to be her way of hiding her nervousness, but Kate had remembered Jenny as warm rather than sharp.

They had met the year before at Northern TV. Kate had escaped there for a while after resigning from a London network company, and her own crisis of confidence and Jenny's insecurity had made them firm friends despite the difference in their ages. It was an unusual friendship which Kate valued. She hoped she hadn't spoilt it by asking Jenny to work for her.

Jenny Sims was in her mid twenties, still slight and rather intense, and she had resisted fashion to keep her long thick curly hair in Rossetti ringlets. But eighteen months' intensive experience in TV had made her face more sculpted, and her eyes wary. She was highly intelligent but her brightness was easily dimmed if someone else stood in her light, and Kate knew she needed nurturing.

The phone crackled. There had been a long silence and Kate realised that Jenny was waiting on the other end for her to go on.

'Sorry, Jenny. I wondered if the artwork for the channel logos arrived last night after I left?'

'Well, I'm a bit worried. The storyboard is here, but there's no sign of the tape . . .'

'Oh, dear, never mind. What are the pictures like?' Kate hoped she didn't sound too anxious herself. After all, she was the boss.

'They're great! We just have to hope they look as good on tape as on paper. And more good news. We got a fax last night from Northern TV. They'll start negotiations to sell us the "Cook of the North" series.'

'Great! It'll be hard getting them to agree to sell it for a price we can afford. But at least they're talking. Well done for asking them. I'll phone Northern TV at nine o'clock.'

'Couldn't I do that?'

'Oh, I don't think so. Not yet. Wait till you've had a bit more experience. Thanks anyway.'

Jenny said a subdued goodbye, and Kate felt uncomfortable. She was aware that the younger woman was unhappy but, as manager, Kate had to do what was best for the project as well as what was exciting for Jenny. They had discussed trying to buy 'Cook of the North' and Jenny had been keen to make the opening moves. But the real negotiation for the rights to something as prestigious as this programme would be delicate, and in Kate's opinion, Jenny was not yet quite ready for that.

After ten minutes, Kate realised she had reached the A4 without even knowing it. Driving through the suburbs so early in the morning was almost restful, past the lush gardens round houses varying from the mock Tudor to the real Victorian. But when the back roads gave way to clogged lanes of impatient cars, like shiny coloured beads shunting in clusters down a thread, she needed her wits about her. She was about to accelerate forward when a boy racer in a beaten-up van swerved in front of her, waving cheerily. She was tempted to wave back, but the van had gone before she could even think about it. Then it was her turn to cut across the traffic, with rather less panache, and she turned off into a lattice of terraced streets, towards Brentford. For the next few minutes, driving took up all Kate's concentration. In this urban jumble it was perfectly possible to lose your bearings. The only sure point of reference was the river, an unseen presence somewhere to the right, breaking up the buildings with a hint of feathery foliage and the sense of translucent sky.

But Kate was heading towards the canal.

On the left-hand side before the bridge, a huge white shiny sign proclaimed 'Canal Bank Project. Superb Office Accommodation in Sensitive 19th Century Style Renovation'. Underneath, a poster hung on with its corner flapping to announce 'The Warehouse Office Block. Sq. footage still available. Apply Canal House'.

Kate drove straight on, to pick up the papers at the newsagent's before going to the office. The other side of the canal bridge had escaped 'sensitive renovation', and in a way seemed more

Dickensian to Kate. A terrace of squat brick buildings, once labourers' cottages, was now hacked into shop fronts gleaming with Special Offers, but they clustered under dusty flat frontages more than a hundred and fifty years old. Behind them another half-derelict warehouse loomed, absorbing the light and casting the opposite bank of the canal into deep day-long shadow. Kate stopped outside the newsagent's where the pavement was filled by the round backside of Mr Chandip. He pulled himself upright and started to heave a pile of newspapers into the shop. Kate could tell by the way he strained ahead of her that he was later than usual, and vexed. She stopped here every morning for the dailies, and the numerous health and food magazines Mr Chandip ordered for them.

'Morning, dear,' Mr Chandip called. 'I'm behind schedule today.' He tutted. 'We had a lot of disturbance here last night.'

Mr Chandip and his family lived over the shop, and despite their short acquaintance he tended to confide in Kate his worry over western ways. His complaints were always about activity on the towpath, where he believed kids or lovers or sex professionals – all equally scandalous to Mr Chandip – gathered in degenerate droves.

But this time, something drew her attention away and she lost the thread of his remarks, distracted by a strange sound. She turned around to see where it was coming from, but her eyes were dazzled as she turned. Yet she continued to peer painfully into the gloom opposite because the noise disturbed her. It had a compelling rhythm, soft but intense. Kate squinted, and narrowed her eyes.

The angle of the sun caught only the top windows of the Ware-house opposite, the panes so bright that the black silhouette looked like a cardboard cut-out. Kate blinked. She put her hand to her fore-head, visor style, but was aware that the hand was shaking. What had she seen? She took a few steps forward to look.

And the running figure was still there. It hardly seemed to move, for all the appearance of urgency. It was a girl, struggling along beside the Warehouse, in soft relief against the black shadows. She seemed to be trailing her dress, her hand clutched to her bosom like a distraught Victorian virgin in flight.

Kate refocused. But the girl was still there, virtually running on the spot. Her face was turned away from the water, and she was pounding her breast, yet hardly moving through exhaustion, her shoulders bowed and her thin chest heaving. Long locks of black hair poured from the knot on top of her head like waterweed. And the loose white shift could not disguise the emaciated outline of her body, making her seem more wraithlike than human. Kate shut her eyes consciously for a second time, knowing that if the girl was real, she would have to do something to help. As she stood with her eyes closed, her imagination snatched at half-remembered stories of suicidal factory hands or servant girls drowning their unborn shame. Kate breathed deeply, and told herself to calm down. To her intense relief, when she opened them, the figure was gone. But at the same time, the disappearance made Kate feel seriously shaken. She shuddered so violently that Mr Chandip put out his hand to her.

'You all right, miss? Here's your parcel. More than usual. Can you manage?'

'What? Oh, sorry, Mr Chandip. I thought I saw a girl, running . . . but it was horrible . . .'

'Oh, this jogging! I think it very silly myself. They are asking to be mugged or worse. And the clothes . . .'

'No, no, this wasn't a jogger, this was . . .' Kate faltered, wondering just what she had seen.

'Oh, those young girls, with their cans of lager and their loud voices! Don't talk to me about young girls today . . .'

No, I don't think I will, Kate thought. Mr Chandip was clearly thinking of a very different type of young animal from the wraith Kate had seen. She felt the sun burning the back of her neck, and she physically relaxed to let the warmth flood her body. She had been tensed, fighting the heat, squinting into the dark. 'I'm sorry, Mr Chandip, I'm in another world this morning.'

'Oh, busy lady. Now please take these papers from me before my arms give way. I think carrying all those exercise magazines is what keeps you fit!' he chortled.

Kate laughed with him, her voice sounding false and patronising, which she hated. But she needed to respond to him and to hear her own pointed laughter. Then she staggered back to the car and dumped the papers on the front seat.

She could smell the warm twentieth century aroma of leatherette.

Already, she was making the vision of the girl recede. It *had* to. A pickup truck hurtled aggressively over the bridge, horn blaring because Kate had parked half an inch too close to the main road. The canal caught the sun and glistened like wet silk, and Kate made herself think of John and normality.

Why had she felt such fear? The running girl had deeply disturbed her. The whole scene had seemed both sinister and unreal. She straightened her back, started the engine and drove back over the bridge, down to the bright glass automatic doors of the Warehouse.

Matthew Lavelle liked the smell of the gym now, though the first few times he had thought, phew, what a whiff. Inside it was brighter than the day outside, where the early sunshine still left huge black shadows behind. But here in the large square room the neon strips flushed the light from floor to ceiling with no cowardly shade allowed. It was designed to illuminate every glossy muscle and make every piece of metal gleam.

Matthew raised a hand in greeting, and the two trainers in turquoise shell-suits acknowledged him. He noticed the nod of approval that he earned. Then he turned into the changing room, put his bag in the locker, and took off his track-suit top. The previous day, in his lunch hour, he had popped into the local sports-wear shop and bought a black vest with cutaway sleeves. Turning his head to one side in the pretence of warming up his neck muscles he could see his traps, as he'd learnt to call his shoulders. The new thin black straps showed up the bulges in relief much more than the old grey tee shirts he had worn before. His shoulders had never been so broad nor his pecs so sleek. He was changing weekly, and he hadn't realised he was the core of such a malleable frame. The previous height of physical response . . . the stretch of his running muscles, the force of kicking a ball, the tingling excitement of erections and the satisfaction of smooth functioning bowels, all seemed trivial compared to the realisation that he had the power to change his body shape.

He walked back into the gym, swaggering. Then he picked up the skipping rope and twisted it over his head. It cracked on the floor and his feet flexed and leapt, his legs taut, his eyes closed, and his body moving lightly at his command.

When he finished his whole routine, he came out of the shower with his towel loosely round his waist, feeling slightly contemptuous of the lads who had only just arrived in the changing rooms. They looked unshaven and unkempt compared to him.

'Hi, Matt,' said one of them, with whom, months ago, he used to go drinking. Matthew grunted back and murmured, 'Putting on the pork, mate?'

'Yeah,' sighed the other man. 'Better get back on the weights.' Then he stood up and scratched his testicles, so the flab of his lower stomach welled for a moment. Matthew couldn't understand how he could be so cheerful about backsliding.

'Coming for a drink for a change?' said the other man.

'I don't think so,' Matthew replied.

'Oh, you've pulled have you?'

Matthew looked back at him. 'No,' he said without embarrassment. His previous 'pulling' exploits seemed to him now like the fumbling of Mr Blobby. It occurred to him fleetingly that the last time he had had sex was when he and this clown had met two less than fragrant girls in The Narrowboat. He ought to think about doing it again, now he was looking so good, but this time with a classier partner. He felt activity in his groin, the sort of unexpected physical response that annoyed him now, and he turned away quickly.

'OK, sod you then,' he heard the other man say. But Matthew was busy unpacking his work clothes, and pulling on his new briefs. The other man had gone by the time Matthew zipped up his flies, but he wasn't concerned. He didn't have time for arsing about now. Not with training, and his job as Deputy Facilities Manager at the Warehouse TV Centre.

He walked outside, head high in the morning sun, and clicked the remote control to unlock the doors on his car. His arms rippled continuously into the smooth working of the machine and with ease and precision he drove over the canal bridge and down to the Warehouse. There, he waited patiently behind the head of the Food and Health Channel who was struggling to back into her space. Then in one manoeuvre he placed his car perfectly in the bay next to hers.

*

Jenny Sims stood by the window in the huge empty open plan first floor office of the Warehouse, looking down to the sunny courtyard. She saw her boss, Kate, parking laboriously, and then she watched Matthew Lavelle swivel his long legs out of his car next to her. Only Jenny, Kate, their three researchers and a bored receptionist were located in the Warehouse itself, and normally Matt would have strode away to his offices in the administration block, which had been old stables, and which ran at right angles to the main building. But today she saw him offer to carry the papers for Kate, who handed him the bundle which he tossed casually onto his shoulder. Jenny heard their footsteps clatter over the cobbles as they made for the main building. She wondered fleetingly if someone at Matt's level worried about letting out the Warehouse. It still smelt of fresh paint and prospects, but there was an underlying scent of emptiness settling in. West London was full of other exciting and interesting new office blocks, and this one should have been busier. Jenny wondered what was keeping tenants away.

She continued to look out of the floor-to-ceiling window, which flooded their space with light, and didn't wave back to Kate, who had raised her hand. Jenny felt resentful over the 'Cook of the North' negotiations. She admitted grudgingly to herself that perhaps Kate was right and that she needed more experience before attempting to bargain with an ITV company. But she didn't want Kate to treat her as untried, like the others who worked on the channel. Jenny was aware of the confusion in her own mind. At the same time as wanting to be independent and adult, she was jealous of the attention Kate gave the office juniors.

Jenny had tried to understand Kate's problems. Staffing a project like Food and Health TV was fraught with difficulties. Kate had told her that she had been inundated with letters as soon as the potential launch of Food and Health had been noted in *Broadcast* magazine. Most of the unsought applicants were kids from college. Frequently they had enough parental influence to get work experience in small TV companies, where they acted as unwaged slaves for the sake of the great opportunity. But Kate had been determined not to let that happen here.

Jenny could see the whole team in her mind's eye. Kate, forty-something with shoulder-length auburn hair, had chosen to sit in the middle of the wide open plan office. Chloe Carr, in her early twenties, sat in the corner, tall and slender, with a white face and cropped black bob, wearing a Yin and Yang earring and a bolshie air so as not to seem grateful. At the next desk sat plump, bulging Debbie Allen, a little older and by contrast a positive jelly of gratitude, with her lank hair and pale spotty face. And then there was neat, conventional Laurence Smith, a former telecoms engineer who had decided to go into TV. He was twenty five going on fifty, and if anyone deserved a prize for keenness it was Laurence, though he was as devoid of imagination as the mug on his desk.

They all tended to rattle round in the empty premises, a little group who hardly knew each other yet, but already there was a dynamic between them, and it was not always positive. Jenny felt as if she was neither management nor worker, and that her uncertainty was really Kate's fault.

People had already made efforts to mark out their territory with their things. It was fascinating, Jenny thought, to see how their roles and aspirations were defined by desk top objects. Kate had least personal clutter because she was most established. Debbie had two overflowing desk tidies full of multi-coloured pens and pencils and rubbers. Chloe had a pottery ash tray, although it was a no smoking building. And on Laurence's desk, all in immaculate order, were the necessary files and forms, with one token personal object, a mug displaying a pig in Y-fronts, in the exact centre of his own black drip mat. In the emptiness, Jenny felt as if the objects were as meaningful as the people. She looked at Chloe Carr's ashtray with particular loathing.

Behind Jenny, Kate and Matthew Lavelle swung through the double glass doors from the landing. Reluctantly Jenny turned round. Matt had dropped the papers on Kate's desk, and was still standing there. Jenny had seen him from a distance before, but had never actually looked at him. He had a classic body which bulged in a way she found disconcerting. There had been no men at Northern TV with the same sort of smooth tan and cultivated good looks and Jenny still tended to assume well-groomed men were effeminate. She was prepared to dismiss Matthew Lavelle, but suddenly he smiled rather self-consciously at her over Kate's head, before turning to walk away.

Kate had sensed the atmosphere, and said nothing more than 'Hi, Jenny'. She was busy cutting the string round the bundle from the newsagent, then almost involuntarily she said 'Ouch' and straightened up.

'Hi. You OK, Kate?' Jenny had meant to sulk, but Kate's sharp exclamation of pain surprised her.

'Yes, fine. I feel a bit tired, actually. And I saw something weird this morning . . .' But to Jenny's annoyance Kate stopped talking to her, bit her lip, and put her hand to the small of her back. Jenny turned back to the window.

'Hiya!'

Plump, spotty Debbie Allen was naturally quiet and had come in unheard. Now she stood behind the two senior women, a bulky figure in her shapeless budget clothing, seriously proffering a Prêt-à-Manger bag.

'I picked these up at the shopping parade.' Her timid voice with its Manchester accent took the sting out of the atmosphere like blotting paper. It was hard to resent the blob-like Debbie.

'Ooh, thanks.' Jenny grinned encouragingly at her. 'Chocolate croissants. Very appropriate for the Food and Health Channel!! Where's yours, Debs?'

Debbie Allen brushed some crumbs off her bulbous black jumper and said, 'I ate mine on the way. Couldn't wait.'

Jenny laughed. 'You did? You've got no inhibitions about your figure, have you, Debbie? Not like me! I've put on three pounds since I've been in London.'

'You don't need to worry about that,' the plump girl murmured ruefully, patting one of the many bulges in her jumper.

'I don't know!' Jenny said. 'To be honest, I'd like to lose more weight.'

'But not too much. Looks aren't that important,' Kate said with a laugh, but she was suddenly aware she was being excluded, and that despite her smile the others had sensed a censorious edge to her voice. Why was managing people so much more difficult than it appeared?

'Oh no?' Jenny's tone hung on the fringe of irritation. 'Tell me that when we see the first bald President of the USA.'

Well, what about Gerald Ford, Kate wanted to counter, but she was nervous of the younger woman saying 'who?'. She and Jenny both seemed to be teetering on the brink of a row, which Kate desperately wanted to avoid. So she chose to laugh. The room was large and empty enough to turn the sound into an echo. There had been some suggestion of subdividing the room into smaller offices, but Kate had made a decision to sit with everyone else. Her staff numbers were so small that she thought it might be ridiculously hierarchical to cut herself off. She had imagined a close, family atmosphere in the big room. But it hadn't happened and now she found she was laughing alone.

The arrival of the other female researcher, as always making a late entrance, added to the strained atmosphere.

'Good morning, Chloe,' Kate beamed and Jenny raised her eyes to heaven. Why Kate always treated Chloe like the prodigal daughter she did not know. Jenny believed Chloe had taken advantage of Kate's conscience, and she suspected that the girl in her tiny shiny A line skirt and sawn-off top was more interested in spending time in the ladies' loo with her make-up bag than viewing tapes or learning to schedule programmes.

This morning Chloe was on form. She screeched, 'Where's our token man, Mr Laurence Smooth? I'm thirsty and I want a coffee. He's late, isn't he? If this goes on he'll never be a Chief Executive before he's thirty.'

Kate couldn't help smiling, although Jenny refused to catch her eye. Chloe's sharp tongue often hit on the truth. Laurence was helpful and organised, and made no secret of the fact he wanted to be an executive. He would undertake any task with cheerfulness, which was why he made the morning coffee. He was unmoved by the all-female office, even when Chloe told her favourite anti-male joke in a loud voice, screeching, 'What do anniversaries, toilet bowls and clitorises have in common? Men miss all of them!'

Laurence Smith had smiled, but immediately turned the conversation back to digital distribution. He had never mentioned a girlfriend – or boyfriend for that matter. 'He thinks a clitoris is a BT widget,' Chloe Carr had moaned.

Kate was concentrating on her computer, but she was thinking about Chloe's remarks. Chloe was right, Laurence was usually one of the first to arrive. Where was he? Then Kate was distracted by the pain happening again. She felt a wrenching ache in her stomach, and looked back at her computer screen and willed the sensation to stay away. It had just been cramp because she was sitting awkwardly. She shifted in her seat. But the next stabbing pain in her back was unmistakable. Kate stood up sharply, then snatched up her bag and made for the double doors.

Strange, thought Jenny. There was obviously something wrong. Kate looked genuinely distressed and Jenny felt a rush of the old affection. She waited a moment, and then stood up herself and followed Kate to the loos. One of the three stalls was occupied.

'Kate?' she said tentatively.

'What?'

'You OK?' asked Jenny.

The toilet flushed, the door swung open and Kate came out. Her face was white, but Jenny thought it was more from anger than pain. Kate moved unsteadily past her and gripped the wash basin.

'What's up, Kate?'

'Nothing. Just my period, actually. A week late.'

'Well, that's a relief,' Jenny said brightly, trying to help.

'A relief? Good God, Jenny!'

'What? You mean you aren't pleased?'

'No! I'm not.'

'Oh!'

Kate looked at Jenny's astonished face. And I'm crying, Kate thought in horror. I'm the boss, and I'm crying in the toilets because I'm not pregnant. The fact she was being so weak made her cry more. She was aware of how ugly she was, snivelling as she tried to wipe away the tears and the matted mascara like tyre marks under her bloodshot eyes.

'God, Jenny, this is so stupid. Leave me alone. I'll be all right. Really.'

'No, Kate, I'll wait with you. I'm sorry, but I'd no idea! It just never occurred to me.'

'Well, perhaps it is ridiculous, at my age!'

'No, Kate, I didn't mean that! It's just that I thought everything was perfect for you now!'

'But that's exactly it! Everything's right, for the first time in my life. So why not this? Since I sold the flat we've even got enough money!'

'But it doesn't always happen straight off, does it? I mean, perhaps next time . . .'

'Next time. Next time? This is the sixth month. All these years I've stuffed myself with rubber and wire and swallowed chemicals, and then when I'm in the right place at the right time with the right man, nothing. NOTHING, except blood!! I can't believe it. And it's not as if it hadn't happened before! What sort of God does the Reverend John Maple think exists, who would get revenge out of doing this to me?'

Aware of what she was saying, Kate stopped suddenly. 'Oh, Christ, Jenny, I shouldn't have said that. I really didn't mean it. And I know there are far worse things than not having a baby. But other people can do it! I'm so *angry*.' She kicked the wash basin pedestal. 'Look, I kick this bloody sink and I no sooner want to do it than I've done it and the porcelain is shaking. My body does everything I want it to do, when I want to do it. All except conceive! I feel like the walking wounded, but no-one can see the damage!' She stopped abruptly when Debbie Allen's moon face peered round the door.

'Oh . . .'

'We're just talking about periods,' Jenny said quickly. The girl looked blank, smiled diffidently and scurried past into the toilet. Then she reappeared, to wash her small, surprisingly thin hands. Like a lot of shapeless people, Jenny thought, Debbie Allen had one feature that was beautiful, and in her case it was her long tapering fingers and perfect nails. Then, like a little fat mouse, she hurried out.

Kate put her head down over the basin. Then she gasped her breath back, and said, 'So that's that, Jenny. Let's change the subject. Talk to me about something else, anything else, while I pull myself together.'

'OK.' Jenny paused. 'You mean anything?'

'Yes. Preferably something practical and professional so I can come back to earth.' Kate leant her back against the cool tiled wall.

'Well . . .' Jenny started warily. This was possibly the only chance to claw back the closeness she and Kate had once shared. If she let this go by, Kate would probably glide upwards on the escalator of management and be on a different floor for ever.

'Look, Kate, there is actually something I ought to say to you.

I should have mentioned it earlier, but . . .'

Kate still held her head down and her voice echoed up from the washbasin. 'I realise it's not been that easy for you, Jenny. I'm sorry.'

'I'm sorry too. Look, the problem is that I feel you're far too protective of the juniors, and too distant with me!'

Kate still kept her head down, but the surprise of what Jenny was saying was distracting her from the wrenching ache. 'Distant? Surely not, Jenny. And if it seemed that way, I didn't mean it.'

'I realise that. At least, I hope so. But that was how it looked to me.'

'You know that keeping you at arm's length is the last thing I would want. You're my deputy, for goodness sake!'

'Yes, but it doesn't seem like that while we're all bunged in together. Kate, it's madness your sharing the open plan office with us. To be brutally honest, the researchers don't want to feel the boss hanging over them. But sometimes I do! I'm the one that needs a bit more attention! You need to make it clear that I matter!'

Kate lifted her head up, steadied herself, and took a minute to think, remembering her own forced laughter echoing round the office a few minutes earlier. Perhaps Jenny was only asking for what she, Kate, as a good manager, should have offered in the first place – a small indication of status. Kate felt physically sorry, as if her stomach ache was a practical reminder. Here she was, trying to be the perfect boss and she had hurt the person who mattered most. She reached out and touched Jenny's arm.

'You're right, Jenny. I haven't been thinking straight. Perhaps I *should* have an office, and you should have some space of your own. I can see what you mean.'

'You can?'

'Of course. God, you must think I'm so insensitive! Look, let's go back now and think about where we could put some partitions. Then you can go and see Matt Lavelle about it. I do understand. It would be better.'

Jenny breathed out, relieved. 'Thanks, Kate. You won't regret it.' She looked at Kate with genuine affection, and her friend smiled back.

Half an hour later, Jenny picked her way over the cobbles which cosmetically fringed the front of the Warehouse, feeling happier than she had done since coming to London. She couldn't believe how warm it was. On the south facing side where the courtyard was, the Warehouse had a calm stone solidity which soaked up the sun. Here, in the sunny silence, Jenny was reminded of the deserted valley mills at home. Only the flatness and the pale, never-ending sky, plus the muted sound of moving traffic, assured her she was really in the capital. But on the north facing side next to the canal, it was very different. The same stone walls seemed as dark and dense as the water, and always made Jenny feel shivery. It was as if the building echoed her two moods, the sunny, optimistic one which now prevailed, and the blacker one she had shaken off earlier.

Now, she was looking forward to talking to Matthew Lavelle, even about something as mundane as partitions. It had been kind of Matthew to carry the papers for Kate. With the exception of Laurence Smith, Jenny hadn't met any men since moving down. She wondered how much Kate knew about the on-off affair she had been having back home, which was now decidedly off. The man she had left, Nick Malcolm, was a volatile and creative editor at Northern TV. But he had also been completely unreliable. He had been away on location, shooting a documentary in Eastern Europe for Channel 4, when Jenny had handed in her resignation.

She went into the coolness of the admin block, and past Matthew Lavelle's secretary, who was struggling on the phone and who waved her through into his office. The moment she entered the room the phone shrieked again.

Before answering it, Matt smiled at her in happy surprise, his eyes flickering over her in a way that made her feel, not sexy, but . . . and she searched for the word . . . pretty! She sat down, and only then listened to what he was saying, noticing suddenly that his face was crumpling.

'Sorry, who are you putting through? What? Security? OK. Hello, Security. Yes? Pardon? Police activity? On the canal side?' He paused. 'Oh God. Should I come down? My boss is away at a meeting.' Then, 'Okay, I understand. Let's hope not. Look, call me when you know for certain.' He replaced the receiver, and looked at Jenny, his handsome face unsettled.

'Hi,' he said absently. 'I know we've met recently, but sorry . . . you are?'

'Jenny. Jenny Sims. Senior Producer on the new Health and Food Channel.'

She could tell he wasn't listening, and as she watched him, the phone pealed out again. He jumped, perceptibly. Then he picked it up.

'Oh, my God,' he said. There was a long pause. 'OK. I'll come down. Christ!' He replaced the receiver. Then he stared vacantly at Jenny.

'The Food and Health Channel?' The realisation bleached his face. 'God, then you must know Laurence Smith, mustn't you . . .'

'Oh yes, Laurence is one of our office juniors.'

'Was. He *was* one of your office juniors. It's terrible. He's just been fished out of the canal. He's dead.'

CHAPTER TWO

An hour later Kate was still feeling the shock. She sat staring bleakly with her head on her hands, her elbows stuck out and her coffee mug thrust to one side. It still made her shake, and she found she couldn't concentrate. The police had just left, after telling her officially about Laurence. The cold metallic smell of the canal had clung around them despite the warmth of the sun through the window.

Kate shivered. 'Have Debbie and Chloe gone home yet?' she asked Jenny. 'I said they could, and it's midday.'

She had been advised by the General Manager of the Warehouse that he did not want superfluous people on the premises. But it was hard to detach the two younger staff who seemed to want both involvement and no responsibility. Kate was struggling to find the right level of authority. What was reassuring? And what was patronising? She was vaguely ashamed of just wanting them to go home.

'No, they haven't, surprisingly. Chloe's having a fag outside and Debbie's hovering in the kitchenette.'

'I don't see what more I can say to them. The canal bank is quiet now, isn't it?'

'Yes. They've taken it . . . him . . . away.'

Matthew Lavelle had already been up, ostensibly to tell them more. But he seemed to find their office a haven and his pride was salvaged because he could pretend to be there through gallantry. Kate understood this and, though she could have accused him of being condescending, she realised he needed an excuse to escape from the ghoulish stares of others.

'It's kind of you to come and see us,' she said gently. He nodded, and was triggered off to go through the whole thing again. He had been there when the police supervised the removal of the body from the towpath, and out to the ambulance in the car park. A week ago he would have thought something like this would be a fascinating experience for a building manager. But the reality had made him feel nauseated.

'The police hinted that Laurence was probably unconscious when he hit the water,' Matthew had repeated, as if that somehow made it better. 'He had a scratch on his head. It looks as if he threw himself off the bank, hit his head on the side, fell in unconscious and was trapped by underwater debris. They reckon he was in the water all night. There was no sign of violence. His clothes and belongings were all intact. So they all seem to assume he went in deliberately. And it would be hard to stumble just there.' For a moment Kate remembered the noise she had heard that morning. Had that strange girl run past the body? Was her distress caused by seeing it? But the dry shuffling sound of the eerie feet meant there had been no mud on the canal bank.

'It's certainly not wet and slippy,' Kate said thoughtfully. 'Could he have been pushed?'

'They don't seem to think so. And there would seem to be no reason.'

'So suicide's an easier theory. An occupational hazard of being young.'

Thanks to the open plan office, everything they said had been heard. Debbie Allen looked horrified and stood with her arms across her chest and her little hands clawing the sleeves of her jumper. She wore a long full black skirt that billowed round her calves and bulged at her hips, and her mousey hair hung lankly. Chloe Carr looked shattered, her jaw slack. But she still kept up her supermodel pose, arms akimbo and leg thrust out to one side with her micro skirt flapping like a loose curtain and her boot laces undone and snaking around her feet. 'Christ, I wish I'd been nicer to him,' she muttered.

'But you didn't know this would happen, Chloe,' Debbie whispered.

Chloe ignored her. 'Do you think he did it? Killed himself? He can't have, can he? I mean, he was the one who was going places . . .'

'We just don't know,' Kate murmured, and Jenny said, 'Look, why don't you two go home?'

'Go home?' Chloe's voice rose. 'But it's been awful for us too. What about help for us? Counselling or something?'

'Oh come on, Chloe,' Jenny snapped. 'You only worked with Laurence for a few weeks.'

Kate watched wondering if Jenny's sharp words would provoke a tantrum. But Chloe was merely petulant. 'Well, I don't feel like going home.'

'We can always make more coffee,' Debbie suggested.

'Good idea,' Kate agreed. 'Why not do that? And look after the phones . . .' The sense of shock yawned, exhausting them all. Chloe and Debbie both sidled away towards the tiny pantry which they used to make coffee or prepare lunches to eat at their desks.

'Where was Laurence from?' Jenny asked Kate.

'He was local. I don't know why, but I was pleased about that. So many of the applicants were from much smarter areas, and media families. We spoke about it at his interview. I wanted to know how all the juniors would travel to work. Chloe has a flat virtually round the corner with that scruffy boyfriend of hers, and Debbie has a room over the pub. She barmaids there on Fridays and Saturdays.'

'What, at The Narrowboat? She's hardly Bet Lynch, is she?'

'Boobs aren't everything. Mind you, Debbie's plump enough, it's just that she's so . . .'

'Formless?'

'Yes, that's right.'

'The police will have broken the news to his family, won't they?' Jenny asked.

'Oh yes. Laurence lives with his widowed mother. Poor bloody woman!'

'Is she OK?'

'As well as can be expected, I suppose.' God, what a lot of clichés we all use, Kate thought.

Later, after a sandwich lunch brought in by a subdued Debbie, Kate phoned John and managed to catch him at home. She faltered through her account of the morning's tragic news, expecting predictable responses, so that when he finally spoke she had to ask him to repeat himself.

'What did you say?'

'I said I'm so sorry. It must be such a shock for you. But it's been a shock for me too.'

'You? What do you mean?'

'I knew already. What you've been telling me. About Laurence Smith. I heard from his mother this morning. Mrs Smith is one of my parishioners.'

Of course. If Laurence was local, there was a good chance his family would come under John's pastoral care, even if they never darkened the door of the church. John's church had a tiny congregation, but his parish area covered several miles of dense Edwardian housing, stretching along the river. Even the non-churchgoers had taken a liking to him, and Kate could imagine how a distraught mother might reach out to him. He had a son himself, by his first marriage, a boy about the same age as Laurence Smith.

'His mother actually comes to church from time to time. Kate, what do you think really happened?'

'Well, there doesn't seem much doubt around here that it was suicide. Hard to believe though . . .'

'Absolutely. And his mother won't go along with that either. She's convinced that Laurence was . . . well, pushed.'

'You mean someone did it deliberately?' Kate stopped and looked up to see the horrified faces of the others in the office. Then, as if her strings had been cut, her face like plastic and her lips turning purple, Chloe finally gave up her posing and folded on to the floor.

'She fainted. We propped her up in the chair and put her head between her legs, and she came round and groaned. Debbie had some strong coffee waiting. I don't know if that's the right remedy, but it seemed to work. I've told Chloe to take the day off tomorrow. I'm sure half the problem is that she doesn't eat properly.'

Kate snuggled up to John on the bed which was the only piece of furniture in their gutted house. He held her, feeling the involuntary tremors of shock that were still going through her. She had come straight round to the house after work, and despite the heat she was wearing one of his jumpers, with long sleeves which flapped off the end of her arms. He held her close while she told him about Chloe's collapse.

'Anyway we revived her, and then Debbie took her home in a taxi. I don't know what we would have done without Debbie. She really is a source of strength. Jenny's been great too . . .' Kate's voice faded. The scene with Jenny in the ladies' loo that morning seemed light years away, and she didn't want to talk about it. It had been John who suggested to Kate they should have a child but now he never mentioned the subject, and Kate refused to disturb the new peace of their relationship by talking about her disappointment every month.

'John, tell me about Laurence's mother. Is she normally a reliable character? What did she mean about his being pushed?'

'I don't know. I went to see Joyce Smith as soon as she called me. She was distraught, so it was hard to understand what she meant. The one thing she said was that her son was really happy. Happy and successful, those were the words she used. I gather the police took no notice of her, because she had nothing to go on. I'm going back tomorrow, of course. A neighbour is staying with her tonight.'

'Poor you.' Kate leant up and smiled at him. 'All I've got to do tomorrow is keep the staff calm and tell the shareholders. Not much, compared to providing the sheet anchor for a bereaved mother!'

'That's my job, Kate. Yours is just as bad in its way. You've got to run a business as well as cope with all this pastoral stuff.' He kissed the top of her head. 'I'll make some tea and toast. Oh, and something else, Kate, to take your mind off all this. Andrew's hoping to come to London to see us.'

Kate sat, motionless. Andrew was John's son, the living proof of her own failure to conceive. John went on, 'He rang me earlier tonight and said he wanted to come down this summer. I told him it was a good idea and that it would give me an incentive to get the plastering finished in the spare room!'

Kate felt cold again, and huddled into the jumper. John felt her shuddering movement and knew that he had disturbed her, but instead of asking why, he got up from the bed and walked over to look out of the window. John knew he ought to talk more about the past to Kate, but he could not bring himself to do so. He was extremely sensitive about his divorce. He knew that one of his worst failings was that he hated to admit to his mistakes, but he also knew that he needed to own up to them. And one of the things he had valued most about Kate was the way she never indulged him. She was a born questioner and, much as it irritated him, her analysis stopped him sliding back into the cycle of evasion and depression which had bedevilled him throughout his first marriage. To talk to her about it would do him good, he knew. But he couldn't face it. Not yet.

John and Kate had both been married before, but Kate's relationship had dwindled unlamented into decline. She had lost a baby whilst the marriage was foundering, and prior to that, during a wretched affair in her twenties, she had had an abortion. But pregnancy had not been on her agenda for years. John's history was more conventional. He had thought himself happily married, and as a result his divorce had been much more critical. He had once been the golden boy of his small town in the north, a rugby star who had managed to retain respect despite entering the priesthood in his late thirties. His wife had accepted it at first, and with the egoism of his sex and age he assumed that his choice was her preference. But when he decided to give up his local status and move to London to work with the homeless, his wife finally announced she had had enough, and left him, taking their son.

After that, John Maple had slowly begun to question his own adequacy as a full-time priest. If he had made selfish assumptions about his wife, how fit was he to lead a parish? He had eventually opted out, and taken a job as a security guard at Northern TV. There he met Kate, who had had no idea of his real vocation. But their relationship had grown out of their mutual need and, though the last year had been an emotional roller-coaster, they were now settled. He believed it was God's will, and she, an agnostic, put it down to her own. But it had undeniably worked, John thought gratefully.

'Andrew says he'd love to meet you again, Kate. His phone call was the one decent thing to happen today.'

'Well, that plastering certainly needs doing!' Kate said with some effort and turned to smile at him. John grinned back in relief, and went downstairs to plug in the kettle in the near derelict kitchen. He was terrified of losing her. He thought that to keep her, he had to be perfect in her eyes, and he had no idea that to admit to weakness might make her love him more, not less.

The next day at the Warehouse was business as usual on the face of things and, as a result, Jenny found herself making programme judgements for the first time, while Kate spent hours on the phone to the various contacts who had heard about Laurence's death on the grapevine. It was a dress rehearsal for the all-important phone calls to the shareholders which were looming.

Kate realised that she should have confided in Jenny about the hierarchy of the Food and Health Channel much earlier. Kate had been approached originally by the Chief Executive of Mediaworld plc, Joan Thompson, one of the few respected women in TV, when the company had first decided to invest in a new channel. Mediaworld was to be the major shareholder in Food and Health. The other principal equity holder was a US cable TV group, again of impeccable credentials.

Kate had met their representative, Charlie Mansfield, on one of his visits to London. Like most Americans, despite their reputation, he was less covertly sexist than his British counterparts. He and Kate had hit it off immediately and Kate's appointment had been on the cards.

But in the UK, Charlie had recently taken over a publishing house, and one man on the board was an ageing and difficult multi-millionaire whom the others had trouble keeping happy. When he offered private funding from his own resources to back a TV project it would have been undiplomatic for Charlie to reject it.

Years before, Antony Chester-Lang had made his money out of a small stable of magazines, some with rather sleazy content and all of which copied more established titles. He had been bought out by a bigger magazine group, in corporate irritation at his success, but he had retained a large personal fortune which he had invested in private publishing. Since then, he had produced a series of fitness books written by his wife. The books had been a limited success, particularly as Antony Chester-Lang had used his remaining clout to get them promoted, but they now seemed dated in tone. He was in his late sixties, and his wife could have been anything from ten to twenty years younger. To Kate it was blatantly clear that he had become an investor in Health and Food in order to get his wife on TV. He had assured Kate that this was not the case, telling her that she was under no editorial pressure to use the books.

'Of course not. It's not an issue,' Kate had replied pleasantly. Antony Chester-Lang had smiled like a starving crocodile, and Kate had filed the impression that here was trouble for the future.

Now, she said to Jenny, 'I'll call Charlie in New York about Laurence's death this afternoon. And I'll phone Joan Thompson at Mediaworld too. She'll be really supportive, I know.'

'So your only real nightmare is what the Chester-Langs will say?'

'Absolutely. They don't like me and they really want another manager who will put Mrs Chester-Lang in a starring role, though they would never admit as much. They'll see Laurence's tragedy as a way to get at me. I'll speak to them now, and get it over with. Debbie can call them and put me through. That'll sound very official!'

'Good old Debbie. She's worth her weight in gold. And that's saying something!'

Kate smiled despite herself, and felt her face stretch because the sensation was unfamiliar. She had arrived at the office ridiculously early and all morning she had felt apprehensive and jaded. It was still barely eleven o'clock, but in the open room, under the window, the sun was fighting the air conditioning with the fierceness of midday, and the brightness made them all feel hot.

'Debbie,' Kate called. 'Can you look in the computer and find Antony Chester-Lang's entry? Then phone him for me. He plays golf a lot so you'll probably get his wife, Sonya.'

When Tony was out Sonya Chester-Lang exercised. But when the phone rang the only action she was taking was that of rifling through her husband's clothes with her right hand. She froze. Then she waited for the footfalls of the secretary downstairs to clack across the parquet flooring of the large sunlit hall of their huge mock Tudor house. But even as she waited, she could not help furtively fingering the soft cloth inside the pocket of his baggy weekend trousers, neatly hung inside the wardrobe.

Earlier that week she had caught her husband in a whispered

phone conversation. It was the latest in a series, which had perturbed her. But there was no evidence of an affair here, no crumpled piece of paper or discarded credit card slip. It was as empty as all the other pockets. Sonya waited motionless until she heard the crisp, slightly irritated tones of the secretary.

'Mrs Chester-Lang? Are you upstairs? There's a phone call for you.'

'Yes,' she called forcefully. 'I was in my gym. Couldn't you take a message? That's your job.' In Sonya's opinion it did no harm to keep the secretary in her place.

'Not really, Mrs Chester-Lang.'

'Why not? What a nuisance when I'm busy! Well, put it through to the bedroom. Who is it?'

'It's the Food and Health Channel woman. She said she needed to speak to you or Mr Chester-Lang personally.'

Sonya Chester-Lang sighed loudly and walked into the huge master bedroom. At once she was greeted by the reassuring image of herself several times over, in the huge sepia mirrors that surrounded the room. She breathed, and took stock, before advancing to the phone on the bedside table.

She was a tall woman with the coat-hanger looks of a model, but in reality rather than the mirrors' glossy reflection, her body had the texture of well cooked brisket. Her brown muscles were stringy, and her torso was covered in a shiny dark leotard of liquid Lycra which coated her like sauce. Out of this her neck craned to her long face with its large mouth and full lips. Her teeth were stunningly straight and gleamingly white, and her head was crowned by a full dark blonde bob. At a distance she looked disconcertingly like a teenager.

Pleased, she glanced back at the mirror for a moment, her unlined reflection looking like smooth wood, whereas in reality her skin supported tiny creases like crumpled clingfilm. But you couldn't see them in the glass. She nodded at herself. She liked mirrors. Especially smoked ones.

The decor had started as the lavish extension of personal erotica which only the rich could afford. A few years into their marriage, Sonya had wakened to the sleeping lump of lard which was her husband and had experienced a serious shock. She prided herself on always being available for him, pulling and stroking and cajoling the tag of skin that was his penis until her hands ached, always denying that there might be a moment he would prefer to be left alone. Achieving his orgasm was as much of a goal for her as a budget was to a businesswoman. But that day when she woke, she saw him glance at her out of the corner of his eye, and then feign sleep.

Sonya was appalled. If they no longer had sex, she would surely be redundant, and Tony had already rid himself of two wives. But what was wrong? Shouldn't the right diet, the right exercise, and the right attitude mean she was as attractive as any woman her age could possibly be? So did he want a woman who wasn't her age? Sonya had always lived in terror that Tony would move on to someone else, someone younger.

Agonised, the next weekend she had wheedled her tetchy, domineering husband into a long love-making session. She had seen it as a challenge rather than a joy. Sonya had not experienced a climax for years, and she had never thought of pleasure as part of her job.

But that night, she had accidentally caught sight of them both in the mirror on the open door of their fitted wardrobes. Tony's large fleshy body had been spread out, as he lay on his back, with his fat hips oozing between her knees, his big red face under the dyed black frill of hair contorted by the need to get to an ejaculation. But Sonya hadn't done much more than take in his appearance with distaste. It was herself she saw.

In the dusky bedroom lamplight, the mirror showed the outline of a beautiful young woman. She was riding on top of her supine husband, as thin and subtle as a weaving brown snake, her head nodding as she moved, as if to mesmerise him. When she turned to see more, her hair lifted round her like a cloud, then settled. Sonya had been pouting and groaning to show Tony how much she was enjoying this, but his eyes were shut, contorted with effort. He missed her show, but she saw it herself.

She felt for an ecstatic moment as if she was a gaping, sex-wild centrefold from a men's magazine, a figure who would drive males to instant erections and engorged frenzy. Until then, achieving her own orgasm had been as unlikely as boiling water with a match.

But his grossness, compared with her own flat stomach and small muscular breasts, excited her so much her body had bubbled over in excitement.

Her genuine orgasm had provoked her husband to come, and he had been sweaty and almost affectionate with relief. From then on it had been easy to turn him on to mirrors, coyly at first, then making little displays with herself in the glass, like the lesbian fantasies she suspected fed his sense of power, until her performance became a key part of their sex life. But it was herself she looked at, as she straddled and heaved and splayed on top of him. Catching sight of the grosser corners of his bulk, his broken veins, vast shiny knees, or welling stomach, just added to her appreciation of her own looks. It was the only time Sonya ever felt in control, although the trick was not to let Tony know, of course.

The secretary had put the call through and the phone rang out. Sonya picked it up greedily.

'Kate, marvellous. So nice of you to be serious about keeping in touch and phoning us with updates. But you know, you can always leave messages with our secretary.' It didn't hurt to put Kate Wilkinson in her place too.

'Mrs Chester-Lang, I'm sorry to disturb you.'

'Oh, don't apologise – er – Kate. We always have time for you. But I'm afraid Tony is on the golf course, so it will have to be me.' Her voice tinkled self-deprecatingly. 'Now, what is it?'

Kate explained what had happened, slowly, twice. Sonya's baking board chest started heaving and her eyes dilated.

'My God, how awful,' she breathed, deeply excited. 'Kate, how can you possibly cope? My dear, you need a man there. Really, you do, there'll be so many arrangements to make. Tony and I will be over as soon as I can get hold of him. And we must take you out to eat. You'll need support . . .'

'No, Mrs Chester-Lang, I'm all right . . .'

'Sweetie, of course you are. But I know Tony will want to see for himself that all is well. Book lunch at L'Escargot. We'll get the driver to bring us over, we'll pick you up and drive into town and we'll be there by one.'

'Well, if you really think . . .'

'I do. I doubt any other shareholders are to hand.'

'No. Er, thank you.'

Sonya put the phone back on its pale pink stand and smiled with satisfaction.

'Good,' she murmured to herself. Then she rang the secretary with strict instructions to bleep her husband. He wouldn't be pleased, but at least this meant something to do. Would her black dress be too obvious? She sighed happily.

By noon Kate Wilkinson had phoned the other shareholders and stressed that the tragedy of Laurence's death did not appear to be linked to his job. Joan Thompson expressed suitable shock and sympathy but neither she nor Charlie Mansfield questioned Kate's ability to manage. Nor did they seize on the event to turn it into a crisis. If anything, Kate was feeling reassured that she had their confidence.

But she was furious at being trapped into lunch with the Chester-Langs. Just as she had been trying to think of an excuse to phone them back and cancel, the general manager of the Warehouse, Matthew Lavelle's boss, loomed into the office. He was a harassed, pompous man in a short-sleeved white shirt, and a tie which gave up before it reached his waistline. He held a sheaf of plans under his arm and was clearly put out at having to leave more vital matters in order to attend to dreary problems like the death of one of the workers.

'The timing is terrible,' he huffed, after satisfying himself that Kate and Jenny hadn't personally encouraged Laurence Smith to smear the name of his premises. 'I just hope it doesn't put this other new channel off coming here.'

'What new channel?' Kate asked sharply.

'Oh, I mustn't speak out of turn,' the man smirked. 'The ink isn't dry yet but by the end of the month it should be.'

'What's it about?'

'Oh, it's along similar lines. Women's stuff. It should be very popular. But I'm not at liberty to say what it is. Of course, as facilities providers we at the Warehouse have no interest in the subject matter.' He smiled smugly.

'Don't you have a problem about competitive interests?'

'Us? No. We'll transmit any channels which come to us.' He

shifted a little more uncomfortably at Kate's accusing glare. 'Look, it's not easy getting an office block or facilities house up-and-running these days. This death is going to make things worse because . . .'

'Because what?'

His smile had gone now. 'We have enough problems getting tenants. This isn't the easiest of places. Some people don't like the thought of this place, if they're bloody nervy.' He stopped abruptly. 'Look, anything else you need, like those partitions, Matthew Lavelle will deal with it,' he said. 'I need to get to a Council planning committee meeting this afternoon.'

He left the door swinging behind him and Kate got up to close it, before exclaiming, 'Oh God!' She paced round. 'How many channels do they think the public can take? Anything similar to us could slice us by half, and we need to reach two hundred thousand viewers a week to make this work.'

'But would the Warehouse run two competing channels?' asked Jenny.

'Why not? They're just the technical people, like he said. They get rent and facilities fees from both channels.'

'Is this really a threat to us, Kate?'

'I'm not sure. Look, don't worry about it. If our product is good it'll work. Talking of which, we never did get that tape of the new logos. Why don't you go and see if perhaps it arrived, and then got lost in yesterday's fuss?'

Kate clearly wanted time to think. The man's remarks had alarmed them both. Jenny walked downstairs and out into the well of heat caught in the cobbled courtyard. She could see Matthew opposite, looking up, his broad shoulders braced so he could stretch and stare at the building work on the new transmission section.

'Hi.'

'Oh, hello.' He turned and smiled at her, and she noted how tired he still looked.

'I hope you've got time for a relatively minor problem, Matthew. We've mislaid a video tape of our new logo. Seems trivial in the circumstances, doesn't it, but Kate wondered if it had turned up in someone else's post.'

'I'm not sure. I can check, though,' he said.

'And by the way, did you know we've just been honoured by a visit from your boss? He seemed to take Laurence Smith's death as a personal inconvenience.'

'Yeah?' Matthew shrugged. 'Well, he can be a bit thoughtless. But we're under a lot of pressure to get the space taken. Mind you, I don't think we'll have much trouble getting the Council to nod through the latest plans. We need room for more TX machines now that . . .' He stopped suddenly.

'So you're transmitting another channel are you, Matthew? Could this compete with us and harm us?'

Matthew looked awkward. 'Look, Jenny, it's completely confidential at this stage.'

'But what would our shareholders think? You can't believe this is justifiable can you?'

Matthew grimaced. He was beginning to feel a little hectored. Jenny was pushing him, and he wasn't used to prolonging conversations with girls who took the reins. Automatically he hit back.

'We've got to take what we can get here, Jenny. This is a difficult place to attract tenants. You're only here because one of your shareholders has an interest in the place. And as a matter of fact I don't think he'd be too bothered about the new channel.'

'What do you mean?' Jenny had flared up and her anger goaded him to reply.

'It's one of your own directors who's starting up in opposition anyway!' Abruptly, he turned away from her, and began to stride back to his own office. But in mid step he turned to look back at her, so that she broke from the grip of her surprise, and ran to follow him.

'Matthew. Hey, wait . . .'

The phone rang on Kate's desk.

'Kate?'

'John! Where are you?'

'I'm back at the house for a minute. Look, I went to see Joyce, Laurence's mother, this morning.'

'Is she feeling better? Sorry, that was a crass thing to say. How losing a child ever gets better I don't know.'

'It doesn't get better. People get used to the agony. Anyway, she's a long way from that stage. I think she's angry. She still insists that there was foul play. I agree, she's not very clear on who would do it, or why. But she wants to get in touch with Laurence's girlfriend.'

'Laurence's girlfriend. You're joking!'

'Of course I'm not joking.'

'That's ludicrous. Laurence never mentioned a girlfriend.'

'But you were his boss, not his friend. He may not have talked to you.'

Kate reluctantly agreed. 'He never said anything to anyone as far as I know. But I'll ask the others.'

'Thanks. Joyce Smith seems certain. And if we can find the girlfriend, at least we're doing *something* for the poor woman.'

Kate put the phone down, and looked at Debbie Allen who was working away, earphones over one ear and pencil at the ready, her faded grey jumper hunched over the desk despite the warmth of the day.

'Debbie,' she said. 'Did you ever hear Laurence mention a girlfriend?'

The plate-like face of the younger woman paled at the mention of Laurence's name but her small grey eyes held Kate's.

'Absolutely not,' she said, in her Manchester voice. Kate noticed the ring of authority which it held, with surprise. For the first time since hearing the news of Laurence's death, Kate felt some consolation. Debbie at least had been a good choice.

'You're sure about that?'

'Completely.' Debbie smiled at Kate with new assurance.

Jenny sat in Matt's office drinking diet Coke. She had followed him like a terrier, and to his own surprise he had invited her in, and shut the door behind her. Of course bossy females weren't his cup of tea, but there was something about Jenny which he found inviting. He was used to more glamorous women but it pleased him to watch her sitting opposite, her brain working so hard she was unaware of how she sat, or the way her hair was mussed up. To Jenny, Matt seemed slightly ponderous. But she found, surprisingly, that it gave her a sense of suspense rather than irritation.

'Look, I've told you all I can . . .' Matt said, looking genuinely embarrassed, '. . . except that this other channel isn't *exactly* like yours.'

'And the shareholders you mentioned?'

'Well, it isn't *all* your shareholders.'

'Who is it then? Come on, Matt, you haven't signed the Official Secrets Act. And if this channel is going to happen, there's no way the ownership can stay a mystery for long. Look, is it anything to do with food?'

'No.'

'Or fitness?'

'No.'

'Well then, I'm not going to get my knickers in a twist over it.'

Jenny grinned broadly but to her surprise, Matthew now looked even more uncomfortable. She wanted him to like her, and found his handsomeness fascinating, but she guessed that her tenacity was alienating him. She stood up.

'Well, thanks for what you've told me,' she said. 'I appreciate that I've been badgering you. It's a pity the Food and Health Channel isn't on the air. We'd be sure to have some antidote to all this stress and strain. Home-made soup, perhaps? Or a quick session of step aerobics?'

Matthew Lavelle smiled gratefully at the change of subject, his white teeth shining. 'You aren't into fitness then, Jenny?' His use of her name made her neck feel hot.

'How did you guess? Although I would like to take up some sort of exercise, now I'm in London. I used to go swimming a lot up north. I'm a really good swimmer, but perhaps I need something a little more demanding . . .'

'Well if you want to tone up . . . Not that you don't look great, I'm sorry . . . I didn't mean . . .'

Jenny stood by the door, holding her breath . . .

'If you'd like to try working out, there's the gym I go to. Would you be interested?'

'Well, I might.'

'How about Thursday night?'

'Oh . . . OK, why not!' Jenny tried to sound unconcerned, but stood up hurriedly to quit while she was ahead.

'Fine. Bring a leotard or tee shirt and shorts. I'll pop up to your office for you after work.'

She grinned at him, delighted. But as soon as she turned away, her face furrowed up, and she hurried downstairs to pass on her news about the new channel to Kate. She was too late. She was momentarily blinded by the sun glinting fiercely on the rich coffee metallic roof of the Chester-Langs' Bentley as it bore Kate away.

Jenny mooched more slowly now back to the Food and Health office. She walked past reception, up the wide modern stairs and through the glass doors. The place was hot, still, and totally silent, and the plastic smell of sun-strafed office equipment hit her like the aroma of cooking.

It made her feel slightly sick and definitely not hungry. She peered into the kitchen to see if Debbie was making a Cup-A-Soup, spooning lumpy cottage cheese on to cardboard biscuits, or eating Twix bars in her usual messy way, leaving packets and wrappers everywhere. But the place was empty, and Jenny remembered Debbie's arrangement to do occasional barmaiding stints at the pub, lunchtime and evening. She looked out of the big window on her right to the canal, flat and shiny like a stream of treacle, with no coloured narrow boats or happy dog walkers. Not many people strolled through the narrow chasm, caused by the Warehouse on one side and the other derelict building opposite, which mugged the sunshine leaving them in the dark. In contrast, through the window on her left, the courtyard side of the building seemed bleached by bright sunlight and dotted with the welcoming red splashes of potted geraniums.

Jenny realised for the first time that she was completely alone. The receptionist was at lunch. Kate was away with the Chester-Langs, Chloe was off after her collapse the day before, and Debbie was presumably barmaiding. Jenny turned to walk back to her desk, and as she did so her phone rang out, crashing and jangling through the hot soupy silence like a full peal of bells rather than just one phone. Jenny picked it up confidently and said, 'Food and Health. Jenny Sims.' There was no reply. 'Hello?' she said again. But she could hear nothing although she had the unmistakable sensation of the lightest of breathing at the other end of the line. 'Hello!' she said angrily. Then a very soft voice said, 'Can I speak to Laurence?'

Jenny sat, immobile. The thought of what she had to say next horrified her.

'I'm awfully sorry,' she said, her eyes filling with tears. 'Didn't you know?'

She waited for the caller to say the inevitable, to ask in a louder, more alarmed tone, 'Know what?'

But instead, there was absolute silence on the other end of the phone. And then, to Jenny's horror, she heard what she could only describe as a light, androgynous giggle. Appalled, she looked down at the phone. Then she heard the soft sound of the call being slowly disconnected.

She put down the receiver herself, and shuddered. Her eyes were drawn to Laurence's empty desk, still uncleared, where his pile of unviewed tapes and a few letters sat. The desk looked incomplete, as if Laurence had just gone to get himself a coffee and would be back any minute . . . he couldn't possibly be dead. For a mad moment she wondered if it had been Laurence himself who had called to tease her, and it was all some silly joke.

'Don't be stupid,' she said out loud, to her own surprise. But she wasn't being stupid. The voice on the other end of the phone had sounded soft and sweet and unmistakably malicious.

Jenny jumped up as if the desk was poisoned. She turned away from the phone to take a deep breath, and look out of the window. She could see an untidy figure in baggy clothes bustling through the car park clutching a brown paper bag of goodies. Debbie looked up at her, shifted the bag from one arm to the other, and waved. She had obviously only popped out to the shop for her supply of comfort food. And Jenny suddenly felt better, and lifted her arm and waved back with enormous enthusiasm.

Then she turned back to shake the stupid phone call from her head, and settle to some sensible work. But there was something else on her mind, something trivial and irritating which wouldn't go away. She raked over the affairs of the morning. The news of the rival channel was disturbing, but it wasn't that. The phone call had been horrible, but offices were frequently the focus for weird callers, and anyway, what could she do about it unless it happened again?

No. The thing which was worrying her was silly but even so,

deeply disturbing. She looked round the office again. What was wrong? Like most people, Jenny had a blueprint in her head of how her place of work should look . . . where the desks were, what would normally be left lying around, people's private knick-knacks. Her eyes went over it again. Something was missing. Something she knew was unimportant in itself, but whose disappearance was making her flesh creep. She looked at Kate's desk, then Debbie's desk, then Chloe's desk, then Laurence's . . .

That was it. Laurence's desk, supposed to be left untouched, was just the same, except that his silly mug with the pig on it was gone. Jenny started to shake. She was sure no-one in the office would have taken it. The thick, Victorian walls of the Warehouse seemed to press in on her. She had a sudden sense of hundreds of wretched Dickensian workers laughing at the new renovation and creeping through their new, spanking, sparkling offices, peering and prying among twentieth century paraphernalia. For some crazed reason her breath was coming in great hoarse gusts when the glass doors opened and Debbie came bounding in.

'Hey, Jenny,' said the plump girl. 'You look as if you've seen a ghost.'

'What? God, of course not. I'm sorry, Debbie, I was just startled when you came in. We'd better start viewing those old Delia Smiths.'

But as she went back to her desk, Jenny noticed almost dis-passionately that her own hands were shaking.

CHAPTER THREE

Kate liked the glowing, jewel-like colours of L'Escargot restaurant. It was grand enough to give a sense of occasion, warm enough to make her feel comfortable, and smart enough to satisfy the desperately fashionable Sonya Chester-Lang. Sonya was one of those women who always remark on other women's clothes as soon as they meet, with an air of noblesse oblige. As Kate had awkwardly scrambled into the chauffeur-driven car beside them Sonya had said, 'Kate, what a lovely jacket,' in a tone which made Kate wonder what was wrong with the skirt.

But Kate did not react. She was determined neither to be unnerved nor to try to please, although she knew that dealing with shareholders was a job even the most successful executives dreaded. For the next few minutes a heavy atmosphere hung round the back of the Bentley along with Antony Chester-Lang's cigar smoke. Then he spoke, without looking at Kate.

'Terrible news about this chap. Didn't you suspect there was something odd about him when you took him on?'

'No,' Kate replied. A few years earlier she would have gushed with explanations, but she was learning that often with these people silence was the best weapon.

'Humph. There's no way our venture could be implicated in this death?'

Kate thought carefully before answering. 'I can't see why. My own belief is that Laurence slipped and fell, and the coroner's verdict will probably be accidental death. The chance of anyone from the press bothering to rake up Laurence's accident and link it to the channel, however misguidedly, is slim.'

'Mmm. Well, I think you've been bloody stupid. You should have gathered the chap was a bit peculiar. We don't want weirdos working for us. There better hadn't be a next time.'

I'll remind them not to kill themselves when I give them their tax coding, Kate felt like saying, but she bit her tongue. She wondered if people on the outside knew just how rude and dismissive the rich and powerful could be. Friends assured her that Chester-Lang was just one of many offensive shareholders in the world of media, but she privately thought he was the worst. He now relapsed into a grumpy sulk. So much for the help his gushing wife had offered.

The lunch was a tortuous affair for everyone but Sonya. Her husband was clearly irritated by having to be there at all, but she was almost likeable in her delight at the fuss from the waiters and the table in the window looking out on the Soho street. Chester-Lang watched in bad-tempered silence, ignoring his wife's little-girl comments and contributing only two loud belches to the atmosphere. But he certainly put away a large amount of expensive wine, and when it came to choosing a main course, he turned tetchily and said, 'Oh for God's sake Sonya, have the lamb. With potatoes and vegetables. You know you love it, and your own bloody books say that someone who eats sensibly can have a jolly good dinner every so often.'

'Oh, yes,' Sonya squealed. It was surprising how small she could become. She was supple enough to curl her spine up so she looked like a kicked King Charles spaniel, all quivering body and bulging eyes, focused on her husband but with a sort of cowed slyness. And to Kate's surprise, she ate every morsel on her plate with the delicate intensity of a greedy cat.

'Sonya,' her husband said suddenly, after the pudding, 'better go and powder your nose. I want a word with Kate.'

'Oh,' she said, resentfully, 'well, fine,' though it sounded like 'faine', and she tottered away towards the stairs to the ladies'.

'Umm,' said her husband, after a sultry pause. 'Kate, are you planning to go to MIP at the end of the week?'

'Sorry?' Kate wondered if she had heard correctly.

'MIP. In Cannes,' he growled. 'I'm not completely ignorant about television. Are you going to it? Or don't you know what I'm talking about?'

Kate knew very well what he meant. But she was genuinely

astonished. Chester-Lang was not a man who ever said unpredictable things. He preferred to bludgeon rather than surprise.

'Yes, I know,' she said. 'MIP, the European TV programme buying market.' She had no idea why Chester-Lang should show any interest in MIP at all. 'I've been before, but I don't see much point in us going at this stage. We already have most British and US catalogues and I don't think it's a useful idea to waste money looking at Spanish slimming series or Italian talk shows.'

'Well, you should rethink.'

'Really? You must know we have no budget for such things.'

Chester-Lang did not offer to help her find one. He merely looked back at her with a sort of sneer.

'You can move money around, Kate. The budget is your shout. You should go. I don't want this channel to miss out on anything, and you never know what programmes you might be overlooking. And while you're there, I want you to help someone.'

'I'm sorry?'

'I want you to help someone. Someone who is setting up another channel for me. A second channel which will be broadcasting from the Warehouse, but will be completely owned by us, the Chester-Langs. I'm sure you can see your way to giving us every help and support.'

Kate stared, then collected herself. So that was what the works manager had meant that morning. In the mirror across the room she saw her open mouth and the black pits of her astonished eyes. 'I don't see why I should support any venture which might be in competition with the Food and Health Channel.'

'Don't be ridiculous. There's no contest, because the new channel will probably be bigger than yours could ever be. It's a whole new, exciting concept.' The thought made him smile. 'My man can meet you for a breakfast or lunch at the Majestic Hotel on the Croisette at Cannes. I gather that's where everyone who matters does business.'

'May I ask what this other channel is?'

'You may ask, but I can't give you an answer. It's under wraps as yet.'

'And what do the other shareholders say?'

'I don't care what they say! They were vague enough when it

came to getting my money out of me, now it's my turn for a little quid pro quo.'

And I'm the pro, Kate thought angrily. But antagonising shareholders was never a very good idea in the insecure world of TV boardrooms where huge sums of money funded even bigger egos. Chester-Lang was growling, 'Charlie Mansfield and Joan Thompson both know I'm investing in another venture. There's damn all they can do about it. Anyway, cable TV is full of people with a lot of fingers in a lot of pies. Flextech, Cox, Pearsons. They're all at it.'

'But their ventures don't conflict.'

'Who said anything about conflicting? God, you're paranoid as well.'

As well as what, Kate thought? The implication was clearly that he thought her incompetent too. But she said nothing and waited for him to go on.

'My, er, manager particularly wants to talk to you. He seems to value your . . . experience. It's a very special project, and it's going to be big. Too big, eventually, for the sort of person who's needed on Food and Health. But at this stage we might be able to use your basic expertise.'

Kate tried not to splutter into her coffee. Chester-Lang, she knew, was trying to rile her. 'Fine,' she said calmly. 'Where's he staying?'

'At the Carlton.' The best hotel in Cannes.

'Really? And his name?'

'Daniel Chester-Lang. He's my son.'

Kate hid her genuine surprise and instead raised her eyebrows archly. Chester-Lang was well aware that she was silently accusing him of nepotism, but he merely smirked. He was unconcerned about Kate Wilkinson's strictures.

In the pause that followed Kate excused herself, saying that she too needed to visit the ladies'. She followed Sonya's route, expecting to meet her coming back, but there were two sets of stairs to the first floor of the restaurant. When Kate opened the door of the elegant ladies' toilets, she wasn't sure whether or not Sonya was still inside. But as she looked for her, she heard retching. It didn't sound like normal, involuntary vomiting; instead, it was a controlled, almost discreet sound. Quickly, Kate went in and locked the door. She heard someone leave the cubicle, turn on the taps, throw the hand-towel into the basket, and then the main door flapped.

Kate left her cubicle, and went through the washroom where two other women were washing their hands. She wondered if either of them had been sick, but both looked totally composed. She hurried back to the table, where Sonya too seemed unruffled, her face angled up brightly. Kate was now desperate to escape from the meal. As she waited for Chester-Lang to finish his coffee and petits-fours, Kate could tell that Sonya was already searching for a new way to use her, to fill up the rest of her empty day.

'Well, if you don't want us to come back to the office with you, at least let us give you a lift,' Sonya squeaked.

'Thank you so much, but I actually have a meeting to go to now. I really mustn't waste more of your time.'

'Oh, well, if you're *certain*!' Sonya was still unsure whether to argue, when she was yanked away at the elbow by her husband who bawled at Kate, 'Coming?'

'No, no, thank you, Antony, I have an appointment.'

He hardly listened. 'OK,' he growled. 'I'll be on to you with more details about that arrangement for MIP.'

'Fine,' Kate lied, and he immediately turned away. But Sonya turned back, for the regulation media kiss. Kate raised her face to her, and in that second, as Sonya's tipsy lips just missed her cheek, she smelt the unmistakable tang of mint flavoured vomit. Then Sonya was borne off, her tip-tapping stilettos rattling on the dry pavement.

So much for the secret of Sonya's dietary success. Kate wondered if her husband guessed. Then Kate's mobile phone rang out, competing with the incessant noise and traffic so that it was only after a few seconds she heard and answered.

It was Jenny. Her voice sounded high and panicky, but she whispered at the same time.

'Kate, can you get back here? Now?'

'Of course I can. Are you OK?'

'How long will you be?'

'Twenty minutes? What's the problem?'

Jenny's voice suddenly stiffened into a more formal tone as if someone had moved back into earshot. 'We've got a visitor, Kate. He won't go until he's spoken to you.'

'All right, Jenny, I'm hailing a cab as we speak. Now, tell me more.'

'It's Chloe Carr's boyfriend. Just get here, can you?'

'Is Chloe with him?'

'No. She's still off.'

'And is Debbie with you?'

'She's . . . she's in the kitchen.' Jenny's voice quavered again. 'Please, Kate. He says he'll wait.' Kate had the clear impression Debbie was hiding and Jenny was under siege.

'OK, I'm on my way.'

Kate plunged into the street to stop the first cab with a yellow light. The driver assured her that it would be fifteen minutes from the West End to the Warehouse TV Centre. Bouncing in the back of the cab, still recovering from the three glasses of Bordeaux she had been forced to take with the Chester-Langs, Kate wondered why Jenny had sounded so alarmed.

The cab pulled in at the Warehouse, and Kate leapt out and paid. Opening the office door, Jenny was hardly visible, with the back of a young man, in filthy ragged jeans and a strangely glossy leather jacket bent across the desk immediately in front of her.

'Kate! You need to deal with this.'

The young man turned round.

'So you're the fucking boss here?' One of his arms, as if in a stray, almost involuntary gesture, swept the remaining papers off Jenny's desk and on to the floor. Jenny flinched, but did not move.

'So you're the fucking boss!' he said again.

'Yes.' Kate felt an unusual sense of cold detached calm which she realised in surprise, was anger. The man was on her territory. How dare he disrupt what they were doing? 'What do you want?'

'He's been waiting for about twenty minutes, Kate.' Jenny's voice was loaded with warning, but Kate felt equal to the man's challenge. He had bullied Jenny because he was waiting for the boss, and now the boss was here.

He looked menacingly at her but Kate held her ground. He was clearly shaking with rage, made worse by coming face to face with a middle-aged woman slightly smaller, and much slighter, than he was. Yet that gave Kate an advantage, so that she waited calmly for his explosion. When it came, in a high pitched shout, she wasn't ready for it.

'I want my money.'

'What?'

'*My dosh. My fucking money!*'

'What money?' Kate asked. She noticed the trembling of the man's arms as he turned away in frustration, his back to her again, his arms splayed and his hands resting on Jenny's desk. Then like a toy he jumped and bounced round towards her, six feet of hyperactivity inches from her face. Kate knew about being high, but this man was as taut as a piano wire, quivering with suppressed action.

'I want the money that other bastard promised me. I need it.'

'What other bastard?'

'That dead shit. He promised me money.' Again, the man's arm leapt out like a thing possessed and swept the remaining debris on Jenny's desk on to the floor. He brought his face up to Kate's so she could smell his strange, acidic, unnatural breath.

'What was the money for?' Kate asked again. She wasn't afraid because this man was almost pathetic in his intensity. But as she watched he began to fumble in his pockets and for a second she thought he was grasping for a knife.

'Here,' he half-screamed at her. 'Look!'

A tiny scrap of paper fluttered under Kate's nose. She tried to focus on it. The words, neatly written in biro, said, *I owe you fifty pounds.*

The word 'SIGNED' was written in block capitals in an almost childish way. And underneath was the clearly legible signature of Laurence Smith.

'Why did he sign this?' Kate said evenly.

'A delivery. A fucking delivery. You know.'

'I'm afraid I don't.'

'*Where's my fucking money!*' he bellowed again. Kate opened her bag. 'There's twenty five pounds,' she said. 'If you're owed the rest, you'll get it, but we really don't have any cash here.'

The young man's face went from surprise to aggression.

'I want the rest NOW!' he screamed. Then Kate saw his eyeline flicker. Behind her, Matthew Lavelle had come quietly up the stairs and in through the double doors. He was standing, outstaring the lanky young man in his trembling tension.

Suddenly the boy calmed, and seemed to loose inches in height and weight.

'OK, s'alright,' he said sloppily. 'OK, OK. I'll go now.' He shambled away from her, the notes crinkling audibly in his shaking hands. Thank God, thought Kate, closing her eyes for a second in relief.

But as the man . . . boy . . . reached the doors, he suddenly turned round to shriek again, the uncontrolled loudness of his voice as frightening as anything else about him.

'And where's that bitch? That thin bitch?'

'Who do you mean?'

'You fucking know. That long scrawny cow always sticking her fanny at you. The one in the long white silky stuff who thinks she's God's gift. She'll have my money.'

'I think you'd better leave, mate.'

Matthew Lavelle's cold voice cut through the office. Kate could see that he too was scared. All that muscle, she thought irrelevantly, and Matt is frightened by the crazed unpredictability of drugs.

Then the young man's words sank in. Who did he mean? Kate remembered, for one mad moment, her ghost on the towpath.

'Hey,' she called, wanting to find out. 'Hey, wait a minute.'

But he had gone, lurching down the metal staircase and out into the sunshine. Behind her, Kate sensed Jenny physically relax.

'Good riddance,' said Matt. 'I'll talk to reception about letting in slobs like that.'

'What a wally,' Kate said conversationally, hiding her horror and noting how it was she who had the responsibility to control the atmosphere, to reduce the tension by her own remarks.

Jenny, still trembling at her desk, felt the watery sensation of panic in her knees. She wanted to burst into tears and hug Kate in relief, to blurt out about the nasty little phone call and her confusion over the missing mug. Instead, the sound of Debbie slowly opening the door of the little kitchen, and then her round, pale face peering out, reminded her to keep calm.

'It's OK now Debbie,' she called brightly instead, 'he's gone.' As the other girl crept wide-eyed back into the office, Jenny smiled around her at Matthew Lavelle, who nodded back, impressed, and said, 'Well done.'

Kate left work at six and drove home in the stop-start traffic. It was hot enough to open the window of the car and rest her elbow on the sill. At the traffic lights, the cars came to a standstill.

Kate felt irritated by the hold-up until she reminded herself she was in no hurry. That night, she was going back to her bedsit, not to the house. Thanks to Chloe's boyfriend, she had been unable to get away from work until they had tidied the office, straightening the mess of tapes and papers he had swept on to the floor.

Kate wished John was around that evening. But he was with Mrs Smith, making funeral arrangements. The family hoped the coroner would release Laurence's body for burial early the next week. The full inquest could be months later, but the predicted verdict seemed to be accidental death.

Kate knew that coroners rarely considered suicide unless specific notes were left, but even so, the police had said privately to her that it was enough of a possibility to rule out further investigations. There were definitely no signs of foul play, she was told. His body had been found with a wallet full of cash, and two credit cards in his pocket. Traces of his skin and blood were found on the edge of the path. He had no other marks on him.

So why might he kill himself? Money worries? Unlikely. He had been much better off than the other two researchers. He had told Kate proudly that he had savings in reserve to see him through any short term problems while he made the move into the ultimately more lucrative world of TV.

Sex problems? Kate thought again about Mrs Smith's insistence that Laurence had a girlfriend. Yet Debbie had been adamant that Laurence was uninvolved. And when Kate thought of him, her overwhelming recollection was of a self-contained, perhaps self-satisfied young man. There had been a sense of purpose about Laurence Smith, with none of the uncertainty or stress that characterised most young people's private lives. If he had had a girlfriend Kate was sure she would have been on display, a pleasant asset to Laurence's career prospects.

So why had Laurence been on the towpath at all? The one thing which motivated him was his job. If someone had said, 'Hey, there's a tape delivery coming by barge at eleven o'clock,' Laurence would have been there, ready for it despite the madness of the request. It was total nonsense, but the psychology of it – Laurence waiting there, bright and helpful, because he had been asked by someone in authority – rang true.

As did the strange, organised way he had given an IOU to Chloe's ghastly boyfriend. What had that been all about? Yet the very innocence of Laurence's big round writing, and the fact that he had bothered, characteristically, with something both as juvenile and as formal as a tatty little receipt, seemed to suggest to Kate that although it was strange, Laurence's involvement wasn't sinister. Chloe would know, of course. That young woman would have a lot of explaining to do when she came back to work the next day. Her fainting fit was hardly the result of mere sensitivity. Her boyfriend and Laurence were linked, and Kate wanted to know how.

She shifted in her seat. At least she felt better physically. She was aware that the bloated sensation and backache had gone. No wonder her period had been late. She hadn't realised how much the anxiety of management had affected her. It had been one of the worst weeks she could remember, but there were still some compensations, like Jenny's revived friendship. Jenny had handled the threatening visitor with real competence. Kate had remarked to her on leaving how well she had coped. To her surprise, Jenny had said, 'But at least he was real. We could do something about him.' Kate had glanced back at her, but Jenny had already been packing up to leave. Now Kate thought again about the odd comment. What did Jenny mean?

Still, the solid calm of the houses and spring gardens reassured her and once the cars coughed and moved forward like old people out in the sun, she almost enjoyed the last half mile of the drive, past an office block and a small row of shops, round a corner and into a tree-lined avenue of Edwardian houses.

Most were still large family homes, with attractive overgrown gardens. Kate's bedsit actually contained a bedroom, en-suite bathroom and kitchen alcove, and was at the top of a big, well-maintained house at the end of the row. She had to go through the front garden and round the side of the house to a metal stairway at the back, to climb up to her front door.

The road was on the fringe of John's parish. He had an active congregation of thirty at most, in an ugly little yellow-brick church on a corner between a Bottom's Up off-licence, and rows of red-brick villas, and was eclipsed by a wildly fashionable Anglo-Catholic church in acres of green grounds, a mile to the west. John had already started a project to renovate the grounds round his church, but his parishioners were as sparse as the plants.

As Kate walked through the garden she stopped, halted by the rich, sudden smell of the purply wisteria which was flowering on the southern facing rear of the old brick villa. The laburnum tree was just coming out too, encouraged by the early heat, its sweep of yellow blossom dusting the top of the garden shed. A cat scurried out from under the shrubs, and overhead a plane droned. Kate paused, hoping the peace of the garden would creep up on her. Then she saw one of the children from next door, sitting on her swing, kicking with her legs at the struts and singing with great sweetness:

'What do you do if you're needing a pooh
In an English country gaaaaaaarden.'

Kate started to laugh.

'Pull down your pants
And suffocate some ants
In an English country gaaaaaaarden.'

'Sarah Louise!' The voice of her mother rang out. Kate had heard this voice one or twice before, usually raised in some sort of outrage. 'Get in here NOW. You need a bath.'

The child leapt off the swing, then she saw Kate through the trellis, overladen with rampant ivy, which formed the boundary between the two gardens.

'Hello,' she said. 'Good song, isn't it?'

'Very good. Does your mum approve?'

The child pulled a face, then shied as a woman came flying down the path and grabbed her by the arm.

'You little horror!' The child squealed in simulated terror, well aware of Kate's eyes. Her mother stood up, disconcerted.

'Oh,' she said. 'Hello.' She paused fractionally. 'Are you Kate?'

'Yes?'

'That's great! I'm Polly!'

'Oh, hi.' Kate said lamely. Polly who?, she wondered, her mind raking desperately for a clue.

'I'm so glad to have caught you! Look, let me get this little madam inside, and then would you like a glass of wine and some nibbles?'

Socialising that evening had not been on Kate's agenda. But the woman went on. 'Do say yes. My husband won't be back for hours, and of course I feel as if I already know you.'

Do you, Kate thought. Why?

She looked at the woman, who was as tall as she was, but plump in a curvaceous way, with the glossiest bob of dark hair Kate had ever seen, except for two streaks of grey which ran down from her parting. She was wearing a long thin Indian fabric skirt from which brown legs in sandals emerged, solid but smooth. She's big but beautiful, Kate thought, glancing down for contrast at the wiry little girl.

'Well, thanks,' Kate said, still hesitant, but afraid of sounding ignorant.

'Great! I've been desperate to meet you since I heard about you of course, but I didn't want to push myself or my hectic family on you!' Polly beamed. She had an inconclusive way of speaking, as if every sentence had to be rushed out for approval, or gabbled before a child could interrupt.

'Mu-ummy, what about my bath?' squawked the child, just as Kate was about to ask what the connection was.

'So I'll see you in about an hour?' the woman asked, as the child pulled her away.

'Yes – er – that would be lovely.'

'Great! And we can talk about John.' And then the woman had gone, dragged along by the child who was squeaking like an uncomfortable puppy.

John? Polly must be a parishioner, Kate thought in surprise, as she climbed the stairs up to her front door.

She chucked her briefcase so it landed on the bed, behind which piles of packing cases dominated the small room. She undressed slowly, enjoying the change of pace, cleansing the remnants of make-up and scrubbing her face, putting on jeans and a sweatshirt and trainers. She brushed her auburn hair back, and looked at her rawness in the little mirror above the wash basin. The real, vulnerable Kate. Being alone tonight seemed a bleak prospect and she suddenly felt very grateful that someone was waiting for her, even if it wasn't John Maple. She hurried out, down the staircase that ran down the back of the grey brick villa, and into the garden.

She was about to go around to the front and knock formally when she heard Polly call, 'Hi, there you are! Come through here.' Kate brushed through a gap in the fence, and into Polly's back garden. Her house had a small conservatory at the back, opening on to a lawn. The unusual dusky warmth of the April evening was cuddled there, undisturbed. The wide double doors of the conservatory were opened and just inside there was a pale wooden table. Besides the table, two low cane sofas held fat cream and green cushions just the right side of being too clean to sit on. Kate had a sudden desire to collapse into them, except that a lopsided pile of brightly coloured children's books were in the way.

'Just dump them on the floor. If you can find the space.'

'Fine.' Kate moved the books. But on the floor, the remnants of some sort of board game had to be pushed to one side.

'I haven't got a huge variety of bits and pieces to eat!' said Polly. 'Sit down, or follow me to the kitchen while I find something you'd like!'

'Oh, anything will do, really. I had a big heavy lunch and it's great not to have worry about microwaving some instant dinner!'

Polly laughed ruefully. 'Yes, must be awful. You work full-time, don't you? John told me. It's so nice, you living next door!'

Kate smiled noncommittally, wondering why. She followed Polly into her big pine fitted kitchen, and watched her rummage about. She felt a frightening sense of inadequacy at seeing an earthmother so easy with technology, as Polly tipped home-made crackers out of a tin with one hand, and with the other pressed a button on the most elaborate food mixer Kate had ever seen.

'We should start with daiquiris,' Polly said. 'Don't get me wrong, I don't drink much, but Nigel and I have discovered a taste for cocktails lately.' Then she turned away to the fridge, taking out a jug of ready crushed ice to pour into the mixer.

'So you know John from St Mark's?' Kate hazarded, over the pounding noise of the whirring blades.

'Pardon? Noisy, these things, aren't they, but the drinks will be delicious. Yes, John's a marvellous vicar . . .'

Kate was unsure whether Polly had misheard her, or whether it was her disjointed way of talking, but she felt they had lost the thread of the conversation. Polly was unwrapping pieces of cheese, and the moment to query her had gone. But Kate allowed herself to feel flattered on John's behalf. If you were involved with a priest, it helped if he was a good one! With a practised hand Polly stopped the machine, tipped out the beautiful pastel drinks into fluted glasses, and at the same time reached for a large blue and white cheese dish.

'Let's eat,' she said. 'I'm peckish too, now. I haven't cooked a big meal tonight because my teenage son is at his friend's, and Nigel's working late.'

'How many children do you have?' Kate asked.

'Oh, a whole tribe! Ghastly, isn't it? There's Richard, my eldest, he's seventeen, then Sarah Louise, aged eight, and my baby, Laura, aged six.'

'So how do you cope with stray guests demanding cocktails?'

'Oh, tonight the two girls are putting themselves to bed. Chaos, of course!'

Kate followed her into the conservatory and went to sit down. Again, before she could, she had to move one of the little girl's tee-shirts, flung on to the sofa. There was an all-pervasive family atmosphere, and to Kate's irritation, she felt an unprecedented stab of envy.

'God, those children make a mess,' Polly said. 'Hey, I'm sorry for going on ten to the dozen. I'm just so pleased to have someone to talk to. My husband is working till all hours this week. He's auditing at the moment.' She flopped heavily into the opposite sofa. 'I haven't seen John since Sunday. We don't often have the benefit of a parish visit which is understandable in the circumstances. Nigel isn't too keen on the friendship, as you probably know.'

No, thought Kate, baffled for a moment. I don't. But Polly was already rattling on, at the same time piling cheese onto her crackers.

'I think he really should put the past behind him. I suppose John's told you about all that! Do eat some of this cheese up! Anyway, you know how discreet John is. I didn't really get all the details about you, though he told me you had a wonderful job. Where do you work?'

'In TV.'

'Oh! Well, we don't get a chance to watch a lot of it.'

Kate smiled weakly. Most people said that.

'And is it hard work?' Polly went on politely.

The evening was threatening to become an exchange of clichés. Kate carefully sliced herself some Stilton, put it on a cracker, and made a decision.

'Actually, Polly, it's bloody hard work. In fact, this week my job has been absolute unmitigated hell!'

Polly's head jerked up in surprise at this sudden breaking of the usual conversational code. Career women and career mothers were usually locked in uncommunicative competition.

'Good Lord! Tell me more,' she said, her mouth full.

Kate finished her cheese and biscuit in the expectant silence, and then leant forward, and slowly repeated the details of Laurence's death. Polly's eyes widened. But like John, she had already heard about the tragedy.

'But I know who you mean! Poor Joyce Smith's son. I know Joyce quite well. I went round to see her this morning.'

'So you knew the family through the church?'

'Yes!' Polly sat with her cocktail midway between the coffee table and her lips. 'Or at least I know his mother. Of course this means that you'll be able to help her!'

'Help her with what?'

'Finding Laurence's girlfriend! You must know her! I mean, Laurence met her at work, didn't he? That's what Joyce says. Laurence'd never had a girlfriend before apparently. To be honest, I always thought he was rather, well, asexual. But Joyce Smith thinks this was really serious!'

'Hang on, Polly, let me get this straight. You're saying Laurence Smith's girlfriend worked at the Warehouse TV Centre?'

'Yes! If that's what you call it. I just told you, that was where they met!'

'But that's not possible. No-one has a clue who she is. In fact my staff are adamant Laurence wasn't involved with anyone!'

'Well, that's very odd. Look, I can't exactly leap up and phone Joyce Smith, she's still in a very rocky state. But I'll ask her for more details and pass them on to you.'

'But I don't see how I'll be able to identify a girl who doesn't exist. Could it be that Laurence just told his mum he had a girlfriend to keep her happy?'

'It's possible, I suppose.'

They sat in reflective silence for a moment, until Kate asked Polly a few polite questions about her children. To her surprise, Polly did not indulge in the usual long parental ramblings, and instead asked Kate more about her job. After the tension of the last few days Kate found Polly's interest seductive. She heard herself reciting all the other horrors of the week – the news that another channel might be transmitting from the Warehouse, the self-seeking sympathy of the Chester-Langs, and her own fears for the young people who worked with her. Polly listened to it all. And before Kate realised it, she was telling Polly about the moment outside Mr Chandip's shop, when she had seen the apparition on the other side of the canal, running in desperation yet getting nowhere.

'It was so strange, this emaciated figure in such a long white dress. She looked like something out of Dickens.'

'Spooky, as my daughter would say! Did you think you'd seen something supernatural?'

'Yes! *No!* Of course I didn't.'

'Sure?'

'Well, OK then, I'm not sure. Even now.' The admission made Kate's flesh creep. It's the wine, she thought, and of course it's getting cooler. Polly read her thoughts, or saw her shiver, and got up to close the conservatory doors.

'Why did you think it was a ghost?'

'Well, she didn't look real. It was the clothes . . . and the light . . . and she was so thin and wraithlike.'

'Thin.' Polly said the word as if it had special significance. 'Well, I don't believe in ghosts. And if she looked like Kate Moss I very much doubt she was the spirit of a nineteenth century maiden. This obsession with being thin is very twentieth century, you know.'

Kate thought for a moment. The ghost girl had been as emaciated as a modern model, and it had been the long white dress and the flowing hair falling from some twisted knot which had given the impression of Victoriana. She realised she was no longer listening to Polly, until something the other woman said struck her.

' . . . and your job sounds fascinating. Now Laura is settled in at school, I feel I should get a job myself. But I don't know. Between you and me . . .' – she leant forward conspiratorially – 'what I'd really like is another baby!'

Kate froze, then rallied. If she was going to feel her heart wring with tension every time someone mentioned pregnancy, she was getting obsessive, and some restraint within her wanted to stop short of that. She raised her eyebrows at Polly. 'Really! Then you'd have four?'

'Yes! I suppose it is a lot! Like our own dear Queen, and see what happened to her brood! Oh dear, I'm going on, aren't I? And look at the time! And still no sign of Nigel. I would have liked you to meet him.'

'Another time, I hope. I must thank you, Polly. I needed to talk, tonight.'

'Well, when you and John have finished doing up the house, you must invite me over for a nosy! And of course, I know his son Andrew is coming to stay, though I'm surprised his mother will let him! But we've hardly talked about John at all, have we? And I really meant to have a gossip with you and swap notes. Never mind, it was lovely to find so many other things in common. We'll have to leave John till next time.'

Oh, will we? Kate thought, suddenly stunned. How on earth did Polly know so much about John? He was extremely reserved when it came to talking about his first marriage, and Kate was surprised, and a little bit annoyed to find that Polly was so familiar with his past. John must have been opening up to this big woman in a big way.

But Polly hadn't noticed her consternation, and was standing up, smoothing crumbs from her voluptuous bosom. Kate stood too, and as she did her eye caught the silver framed photograph on the antique bureau just inside Polly's living room.

'Oh, your family?'

'Yes, all looking clean and tidy for once.'

Kate looked again. The husband stood proprietorially at the back of the group. To Kate, his large, dark looks seemed familiar, which probably meant she'd seen him putting the dustbins out or going for an early morning walk. She turned back to say goodnight to Polly.

'Thanks again.'

'Pleasure. Bye. Sleep tight . . . after the daiquiris you should!' Polly laughed merrily.

But when Kate left by the double doors and looked back, Polly was standing framed in the low lights of the conservatory, standing in a dream, cuddling the little girl's fluffy dog like a baby. She held the toy in a grasp that seemed almost desperate, and to Kate, who found the thought alarming, she looked both maternal and mysterious at the same time.

Kate went up the stairs to the bedsit, quickening her pace as she heard the phone ringing. John, she thought. But when she picked it up, it was Jenny.

'Kate, thank goodness I've got you. I've been trying for half an hour. I'm at work. I came back 'cos I needed to do some more tape viewing. And it's awful! That bastard boyfriend of Chloe's must have broken in. The petty cash tin has been forced open and the place is in a shambles. He's wrecked it!'

CHAPTER FOUR

'I'm not on drugs!' Chloe Carr raised her voice angrily. 'You've got to understand, Kate. Jason scores, but I don't. I've got too much to lose now.'

'OK, OK.' Kate sighed. It was eleven o'clock in the morning in The Narrowboat pub, the only place where she could find any privacy to talk to Chloe. Matt Lavelle was putting up the partitions in the office that day, along with locks on all the new internal doors. The conversation, the smell of beer and polish, the bright hard sunlight, all gave Kate a sense of unreality. That and the lack of sleep. She and Jenny had been at work until midnight the night before, sorting papers and tapes from the huge muddled mess on the floor. The vandal hadn't smashed any equipment. But files and tapes were flung everywhere.

'All right, Chloe, so you're not . . . scoring . . . but your boyfriend Jason is. And he was pretty hostile to Jenny and me. So what was this "delivery" he was talking about doing for Laurence Smith? Was that something to do with drugs?'

'Drugs? Laurence? You must be joking.' Chloe's lips curled in contempt as she lit yet another cigarette. 'Laurence wouldn't let a little thing like excitement get in the way of his fabulous career plan.'

'So how well did you and Jason really know him?'

'Hardly at all. Christ, Kate, you must believe me.' Chloe's arrogance ebbed and flowed like water slopping round a bowl.

'Look, Chloe, I'm trying,' she said. 'But you must tell me what has been going on. As much as you can. Please.'

'I've told you, for God's sake. Why are you so bloody worked up about it?'

'I'm worked up about it because I believe Jason came back last night and trashed the office. It wasn't a normal break-in – whoever did it came in through the front door. He wanted money he says he was owed by Laurence. They seem to have been involved in some scheme together. I can't accept it wasn't drugs, but, of course, you would know more about that than I do.'

'Oh, for Christ's sake, give it a break. What Jason does is nothing to do with me. He says he's moving out anyway.' The girl's lower lip began to tremble.

'So should I report his vandalising the office to the police?'

'No! Jason wouldn't do that. And how would he find the code to get in anyway?'

'Perhaps he wouldn't have to, Chloe. You're the one with the swipe card to get in through the door, aren't you?'

'What the fuck do you mean?'

In answer, Kate held up a little dangling object to the light. It was Chloe's Yin and Yang earring.

'This was in the middle of the mess we found, Chloe. Were you there with Jason, for whatever reason of your own?'

Chloe wavered, swinging once again from being boldly contemptuous to loudly defensive. 'No, *no!* Oh no, Kate, please, I know I'm not great to work with, but I'm not destructive. I wouldn't damage anything to do with the Food and Health Channel. This was my last chance of a real job in telly.'

'You're damn right. Let's be honest, Chloe, your CV was one long list of failing to get taken on in permanent jobs after endless work placements. I know how people can be exploited and I also know how many media companies are taking advantage of kids. But you haven't done yourself any favours. Now, if you insist that you weren't involved in last night's shambles, I'm prepared to believe you. I've invested a lot in you, Chloe, and I don't want to throw that away.'

It would have been the most justifiable act in the world to dismiss Chloe on the spot, but that would mean Kate admitting she had been wrong. After Laurence's death, she couldn't face the possibility of another misjudgement.

She waited. She could sense the pent-up misery in the girl's long but beautifully proportioned body. Chloe Carr could have been described as lovely, except for the sulky cast of her mouth. Now, though, she was ugly with stress.

'All right.' She plonked herself suddenly down on the stool. 'But I told Jason I would never tell anyone. So if I keep faith with you, I break a promise to him. But maybe I should.' She took a deep breath. 'Yes, he does have a drugs problem, and I've been there too. Loads of people have, far more than you think. It's amphetamines. Ecstasy. It makes you hyper, speeds you up, like doing a massive workout. You don't need to eat, that's why I used to like it. It keeps you slim. But afterwards you get very tired, as if you'd been on a humungous exercise jag. So you need more. And so it goes on. Jason needed the pills so he tried to take on all sorts of odd jobs to finance the habit. And Laurence found him some work. They met here in the pub, a couple of Fridays ago, when we all came up for a drink.'

'And what was the work?'

'Just picking something up and delivering it. Jason never talked to me about it. Although he did say . . .'

'What?'

'He said it was awkward to carry. Bulky. Not heavy but bulky.'

Puzzled, Kate finished her mineral water. It didn't sound like drugs, she had to admit.

'One more thing, Chloe. Was it the connection between Jason and Laurence which caused you to faint when you heard that Laurence might have been pushed?'

Chloe bit her lip, then gave a tiny nod. When she spoke, it was in a quiet, measured voice very different from her usual tone.

'OK, yes, it did cross my mind. Jason has some dubious contacts. But I honestly didn't know what was going on. When Jason asked me to join in with this delivery business, I said I had enough on my plate, making a go of Food and Health.'

At least Chloe had displayed some limited loyalty, Kate thought. She really didn't want to sack her, though she recognised both pride and some sentimentality in her justification. It must be hard, Kate thought, trying to enter this competitive world with no family or friends behind you. When Kate had begun a career in TV, it had been almost impossible to get started, but once recruited you were part of a big company with a formal training scheme. It wasn't like that now. How would she have turned out, if she had been in Chloe's place? She couldn't imagine it.

She said, 'Here you are,' and put the earring back into Chloe's trembling hand. The young woman found it difficult to control her relief. She was shaking as she rose from the table. At the pub door, she turned round.

'I'm sorry all this has happened, Kate. I know I've been a pain sometimes. I'm going to try and be a bit more like Debbie now. Keen and reliable. You won't regret giving me the benefit of the doubt. Thank you.'

Kate smiled back, and watched Chloe slope out in her skimpy striped trousers and absurd cropped tee shirt. She wanted to believe her. But even now, she couldn't be sure.

'So how are you all coping?' Matt asked Jenny later in the evening in the lounge of the same pub. Jenny remembered her own fit of the shakes when Laurence's mug had disappeared, and how Jason's intrusion had at least seemed concrete and to be coped with by comparison. But she didn't want to talk about either of those incidents to Matt on their first date.

'Well, we're all right, I think. After all, it's only two days since Laurence's . . . since Laurence died. Chloe's still a bit flaky and inclined to overreact, but Debbie's the salt of the earth. And Kate is so calm.' In fact Kate had described herself as like a duck, unruffled on top but paddling like crazy beneath the surface.

'And do you like your new partitions?' Matt took a rather innocent pride in the work he did on the office.

'Yes, very much. Funny, isn't it? When we were all in the same room together Kate spent half the time keeping me at arm's length, and being over friendly to the others. Now we've got the partitions, Kate can retreat whenever she needs to, while I keep the rest in order.'

'And you like doing that?' Matt smiled playfully.

'Yes, I do rather!'

Jenny had realised that Matt did not approve of authoritative women. He's not educated in the same way as I am, Jenny thought, and he can't hold the sort of conversations I want to be part of. I should get away, now . . .

'Another spritzer?'

'I'd love one.'

So much for resolution, she thought. The desire to stay in The Narrowboat, talking to an attractive man, mesmerised her. I should go home and read through the transcripts of those boring health shows, she thought, but her own bottom stayed on the uncomfortable stool, and her eyes followed Matt's as he moved toward the bar.

She wondered if all this emphasis on the body was making her randy, yet previously she had always associated gyms with asexuality. Earlier that evening she had met Matt for their first exercise session together. She had been introduced to his trainer at the gym, and had started the programme. The inadequacies of her own body had struck her, and her satisfaction with her general appearance had dimmed. She needed to be more muscular, fitter, less saggy. She admired Matt's smooth physique.

And she wanted him to think her attractive. Matt had watched her with an objective, unsensual appraisal as she finished on the exercise bike.

'Bit of a tum, but not bad,' he had said, without any fear that he might be offensive. Now, sitting on the stool, she breathed in and held her stomach tight, clenching her buttocks too, aware that they might be drooping over the edge of the upholstery. Matt ambled back, sat down and pushed the wine and soda to her. She noticed that he had mineral water with ice and a slice of lime again.

'You don't drink?'

'No, not much these days. Too many chemicals and carbohydrates.'

'And eating?' Jenny asked tentatively. She wanted to spin out the evening. Matt was probably the handsomest man she had ever seen, face to face, inches away from her. She squirmed.

'Well, Jenny, I'm careful what I eat and I don't eat out much for that reason.'

There was a long pause. She waited uncomfortably until he added, 'Hey, why don't you come back to my place and share dinner with me?'

It was all turning out very differently from the way Jenny had expected. She'd anticipated his making a pass at her, and imagined weighing up the offer and gently declining. Instead she gabbled, 'What a great idea, Matt. Shall I drive us there?' He smiled, used to female compliance.

And then Matt's flat reinforced her insecurity. The building was turn-of-the-century red brick, encrusted with plaster mouldings, although the feminine frosting of the frontage gave way inside to a sleek modernised hallway with lowered ceiling and lightspots. Jenny could see at once that Matt's apartment had a clean-cut male style which she had rarely encountered. The single men she had known at Northern TV lived either in grisly flats where social success was measured in used bottles and discarded underpants, or small houses decorated predictably by Habitat or John Lewis.

This was different. All the walls were white, and the floors were carpeted in thick cream rugs over black shiny floorboards. He had no plants, pictures, bric-a-brac, or matching furniture. And it was brutally modern, from the steel-fronted kitchen units to the wrought metal coffee table, black leather sofa and grey shelves.

'Nice place you've got here,' Jenny said with unnecessary sharpness, and he smiled pleasantly. But she was starting to realise that his sweetness was not all. The flat gave every sign that Matt saw himself as someone of consequence.

'Don't you have anything more exciting to drink?' she said aggressively, eyeing yet more mineral water.

'Oh, yes, sure. For visitors. On the table through in the big room.' Matt did not have a lounge or sitting room like everyone else. His 'big room' was a knocked-through arrangement, which was reached via a large arched opening from the kitchen, but which held hardly any furniture other than his black hide chesterfield and a lamp resembling tortured iron railings. She poured a generous portion of whisky into a glass, and went back to the kitchen for ice.

Matt opened the freezer for her and she noticed that his ice cube moulds were black plastic. It made her laugh. For the first time since leaving the gym, Matt looked disconcerted.

'Something funny?'

'Yes. Black ice trays. Good God, is there anything here that isn't advertised in GQ magazine? It's too smart to be true! I'm frightened to sit down!' She had meant to be amusing but it sounded merely mean, and Matt recoiled from her as if she had slapped him. Jenny immediately felt guilty at her waspishness.

'I'm sorry, Matt,' she said quietly. 'I'm a bit defensive. Since coming to London I sometimes find myself out of my depth, and then I get mad at myself because there's no reason why I should be. I tell myself I'm as smart and bright as anyone here, with a dash of northern spirit to make me even better . . . then I see black plastic fridge furniture and I lose it!'

Matt stared back at her gravely and for a moment she thought she had blown it. But then he started to grin.

'Well,' he said slowly. 'Jenny, you've certainly got a way with words.' She looked back at him, suddenly and awkwardly self-conscious. He noticed the first tiny lines under her eyes, and her trembling mouth. He had expected his next woman to have the smooth perfect skin of a model, yet he was fascinated by the mixture of sharpness and softness in Jenny. And she was shaking slightly, desperate to be touched.

This is it, he thought . . . this is a class act. And perhaps for that reason, he was almost scared to play his usual game of making women wait till they were so relieved at his eventual touch, they fell into his arms. And Matthew knew he was worth waiting for in the sack! Yet with Jenny, he was losing his customary calculated calm. He felt that if he didn't grab the moment, she would pull back and they would sit and make bright conversation over a limp salad. So he encouraged the pulsing in his penis, and pulled her towards him.

He's going to kiss me, Jenny thought, and as his warm, dry mouth pushed against hers she knew that it was probably going to be all right with Matthew. Not great perhaps, but all right, and she felt herself soften and moisten. The sensation made her knees sag, so she relaxed into his muscular body and felt with relief that he was hard under the floppy, loose cotton of his track suit pants.

'Do you want to eat first?' she whispered.

He laughed. Her directness was new for him. 'You're not shy, are you?' he said.

Jenny reminded herself this wasn't her old lover, with his post-feminist expectation of straightforward dealing, but Matthew Lavelle, studiedly non-intellectual, scared of being a luvvie, and accustomed to girls who should swoon into his bed. And that wasn't such a bad idea, she thought. He had his hands round her waist, and was pushing her backwards across the kitchen, through the living room and then through his bedroom door. As he tipped her gently backwards on to the bed, she was distracted by the black sheets. But Matthew was kissing her with the seriousness of a sexual expert, and she thought it advisable not to laugh.

They made love with self-consciousness rather than passion, but there was enough skill on both sides for it to be successful. They hardly spoke, but worked with a sort of sensible intensity on each other, like lovemaking from a guide-book. He would indicate what he wanted her to do, and they went through several routine positions. Jenny knew she would not climax, but she enjoyed the feel and smell of Matt, and he seemed to appreciate her, which she liked. She genuinely groaned and gasped a little, and he did not pressure her, although he was more athletic than she was. At one point Jenny thought, this is an exhibition, a super exercise, but Matt murmured 'that's nice' in a voice that seemed full of real pleasure, and she put aside her reservations and went back to concentrating on keeping her balance. A few minutes later Matt rolled away from her, and she could literally breathe a sigh of relief. It had gone well. He lay beside her, breathing heavily, his sculpted chest rising and falling.

'Do you want to eat *now?*' he laughed. Then he kissed her lightly on the nose, and chucked her clothes over to her. 'I'll get dressed then finish off making the salad,' he said as he sauntered away from her, his brown back narrowing to the neat cleft of his buttocks.

Jenny had been virtually inexperienced sexually when she had begun her affair with the older, much more sophisticated Nick Malcolm at Northern TV. She'd enjoyed her sensual education, but it had taken time, and she still often found complete satisfaction elusive. She had certainly not planned to fall into bed, literally, with Matt Lavelle. But the very fact that there had been more expertise than passion meant that she didn't feel disappointed and empty, as she had often done after her climactic coupling with Nick.

Matt was nice, a much derided word but right for him. She put her feet on the floor, felt the cold shiny floorboards, and reached for her socks. Then she stood up. I don't look too bad she thought, and swivelled, holding in her stomach slightly so that if Matt came back from the kitchen he would see her streamlined profile. The thought of her own naked body, not as classic as Matt's, but not bad, clad only in fluffy socks, made her laugh silently. Hardly a wonderful sight! But she was sure that soon, with all the exercise she planned, she would look as finely-tuned as he did. She turned again.

And then she slipped. As her feet went from under her she reached out to grab at the bed, then missed as the socks skidded, shooting her across the room so her naked bottom came down with a heavy thud on the polished floor. The force left her winded for a minute, her legs askew. And to her horror she had kicked inadvertently at what seemed to be the only incongruous piece of furniture in Matt's flat, a rather drab cloth-covered bedside table.

But it wasn't a table. Her kick had dislodged the cloth and revealed a stack of five white cardboard boxes. The boxes skidded too, and then the top one began its slow descent, and the lid split open as it slid off the pile.

Jenny looked at it, then blinked and looked again. Out of the box had fallen a cream and white lace robe, followed by a pair of frilly knickers, and a twist of cream wire that could only be the ultimate in minimal bras. Another even stranger bra, with a peephole effect on each cup, lay beneath them. Half in guilt, half in horror, she glanced round, but Matt was nowhere to be seen, though he could be heard playing Simply Red in the kitchen. Jenny shuffled forward and stuffed the lingerie back into its tissue-filled box, then hastily placed the box back on the small stack and covered it.

What was Matt doing hiding women's underwear? It was unworn, boxed and ready, but for what? Or whom? It struck Jenny as particularly distressing that despite what they had just done, she didn't know Matt well enough to ask him why he was hiding cartons of lingerie. She stood up and started to pull on her clothes. Then Matt's face, a picture of uncomplicated happiness, peered round the door.

'How about steak?' he said. 'After all, we've had the exercise!' And taking her startled silence for assent, he disappeared. As she dressed she could hear him in the kitchen, singing.

The next afternoon, towards five o'clock, Kate plonked down the phone in fury, and turned to Jenny, who had seemed quiet all day. They'd been discussing the possibility of taking 'Ready Steady Cook' repeats, and Kate had just been about to ask her what was wrong, when the phone interrupted. By the time Kate had finished the call, she was too furious to think of anything else.

'Those bloody horrible, awful people! Antony Chester-Lang knows damn well that I do *not* want to go to the wretched TV programmes market in Cannes, and he's getting the greatest pleasure from making me. And he also knows it will be well nigh impossible to book a Sunday flight at this time on a Friday, but he's virtually ordered me to have breakfast with his son at MIP on Monday morning.'

'So you haven't much option?'

'No, I bloody well haven't. I really don't want to go, but I think I'll have to give in. The trouble is, there's no point getting there till Sunday, and I *must* be back for Tuesday.'

Laurence's funeral was planned for that day.

'Well, the schedule is tight, and it's a nuisance,' Jenny said sensibly. 'But it's not impossible and at least you'll find out what's going on!'

'Yes, but it's the blasted cavalier way he orders me around. I suppose I'll have to go, but why this son of his can't talk to me in London I don't know.'

'What do the other shareholders say? I mean, this is quite an expensive trip, isn't it?'

'Oh, Chester-Lang has been quite clever. It's now half past four on a Friday night, and Joan Thompson is having her well-deserved weekend break. Charlie Mansfield has left New York for a trip to Sydney, so he'd be on his way to bed even if I knew how to raise him. I'm going to have to go to MIP, Jenny.'

'Well, you mustn't worry. I'll cope.'

'Of course you will! Look, there's only one thing that needs doing urgently and that's the final negotiation for "Cook of the North" with Northern TV. I said we'd finish the deal off on Monday morning first thing. They've got a new head of Programme Sales starting then, and they're keen to get the deal done. I think there's some competition for the show, so it's all rather crucial.'

'Well, I wouldn't mind doing it.'

'It'll be a tough deal to cut your teeth on. The details and draft contract are safely in my drawer. Look, take it now and put it in your folder, and see if you can get some time to look through it over the weekend. I'm sorry I've had to land you with such an important negotiation, especially when I expressed my reservations so freely earlier. That'll teach me to talk down to you.'

'Well, I'll have to prove you wrong. This is a big chance for me. Don't worry, I'll manage!'

'You'll have to, Jenny, you'll have to!'

'Damn right I will!' And Kate noticed that for the first time that day, some of Jenny's sparkle was back. She smiled at Kate, flicking her mass of thick brown hair behind her ears before refocusing earnestly on the draft contract, and Kate thought how Jenny at her best had a unique combination of warmth and enthusiasm.

In turn, Jenny glanced up at Kate, who was biting her lip, concentrating on writing some last minute memo. She looked different now, Jenny realised. Her face was thinner, and she was obviously tired, with new lines around her eyes. But she had lost the hunted look Jenny remembered from their time at Northern TV. The responsibility suits her, Jenny thought – and she's good to work for. Despite all the horrors of the past week, Kate was still in there, not milking the drama or collapsing under the strain, but keeping going.

It was strange, Jenny thought, that friendship could be such a compelling feeling, but that the words used to express it were so feeble. What could she say? Kate, I really like you? I respect you a lot? It was not in Jenny's northern nature. Yet she needed to affirm it.

'Kate?'

'Mmmm?'

'Things are all right in lots of ways aren't they? I mean we're not going to let these nightmare problems, well, end the project are we?'

Kate looked up sharply, her fingertips making a rippling sound on the keyboard as she swivelled in surprise to face her.

'No,' she said decisively. 'No, Jenny, we're not. This is a damn good concept, and we're damn good operators. At least, together we are.'

It was what Jenny needed to hear. She grinned.

'Thanks, Kate.'

'Keep the faith, Jenny! There's no way anyone is going to make us give up.'

*

For Kate the weekend passed in a crazed rush of packing and making arrangements. On the Saturday night as dusk fell she and John walked down to the Thames. Her bag was ready and waiting in the uncarpeted, bare brick hallway of the house. The bedsit was locked up. For the hundredth time she asked herself if she had her passport and tickets, until the rhythm of her own walking feet soothed her, and they reached the river. They stood, quietly watching the water swell against the muddy sides. Kate saw a heron banking, huge wings outspread above the stick thin foliage, where the budding leaves were sprinkled like pale green sugar against the heavy, greying, overheated sky.

There were a few other walkers, but even so, the river was quiet now, no rowers carving through it, or pleasure boats with vomiting revellers splashing down the current. The Thames was tidal up to Teddington Lock, and she could sometimes imagine that she smelt the docks, and the wharves full of oily ships, and the spread of the sea flowing from London to the east. But above the lock it was just a river, with a pale frilled greenness that reminded her of willow-fronded pastures with no hint of the ocean.

'Bloody flat, isn't it?' said John, exaggerating his northern accent.

Kate laughed. It was the first time for days they had been together without someone else's crisis looming. 'We can't all be lucky enough to live north of Watford,' she answered. 'Come on, John, you must admit this is lovely in its way.'

'Aye, I do that. But you never get a sense of being, well, really outside, do you? It's all a sort of interior.'

'You won't say that when it rains. Don't spoil things, John, by wishing you were back home. You *are* happy here, aren't you?'

John laughed teasingly. 'Of course I am. With faith and love you can make a go of anything, even the bland and passionless London suburbs.'

'I'd hardly say it was bland around here after this week! Although it seems to be getting back to normal. What will happen after the funeral, John?'

'Nothing, I suppose. But despite what the police and everyone else says, Laurence's mother will still believe he had a mystery girlfriend, and that he was pushed. You never subscribed to that theory, did you, Kate? In fact, no-one did but poor Joyce Smith. And me, I suppose. But you thought I was over-influenced by her, didn't you?'

'Yes, I did.' Kate paused. She had reflected a lot about Laurence's death, and she still couldn't make up her mind what to think. She was aware of a dilemma in her own mind. If Laurence had committed suicide, it was a tragic mystery they could put behind them. But if he had been pushed, the implications for all of them were horrendous. Say Jason had been involved? Where would that leave Chloe? Kate felt a cowardly temptation to leave well alone. What good would it do anyone if she started raking up more confusion? And the next day she was flying to France, with a whole new set of pressures. It was easier to think of something else.

'Talking of passion, I thought your friend Polly seemed intense enough the other night!'

'Really?' John looked up. Kate had mentioned her evening with Polly in passing, but he had seemed loath to discuss it. And at the moment, Kate was disinclined to spoil the peace between them with her old interrogatory technique. She wanted to be more restrained with John, more serene, and not risk the rows that used to rock them. She went on gently. 'Yes. She was telling me she wanted another baby.'

'Did she?' John stopped in surprise. 'Well, she is quite remarkable in that respect.'

Kate felt a shiver of vexation, but crushed it. She had hoped her remark might encourage John to talk about their own situation, but he said nothing, looking down and scuffing at the dry shaley path.

'So you got the lowdown on Nigel?' he said after a pause.

'Yes, I think so.' There must have been some parish row between John and Nigel, Kate surmised. She did not want to pry, and she hoped John appreciated the newfound discretion she was trying so hard to apply.

'I suppose I should have told you.' John looked embarrassed. He hated acknowledging any conflict with his flock, but they both knew church politics could be vicious. 'I really didn't want to talk about Nigel and Polly. All that's another life.'

'Fair enough.' Kate was quiet for a moment. The sun seemed to be setting unnaturally early, but it was merely the illusion caused by the surprising April heat, a phoney summer giving up by seven o'clock each night.

'Let's go home to bed,' she whispered. 'Look, even the heron's coming back to roost.'

And the big bird laboured over them, drifting heavily towards the mud and gravel of the bank where it landed on feet as delicate as pins, then stood on one pencil of a leg, reminding Kate of a sad grey stork.

Antony Chester-Lang hated the suburbs. His car rolled smoothly through Kingston on Thames, and over the bridge, while the fat man behind the smoked glass partition looked down at the riverside strollers and clustered drinkers as if they were models spilt from a toybox. Chester-Lang had been brought up in the large tree-lined roads over the bridge, and tended to sweat as they drew nearer. Sunday evenings reminded him of his mother, which was another reason why he chose Sunday for his weekly 'outings' as he euphemistically called the trips.

His mother had been a gentle woman, with no interest in his father who had died when Chester-Lang was twelve. The same summer, in the pleasant Edwardian home where Mrs Chester-Lang senior had sighed with relief and expected to sink into relaxing respectable widowhood, her son had discovered something about himself. One day, in the garden, he had seen his mother sitting, drooping over her cup of tea. It was a sunny July evening, and he had expected his meal to be ready by six, but she still sat there, dozing. He knew their housekeeper had the food ready. The whole household was just awaiting his mother's word. And she was asleep. He had marched up to her deckchair and bawled in her ear.

'Mother!' he had shouted in a parade ground voice. 'Supper!' She had opened her eyes wild in sheer panic, and had jumped so much the teacup leapt in her lap. Even now, he could still see the tan stain seeping over her blue crêpe lap, as if she had wet herself. She had put her shaking, crinkled white hand to her bosom, which was heaving in fear. 'Yes, Antony. I'm so sorry,' she had said weakly, without any attempt to remonstrate. It was a tiny event in her

70

uneventful life, but it was to change Chester-Lang's view of the world.

And it changed his mother's life too. From that day on he bullied her with the passion of a dedicated lover. The pleasure her fear gave him was indescribable, and shaped the whole of his sexual future. He had made the woman wretched till she died, worn out by him, in his late teens. By then he was ready to join the army, and foreign postings had enabled him to refine his tastes. In the seventies and eighties, the slow spread of sexual literature had honed it further. Chester-Lang knew he was addicted to a specific sort of sex. He had been married three times, each time to women he could bully, which remained the ultimate turn-on. But a few years earlier he had realised that he needed more explicit aid. Sonya had found her own turn-on at the time, and her pathetic reliance on the mirrors had amused him, and even helped. But he needed much, much more than that. Hence the outings!

And tonight was to be better than usual. Chester-Lang visited a number of clubs, changing them regularly when they had reached the heights he expected. He usually made private arrangements with the performers, hanging around for them after the shows, and persuading them to go a little bit further the next week, for money. Most of them would do anything for cash, he discovered, and the knowledge that people conspired in their own degradation excited him even more.

That night's venue was called Collars, a club in Soho, excitingly near to the restaurant where his whining wife had dragged him earlier that week. Chester-Lang left his driver, arranging to be picked up in two hours, and walked through the darkening streets. There was something about Soho which made him feel confident. There were so many respectable reasons for being there, yet the source of his pleasure was so close. If he bumped into a colleague, unlikely anyway these days when he was so nearly retired, it was easy to act as if he was on his way to a smart restaurant or power meeting. He was almost jaunty as he walked.

But behind him, half acting like two giggling lovers, a young man and woman followed. They had tried trailing Chester-Lang once before, on a hunch of the girl's, and had hit pay dirt. They had banked on Chester-Lang doing it again. They hadn't gone inside the club last time, but this time the male of the pair was planning to follow him.

The club was down in a basement, like most of its type; a few spindly tables surrounded a stage literally fifteen feet away. Chester-Lang ordered a double gin and tonic, and arranged himself on the tinny chair for maximum comfort and flexibility. The young man in pursuit lounged against the wall at the back. He thought himself a street-wise type and had spent a couple of routine nights in shop doorways, and believed that he was pretty clued up. He did not expect to be shocked, and for a while he wasn't.

The first act was routine. A black-haired woman weighing about eighteen stone paraded a man as a dog around the stage to some silly anodyne music. But Chester-Lang was not impressed. He yawned. It was the wrong way round for him. The second scene was better. Here, a man and woman went through a mild bondage routine, the woman smiling rigidly the whole time to show it wasn't really nasty, and the man, who looked slightly camp to Chester-Lang's discerning eye, displaying various exotic ropes, cuffs and collars. It was fine, for soft stuff.

But it was the third act he had come for. Chester-Lang sat up in his chair, and at the back, the young man watching him became aware of something unscheduled that was about to happen. He had watched Chester-Lang for so long, spurred on by the girl who was waiting for him in the wine bar having given her orders, that he believed he knew the fat elderly man's every gesture. He realised Chester-Lang was really interested now, but to his own surprise the thought filled the watching young man with something between disgust and fear, emotions he had not felt for some time.

A much larger man appeared, with a small bottle-blonde woman in leathers. She stripped as he watched. Then he pushed her to the floor, pulled her up again, and proceeded to start to tie her up. This time, the bondage was far fiercer. There was a post at the side of the stage which was the nearest they got to props. Slowly, tantalisingly the big man lashed the girl to it. For a while, as if dazed, she too displayed the same painted sleazy smile which all the women wore as some sort of symbol of enjoyment. But then it became clear that this time the bonds were actually hurting her. Her face contorted and her strained smile was wiped away. She was in panic! Chester-Lang sat upright with a little jolt and the young man watching him began to feel slightly sick.

The performer was whipping the woman now, with a long stagey whip, but it was flying though the air to the music and hitting so hard that even above the thumping beat they could hear her cries and whimpers. Chester-Lang was smiling.

The woman was looking terrified as the man circled her, and the music kept up its trivial little beat. Her partner stopped, and turned to the audience. He was wearing black leather pants and nothing else, and a chain twinkled from nipple to nipple. Pulsing his hips to the music he began to undo his flies, and Chester-Lang sat forward, his tongue flickering over his fleshy lips.

Then the performer turned to the woman and Chester-Lang laughed out loud, the jarring sound making even the other creeps in the club flick their eyes to him, and the young man shuddered. The dancer turned in profile, and right on the climax of the music an arc of yellow urine sprayed in the lights as it fell on the face of the terrified girl, who coughed and spluttered in degradation. Chester-Lang crumpled with delight in his seat, and the boy at the back turned away, for once appalled.

Quickly, Chester-Lang leapt up. He was not the sort to be sated and bleary, and the boy, who could begin to feel the cold yearning for drugs which a shock often brought on, had to sidestep into the shadows to avoid him as he hurried out through the dark exit. Not that Chester-Lang had ever seen him, of course. That was his new girlfriend's job. Even as the boy recognised his own jerky needs, he was aware for the first time of being scared, not just because of Chester-Lang's power and perversion, but because of what it meant about his girl. Hurriedly, feeling more and more disgusted and enraged, the boy followed him upstairs to the paybooth at pavement level.

Chester-Lang was talking to the dancer at the door, and slipped him the money, then went out into the night, feeling refreshed and spry. He rarely let his guard down, but in those few sweet minutes waiting for the driver each Sunday night, the fat man came as near to being relaxed as he could.

That was why the voice behind him caught him unawares. Worse still, the sensation of his left arm being forced brutally up his back shocked him so much he was breathless.

The boy felt quite different now. What he had thought of as almost a laugh – following a fat old pervert into a seedy club – had hardened through disgust and fear into anger. And with the anger was confusion about his own girlfriend and what she knew and would do. He jerked Chester-Lang's arm up his back more fiercely. You disgusting old bastard, he thought, but that was not what he had been told to say.

'Hi, Tony.'

'Good God! Let go.'

'No way. Listen, you need to know that we're on to you and your fun and games, and we need money, now, and we're going to get it. A grand will do. If not, we'll talk. To anyone. And you wouldn't like that, would you? After all, you have a reputation to keep up.' The boy's voice laughed brightly.

'What do you mean, a grand? I haven't got that on me . . .'

'We're not talking about now, you fat slob!' The boy cracked the arm again. 'You know the deal? The one you've got with the girl?'

'I . . .' Chester-Lang felt his heart heaving. He had been told to take it easier. My blood pressure, he thought. 'Yes . . .' he gasped, realisation sinking in. 'All right. *All right!* There's no need for this.'

'Oh yes, there is. Leave the money where you leave it for the girl. A grand. Or we'll talk about this to whoever will listen. Your lovely wife perhaps? Or all those respectable TV types you work with . . .'

It came to Chester-Lang that the inevitable was happening. For fifty years he had lived with the threat of blackmail until it felt like a familiar harmless pain, a sort of moral headache that would never get any worse. But now it popped in his head like a firework flaring. It had happened at last. He writhed and gasped and realised he was not having a heart attack, merely a major shock. Shock and realisation. The biter was bit. He was having screws put on him, and by someone he needed, and even had grudging respect for. It was a complete turnaround and he recognised it and for the first time in his life, felt the mirror image of his own perversion, a masochism which fascinated and appalled him. He was being humiliated in turn. And he admired her for it at the same time as hating her, whilst fuming in the arms of the fit, edgy, smelly youth who had pinioned his hands up his back.

'I'll do it,' he croaked. That fucking girl!

'OK, so we're off now, Tone. But remember, a deal's a deal.'

The pressure on Chester-Lang's arm slackened. He staggered forward slightly, before righting himself and lumbering round. The alley behind him was cluttered with Soho night-life and lowlife. But he could still see them, laughing and moving away in the distance, his assailant and that bloody girl whom he should never have trusted.

But she had been so damn persuasive. He remembered how she had wiggled her arse at him, and wheedled those clothes she wanted out of him, and listened to his plans, and been oh so helpful as she bent over the desk invitingly while she talked to him, daring him to give her a bloody good slap on the backside! The fact that she had been so scrawny had excited him, making her seem vulnerable.

He could see her bum waggling now, as she scurried away down the alley. He felt the fury of the humiliated bully. He knew that both of them were sniggering at him. And her power over him, the power of the only woman ever to get the upper hand, left him with the same sense of aching sexual frustration that he had savoured in the club. He knew then that things would come to a head at last with Sonya. After all, he told himself savagely, she was his wife, and he could do what he wanted with *her*.

As Chester-Lang lumbered to his feet, his mind spinning with confusion for the first time in years, the two lovers sidled round the corner into the alleyway running between two of Soho's most famous streets. The boy suddenly stopped, his body still jerky, but his arm as heavy as lead as it slipped from the girl's shoulders.

'What do you do for him?' he asked hoarsely, hugging his chest suddenly as if freezing. 'It was all fucking horrible in there. What do you do for him?'

'Nothing. Yet,' the girl said, looking at him sexily through narrow, heavily encrusted eyes with huge eyeliner striped in lines almost to her ears. She smiled. 'Our relationship is business so far. But you never know . . .' She shimmied provocatively in front of him.

'*No,*' shouted the boy in the uncontrolled voice Kate and Jenny had heard in the office.

'Oh, for God's sake.' The girl brought her sneering face down to his. 'Get a grip, Jason.' Then she slid away from him up the alleyway, her tight slinky dress clinging to every line and crevice of the thin buttocks she wiggled at him before disappearing round the corner. Jason was left to hug himself and lurch towards the square, and more supplies. 'Fucking, fucking horrible,' he mumbled, as he stumbled up the alley.

CHAPTER FIVE

By late Sunday afternoon, Kate was in the south of France. On her left, the promenade at Cannes, the Croisette, curved into the distance, fringed by luxury apartments. On her right, the Mediterranean sparkled like a silver dress on a supermodel.

It was bakingly hot. The heatwave which was still taking the chill off the ground in Britain had already turned the south of France into something at the bottom of the frying pan of Europe. Kate felt like a greasy blob, laden with her overnight bag, handbag, and bulging complimentary MIP holdall. The weight made a cruel dent in her shoulder. To her alarm, the sweat on her thighs was busily working its way under the tops of her hold-up stockings. And she wasn't sure where she was going.

She heaved the bags up, and moved on. She had been to MIP once before, in the eighties, when British ITV companies took small yachts on the Jetée Albert Edouard. Kate had worked for London Vision, and had come out to Cannes as a perk. Those had been the days, when the politics mattered more than the programmes, and whole weeks could be amply filled with speculation over union agreements, pay rises, and white wine. Then, she had stayed at the five star Grey d'Albion. Now she was looking for the two star Hotel des Cyclades. That was real commercial TV for you!

Hot and bothered, her vexation was compounded when she saw two men she remembered from the past strolling up the palm fringed boulevard towards her. The name of the taller one escaped her, but the other was Jeremy Woodley, ex-London Vision, and now a consultant. He was reputed to be a whizz at dealing with the Independent Television Commission or ITC . . . the fickle regulator. Jeremy was dressed in a linen jacket, his ample tum coated in a crisp navy cotton shirt, and his friend was sporting a thick blazer, shirt and tie without a trace of the sweat which was making snail trails down Kate's face, not to mention the tops of her legs.

Before she could hide behind the foliage, they were there. 'Kate! Kate Wilkinson. What a lovely surprise.' Jeremy bore down on her for a lipsmacking kiss. 'Derek!' he called loudly to his companion, who was only inches away. 'You know Kate, don't you? Ex-LondonVision, like me. Kate, you've met Derek Boulder, haven't you?'

'Yes, I'm sure I have.' Kate smiled back at the other man who stood aloof.

'Derek is a commissioning editor now,' cooed Jeremy. She was unsure whether or not to hold out her hand. But the man, annoyed by her hesitation and used to sycophancy, turned away and stared out to sea with an air of long suffering patience. Jeremy sniggered. 'Are you well, Kate?'

'Fine,' she said, trying to smile sweetly through the bile. Not only that, she could feel a sticky stocking top gently unpeeling from her thigh, and knew that the weight of the rubbery welt would bring the rest of the stocking rolling down her leg in seconds. If the two men would only move on, she could sidle towards the fringe of palm and bougainvillea and discreetly haul her hold-ups back again.

'Well, must dash. We should meet up for a drink sometime while you're here, Kate, though these things are such a thrash. I'm in the middle of trying to get the ITC to allow a shopping chain to fund a gameshow for teenagers.'

Kate stared back at him. She could remember the early eighties, when Jeremy Woodley would have died rather than toady to fatcat big business. But he had forgotten all that now. Waving grandly, he resumed his royal progress down the Croisette.

Kate watched him go, Derek Boulder strolling slowly after him, then realised she was lost. She needed to stop and grope in the cavernous depths of her free conference bag for a street map. As she bent down, her left stocking gave up, and came down, slowly and infuriatingly. In sudden impatience she dropped her holdall, hitched up her skirt and whipped the stockings off, rolling them in a ball and stuffing them in her bag. It had all taken less than thirty seconds.

But ten yards along the promenade, Derek Boulder had paused, looked back, and taken in the whole of Kate's undignified strip-tease. She caught his contemptuous glance before he turned to stroll away.

In Britain the welcome sense of early summer meant the doors were wide open to The Narrowboat, and the pub garden which stretched down to the river was filling with pale couples in their first weekend tee shirts of the year. In the neat flowerbeds the pink and yellow blooms were pert and fleshy, no hint of the wilting to come, and the publican had grabbed a quiet moment to water them so the scent rose freshly. The grass was still damp in half moons along the borders.

Jenny was aware that Matt was guiding her by the elbow to one of the benches at the bottom of the garden which looked out on to the Thames.

'Now, you can't sit here and say London has nothing to offer!' he said.

'I never said that!'

'No, you didn't, but you think it. I know what it's like, Jenny. I mean, I'm not a northerner, and it's not exactly the same, but when I moved up here from Slough, it took me a bit of time to get used to it. Drink?'

'Oh, thanks, a spritzer.'

Jenny turned to look out over the muddy river, where two snooty swans floated past. Bushy little islands obscured her view of the Georgian houses on the other bank. Matt said, 'I was very pleased when I saw you at the office today. I thought it was only me who had to work Sundays. Weren't you were planning to go back "oop north" this weekend?'

She ignored the silly accent. 'I was. But Kate had to go to France, so I'm in charge.'

Jenny was aware of the nervous tumbling in her stomach. Things were already going badly wrong. She had come into the office determined to be absolutely on top for Monday morning. But her confidence had been shattered by the discovery that the one thing Kate had expressly asked her to work on had disappeared. Jenny had searched everywhere for the draft contract for 'Cook of the

North'. It was a highly sensitive document, detailing the terms which Kate was prepared to offer Northern TV to sell their most popular new programme, and Jenny couldn't face the thought that she had lost it. Her desk was strewn with logging notes and programme cue sheets, but no draft.

But something else had happened to make it worse. She had been rummaging rather desperately in the pile of papers on her desk, when the phone had pealed out. Half distractedly she had picked it up, sure it would be Kate. But there had been silence. Jenny waited. She had forgotten about the phone call the day Jason had blagged his way into their office. Now, it was happening again. And at the other end the same weird, high, sexless voice was saying, 'Can I speak to Laurence Smith, please?'

'Who are you?' Jenny said loudly, her own voice echoing round the hot empty office.

And then the giggle.

Jenny slammed down the phone and took a deep breath. There was a number you could ring to trace a call, she knew that, but the digits had gone out of her head. 1457? 1475? If she phoned the operator to ask, would that new call obliterate the traces of the nuisance caller? This time, she thought, she would have to tell Kate about it. It had gone beyond a need for Jenny to keep her own council and stay cool for the sake of office calm. They needed to find out who it was and deal with it. What sort of creep would get his pleasure from this?

She had been starting to rummage again when Matthew had bounced through the door, clearly delighted to see her. And because she was still shaken after the horrible phone call, she looked up at him with a welcoming glance. In the scouring summer light, he looked absolutely normal, and the issue of the lingerie in his bedroom seemed to recede. There had to be a simple reason which she hadn't sussed. And he was clearly thrilled at the chance to invite her for a drink. After all, she thought, there could be nothing sinister about a walk to The Narrowboat and a quick glass of white wine, and she felt that an hour off the premises might clear her head. So here she was.

'Penny for them?' Matthew said imaginatively.

'Oh, nothing, Matthew. Sorry!' She smiled at him guiltily, and for the first time since she had left his bedroom, she looked him full in the face.

After her discovery of the boxes, she had just wanted to get away. But Matthew had taken her silence for shyness after their sudden lovemaking. And he had been flattered. He had thought Jenny a clever sort of girl, and when she went quiet, he felt both superior and sympathetic. So, driving her home that night, he had confided in her more than in most girls he had taken out. He told her about how he had been determined to be successful, and how he had done a diploma in business management at Kingston Poly after an unpromising start as a salesman. His job at the Warehouse was a real opportunity, and he glossed over the slight problem they had filling the floor space with tenants. His life story sounded organised, successful and properly paced, and the more he talked, the less Jenny felt she could ask, 'So why have you got boxes of bras in your bedroom?' But when he dropped her at her flat, Matt had clearly been surprised that she turned down his offer to 'work out' together later that week.

Jenny had resolved not to see him again, but bumping into him at the Warehouse on a Sunday was a rather different matter.

'Hey, smile!' Matt beamed. 'Look at this lovely weather! Aah, that's better.' And he winked in a conspiratorial way so that his delight was obvious and she had to grin back.

'Oh Matt,' she said, and on a sudden whim leaned out and put her hands over his. Surely she could just ask him, straight out, about the clothes? Perhaps he had a friend in the wholesale business? The thought, so simple and for some reason so funny, made her laugh again. 'Matt . . .' she began.

'Don't say anything, Jenny. I know you think I rushed things last Thursday. Well, I didn't know how else to do it. But I really want us to get to know each other now.'

She looked back at his bright, hopeful face.

'I suppose the sort of guys you like, Jenny, are all politically correct and into music and the theatre . . .' In the last few days, he had tried to work out why Jenny had withdrawn from him. Intellectual snobbery seemed one possibility, and made him less confident with Jenny than with the other women he had laid.

Jenny said quietly, 'And the girls you like? I suppose they have flat tums and live for step aerobics?'

'Actually, a lot of the girls I've been with have been pretty gross! But I've had one or two really nice girlfriends. Like my boss's secretary . . .' He waited. Could that be the problem? Had she heard about Michelle?

Jenny knew at once who he meant. The girl was called Michelle something and was the luscious type. So you're a normal guy, with a normal sex life, Jenny thought. And suddenly she felt relieved.

'That doesn't bother me . . .' Quite the reverse, Jenny thought. Surely in a day or two, over a drink, having a laugh, she could question him about the lingerie and be reassured?

'So what do you say, Jenny?' He picked up her hand from the table, and kissed it. His physical vigour seemed to flow down his arm and into hers, strengthening her.

'Oh, Matt, you are sweet! Thank you so much for asking me. I can't say I've been propositioned like that before. Especially after the event!'

'So you'll see me again?'

'Why not? I enjoyed the work out! In every sense!'

He smiled back. Then he turned, satisfied, to look out at the river. Jenny watched his untroubled profile. Conversation, she guessed, would not be his strong point. But his calmness, almost his lack of imagination, was soothing. For a moment she let her mind float along the brown river with his, until his quietness let her return to her real preoccupation.

Where the hell was that lost contract? She would give it one more go.

Eventually, saying little, she and Matt walked back up to the office, and she persuaded him to leave her while she went back inside for yet another search. She knew he was eager to get to the gym and heard his car revving away as she entered the stuffy building, as always aware of its creepiness now she was alone. It was as if sometimes, the dark canal side seemed to dominate, however bright the sun was as it splashed round the courtyard. Jenny walked slowly upstairs. She was hot and tired, and there was no way the contract could be in there, undiscovered. She really had no idea where it could have gone.

She opened the glass doors, and as always, her eyes went round the room, re-assessing it now there were the new partitions. To fit everything in, Laurence Smith's desk had been pushed to one side. They still needed to go through all his papers and tapes, but there had been an unspoken feeling that that should be left until nearer the funeral. Even so, Jenny had felt sad to see his stuff moved. Once that desk was cleared, she knew, Laurence would be officially dead to the office.

But this time, Jenny felt the heat off another person, as clearly as if somebody had been standing there. She was convinced someone else was in the room. She looked round wildly for some sign that she was not alone, but apart from the tremor on her neck and the warmth which should not have been there, there was nothing.

Then Jenny realised. The warmth, which seemed to so clearly suggest Laurence, was actually coming from Laurence's desk. The pig mug was back, and from it rose an unmistakable smell of hot coffee and the slightest of vapour trails against the dark increasing gloom of the canal side of the office. The scream caught in Jenny's throat and she backed out of the door and stumbled down the stairs and out into the courtyard.

In Cannes, Kate sat on the narrow bed at the Hotel des Cyclades and felt hopelessness creep up on her like the damp on the crusty pink wallpaper. Patronised by the past in the bloated shapes of Boulder and Woodley, she felt oppressed by the problems of the present too. She had hoped that the Food and Health Channel would be her great success, restoring to her the status she had once enjoyed at LondonVision. But it was going to be a long slow haul.

The hotel room managed to be both bleak and crowded. She had to close the main door before she could open the partition to the so-called en-suite bathroom, a tiled shower cubicle where the grout had been replaced by an ecological green growth. It now appeared to be a haven for scuttling creatures which fled when she turned on the light. There was one window, so high and small that it provided neither sunshine nor view, and the large flat continental light switch was hanging from the wall, attached only by a vein of plastic coated wire.

She looked suspiciously at the phone. At least there *was* one, but its dirty beige plastic handset repelled her. She lifted it as if germs might crawl out of it and into her ear. Gingerly she tapped in the code for the UK, only to hear the furious outraged gabbling of the woman downstairs. She dropped it as if burned.

By now, Kate looked and felt terrible. She stood up, unzipped her bag and shook out the one summery dress she had bought. It was as crumpled as a toffee wrapper, but there was a wire hanger lolling from a rack, so she hung up the dress in the hope that the creases would drop out overnight. In the morning, she would brave the shower, then towel-dry her hair.

She decided to change into casual trousers which were designed to look rumpled even when she ironed them, and stroll back to the Croisette. Perhaps the fresh air would make her feel better

But in the evening warmth, she found that the disorientation made her feel queasy. She lurched forward, and put her hand out to the wall on one side, propping herself up while she got her breath back. Then she felt a soft touch on her shoulder, and jumped inches in the air.

'Kate! Hi! I didn't mean to alarm you. Are you OK?'

She turned round to find one of her long-standing acquaintances, Pat O'Shane, looking worriedly at her. Pat was an executive producer for Actionpacked, one of the leading game show producers in Britain.

'Hey, what's up?' Pat was even taller than Kate, and instead of the routine media kiss inches from her cheek, Kate felt Pat hold her like she would hold a child.

'Come with me,' Pat said masterfully. 'It looks like you need a drink. You're not the only one to be suffering from some wretched bug. Most of Granada's laid low.'

Pat shepherded the pale and stumbling Kate along, explaining as she did that every year Actionpacked took an apartment with a big balcony looking over to the Palais where the market and conference was held. It was the perfect place for weary TV executives to pop for chilled white wine after a hard day's buying – what was more, Actionpacked executives could see everyone come in and out of the hall.

Pat made Kate sit out on the balcony, where the last rays of the evening sun hit her full in the face and her body began to slowly balance up again. A cup of coffee and a pastry appeared in front of her.

'Your teeth were chattering and you were white as a sheet,' Pat said. 'What is it? Tum? Or flu? Where are you staying? We'll get you a cab. Or stay here, if you like. We're just expecting a few people, some of them old friends of yours.' Kate shook her head weakly. Pat O'Shane was a rare person, who seemed able to progress in TV without losing her kindness. Kindness is such an underrated quality, Kate thought, and people in power try to stifle it because it's arbitrary, springing up in response to the needy at inconvenient moments.

'Pat, I must go. I'll be in your way. I feel much better now, really!'

'Don't move! Trust me, I'm a mum. You know what they say about working in TV, it helps if you have children of your own!'

Kate laughed feebly.

'There you are,' Pat went on, 'there's a tinge of colour coming back to your cheeks.'

'Yes. Look, Pat, I'll just drink this . . .'

There was the sound of a buzz on the intercom. 'That'll be our first guest,' Pat said.

Oh God, Kate thought, and I look and feel such a mess. She dragged herself up and into the bathroom at the far end of the apartment, and safely locked inside, she shook her head vigorously. When she emerged, two or three clusters had already formed. She could hear Pat introducing people.

'Kate,' she called, 'come and meet Derek Boulder.'

What bloody awful luck, Kate thought. But anxious to please Pat, she edged forward. Another surge of visitors welled into the narrow entrance at the back of the apartment so Kate was cut off by the tide. Good, she thought, Pat would be occupied putting the new guests at ease. Skilfully, Kate squeezed herself behind a little occasional table bearing a huge smoked glass vase of lilies.

Then she became aware that Boulder had oozed away from the balcony and was inching with his back to the wall down the perimeter of the crowd.

She heard him say 'Hello there!' in feigned surprise to a pleasant looking man in a grey suit, whom she had seen Pat introduce to some fawning BBC types earlier as being from Pearson Broadcasting. She watched Boulder's half profile, and marvelled at the change. From being a mask of contempt on the Croisette, his features were now mobile and his voice was lightly bantering, a sort of man-to-mediaman tone.

'God, this place always gets so packed, but I can't resist Pat's wine. She's such a super hostess one can almost forgive her her success!'

The Pearson man smiled, but warily, Kate thought.

'And how's your chairman now? I saw him a few weeks ago at the Royal Television Society,' Derek leered enquiringly. Kate could lip read the other man's noncommittal, 'Fine.'

'I'm glad I bumped into you,' Boulder went on. 'I wanted to avoid a woman whom Pat was calling over. Some lame duck friend of hers who's involved in a little cable channel.' He leaned forward in fake camaraderie. 'Cable! Pathetic. Mind you, there might be some rich pickings. They say Tony Chester-Lang is putting a lot of money into his latest venture. I was talking to Jeremy Woodley about it today. Chester-Lang's taken him on to sweet-talk the regulators. Can't say I know what it's about, but it's supposed to be a winner, and there's already a team behind it. Not that you should worry of course . . .'

Kate leaned against the wall. So what was this *team*? Who were they and where were they based? And why was Chester-Lang's new channel creating so much more interest than Food and Health? Discreetly, Kate crept out from behind the vase, and working against the flow, crept back down the marble steps and out into the still warmth of the street.

It was full of beautifully dressed people strolling purposelessly along, and Kate joined them, letting her muddled thoughts flow. It was a relief to realise there was no-one she knew in the crowd, and on impulse she followed a reptilian old man and his lizard-eyed escort across the road, and on to the Croisette. There was no doubt the place was gorgeous at night, although the fact that every square centimetre was teased into style was claustrophobic. And though she hadn't wanted to come to Cannes, it would be churlish to deny its magic. She was really very lucky. It *was* funny to think she was here, looking out at the yachts moored in the bay, while John was holding the Parochial Church Council monthly meeting in the parish hall.

She shivered despite the warm scented breeze. She felt guilty, suddenly, for enjoying the warmth, and worried for a moment that the trip to France signalled a new divide . . . Kate the TV executive, John the man of the caring nineties. John was always discreet, so did her new success mean he was less likely to talk to her about the human misery that was the substance of his job? Their difference of opinion, however mildly stated, about Laurence Smith's death hadn't helped. And then, there was his reluctance to talk about Polly. When should Kate pry, and when should she respect his need for privacy for his flock?

She walked back towards the squalor of the Hotel des Cyclades. She crossed the road, found the Rue des Serbes, made a few turnings, and was soon at the open doors of the hotel, the rusty old woman giving her a welcoming snarl. But this time as Kate passed, she croaked with painful slowness, '*Pour vous, madame. Téléphone.*' Kate stopped in surprise as the crone thrust a dirty bit of paper in her hand. John's number was written on it, several digits illegible, but the overall impression clear.

'*Madame,*' said the witch, '*essayez ce numéro. Maintenant. Vite, vite.*' With a toss of her greased iron head, she indicated that if Kate sprinted to her room, she would graciously make the connection for her.

Kate leapt up the stairs two at a time and the phone was ringing demandingly when she fought her way breathlessly through the mortice lock into her room.

She picked it up and with a rush of frustration, heard the usual irate garble before, suddenly, John was there. She sank on to the bed so it shook, clutching the headset despite its grime.

'Oh God, John, I do love you,' she said before realising how strange that sounded, out of the blue.

'Oh, hello!' John intoned. 'Have I got the right number?' Kate laughed, with an edge of hysterical relief. 'Actually,' he went on, 'that's only half a joke. It's been a nightmare trying to get you. I've tried four times. But at least you sound pleased to hear me. To what do I owe this enthusiasm?'

'I miss you.'

'Already? Although of course I miss you too. And I love you too, before you go off in a huff thinking that I never say the right things! How's your day been?'

'Horrid. It's a real pain bumping into people from the past. And I just heard at a party that two of our shareholders, the Chester-Langs – I've told you about them – well, they're investing heavily in another channel. I mean, I knew that anyway, but I didn't know they'd already employed people to start running it . . .'

'So you're going to parties? Having fun?'

'No, not really. I just got caught up in this one. I didn't get much to eat though. And how's your day been?'

'Not bad at all actually.' His voice brightened. For a moment Kate felt her spirits fall, but what sort of person would want their loved one to have a rotten day without them? Everyone, she thought, amused at herself!

'I've done two services, and a visit to Joyce Smith which wasn't great. But then I went to see Polly. It's wonderful really how she keeps that family going. She's remarkable.' The enthusiasm in his voice irked Kate slightly.

'I thought you didn't want to talk about them?'

'True. I don't. Hey, I found that stupid black frilly thing of yours in a bag in the rubbish in the hall, just now. Made me think. Are you sure you'll be back tomorrow?'

Cheered, Kate laughed. 'I hope so!'

They rang off minutes later. Kate lay on the bed, thinking that perhaps things weren't so bad. John sounded so much more demonstrative than usual, and that was gratifying. And whatever Chester-Lang was up to, she would find out from his son within twelve hours. Best of all, by ten o'clock the next morning, the 'Cook of the North' programme would be in the bag for the Food and Health Channel.

In South London, Jenny Sims could not settle at all. She had finally left the Warehouse an hour earlier after forcing herself to be rational and face the coffee mug on her desk. She had made herself walk back to the office for her bag, and she had stared at the congealing cup of slimy liquid a good three or four minutes before she braced herself to walk over and pick it up. Then she had strode determinedly into the kitchen, flushed the coffee down the sink, and put the mug back on the rack. It was only a mug . . . only coffee. Anyone could have come back into the office and made it. Look how Matt had strolled in earlier to see her. It meant nothing. Nothing. She would not be terrorised by objects. She had a job to do.

Back at her flat, she needed to concentrate on something concrete. She kept going over and over the possible whereabouts of the missing draft contract. And she had a slight headache. It was now hotter than anything she had experienced in the north at this time of year. She shared the flat with two other women who were both away for the weekend, and she had flung open the sash windows in the bedrooms. But rather than fresh air, all she seemed to feel welling through the building was the updraught from thousands of flats and houses. And the foliage in the borders outside her ground-floor window oozed heat like jungle undergrowth. Worst of all, she could not help thinking of the cool empty spaciousness of Matt Lavelle's tasteful apartment. If this heat lasted from April until October, Jenny would have to rethink where she was living.

She looked round the disguised tat of the living room. Bric-a-brac which the other girls had displayed with pride now seemed like dated clutter, and the plants she had thought flourishing seemed parasitical after the clean lines of Matt's big room. One of the women she shared with had propped invitations to all sorts of functions on the Victorian mantelpiece. Jenny had thought they gave the place a look of Sloaney class, but now she saw them for what they were, curling reminders of juvenile ad agency 'do's' and pretentious press receptions.

The phone rang in the hall. For a moment Jenny was scared to answer it, suddenly cold with the thought that the giggling idiot who had called her at work might know her home number. Ludicrous, she told herself, and stumbled quickly to pick it up. Any contact would be better than prowling round here, from room to room, worrying about that wretched missing contract and trying to cool down.

'Hi,' she said.

'Hello? Is that you, Jenny?' For a minute Jenny could not place the soft Manchester accent.

'Yes, who's that?'

'Oh, hi. I'm sorry to bother you but it's Debbie Allen. I know it's lateish, like, but I thought you wouldn't mind.'

'No, no, not at all. What's the problem?'

'No problem. Just to remind you that I'd booked Kate a call to the Programme Sales Executive at Northern TV for nine thirty tomorrow morning. You'll want to go ahead with that even if Kate's away, won't you?' This time Jenny's stomach turned over for real and she was aware of the gripe deep inside.

'Oh . . . er . . . yes, of course.'

'Great! I think I ought to be there to put the calls through for you, Jenny. I think it's a good idea to make you sound important. You know, with an assistant and everything. This is very significant, isn't it, Jenny?'

'Yes.' Jenny felt sick. 'Very significant indeed.'

'Thought so. OK then, Jenny, see you tomorrow.'

'Fine. Thanks.'

'Oh, that's OK. Tarra now.'

Jenny put the phone down almost before Debbie stopped speaking and was aware of the headache taking up residence in the middle of her forehead. The heat, she thought. She went into the living room and sat on the dumpy blue sofa, clutching a yellow cushion to her chest as if to protect herself.

What could she do? She had no idea what Kate would pay for 'Cook of the North'. There was a price range of thousands of pounds. She had let Kate down and the only thing to do now was to ring her in France. She found the yellow sticker with the hotel number on it in her handbag, and dialled. The tone burped at her. Then it was picked up by a female who sounded as if she was clearing her throat.

'Madame. Je . . . s'il vous plaît . . . parler . . . er . . . speak to . . . er, Miss Wilkinson. Kate Wilkinson.'

A torrent of what sounded like abuse came down the line. Then there were a couple of interrogatory 'eh's?'. Jenny had no idea how quickly her holiday French could desert her. After a few seconds' silence the female slammed down the phone.

Jenny sat on the sofa, paralysed with guilt. Now the moment had passed, she knew she couldn't face telling Kate. It was the first major responsibility she had been given, and she had screwed it up. She might even be in danger of losing the series for the Food and Health Channel altogether, by stalling until Kate got back. There had to be a way of finding out about Northern's negotiating position, so she could forge ahead with the deal.

To do that, she would have to speak to someone important there, but someone whom she could trust, someone who perhaps owed her enough of a favour to talk to her about the way they conducted their sales. One phone call would mean nothing.

She lifted up the receiver, and dialled the home number for Nick Malcolm, Foreign Documentary Editor of Northern TV, and her ex-lover. There wasn't much connection between the Foreign Desk and programme sales, but she knew he would advise her on how to deal with Northern TV, if she swallowed her pride. And it was amazing how low you could stoop when the job was at stake.

Jenny was aware that she hadn't handled her first taste of real management responsibility too well. She had lost the draft. She had failed to own up to her boss. She had been terrified by a stupid nuisance caller. She had been ungracious on the phone to Debbie, who had only been trying to help. I've lost my grip and I'm out of my depth, she thought desperately, as Nick's rather terse voice answered the phone. She took a deep breath. 'Nick? It's . . . it's Jenny.'

Would he help her? If he didn't, she was in the shit, and maybe out of a job.

Oh, God, thought Jenny. For the first time, she understood how the pressure might have got to someone as keen to succeed as Laurence Smith.

CHAPTER SIX

Kate woke in the Hotel des Cyclades to see a tiny patch of blue through the window above her bed, and lay there without moving her head, just in case it was aching. She automatically ran her checklist for the usual business trips blues – hangovers, physical discomfort and insecurity. No hangover. The discomfort she could live with. And insecurity? She thought again about Derek Boulder and his remarks at the party. In an hour she would be seeing Chester-Lang junior, and she could find out more for herself. She wondered what he would be like, and imagined a thirty year old version of his father, in a sharp but expensive suit, patronising her with business school jargon.

She swung her legs out of bed and advanced on her dress, drooping from the coathanger on the wire across the corner of the room. Good, the creases had dropped out of it. It was calf length, navy with tiny white flowers, and was inexpensive and conventional, but it always looked good, making her appear flatteringly slim. She showered, appreciating the red hot water and realising that the little window actually let in the bright sunlight of morning, but kept out the fierce heat of afternoon. The hotel wasn't quite the hellhole it had seemed.

She rubbed her hair on the scrap of towel until her scalp felt raw and achingly clean, then brushed it and rubbed it again. Then she combed it back and surprised herself by looking rather sleek and fashionable. The dress fell round her in its usual graceful way, this time more so than usual because there was less stomach in the way. More by good luck than good management the shoes she had brought were low-heeled, navy court shoes which looked great with the dress, and the conference ID and holdall added to the picture of an organised executive. Amazing, Kate thought. If she'd planned an outfit down to the last detail she would probably have looked a mess, but the things she'd thrown grumpily into the bag at the bedsit had actually worked.

She felt surprisingly self-assured when she arrived at the Croisette and the long curving drive to the Majestic Hotel, but it only took one glimpse of a laddish Programme Controller from ITV to remind her that this was MIP, an event she would have normally avoided. She walked less cheerily up through the lethal swing doors, into the reception. Her arrangement, via his father, was to meet Daniel Chester-Lang in the lobby.

She spotted a magazine rack, moved to the side of it, and allowed herself to stop and look round. Various people dotted the room. By the porter's desk, a large woman in bright clothes was giving orders. A sleek grey-haired business man lounged cross-legged on a sofa reading *MIP News*. A busy-looking woman, one of the few female executives in the BBC, walked past with an anxious man at her elbow. And a tall slim young man waited by the jewellery case. Kate stared at him, hoping he couldn't see her.

He looked slightly crumpled but smart, in a loose cream-coloured linen jacket, with jade green trousers and a dark polo shirt. She felt he was too colourful to be Daniel Chester-Lang, and her opinion was confirmed when he turned towards her, catching her stare, and revealed a red Aids-awareness ribbon pinned to his lapel. She smiled vaguely at him, mildly embarrassed at being caught, and turned to look at the magazines.

Then she sensed something happening, as if a parade was approaching. Out of the breakfast room swung a group of men, led by a person she recognised as an international children's programming executive. He was followed by the routine cluster of clones.

'If the ratings fall, spend on the marketing. We want every kid in Britain to need our culture,' boomed the overgroomed executive. Kate smiled, wondering how admiring parents in the UK would feel about the innocence of cartoon creations if they saw this bunch moving through the lobby like piranhas. As she watched, one of the minor feeder fish was forced away from the others by having to hop round the jewellery case. There was an expression of panic on his face as he hurried to catch up with them, and was hailed instead by the thin young man in the cream jacket who seemed to recognise him.

'Hi, wow, how're you?' the young man called in a light, American voice to the gasping acolyte. The executive seemed visibly to jolt, blink and stare, and then refocused right past the young man and hurried on two steps at a time, desperate to rejoin the shoal. The young man looked crestfallen, and Kate's heart went out to him.

'What the heck!' he said. 'The meek may inherit the earth! But people like that will make them pay tax!'

Kate laughed sympathetically, warming to his light voice and soft accent. His voice had an unmistakably camp inflexion. 'MIP can be hell,' she said gently.

'Yep, 'fraid so. And I suppose that's what happens when you come out of the closet, and others still have a foot in the door!'

'I should think being snubbed by people like that is a small price to pay,' replied Kate stoutly. She was aware she sounded almost unnaturally British as a reaction to the Hollywood heavies. The same thought seemed to strike the young man, who suddenly twisted round with easy grace to try and read her conference ID, which was turned the wrong way round. Obligingly she flipped it towards him.

'Well, I'll be darned!' he said pleasantly. 'You're Kate Wilkinson. Hi, I'm Dan!'

He stood in front of her, beaming.

'Goodness! Hello! I'm pleased to meet you.'

The young man was not quite as young as she thought, close to. And she hadn't known he was American. He was tanned, open-faced and pleasant, as unlike his heavy red-faced father as possible. He leaned towards her.

'No, you're not pleased to see me, I can tell. Of course, Dad set me up too. He told me to look out for a middle-aged battleaxe, and after seeing the seven dwarfs go by, I was expecting the wicked stepmother! You may be disappointed in me, but I'm delighted by you! What a lovely surprise.'

Kate tried to collect her defences. This man was supposed to be there to asset-strip her experience. But somehow she couldn't see it. There was an air of spontaneous self-mockery about Daniel Chester-Lang, who looked about as calculating as a puppy. And he was obviously gay, unashamedly so, he had told her as much in the first words he had spoken. Kate was used to being shrewd enough, particularly on her home ground, to spot and place most types of people. But Daniel Chester-Lang had her stumped. And here he was, almost laughing at her, clearly noting her confusion.

'Hey, do you really want breakfast in there, eyeballing executives? If you were here to be seen, you wouldn't be hiding behind those racks of *Marie Claire!* Let's get out of here and find somewhere more informal.'

'Why not?' she said. And it would certainly be easier to talk to him, away from the atmosphere of display she anticipated in the dining room. He beamed at her, and indicated the way forward and they strolled easily together out of the swing doors, away from the heavy smell of breakfast linen and starched executives.

'I love these pavement cafés,' Daniel was saying. 'Much more fun. Hey, how about a Kir Royale, and coffee and croissants to celebrate our meeting?'

The idea of champagne and cassis at eight in the morning suddenly seemed daring yet appropriate. She wondered fleetingly if he planned to get her drunk so she would tell him trade secrets, but there were no secrets to which his father did not have legitimate access. So what was this about?

Daniel spotted a café opposite the harbour, with just a few people and the benefit of the full morning sun, and they sank on to the plastic cane chairs. He was able to attract the waiter's attention in seconds, and Kate sat blinking out at the glamorous world of the Riviera as he commanded hot coffee, fresh croissants and two fluted glasses of deep pink bubbly liquid.

'Here's looking at you,' he said cheerfully and it was the most natural thing in the world to raise and chink glasses with him.

'What the hell am I doing?' Kate thought suddenly, drinking with the enemy!

'You'd better tell me what your father expects us to get out of this meeting,' she said gently.

'Oh shoot, really? Hey, isn't this a fantastic place?'

'Certainly is, but your father didn't arrange this expensive meeting for us to enjoy the view. Come on, Mr Chester-Lang. If I may say so, you're acting the innocent too well. Just what have I been dragged here for?'

*

Jenny Sims walked into the offices of the Food and Health Channel at eight o'clock the next morning. She had been unable to sleep. She had spent a great deal of the previous night on the telephone or lying in bed, working out how to play the day ahead. The night before Nick Malcolm's voice had leapt when he answered the phone.

'Jenny! I didn't expect to hear from you again. I got your little note when I came back from Croatia. You certainly left Northern TV in a hurry!'

'I'm sorry about that, Nick, but Kate's offer came out of the blue. I left quickly because I had some holiday owing.' That was true, but it was also a jibe. Nick had offered to take her away for a skiing trip, but the promised fortnight on the slopes never materialised.

'Oh, yeah,' he said cagily. 'So how are you getting on?'

'Fine.'

'And how's Kate?' Nick had known Kate years before, at LondonVision, and had offered her work at Northern TV, after her fall from grace in London.

'Kate's great. It's all working out really well.'

'Good. So what do you want?'

Jenny paused. 'Look, Nick, I need some professional help. Kate's at MIP, in Cannes. I've got a problem because she's left me to negotiate with Northern TV for "Cook of the North". But her draft contract has gone missing, and I've no idea what price to offer.'

'Oh. That's a laugh. So what do you want me to do?'

'Tell me the sort of money they might want. Please. I know it's not your area, but you're an executive at Northern. It's such a small company that you must have some idea of what they charge to sell programmes to cable and satellite channels. Some of your foreign documentaries were sold on to Discovery Channel, weren't they, Nick?'

'Yes, they were. What a mess this is.' He laughed, harshly.

'Does that please you?'

'That wasn't why I was laughing. What do you take me for?'

Jenny said nothing. The silence lengthened like a strand of cold chewing-gum.

'This is an interesting pause, Jenny. I see you haven't lost your ability to communicate, even without words.'

'What do you expect me to say, Nick, thanks for everything?'

'You could. I wasn't all bad. Jenny, I know you've got more pride than sense, but your curt little note surprised me. I wanted a chance to defend myself, but I'd no idea how to find you.'

'You could have done if you'd tried hard enough.'

'But you were obviously pretty bitter, Jenny. I always told you my job came first.'

'Don't talk down to me, Nick. The job came first for me too. But I always tried to accommodate you. You never even took me into consideration!'

'That's not true Jenny. The Croatia story needed fast reaction. I had to go there. But I was hoping things would calm down when I got back.'

'Oh yes? Look, this isn't what this phone call is about.'

'It's about your needing my advice on this deal?'

'It's not a lot to ask.'

'Little do you know! Things have changed here. I'm going to be a paper pusher now.'

Jenny knew that a management role was the last thing Nick Malcolm wanted. He had been editor of a controversial morning programme when they had met, and had left that for the foreign editor post. Nick had desperately wanted this job to succeed, and Jenny could hear the disappointment in his voice. For a moment she wondered if she should have been more supportive, then she remembered how he had forgotten to book their holiday, and felt vindicated.

'It's more bloody internal reorganisation,' he was saying. 'Making new programmes is mattering less and less, and marketing old ones is mattering more and more. I had to take the job or leave the company.'

'So what is it?'

'You honestly don't know?'

'No.'

'That's really funny. I thought that was why you asked me for my help. Bit cheeky, I thought.'

'What are you talking about, Nick?'

'Well, it would have cost them a fortune to pay me off, so despite my stunning lack of credentials, I'm Northern TV's new Head of Programme Sales.'

'What?'

'Yes. You'll be negotiating directly with me. Now if you shut up, and listen, I'll tell you the lowest price we'll accept.'

'But that means you'll be throwing away the deal?'

'Yep. You see, I'm really not so bad, am I?'

Kate watched Daniel Chester-Lang crumble his croissant on to his brilliant white napkin, and blink his eyes as if the sun was hurting them. But she waited. His open, friendly smile had gone, and he frowned slightly.

He said finally, 'You've got it completely wrong. It was me who wanted the meeting. Not Dad.' Then he stopped. Kate raised her eyebrows in astonishment. She had had the impression Daniel was not an evasive man, seeing the fluttering AIDS ribbon, the expressive gestures and the welcoming manner.

'I'm surprised,' she said sharply, leaning forward. 'Why?'

Daniel squirmed. 'I told him I need information about individual local cable operators in the UK. And I do. But it was really an excuse. I wanted to meet you, and to have that meeting somewhere where Dad couldn't interfere.'

'But you still haven't explained.'

'I know. Let's go.' He stood up abruptly, tossing some money on the table, and she followed him through the undergrowth of plastic furniture and back on to the street. He waited for her, hands in his pockets and eyes downcast.

'Look, Kate, this is all very hard. But let me talk to you about Dad.'

They began to walk down the Croisette, towards the benches that backed into the vegetation, and faced out to sea.

'I hardly knew him till I was in my teens. My mom was a singer in London. Quite a lady. She married my dad in the early sixties. I was just a baby when Mom left him. She took me, and found herself some apartment in Earl's Court, another part of London. You know it?'

Kate nodded encouragingly.

'She went to work for a change bureau, at the counter. I guess there are a lot of people, passing through that area?'

'Yes, lots. Please go on.'

'Well, that's where she met Pop, the man who brought me up. He was a lonely widower in his fifties, on a sightseeing trip to Britain, and he went to cash some travellers' cheques to go home, and met Mom. He thought she was just about the most gorgeous thing he'd ever seen. Mom went out to dinner with him that night, and he adored her straight away. So she married him. She's a cool character, my mother. I don't suppose he meant anything other than a meal ticket to her at first. But to her own surprise, she fell in love with him!'

'What a nice story.' Kate could almost see the disillusioned girl, with Dan's colouring and fair hair in Cilla Black kiss curls, hauling the baby in an old-fashioned carrycot into the hired car of a besotted elderly American. She must have been truly relieved to get the Atlantic between herself and Antony Chester-Lang.

'Mom and Pop brought me up, in Connecticut. But after ten years, when Pop wanted me to take his name, Tony came back on the scene. He said he didn't want me to be a Wannawicz!'

'A what?'

'A Wannawicz. Mom had gone from being glamorous Nadine the nightclub singer, to Mrs Wannawicz, housewife! Wannawicz, not wannabee! It's a mouthful, isn't it? Pop's family had come from the Ukraine during the war. He'd had a bad old time. There were none of his family left, and I don't think he could have children of his own, which I suppose was why he wanted me so much. Mom had to contact Tony to ask about the adoption, and he wouldn't let it go ahead. I guess Mom was scared of Tony and I must have sensed her fear.'

'Why was she frightened?'

'I'm not really sure, but as I grew older, I realised Tony was odd. I think being gay can make you more perceptive about things like that. Like most powerful men of his age Tony wants to control people. But with him, there's more to it than that. He wants to see you *crawl*.'

The nasty, mean little word hung in the scouring hot sunlight. Intuitively Kate said quietly, 'And you're crawling now?'

'Yep, sure am.' Tony turned left abruptly and sat down on a bench, half in the sun, half in the shade. He had taken the sunny half and Kate sat in the coolness. The Kir Royale made her feel slightly unreal. But Daniel's story fascinated her. She too, had begun to assess Chester-Lang as more than a bully and worse than a control freak. Why, otherwise, get involved in something like Food and Health, and then try and go one better and sabotage it? Suddenly it didn't matter so much what the content of the rival channel was. It was more the fact that he had established a rival at all that interested her.

'But Dan, why have you got caught up in all this?'

'When you're as street wise and smart as I am? I guess you're laughing at me!'

He turned to her and smiled sadly, so for a minute she wanted to ruffle his hair. He could, she saw, be very endearing, and utterly unlike his father.

'Well, Pop died, and left Mom quite well off. And Johnnie, my partner, and I did well. I'm not a complete business ignoramus, Kate. I was an actor to start with, and then Johnnie and I started a restaurant together in New York. It was very successful. Tony came over once or twice, and he and Sonya came to see us. Boy, can she eat! I like Sonya. And oddly enough, she liked me.' Kate could see it. There was something slightly childlike about Sonya, and Kate could imagine her loving the hint of the theatrical about Daniel. She could envisage them becoming friends, except for Tony being in the way.

'I was careful to be civil to Dad, but never to give him a hold over me. Until . . .'

'Until what?'

'Well, Johnnie got ill.'

'Oh no!'

'Yeah. He needed endless treatment, and I tried every single crazy cure. I sold the business, and Mom gave me a load of money, and of course it just got worse. Compared to Johnnie's suffering, it was nothing for me to take Dad's money.'

'And what happened?'

'Johnnie's stable now. We've got another year or two, maybe. And I'm in hock to Dad. But he doesn't want the money back.'

'Isn't that OK?'

'What? OK? You're joking! Money's too boring for Dad. He's got plenty of *that*. No, he wants his pound of flesh! I'm supposed to be working off the debt by running this lousy TV channel for him. He's controlling me at last, after all these years!'

Kate listened to the chattering of the passing crowds and the far-off sound of someone calling over the sea. Daniel said nothing more. After thinking for a moment, she asked, 'Is it that bad?'

'Christ, it's hell! I thought I could manage it with just a few trips to the UK, but Dad seems to want me there semi-permanently, and Johnnie still isn't very well. And anyway . . .' He stopped, and blinked at the sea, then went on staring into the sun as if he deserved the discomfort. 'I'm not sure that this channel is strictly ethical.'

'*What?*'

'Dad's got two consultants on it, and one of them is fully occupied talking to the regulators, your Independent Television Commission. I think there's more going on than Dad has told me. And because I'm not in England, I can't get a handle on it.'

'So what do you want from me?'

'I need advice from someone independent. Over the past few weeks, I've heard Dad ranting on about you. He was furious that you wouldn't make Sonya's books into a TV series, and later he described you as an opinionated cow, which seems to be some sort of British insult, so I thought that if you had Dad worried, you were strong enough to help me.'

Kate laughed, but her throat was drying up. It was one thing to suspect Chester-Lang's hostility and another to hear it, even second hand.

'Go on, Dan.'

'Johnnie suggested that we should get you over here on some pretext or other, and if you seemed OK, tell you the truth. And that's what I've done.'

'Gee, thanks! But before I can do anything I need more information about this channel.'

'I can't tell you. Not yet. Look, if anyone spilt the beans, Dad would carve them up. We've all signed confidentiality agreements. If I divulged what his great idea really is, even the little bit I know, then it would give him a legal hold over me.'

'So what can I do?'

'You can listen. And maybe you can find out what the sub-plot is. Because there sure as hell is one, if I know Dad! And then you can help me when I have to come to London.'

Kate turned away from his pleading face. There was clearly
something very odd about Antony Chester-Lang's plans, but even
with all her experience, she couldn't imagine what it could be. Was
it a direct threat to her own project? Or was it something sinister
in its own right?

'Are you still based in New York?'

'Yeah. I just came to France with Johnnie. He needed to see his
family.'

'Family?'

'Yeah. He's French. Named after Johnnie 'Alliday, I suppose. His
mother and sister live in Lyons. That's why all this fitted, and Dad
wasn't suspicious.'

So that's the explanation, Kate thought wearily. She smiled and
shook her head. But now she was personally worried. Standing up
to Chester-Lang senior seemed like a short term career move, and
she had already thwarted him over Sonya's books, and stood her
ground over Laurence's death. If he could play power games with
his own son, what could he do to her?

'Daniel . . . ?' She meant to ask him more questions when she
saw the figure of Jeremy Woodley bearing down on them, jacket
flapping.

'Daniel, dear boy,' he gasped, not seeing Kate in the shade. 'We
must talk about the ITC . . . I waited for you for ages in the
Majestic . . . What happened?'

Quietly Kate stood up. 'Dan, I'll be in touch,' she said, and started
to walk, in a bemused state, back to the Hotel des Cyclades.

Kate had spent so long with Daniel Chester-Lang, she was only just
letting herself into the room when the phone rang.

'Kate, hello.'

'Hi, Jenny. How's things? Did you get "Cook of the North"?'

'Yes. Yes, I did.'

'For how much?'

Jenny told her. 'That's great,' Kate answered, genuinely delighted
and surprised at the deal the younger woman had struck. 'Much
better than I expected. I would have paid about five hundred more.'
Jenny groaned inwardly.

'And Jenny, who's their new Head of Sales? Sounds like you've got a good relationship there!'

She was surprised not only at Jenny's answer, but at her tone.

'Nick Malcolm! Good grief! That's not who I expected at all! There may be more deals we can do with Northern. If I remember, you were always a bit of a favourite with Nick.' Jenny agreed, rather glumly Kate thought, and then added something which took Kate off guard.

'Kate, you remember last Tuesday?'

'How could I forget?'

'No, I don't mean about Laurence. We were expecting a tape of the logos that morning, weren't we? They never arrived. Well, I called the artists and asked them to send another copy. But they say we expressly asked for the originals, the tape masters. They sent everything to us in that package. So the whole lot has disappeared. They have nothing left but the paper version.'

'You can't mean it!'

'I'm afraid it's true. We checked with them this morning.'

It was a real setback. Commissioning logos for TV channels, or even titles for programmes, was an expensive business, sometimes running into hundreds of thousands of pounds. If all the work had really been lost, Kate would have to spend a great deal more money on replacements, money that wasn't in the tiny budget. But the last thing she wanted to do was panic the team.

'Look, don't worry too much, Jenny. I'll deal with that when I get back. There'll be a way round it.' But Kate wasn't sure that there was. She put the phone down and lay on the bed, her pleasure over the 'Cook of the North' deal tarnished by the news of the missing logos. Of course things always went wrong on new projects, and it was her role to cope with, and contain that. She told herself that much else was going well. Despite Laurence's tragedy and Chloe's volatility, she still had Debbie. And Jenny, as the morning had proved, was becoming a competent negotiator who was capable of pulling off an extremely effective deal!

But even as Kate was thinking that, Jenny Sims was sitting at her desk in the Warehouse hating herself for not telling Kate the truth. Her *extremely effective* deal with Northern TV's Nick Malcolm had more to do with his old obligation than her new expertise. He had compromised himself to get her out of a mess, and she had been weak enough to let him. She shivered in the sunshine through the big Warehouse window, and watched it glint on Chloe Carr's revolting ashtray. In Kate's absence, Chloe had ignored the no smoking rule, and grey flaky turds of cigarette ash massed in the horrid little pot. I can't handle this, Jenny thought wretchedly.

On Monday morning, at much the same time, Sonya Chester-Lang woke to the tray of Earl Grey morning tea brought in by her Filipino housekeeper. Behind the woman's silent exit, she unfolded her long legs from the silk sheets. She wore a cream sheath which clung to her body making her bottom look round and shiny, and her breasts neat and easily aroused with the rub of the silk on her nipples. But sex with Tony was not on the agenda that morning. The night before had been a particularly vigorous session, she recalled with a twinge from her buttocks. Tony had forced her over the back of the spindly chair by the telephone table, and even Sonya had found it difficult to become excited at the reflection of her own beautiful face and body as the force of his thrusts had become more violent. The worst of it was that it had been one of those occasions when Tony could not climax.

They often had sex again on a Monday morning, but she had the feeling that after such an effort only hours before, it might be best not to try again until possibly Thursday. By then some of the smarting would have gone.

And this week she had a lot to think about. Tomorrow was the funeral. She couldn't remember the boy's name, but she was certain they should go. They needed to be seen at things like that. After all, they were shareholders in Food and Health and Kate Wilkinson must never be allowed to think that her problems might be overlooked by the Chester-Langs! But Sonya needed to check her wardrobe. It just wouldn't do, if something she wanted to wear needed cleaning!

A funeral! So difficult! She pranced into her dressing room, where yet more mirrors fronted an even longer wardrobe. It took her about half an hour to make a selection of black outfits, during which time her husband woke, drank his tea, and emerged in his huge maroon silk dressing-gown from the bedroom, to stand at her door. Sonya was holding a black silky short sleeved dress against herself. A black straw hat with a spotted veil was at the chair on one side of her, and yet another frock, a flowing crêpe creation, was flung at her feet.

'You look nice in that,' he said in his usual gruff manner.

'Oh darling, I didn't see you there,' twittered his wife.

'I was just watching you,' he said with difficulty, aware now that his breath was coming in little jerks. The stop-start sound of his voice made Sonya look up. With a little tremor of pleasure she realised that her husband was sexually aroused. Of course, it would be a nuisance this morning and might also be rather uncomfortable, but it was always a bonus when he had an erection without too much work on her part. She wondered if it was because she was standing in front of the cheval mirror she used to assess her outfits. They hadn't tried it in here before, and the thought intrigued her. She smiled coquettishly at him.

Stupid cow, thought her boorish husband. 'I like that one on the floor best,' he said breathlessly.

'Do you, sweetheart? Really? Oh, I don't know. I think it may be too dressy!'

'I don't. Put it on for me.'

'What now?'

'Yes, now.'

'Oooh, Tony, it's nice of you to take an interest.' Sonya was genuinely thrilled. 'I know it's an absolute tragedy, darling, but I do think it's important, Tony, for us to go along to this funeral, and to look properly dressed. I mean . . .' Her voice became muffled as she slipped the sheath over her head, and stood coyly naked in front of him, ' . . . it matters such a lot that we're seen to be there!'

'Put the dress on.'

Startled a little by his brusqueness, she blinked, then obeyed, pulling the soft black crêpe over her bony frame.

'And the hat.'

'Oh really, Tony! Do I need to, now?'

'Yes.'

'But I look like somebody's mother in this outfit!'

'Yes!' He reached out for her hand, and grinning in a forced way which started to alarm her, he led her into their bedroom. She followed obediently, a little confused now, and then turned to him with another of her silly simpering smiles. She was worried, but not yet scared.

Then as she looked at him, she began to feel a new realisation through a physical, not a rational, response. Her knees began to tremble before she knew why. Sonya had always intuitively known that Tony was cruel. She knew he liked to promise little treats, then rescind them, or take her to posh places where he would humiliate her by acting with the grossness only open to powerful men. She had thought that these were just the vagaries of pressure; after all Tony was very very busy and often preoccupied and she made allowances by saying to herself that he was just teasing her in a heavy handed way.

But over the years she had suspected worse, and never allowed her suspicions to surface. Sometimes the friendly smacks on her bottom were so heavy they hurt. Sometimes too, she knew that he was holding back during intercourse and that there was something else that brought him to his final climax, something separate from her, but she knew all men fantasised sometimes, and she said nothing. She had lived in fear of his taking a lover, but she had never really dared to think deeply about it and thus work out that his mistress was not a woman, but a state of mind, and that he was sexually dependent not on a person, but on a perversion he had so far kept from her.

He was pulling her now, and she realised he was more aroused than she had ever seen him. She started twittering nervously with the same meaningless panicky voice as his poor benighted mother.

'I think you're looking forward to dressing up for this funeral, aren't you?' he said, in a smooth fatherly voice she rarely heard.

'No, Tony, really I'm not,' she squeaked in panic, knowing instinctively what was coming, and unable to move from him because of the panic tremors rippling down the muscles of her thighs.

'I think you are. And that's not very nice, is it?' Chester-Lang's mouth, spit flying from his fleshy lips, came close to hers, his bloodshot eyes staring deeply into hers until she was almost mesmerised. 'You shouldn't want to dress up for something like that, Sonya. It's rather wicked of you, isn't it? Vain and wicked. You like looking at yourself too much, sweetie. Don't think I haven't noticed. And I think you should be punished for it.' His breath was heaving, and she could see his erection poking through the maroon silk, bigger than she ever remembered, a darker shinier red than the cloth around it.

'Oh, no Tony, that's not true. Oh, Tony, don't be angry . . . stop . . .'

She thought that she was going to faint until he slapped her, once, sharply, and she snapped back to life although she knew it was only a preliminary. But the shock, pain and fear in her face brought him to the final pitch. At last, she was terrified. The sex act he had been unable to complete the night before was now just like a rehearsal, not a failure at all! Once again he was the shaking master of a penis that was huge with excitement and demanding to be satisfied. This time he had no need to urge himself on, gearing himself up for an almost painful non-existent climax. Now he was ready for it and all it took was her terror!

Chester-Lang ripped the dress off his whimpering wife, savouring the awkward way the cloth tore in fits and starts, each tug making Sonya gasp then half scream. She still hoped this would resolve into some sort of playing, until he pushed at her a little, tasting the feel of her submission, laughing at her because she wouldn't scream in case the servants heard her. He knew that down in the kitchen they would hardly be aware of a sound, and that even if they heard he would pay them for their discretion.

So it didn't matter what he did. He started to punch at her flesh. She looked at him in dumb horror, but that wasn't enough. He needed more. He hit again and again, until she was aware only of insistent endless pain in a rhythm like deadly music and then she was agonised enough to scream for her life, screaming and screaming and screaming till he punched the breath from her lungs. Her throat was rasping, an inhuman sound of agony, and the pain had turned her face into a distorted skull. He went into her with the force of a bull, and exploded as her pathetic skinny body bounced hopelessly like a grotesque broken Barbie doll on their king size bed, and then, mercifully, she lost consciousness.

CHAPTER SEVEN

Kate looked at her watch. If she stopped lying on the bed worrying about the missing logos, she would still have time before her flight to get to the Palais on the harbour edge, and walk through the bunker full of TV booths, where numerous glossy brochures would be pressed into her hand, advertising programmes which she either didn't want or couldn't afford. But it was absurd to come to the exhibition and not look round, and she suspected Antony Chester-Lang would interrogate her about what she had seen when she returned.

It did not take long to coast around the few distributors who she thought might have shows suitable for the Food and Health Channel. Clutching a pile of flybills, she trailed back up the stairs, anxious to get away, and out on to the Croisette. Her plane was leaving in an hour and a half, and the next nightmare was to find a taxi. She had just identified a car which was both available and had a driver inside, when she heard her own name being called. It seemed so unlikely that for a few minutes she did not respond, thinking she was listening to the urgency in her own head.

'Kate!' Waving nonchalantly and strolling towards her was Felix Smart, a one-time colleague at LondonVision who had been a consultant in the early nineties and then MD of a small independent production business. He was one of the few 'names' in the TV industry who had bothered to keep in touch with Kate and she was deeply attached to him despite the fact that he was always irritatingly in tune with the prevailing media mood. She wondered what he was working on now. His name had slipped out of the gossipy columns of *Broadcast* magazine recently.

'Kate, you look great! What's all this I hear about you becoming a mogul?'

'Oh, for goodness sake, Felix, you don't have to suck up to me!'

'You always were charmingly direct, Kate. Are you in a hurry?'

'Yes, I've got a plane to catch, literally. If I look back at the Palais I'll turn into a pillar of the establishment.'

'Very witty. Listen, before you go on pretending that power and significance mean nothing to you, let me test your ego. I'm putting together a session at the Edinburgh International Television Festival. It's called "New channels, trash or treasure?". It's the same time-slot Michael Grade and Janet Street-Porter spoke in last year. Pretty high powered stuff. Do you fancy taking part?'

Kate looked at him. Felix was a friend, and he would only ask her if he genuinely thought she could do a good, relevant job. And being asked to speak at the EITF pandered to her vanity. But she also knew that it would take lots of work, feel great at the time, and dissolve into nothing except a few carping remarks from competitive colleagues afterwards.

'I don't know . . .'

'Derek Boulder's graciously consented. He thinks cable TV has all been bollocks, except for L!VE TV of course, and fun things like that.'

'Oh well, "lad's telly". He would. He really is a pompous twit, isn't he?'

'Hah, gotcha! As Kelvin Mackenzie himself might have said! So you'll do it? It's the last weekend in August.'

'Oh, I really can't say, Felix. We're due to launch the channel in October and . . . well . . . I've got one or two personal engagements around then. I'll have to think about it.'

'So you'll say yes. I knew you wouldn't be able to resist being the new Michael Grade. I'll call you.' Felix waved with total complacency, and as always, weaved away looking the part, this time through the clusters of French millionaires.

Kate sighed and turned for her cab, to find it had gone. She stood, laden with bags and spare cardigans, waiting for another taxi, growing anxious about catching the flight. In the end, she missed the direct plane from Nice and was re-routed via Paris, where she had a frustrating, hot and tedious wait for an hour. She landed at Heathrow two hours later than she expected, making it impossible to get to the office to see Jenny. And she was tired, and hot, and grumpy. As her cab muttered through the shiny streets towards Twickenham, Kate sat in hot sticky silence. It was then she remembered something the surprising Daniel Chester-Lang had said. He had talked unhappily about two consultants working on his father's channel. If Jeremy Woodley was one, who was the other? The taxi turned into the main street.

'Hey, first right,' she called to the disgruntled driver. The cab lurched along, with him berating her softly for giving poor instructions.

'This it, Miss?'

'No . . . sorry, er, no, a little further down. Just where that white car is pulling away.'

The white car belonged to John. He had just come out of Polly's front garden, and was driving off with no idea that Kate was in the cab behind him. A cluster of children hung round Polly's gate, and as the cab slowly drew up, little Sarah Louise waved energetically. Kate waved back without enthusiasm. This meant John had made two visits to Polly in two days. So what was the attraction? Or was it obvious? She thought wretchedly that if John Maple wanted to spend his time in a house full of kids, then he might well be wasting it with the barren Kate Wilkinson.

The night before the funeral, Jenny tidied the office. They had packed all Laurence's work into three small cardboard cartons. He had actually done very little programme logging or viewing. Much of his value to the channel had been his work as a runner, fetching and carrying tapes and storyboards, collecting programme masters for others to view. Jenny put his few personal belongings into a black plastic bag, the few coins in his top drawer along with a selection of coloured pens and his payslip. But the pig mug was still on the rack in the kitchen where she had washed and left it. As each day went by, Jenny began to feel more and more as if all she had seen that Sunday evening was a half-drunk cup of coffee left by a cleaner or Matt, or someone else passing through the office.

In Kate's absence, she had mentioned the incident to no-one. Jenny was well aware that women in TV were frequently thought of as neurotic for the slightest reason, and she had no intention of being tarred with that brush. If female executives could be pigeonholed by their male colleagues as mad, it saved the men an awful lot of bother trying to work with them! Like Di and Camilla and Clare Short and Mrs Thatcher and just about every other woman who had ever achieved power or attention, they could be parcelled up, labelled and ignored! Jenny was too young and too self-conscious to be able to cope with that.

She looked around the office she was supposed to be running. Debbie Allen was viewing pile after pile of exercise and diet shows, Jenny noted with wry amusement. And Chloe Carr had arrived at nine thirty, and had worked quietly and solidly, viewing Delia Smith's cookery courses from the very beginning, when Delia had a long glossy bob of hair and wore pinafore dresses. It also interested Jenny that Chloe made surprisingly painstaking notes.

Then Chloe turned to Jenny and said, almost accusingly, 'After getting "Cook of the North" surely you could get a deal from the BBC as well? After all you're supposed to have done a great job negotiating with Northern TV.'

Jenny had nodded, both irritated and also, to her own distress, ashamed. Her phone rang. After the barest hesitation she picked it up, knowing it would be Nick Malcolm. The mad caller might have been almost better. But Nick had said, at the end of their formal conversation that morning, that he would ring her at 'close of play'. Speaking in executive clichés was unlike Nick, and she thought perhaps he was mocking her.

'Jen?'

'Hi, Nick.'

'Well, you can congratulate me. I've survived my first day as Head of Programme Sales and I've managed to do only one useless deal. But of course, you know that! You were lucky my other shit-hot negotiators were in the south of France selling the life cycle of the Lancashire hotpot to willing Canadians.'

'Look, Nick, if you think you've got the wrong price for "Cook of the North" . . .'

'Oh, don't worry. A non-exclusive cable deal isn't going to bankrupt Northern TV. Anyway, I'll tell our board that you're going to produce your own programmes soon, and you might use Northern's studios.'

'But Nick, that's not true. And you know I can't commit to that while Kate is away.'

'When's she back?'

'Tonight.'

'Then I'll come and see both of you tomorrow.'

'You can't, Nick. We're going to a funeral.'

'Nice one, Jenny. Can't you do better than that?'

'We really are going to a funeral.'

'Well, funerals don't last all day. When is it?'

'Eleven o'clock.'

'Then you'll have finished the ham and sherry by two, won't you?'

'It isn't that sort of funeral, Nick. He was just a young lad, in his twenties.'

'OK then, pizza and white wine, but you'll still have finished by two.'

'You can be insensitive, Nick.'

'But not over the "Cook of the North" deal?'

Jenny was silenced.

'It's just business, Jenny. I want to do more deals with you and your channel. I'll be in London from midday tomorrow. My other meeting will be through by two thirty. I'll come to your offices for three. If Kate can't make it, you'll do.'

He rang off, leaving Jenny confused. It had never been easy to read Nick's motives. She looked up. 'You still here, Chloe? It's gone six o'clock.'

'Yes. I've really got into those Delia tapes. I never thought I'd find cookery interesting, but it is. I don't just mean the recipes. I mean the clever way it's shot. It looks so simple, Delia talking you through the method, but it's really quite a complicated exercise, getting the close-ups of the ingredients. Presumably they're all edited in afterwards?'

'Yes, presumably,' Jenny was surprised, both at Chloe's sudden lengthy speech, and her ignorance. The placements she had been on in other companies had obviously not taught her a great deal. 'Didn't you do much editing before you came here?'

'Editing? You must be joking. All I did was make coffee and take messages. Oh, and I know every sandwich shop on Wardour Street!'

Jenny felt a twinge of sympathy. She herself had experienced a hard time at Northern TV when she started out, but at least she had been working with professionals on a real programme. Chloe and Debbie had not been so fortunate. Until now, she hoped.

'Has Debbie gone home?' It was unusual for Chloe to still be in the office after her colleague had gone.

'Yeah. She's barmaiding tonight as an extra. And I expect she needed to get to McDonald's on the way.'

Jenny laughed. 'Well, at least Debbie doesn't seem concerned about her weight. I admire her for coming to terms with it. She has, hasn't she? I mean, you're her friend, you should know.'

'I suppose so. But you can't get that close to Debbie. She's pretty self-contained.'

Jenny was surprised. She had never imagined that Chloe might be the one who was kept at a distance by Debbie.

'Well, thanks for all your work, Chloe. It can be tedious, I know. And you've done a good job today.'

The younger woman beamed, uncharacteristically.

'But one thing, Chloe. You shouldn't be smoking in here. I saw all that ash in your ashtray earlier.'

Chloe's face, which had begun to relax as she and Jenny held their first conversation, suddenly hardened into resentment.

'I haven't been smoking,' she snarled.

'Oh, Chloe, don't give me that! What about the ash?'

'What ash?'

'Well, it's gone now. But it was there earlier. I think you're taking advantage of the fact that Kate's away.'

'I'm not. Honestly, I'm not. It's you. You'd blame me for anything. You don't like me and you've got your knife in me.'

'Chloe, that's not true.'

'Yes, it is. You've had it in for me ever since you arrived. But it isn't me who's got a problem . . .'

'What do you mean, Chloe?'

'What I said. It isn't me who's a bag of nerves. You're the one who's supposed to be running the place, and you can't do it. Every time the phone rings you jump and you must make five cups of coffee a day you don't drink. And there's something odd about that clever deal you've just done, isn't there . . . ?'

'No! Chloe, you're completely out of order.'

'It's not me who's out of order. It's you. In the sense of breaking down! Leave me alone, from now on.'

Chloe gave Jenny a look of disgusted resentment, turned on her heel and banged her way out of the glass doors, leaving Jenny open-mouthed, furious and impotent at her desk.

Kate decided she should tell John she had seen him leave Polly's. Even if that meant trespassing on his pastoral territory, it was better not to muffle the little whisper of suspicion which was getting louder in her inner ear. She unpacked and showered. The bedsit smelt of paint and cooped up air. It wasn't musty, it was too clean and newly furbished for that, but it felt unused. For a ridiculous moment she missed the battered individuality of the French hotel. It had character, at least. The bedsit was fine, but Kate knew it was an emotional transit camp.

She was planning to spend the night at John's. She put clean knickers and her small washbag in her briefcase. She wanted to pack her dark outfit for the funeral in a separate suit carrier. By the time she had found it at the bottom of a tea chest, and set up her ironing board and ironed it, she had spent far more time in the bedsit than she planned. She hurried the rest of her packing. She imagined John might be stressed, and she wanted to be with him. Unless Polly had soothed him, of course, with her wonderful maternal touch!

This would be the first time Kate had seen John conduct a funeral. She knew untimely death was one of the things he found most difficult to explain. Violence was at the heart of his vocation, yet it was something few lay people could accept, and faith was the hardest thing to communicate to the bitter and bereaved. Her heart went out to John and the job he had to do, because she herself had no faith and could see nothing but grief in death, and she doubted anybody's ability to make it feel any better.

Kate glanced at Polly's house as she manoeuvred the car out of her parking space in the road. Another late laburnum tree was erupting in the front, and the late, full, heavy tulips were wilting now, with brown crinkly edges. It had been hot for over a week. Polly's garden was full of mounds of unmanicured colour, as fertile and flourishing as she was herself.

It was an evening as bright and harsh as a stainless steel pan, upturned on the world. The sky, though still bluish, had a grey glint behind it and there was a feeling of being enclosed in a dish that was slowly overheating. Kate wondered if there might be storms, but there were no distinguishable clouds. John's street was a little fresher, owing to the proximity of the river, but even the Thames at this stage had the look of a slimy mud bath. The evening sun hung heavy and orange in a sulphury sky. Kate could imagine hippos and alligators slithering along the muddy banks, the colours tropical and dense and the air too still.

She parked and hurried up the steps to John's front door, her key in her hand. But the door opened before she put it in the lock, and John pulled her into the narrow hall and grasped her against him.

'Oh Katy, I'm so pleased to see you.'

'I can tell! Hey, wait while I put my bag down.'

'I've got some wine chilling. OK?' She nodded, although after the Kir Royale at breakfast, then the hurried lunch on the plane with a complimentary half bottle, she wasn't really very keen on drinking more. But John seemed to need it. She heard the cork pop in the kitchen, and the glug as the cold liquid ran into the glasses.

'Let's take them up to bed,' he said.

'John! I'm not complaining, but why the enthusiasm?'

'Oh . . .' He was already walking up the stairs. 'It depressed me, seeing Mrs Smith to talk about arrangements. And I'm not looking forward to tomorrow.' He stopped on the landing and turned to her. 'But I *was* looking forward to you coming home. It kept me going.'

John was not given to emotional outbursts, even gentle ones like this, but he had missed Kate. And he had felt a little jealous. He suspected that in the past, during what he called their 'bad patch', Kate had slept with someone else, and he couldn't really blame her. At the time he had been preoccupied with finding his way back into active priesthood, and had spent hours struggling over issues like gay clergy, and the ordination of women, yet he had never deigned to discuss these things with Kate. But she was not only as bright as he was, she also possessed the sort of questioning common sense which in the end helped him see the wood for the trees. He was desperate not to make the same mistake again. Hanging over him was the discussion he knew he had to have with her about the past.

Especially as he suspected this baby business was beginning to bother her. Yet at the same time, the thought of raking things up and exposing his mistakes appalled him. It was easier now just to hug her.

He went into the bedroom ahead of her, and pulled her on to the bed and they lay together, fully clothed, until Kate felt his hands moving over the cotton of her dress, and round and round on her breasts.

'It's too hot for clothes,' he whispered and she laughed, standing up to unbutton her dress. He took his shirt and trousers off and came to hug her, undoing her bra as he did. She watched his lean body, with the square shoulders and broad but thin chest. He was still a very attractive looking man, she thought, but it wasn't that which made her want to hug him back till they both melted in this hot, greying heat.

'Put the curtain up,' she whispered, and giggled as he fiddled with the silly bit of towelling they draped over the window.

It was the smell and touch of him she loved, so it was inevitable that slowly and gently they would intertwine. They had nights of great passion, when they made love all over the house. But this lovemaking was even more intense in its way. Kate relished the fact that none of the pleasure was based on novelty, and all of it came from certainty, as they touched and kissed each other slowly all over, and John finally slid inside her. Kate experienced one of those long slow, utterly predictable and reliable orgasms that went on till she felt she was crying with delight, and she knew that nothing could stop her calling out again and again with the intensity of it. It was like several climaxes rolling into one, yet when John finished, she finished too by some miracle of compatibility.

Afterwards they lay without speaking. Then John put on his glasses and leant over her to get his book. 'Coffee?' she murmured happily. He lay back, smiled at her, and nodded. She saw that he was reading Dickens, and leaned down to kiss him.

'There's nothing like a classic!' she said, and left him laughing, while she went to put on the kettle, feeling their mixed moisture running down her thighs. The fact that this was the safe period, the time when she was least likely to conceive, and that she had his fluid in her for no other purpose than their own love, made her happy.

Yet at the back of her mind, she remembered there was something bothering her which she ought to mention to him. Oh, yes. Of course. His involvement with Polly. But it hardly seemed worth worrying about now. It could wait.

It was still hot the morning of the funeral, but the sky had a more metallic look. The sun was shining, but wearily, spreading like grease across the sky. Kate had carefully planned what she was going to do. She showered and dressed in her black skirt and grey shirt, a black linen jacket on top. It might be hot, but she was worried about freezing in the church then sweltering at the crematorium. John was very quiet and slow, padding about the bedroom and bathroom in a thoughtful way. She went up and kissed his cheek.

'I'm going now,' she said softly. 'You don't want me hanging around you this morning. I'm sure you want to think, so I've arranged to see Joan Thompson for breakfast. I'll be at church.' For some reason she wanted to say good luck, but it sounded trivial and even offensive.

But she knew John was worried. The suggestion that Laurence had committed suicide made his funeral particularly difficult. Suicide was a sin. Accidents were a tragedy. In one case man was to blame, in the other, God. Because of his beliefs John had to find God's behaviour easier to accept. Yet if it was an accident, why had God allowed someone like Laurence to die? She could sense that John was still struggling about how to explain this to a church full of disgusted non-believers.

Kate wasn't sure why she uttered it, and she knew as soon as she opened her mouth it was uncharacteristic, but she whispered 'God bless' to John, and turned to leave.

She hoped the surprise on his face meant she had said the right thing.

This has got to be the worst bit, Jenny thought, in a bloody awful week. They were squashed into the front room of the small terraced house where Laurence Smith had been brought up. It had been a moving and dignified service and although she was a determined atheist, Jenny had been affected by John Maple's simple words.

But back at the house, it was excruciating. The appalling tragedy of Mrs Smith's loss made any conversation impossible. And to Jenny's horror, there *was* pizza and white wine, the pizza cut into triangles, the white wine not quite cool enough. Mrs Smith looked drugged and unreal, like an old cracked painted doll, her family hovering over her as ineffectively as moths.

But all the time Jenny was there, trying to say the right thing, she was really waiting for the moment when she would be on her own, ready to meet Nick Malcolm. The thought of him filled her head like hot greasy water in a balloon. None of her other fears had room while her obsession with Nick rolled round and round. Chloe's bitchiness, Jenny's own new quiet routine with Matt, the threat of the nuisance phonecalls and the old terror of the coffee left on the desk, all were squeezed out by her need to see him one more time.

The bus journey to the Warehouse was tortuous, and Jenny's heart was thumping in time with her feet as she jumped off the bus and walked down the bouncing hot concrete strip of road to the industrial estate.

'Any visitors for Food and Health?' she said brightly to the receptionist on the ground floor, a kindly middle-aged lady who replied cheerfully, 'Oh, yes dear, such a nice chap! He's just gone to the loo. Oh, here he is.'

Nick Malcolm came out of the gents, and down the stairs. He was not at all embarrassed. 'Needed a wee,' he said confidentially, with his unconventional charm and the lady on reception smiled indulgently at him. Jenny was instantly aware of her mussed hair and perspiring face. As he strolled downstairs he was lit by the strange shiny grey sunshine which was pouring through the high glass windows.

Nick looked different. If anything he was even more aquiline, and seemed taller. He'd discarded his inevitable donkey jacket because of the heat, and the new, bright blue denim shirt showed off his shoulders and made him look even thinner. Strangest of all, he was wearing a tie, a strange mixture of bright patterns and cartoon characters as reminiscent of an old school tie as a bandit's bandanna. But despite the fact he was smiling, clearly fit and well turned-out, Jenny knew there was something unfamiliar about him. Then two things struck her at once. Despite the clothes he looked much older. And despite the charm, he was nervous.

'Hi,' she said stiffly, aware of the receptionist's interest. 'I'm glad I got back to see you in time. Do come up to the office. I'm afraid Kate may be late back. In fact . . .' she added as they passed out of earshot of the front desk, 'I didn't tell her you were coming. I don't want you to tell her anything about the deal, Nick.'

He followed her into the main office, and then through to her section, and sat himself down on the chair opposite her desk. The office was so small his long spindly legs hit the partition and made it shake.

'So you don't want me to split on you to your boss?'

'You wouldn't?'

'You're right.'

'And what did you really want, Nick?' She knew there was a tiny unwanted flicker of hope catching fire inside her.

He stood up and looked up at the big window. It was stickily hot, and she could see a sheen of a pallid cloud spreading across the horizon, not enough to block the sun but enough to mute it. It looked as if the sky was being stretched like smeared clingfilm, almost beyond its limits.

'Christ, it's hot down here in London. At least at home you get a breeze off the hills. Don't you miss it, Jenny?'

'You were from London originally.' It sounded like an accusation.

'True. East Molesey. Not that far from here. But I've no con-nections with this part of the world now. Except you.'

She said nothing, and waited.

'I was serious when I talked about your channel going into pro-gramme production, Jenny. I could do you a costing. It was expensive for Northern to make "Cook of the North" because we went out and filmed at places like the Sharrow Bay at Ullswater. But you could make your own cookery programmes, using our studios. It would save you money in the long run because you could repeat the shows and perhaps even sell them. And it would make your channel individual. That's what UK Living did, as long ago as '93. And the Granada channels are doing that too.'

'But they're on satellite as well as cable.'

'So? Channel One and L!VE made their own programmes from

the beginning, and they're cable only. It means no-one can say you were running an old repeats channel.'

'True.'

'OK, sod it, Jenny, I can see you're not interested.'

'I am! But I can't commit to anything without Kate.'

'So why are we having this meeting?'

'You were the one who asked for it.'

'But with Kate Wikinson.'

'That's not what you said.'

They sat in uncomfortable silence. There was nothing she could add.

'God,' he said suddenly. 'It's stuffy in here. I want to get a train back home tonight. Look, if you've nothing more to say to me, I'm off. It'll take me an hour at least to get from here to Euston.'

'OK, Nick. I'm sorry. I just wanted . . . oh, never mind. Look, I am very, very grateful.'

'That's OK. Which is the quickest way to town? And don't say "I'll get you a car". I get tired of all London affectation. You southern companies must have money to burn. Anyway I want some fresh air.' He shook himself as if he could break the heat into little shards.

'We don't have any money at all. There's a bus to Richmond at the main road. Or if you walk along the canal to the other end, there's a bus to Hammersmith.'

'Hammersmith sounds all right to me. What about you?'

'I'll walk that way with you.'

She didn't want him to leave, but she had nothing to say. They walked down together, into the wall of heat, then turned up through the courtyard, around the Warehouse building, and on to the dark of the towpath.

'This is a creepy spot, Jenny. Reminds me to ask how was the funeral? You look good in black. You'd make a good widow.'

'Nick!'

He snorted with laughter. As they walked in the shadow she felt herself shiver and talk with more animation as if chattering would ward off the cold shadows. She told him about Laurence, and Nick's feel for a good story made him question her until they both forgot the strain between them and the conversation ran on.

'It's quite a tale!' Nick said. 'I mean a real mystery.'

'Yes, I suppose it is. But we'll never know, will we? I have to say, suicide, accident, murder, they're all such bizarre possibilities when you know Laurence.'

'That's why it's intriguing. Like the Mary Celeste or the giant footprints in the snow all round that village in Berkshire during the last century. Creepy.'

'Yes. And talking of weather, isn't this weird?'

It was still hot but now banks of heavy cloud were massing, as if they were pushing the blue and crushing it into purple. The sky was lurid and packed. And suddenly, for the first time in a week, Jenny felt the shiver of a breeze push under the thin nylon of her black tee shirt, making her nipples stand out. She crossed her hands in embarrassment in front of her breasts. Her folded arms also kept her warm. It was becoming distinctly cooler.

'I wish I'd brought a jacket. But I haven't got a black one. And it seemed so warm.'

'Yeah. I thought that too. Jenny, I think it's going to rain.'

She saw it before she felt it. Huge fat drops made great concentric ripples in the canal. The bushes around them on the bank shivered ecstatically and gave themselves up to the rain.

'Jeez, it's pouring,' Nick shouted, lurching into his long, loping run. She was running too, and together they started to scramble along the newly slimy, slippery towpath to the bridge, feeling the water stinging their backs. Within minutes, in her skimpy summer clothing, Jenny was saturated. The rain poured through her light shirt, down between her breasts and into the bouclé wool of her short black skirt. It would be ruined, she knew it.

Nick was ahead, making for the shelter of the bridge, and when he held out his hand to pull her along, she grabbed it and felt the sinews of his wrist and the warm, wet skin like an electric shock. He pulled her so hard she nearly lost her footing and stumbled after him till they pounded under the bridge, the last drops of rain still hounding them. Then it was eerily dark and dry, and she had to try and stop her legs pumping on automatically. She was so breathless she felt a painful lump in her throat, and she doubled over to get her breath back. She felt Nick's hands on her shoulders and thought for a minute he was helping her up. But he twisted her as she tried to straighten, and pushed her against the wall so she could feel the rough bricks in her back.

'I can't believe you don't want me again, Jenny. I know you don't play games.' She could hear his breathing echoing. The bridge smelt dry and only slightly musty. It wasn't unpleasant at all.

She tried to distract herself from the feel of his body. The bridge was fairly wide. On her left she could see rods of driving rain beating sideways, so the sky and the bushes and the few buildings winding up to the main road were all grey and distant, as if through fog. She turned her head to avoid his eyes. On her right, the rain was lashing away from them. She could no longer distinguish the Warehouse from the clouds and the branches of the stunted, tangly trees.

'Jenny! Look at me. You know if you don't want me I'll go. You *know* that. But I want you.'

'Nick, please! I mustn't . . .'

'You must! You want me, you want me now, don't you?'

'But I can't. Anyway, we haven't got anything . . .'

'Don't worry. I have. There's a machine in the toilets in your building, and I thought, you never know your luck.'

It was so very Nick, to say that. She almost wanted to laugh and cry. He felt so good, so hot and smelt so real. He really wanted her. She could feel him pressed against her, hard and wet. He moved a fraction, so the stone wall cut into her back, and her thighs separated just slightly under her woollen skirt. The fat stiffness of his penis rubbed on her, and she knew then that she had to have him too.

There was no-one in sight. He put his hands up her skirt and pulled at her tights. By heaving her back against the wall she could manoeuvre her own short skirt up to her waist. Her tights were coming down now, and Nick's fingers had pushed her knickers aside and were in her pubic hair, prying for the opening. Despite the restricting nylon around her knees, she parted her legs for him as much as she could, and felt him pushing and probing until he found the way in. She thrust her hips towards him, helping him by angling her pelvis, while clinging to his shoulders. The moment the tip of him prised its way into her, she yelped. Then she clasped on to him and held the shaft between her thighs with a force she didn't know she had and moved with all the muscle power she could find, against him.

Jenny did not climax with ease. But this time the thought that their passion was so uncontrollable they were making love like this, under the bridge, stirred her like nothing else had ever done. She knew it was a crazy, fragile moment and that if he came a moment too soon she would lose it. Usually that very thought was enough to make the moment fade like reaching a hilltop and realising the summit was there, already achieved. But this time, his insistent thrusts seemed to go on forever and to carry her along. She knew he was wanting her to come, and that he would somehow stop himself climaxing until she did, and the thought gave her a surge of pleasure which made the moment inevitable. She knew it would happen before it did, as all the nerves in her clitoris rubbed together like matches about to flame against him. She came in an explosion of light in the darkness and even more wetness, and realised as she came down from the black summit in her head that he had come too. He was sighing against her shoulders, groaning with the release that was almost pain.

Nick moved off her. He tucked himself away in a businesslike fashion. He was turning round to look at the canal.

'No-one coming but us,' he said. 'That was lucky.' His voice sounded normal and matter-of-fact, whereas Jenny was still writhing, trying to peel her back from the imprinted brickwork, her legs shaking, her tights now round her ankles. She could hardly breathe, and she knew her face was wet and dirty, her hair tangled with moss and flaky cement. But worse than the state of her body was the turmoil in her mind. Nick turned back and smiled. 'You look as if you enjoyed that,' he said in his jovial, trivialising voice. 'We're quite a good act, Jenny. I have to say, if there are any more deals you'd like me to fix for you, just say the word.'

Still emotionally raw, Jenny felt another rising tide, but this time it was rage. Nick knew from their past sexual encounters that orgasm for Jenny was a stunning, shattering thing she treasured. It was not the casual scratching of an itch whenever the irritation occurred. And to imply that sex, something which mattered deeply to her, was part of some sort of gruesome deal schedule, a form of payment, enraged her. She leapt forward, her clothes still half off, one shoe lost in the dark gravelly dampness of the path, her hair streaming round her head like a witch. 'You bastard,' she screamed, and lunged at him with her hand.

The blow had such force she heard the crack of the slap catch his cheek before she felt the impact of his hot stinging skin and the pain in her own palm. She pulled her hand back towards her and cradled it under her armpit. Nick looked back at her. Even in the gloom she could see his twisted face.

'That's some thanks, Jenny,' he said quietly. 'Don't turn on me because I can make love to you better than anyone else.' And he walked away from her, out from under the bridge.

Jenny called, 'Nick . . .' But the wind and the heavy rain in the little knotted bushes, and the fierce insistent splatter of the drops into the freckled canal, meant he did not hear her.

Or if he did, he wasn't coming back. Muddy, wet, and deeply disgusted with herself, Jenny turned to trudge back to the only place where she could get warm and dry quickly, the Warehouse. It was still pouring, though the rain was more intense and less dramatic now, a steady, blurring onslaught. As she walked, the stinging downpour took her breath away. And for a moment she thought she saw a daylight shadow. Then she realised it was the long thin form of a girl, in shiny black, hurrying in front of her down the towpath. The girl seemed to flutter, then as Jenny blinked the water from her eyelids, the vision disappeared.

Jenny stopped despite the drenching rain, and tried to make out what she had seen. The girl had been walking along, and then she had gone, completely. But she had definitely been there. Jenny wondered with a sick feeling if she had seen her and Nick coupling in that uncontrolled way under the bridge. But there had been no-one around, Jenny was certain. Yet there was no other access to the canal bank, unless a determined walker beat a way through the bushes that matted their way up from the towpath to the iron railings alongside the road.

So how had the girl got there? And where had she gone? Jenny felt the start of a splitting headache. She couldn't bear the thought of being seen, rutting in that awful, mindless way. How could she have given in to that desperate lust which, now it was sated, seemed so pointless? In her tears of misery and confusion Jenny walked painfully back to the office.

There was no-one there. Chloe and Debbie had both taken the day off. She hadn't seen them at the funeral but the church had been packed, and there had been no room for them at the house. Jenny strode past the receptionist who looked up open-mouthed to speak but thought better of it, and then she walked squelchily up the wide stairs, her low-heeled suede shoes oozing water. She could hear the rain on the glass skylight above the landing, and the Warehouse, seen for the first time without sun streaming through the windows, looked dark and bleak and deserted.

Jenny swung through the glass doors, then hurried, her tights sticking to her legs and her wet hair flapping, to answer the phone in her tiny office. For a moment her heart thrashed like a dying bird in her ribcage. Had Nick got to a phone box? Please let him call me, she prayed to anything which would listen. She picked up the phone. There was a small, ominous silence. Then a giggling little voice said, 'Could I speak to Laurence Smith, please?'. Jenny heard her own scream as she flung the phone down and, swaying backwards and forwards, she cradled her own wet body.

CHAPTER EIGHT

The breaking of the weather turned the end of spring into a real disappointment. For the whole of May, one grey day followed the next, with temperatures in the low fifties, and showers followed by just hints of turquoise blue sky and bright sunshine.

It made Matt Lavelle feel tetchy. In the hot fresh mornings of the freak heatwave, he had started to really enjoy getting up for the gym. Now he found it more difficult to get out of bed and work out, which was one of the reasons he didn't like Jenny staying the night. He wanted to wake up properly, do a few warm-ups, have a crap and get the body into motion, before having to relate to someone else.

But the only person he wanted to relate to was Jenny. He liked her sense of thoughtfulness. It intrigued him. And she was certainly getting fitter, he noted with pleasure. Her stomach wasn't a washboard yet, but her thighs no longer bowed out slightly at the front, or welled at the back. Her arms were a lot firmer, and her legs felt much tauter when he encouraged her to wind them round his neck.

They had tried a few more positions, and she was definitely more supple. It had occurred to him that she never quite relaxed, but he wasn't the sort to pressure her. The female orgasm had always seemed a funny, messy, unpredictable thing to him. Of course, he knew it was important to satisfy her. But what could be better than two good bodies, clean, tanned, and oiled, trying out all sorts of combinations? He wasn't sure he could do more.

It was the end of the month, and pay-cheque time. Matthew padded around the flat in his dressing-gown, looking out at another day when the cloud was as steely as the road surface on the wet, greasy flyover he could see from the corner of his window. A few cars were already whizzing to work, even at six thirty. He liked the buzz and hum of London, never quiet or really in repose, but he recognised that a bachelor flat was not the place to live forever.

He looked down again at the pay-slip which had been delivered in the previous day's post. He had opened it after Jenny had gone home the night before, and then left it on the kitchen counter to peruse again in the morning. He frowned. Despite the boss's promises, and the row Matthew had had with the Inland Revenue, it still wasn't the amount he had hoped for. It was a damn good thing he had the other source of revenue! Paying the mortgage and the car loan was hard enough. But Matthew had opened a new account, and was saving with a view to buying a house. Next year, he would be thirty two. And it was time to consider marriage. Thinking about this, he drove, almost on autopilot, to the gym.

His routine was tougher now. He even chatted in a desultory way with the meatheads. They were discussing some product or other that morning. 'Mix it with egg,' one of the guys said. He looked like a piece of old leather, with deep mahogany creases, knotted and crusted. His face would have been cadaverous if it hadn't been so brown. Yet he loved himself, stopping to pose at the long mirror in the corner.

Matthew still couldn't understand how they could do it. Surely they could see how their genitalia were shrunken into little flaps of useless skin, completely overshadowed by their shelving bodies?

As Matthew worked on the weights, he thought about it. Of course, it took time and over-indulgence to turn you into something as grotesque as the elderly meathead. The younger one looked quite good, by comparison. He even had a little bulge still, between his huge thighs. And Matthew had to admire their dedication. Commitment was something Matthew understood, and he had come to look forward to the two meatheads' unchanging cheerfulness on these grey dawns.

Afterwards, feeling better, he towelled himself dry and took a sneak look at his naked body in the changing room mirror before the others came in. Yes, he was fine. And his balls and prick were in great working order as he'd demonstrated the night before. There seemed no chance of *his* sexuality ever withering.

Outside, the spluttering rain threatened to depress him again as he walked to the car, but he felt cheered. The body, the car, the house! The wife? It was all possible, for the first time. The rain chivvied and spat at him, and he pulled up the hood of his tracksuit top and started to hurry to the car.

He clicked the remote control with confidence then suddenly he felt the heat of another body behind him. The knee that jerked up between his buttocks pushed him forwards and pinned him onto his own car door. The force of a forearm crushed the nape of his neck, and the strength of another arm wrenched his left arm up his back. Matthew was strong and fit, but his shower had relaxed him, the work-out had tired him, and he had been caught unawares.

'Hey, big balls, where's the cash?'

Matthew knew it was best not to struggle. He might win, but at what cost?

'OK, OK, it's coming.'

'When?'

'I don't know. None of us know. It's taking longer.'

'Fuck that. I need it now. So does she. I need a hundred today. Leave it in the usual place.'

'All right. I said *all right*!'

The grip slackened, but only slightly. Matthew felt anger rather than fear. Stupid fool, trying to threaten him like that. 'Now sod off,' he growled. 'Your money will be there. And stop making such a fucking nuisance of yourself. I don't want you near me again.'

The grip tightened again. 'Oh ho, muscle man. Get a load of this!'

'Hey . . .' Matthew was conscious of a tiny tickling sensation along his jawline.

Then the man flicked the knife back into its sheath, replaced it in his pocket, and stood back. As Matthew wriggled away, he raised his hand to his chin.

'Youch, for Christ's sake, what have you done?'

'Just warning you, OK?'

Matthew spun round. 'You've cut me, you bastard!'

'Yeah, yeah, just testing!' The attacker skipped backwards, away from Matthew's flailing fist. 'But you can't catch me, Mr Muscle! I float like a butterfly and sting like a bee, but by Christ when I float I'm higher than anyone!' He laughed and bent backwards and forwards with the rapid, jerky uncontrolled force of the drugged. 'Remember, Superman, I want my dosh!'

Matthew looked back evenly at the young man. 'All right, I heard. But you're getting sodding stupid. You nearly screwed things up once before, and when you get like this you're no use to anyone. Get yourself some pills to calm you down. And then fuck off out of my sight, Jason.'

The next day finally dawned brighter and stayed that way, but Kate couldn't give a damn about the weather, except that it made the walk to the doctor's slightly more pleasant. She hurried past Polly's house. She had dreaded meeting her neighbour this particular morning. In the last month they had hardly spoken, merely exchanging pleasantries if they passed each other, and it was Kate who had been cool.

The change in the weather made all the premature summer behaviour seem like a dream. The embryonic social life of gardens and conservatories and barbecues had never developed. Children no longer hung around in the street, and people hurried past each other in raincoats, with windblown umbrellas and wet feet. It was not a time to stand and chat. But John still visited Polly regularly, usually in the afternoon. Each time he told Kate about it with scrupulous care, and Kate stopped herself questioning him, with uncharacteristic restraint, desperate to be indifferent. And she avoided seeing Polly again.

But even if she had wanted to return Polly's first invitation it would have been hard. Kate couldn't entertain in the bedsit, and the house was in chaos. John was only able to decorate when parish commitments gave him time, and he insisted on employing parishioners who were painters or plumbers, on odd days when they had no other jobs. It was a Christian way to behave but sometimes Kate wished they could just hire a decorating firm and get the damn things done!

That morning she was cross and nervous, but because of her doctor's appointment, not because of work. Now the 'Cook of the North' contract was signed, and the replacement logos completed at huge extra cost – offset by the amazingly cheap deal Jenny had done with Northern TV – the channel seemed to be taking shape.

And pressure from the shareholders was lessening. In the last month Kate had had no communication with Antony Chester-Lang, to her surprise, and his son had only called her twice. The first time had been to thank her, effusively, for a fax she had sent him, detailing all the various cable TV franchises, with a thumbnail sketch of each of the Chief Executives. She had anticipated further contact. But in his second call, Daniel sounded much more distant. Personal problems, he said vaguely, but absolutely nothing to worry about. He added that he had also discovered poor Sonya Chester-Lang was in hospital, after a nasty fall downstairs in her huge luxury house. There had been some suggestion of a break-in. Kate sent her some flowers, and was secretly relieved that her husband seemed to have been distracted.

That lunchtime, after leaving the doctor's surgery, Kate took Jenny to the Italian restaurant in the precinct. She had been so preoccupied with her own body, she hadn't noticed how thin Jenny's face was becoming, although she was a pleasant ruddy colour.

'I was going to say you looked well, Jenny, except that your hips seem to be disappearing! Not to mention your lovely round cheeks . . . I mean on your face!'

Jenny laughed back. 'I know! I feel fantastic, although I'm a bit tired! But Matt is great. He keeps me going. I've lost six pounds already, in a month. And I've bought this great self-tanning lotion, so I look brown all the time. Matt trains every day, but I only go three times a week. I'm thinking of extending it to four.'

Kate grimaced. 'I've been the same weight for a year now. It's about half a stone more than I should be, but it's better than I was two years ago. Anyway, what the hell.'

She wouldn't care how fat and shapeless she became if she could only get pregnant. She had no idea why having a baby was becoming such an obsession. Kate had experienced set-backs in her life before, but none of them had been so final. In the past she had always considered the demands of the infertile on the National Health System to be indulgent, when people were dying for want of kidney machines or bone marrow transplants. Now, though, she felt like screaming, hysterically, 'What about ME?'

'I said, are we having a drink, Kate?' Jenny repeated patiently.

'A drink? Oh, no, I'm trying not to at the moment.'

'Oh, worried that lunchtime drinking will put you off your stride?'

'No, it's not that. It's, well, it's because I'm still trying, you know, to get pregnant.'

Jenny looked surprised. 'Oh, how's all that going?'

'OK. I'm going to have some tests. Twenty-one-day progesterone tests, they're called, to see if I'm ovulating. Trouble is, it can take three months to establish a pattern. And it will be a fortnight before I can start them. Anyway, what about you? You and Matt seemed to be getting into a nesting stage!'

'Kate!' But it was true. Jenny was spending as much time as she possibly could with Matt. He was so solid, the sort of man who would laugh off mad phone callers or moving cups. Kate was saying, 'Well, you spend a lot of time at his flat.'

'That's because mine's a hole. And because he's got an exercise bike!'

Kate laughed too. But she watched the usually hungry Jenny choose clear soup, and salad for lunch, and she began to wonder if this fitness craze was going a little too far.

Jenny took a sip of water, thoughtfully. Could she tell Kate about her current fear, without seeming neurotic? On three occasions in the last four weeks, the phone on Jenny's desk had rung, and the little silence had started. It was infrequent enough to startle rather than terrify her, and at first she had not wanted to make a fuss. But she suspected that if she did nothing, it would get worse. And she was starting to be scared. The last time, she hadn't waited for the voice to ask to speak to Laurence Smith. And the thought of the giggle made her feel sick.

'Kate . . . look. There is something which is bothering me.'

'Yes? What is it?'

Jenny pushed her lettuce around the plate.

'It's weird phonecalls . . .' she began, and paused.

'At the flat?'

'No, thank God. At the office.'

Slowly she told Kate all about it, and with a rush of relief, realised that Kate thought the calls every bit as serious as she did herself. There was no point pretending to be tough with Kate.

'Good God, Jenny, that's appalling. Who could it be?'

'Anyone, I suppose. A friend of Laurence's? His mother even? Someone at work who thinks it's funny to upset us?'

'Did you ring that number which traces the last call for you?'

'Yes. After the last time. In a way, before that, I didn't want to know, I just wanted it to stop. But after the fourth time, I rang to check.'

'And?'

'It was no good. It's either not a BT number, or it's a mobile phone. Probably the latter. Everyone has them now.'

'Well, we'll have it stopped. I don't care how inconvenient it is, we'll get the office numbers changed. Good Lord, Jenny, you take far too much on yourself. Why on earth did you think you had to cope with this alone?'

Because I'm trying to learn to be a sensible manager, Jenny thought. For a moment she wondered about confiding in Kate about the time the mug had reappeared on Laurence's desk. But that would surely be too much. Kate was so matter of fact about the calls, dealing with the problem as an awful nuisance which should be stopped, that to whinge about a cup of coffee on a desk seemed to be asking to be taken less seriously. Looking back, Jenny could even convince herself she had overreacted.

As it was, that afternoon Kate informed everyone in the office that there had been a nuisance caller, and they would soon have new numbers. In the meantime, all the phones would be camped on to her extension.

'Gruesome!' said Chloe cheerfully. Kate had not divulged what the caller said.

'Yes, I really think it is,' Debbie had shuddered. 'But Chloe and I haven't had any strange calls.'

'No. It's mostly been Jenny. I don't know why.'

'P'raps the chap only knows Jenny's number?' Debbie suggested helpfully.

Nick, thought Jenny stupidly for a stunned moment. Her thoughts usually went back to him. Or Matt? Or Michelle, Matt's ex-girlfriend? Why would the caller pick on her?

'Yes, that could be it,' Kate said sensibly. 'But it's probably just a coincidence. The main thing is that we're going to stop it.'

It would take twenty four hours to get the numbers changed, and mean an infuriating waste of time letting people like the share-holders know. But Kate felt it had to be done. She had seen more of Jenny's fear than Jenny had wanted her to.

That night she and Debbie were the only people left in the building, working on a new mailing list. In her office, Kate was just packing her briefcase, when the phone rang. She picked it up. There was a silence. A tinny little voice said, 'Can I speak to Laurence Smith?' Kate waited. Then came the fleshcreeping giggle, and the call suddenly ended, leaving Kate staring at the phone. A few seconds later she looked up dazedly to see Debbie at her door.

'What's up, Kate?' The plump girl's plain, dour face was distorted with concern. 'Are you all right?' Kate realised she must have gasped out loud, for Debbie to be able to hear her in the main office. But this wasn't the time to panic people.

'Yes. I'm fine. That was just my partner on the phone.'

'Oh, I thought . . .'

'You were wrong. You mustn't worry, Debbie. The nuisance caller won't get through again.'

That night, with a lot on her mind, Kate wondered if she should mention to John that she might be having fertility tests. They made love regularly and her periods were obvious. But John had never raised the subject of their having a baby again. She thought it was probably because he was a much more patient, sensible person than she was. He probably expected everything to be fine, and that it would just take time. Kate hoped against hope that he was right. At the back of her mind she was scared of her fertility becoming a crisis.

After supper he said, 'I really should try and fix up Andrew's visit. Though the plastering seems to be taking forever . . .'

'It wouldn't, if you got in a plasterer to do it, instead of that weird chap from the church!'

'There's nothing wrong with him. His plastering is brilliant.'

'Yes, but he only seems to work when it's a full moon!'

'Kate! That's not true!'

'OK, OK. Anyway, what about Andrew?'

'I've been thinking.'

They now had an ancient horsehair sofa that had been given to

John by one of his pensioner parishioners, and he had been too kind
to refuse it. It stood in the middle of the empty living room, covered
by a sheet. John pulled her towards him and started kissing her hair.
Kate felt, as always, that she would melt. John had an uncanny
ability to turn her into a sexual blob whenever he touched her.

'Hey, stop it. Just what have you been thinking?'

'Well, one of Andrew's suggestions was that he should come and
stay over the August Bank Holiday weekend. So why don't we just
get married then? It would be a great time to do it. We ought to,
Kate. The parish is quiet, it's the holiday weekend, you've still got
a few weeks before your channel launches. There's time for the
banns. And most important, the plastering will be finished!'

Kate felt a flurry of panic.

'But I can't do that!'

'Why not?'

Because I won't know then whether or not I'm able to have a
baby, Kate thought wildly. And you want one. And I can't bear to
tell you, in case you marry me anyway, just to be honourable! What
she actually said was, 'Felix Smart has asked me to speak at the
Edinburgh International TV Festival that weekend.'

It was a petty excuse, but it seemed like a godsend, although she
hadn't thought about Felix or his invitation for weeks.

'What? Do you have to do that, Kate? I mean August Bank
Holiday is an ideal time. And if Andrew is coming to stay anyway,
and the time is right . . .'

'Andrew? So we're arranging our marriage to suit your son, are
we?'

'No! Don't be stupid.'

'Don't you tell me not to be stupid. It's you who's been ploughing
on making arrangements without thinking about what I might
want.'

'That's not true. Kate, is this more serious than an argument
about dates? Have you had second thoughts about getting married
at all?'

'No. Of course not. I just don't want it sprung on me, that's all.'

She realised she was almost crying again, tears of rage burning
behind her eyelids at everything being so right and so wrong at the
same time. 'Look, I'm going up to the bathroom. In fact, I'm going

to get a shower. It's so horrible and dusty in here, I never feel clean in this place . . .'

John looked at her, bemused and distressed. Kate had never complained about the slow progress on the house before. He felt a shiver of anxiety, but the worry made him bluster.

'I'm going out. I'll be back in an hour. I need to go and see Polly anyway. And then perhaps we'd better talk about it.'

But the last thing John really wanted to do was talk about it. He just wanted to get the wedding sorted out. As he drove to Polly's the little tremor of fear started again. The longer the indecision went on, the longer he would have for his worries to grow into fully-fledged fears. He couldn't rid himself of the one little worm of corrosive concern from the past which was threatening to ruin everything. He was a sensible, educated middle-aged man, for goodness' sake. His life was being spoilt by something which was probably just an old wives' tale! He must get a grip, and stop fretting.

He squared his rugby tackling shoulders, and took a deep breath, and prepared to put his imagination to one side and listen to reason. But he was unsure whether the voice he heard was reason or his own personal devil.

Jenny too took a shower that evening, but hers was in the women's changing room at the gym.

'You're looking great, Jenny, and you've only been coming a few weeks! Just a little bit of flab left on the thighs, but a few more sessions should bring that under control. Are you coming back to the flat for supper?'

'Please, if you don't mind. I can't stand my place sometimes, especially when the other two are drifting round in hair rollers and dressing-gowns eating junk food and moaning.'

'Yuk! Let's go. I'll make an omelette for us.'

It was a coolish, blowy night, after a much prettier day. Jenny knew where Matt parked, but as she turned towards the car, he said, 'No, this way.'

'Aren't you in your usual spot any more?'

'Nope. I think the car is more secure on the main road, even if it is hell parking and getting out.'

Jenny was surprised. After a just a month she had come to realise that Matthew was a man who organised his life carefully. He knew exactly what he was doing, each day of the week, and this evening she wondered what had made him change his routine. Yet at the same time she wasn't really interested enough to ask. Her affair with Matthew had already become an easy co-existence, not so much a meeting of minds so much as two minds travelling on parallel tracks and occasionally waving.

'You go and change out of that load of layers while I make supper,' Matt said in his usual gently authoritative way when they reached his building. She went into his hallway ahead of him, remembering not to dump her big shapeless tapestry bag on the stripped wooden floor. Matt liked her to leave her bag neatly in the bedroom. She had some soft jeans and a shirt to change into.

She could hear Matthew in the bathroom, then in the kitchen. Jenny wasn't a particularly tidy person, but she knew Matthew was keen on keeping things in order. So she decided to hang her anorak over the chair on his side of the bed. She walked round it, then stopped.

The scruffy table arrangement was back, covered with the drab pink cloth that had seemed so out of place in Matthew's smart flat the first time she had visited. Jenny heard Matthew coming, and turned round guiltily in the act of draping her anorak over the chair.

He said, 'I can't believe how I've let this happen, but I've only got two eggs left.'

'We bought half a dozen on Sunday, didn't we?'

'Yeah. Never mind, I'll just pop out to the Seven-Eleven. Is that OK? I'll be less than five minutes. Put that Van Morrison CD on. I like that old comfy stuff. And get out the crispbread, will you?'

'Sure.'

Matthew nodded and left. She heard the flat door slam behind him, and his feet running down the stairs. Driven by fear and curiosity, she pulled the pink cloth to one side.

The white boxes were there again, but this time they were bigger. Fumbling, listening to her own breath, Jenny carefully eased the tight-fitting lid off the top box. And she stared at what was inside, trying to make it out.

It was black plastic. Then she realised that the shiny patent finish was embedded with tiny studs, and it was the curve of some sort of stiff gauntlet. Gingerly, she moved the gloves. They lay on top of something resembling a bolero top but large, made, she was sure, for a man. It was rigid, enforced with metal hoops and pimpled with even smaller sharper studs. But there was also something leering underneath, which could only be a mask. It was grotesque, the studs punched round the lip at the bottom like little teeth. But worse even than that was the coiled whip she saw lying beside it. She moved the prickling garments slightly, to see two or three magazines. Even their front covers were enough to make her retch. Women, tied to stakes, were battered and bruised, and worst of all, smiling. The copy, in badly printed red zig-zag lettering screamed: 'Pain, I'll take it for you!'

Her face cold with shock and disgust, Jenny pushed the costume back into place with just the tips of her fingers, and replaced the lid and the cloth with aching care. Then, gagging, she ran from Matthew's bedroom to the bathroom where she scrubbed her hands till the memory of the cold sticky plastic and the sharp little studs in the palm of her hands were washed away.

She was still there when Matthew came back.

'Good, I see you're nearly ready. Omelettes coming up.'

'I don't feel well,' she said weakly. 'Matthew, I'm going to have to go back to my place.'

'Hey, you do look pale.' He was genuinely concerned about her white face, and also alarmed at the way she shied away from him, her hands behind her back. 'Are you sure, Jenny? I mean, if you really want to go, I'll take you back now.'

'Yes! Yes, please.'

Matthew guided her by the elbow down the stairs. She couldn't bear his touch, but was too stupefied to be able to shake it off. He settled her in the car like a chauffeur with an old lady, and then drove slowly to her flat.

'Do you want me to come in with you?'

'No! No, really. I'll be fine, Matthew.'

'Well, if you get any worse, will you call me?'

'OK.'

'And I'm not leaving you tomorrow. I'll call round in the morning after I've been to the gym, and see if you're fit to go to work. That's for definite, Jenny. I'll be here at eight. OK?'

She nodded dumbly.

At the flat, she stumbled into bed and pulled the duvet up to her chin. At first she lay there blaming herself for never mentioning the first set of boxes she had seen. But when life with Matthew had become a routine, she had forgotten them. And anyway, once they had gone, what did they matter? But as she fell into sleep, she seemed to spend her dreams running from dark perverted creatures in masks who lurked under bridges, before she drifted into a heavy doze.

Her flatmate roused her by turning the radio on full blast in the kitchen. It was seven o'clock. She dragged herself out of bed and showered, neglecting to do her exercises, and saw that her instant tan was becoming patchy. Her hair seemed dustier today. She tried to make conversation with the two other girls over her mug of scummy instant coffee. But all the time, she was waiting with dread for the doorbell's ring.

'It's for you, Jenny. The boyfriend. Hurry up, he's waiting!'

Jenny picked up her shapeless anorak, and went out. The weather had reasserted itself to celebrate the start of summer, and Jenny felt the warmth and softness on her face. Matthew tried to kiss her with equivalent gentleness, but she flinched away, unable to bear his touch. He seemed oblivious, taking her shudder for lack of balance.

'You're still shaky,' he said brightly. 'But I take it you're going to work?'

She nodded.

'Climb in!' he ordered, in his usual pleasant way. Despite the gentleness of his tone, Jenny knew by now that he always assumed command. She silently obeyed him. But as she bent forward to lean into the low sports car, she stopped. In the back, behind the driver's seat, were the white boxes from his bedroom. She slumped into place, grabbing the seatbelt for support. Matthew bounced in next to her, and put the key in the ignition.

'What are those boxes?'

'Those? Oh, just something for work. If you were feeling fitter I'd expect you to help me carry them in!'

Jenny was sitting upright now, looking out of the window. But her mind was not on the lacy city trees, or the reflected blue sky in the plate glass shop-fronts. She glanced at Matthew as he drove. He was singing to the tune on Heart FM.

'So the boxes aren't yours?'

'No! What did you think they were? An illicit cache of cream buns? Naughty but nice?' He laughed. 'I'm glad you're feeling better,' he said. 'But I quite liked the idea of looking after you.'

He smiled to himself, and left it a fraction too late to pull up smoothly at the traffic lights. Behind Matthew's seat, the cardboard boxes shifted slightly. Jenny turned to look at them, mesmerised, waiting for the lids to slide off again. But they didn't. It occurred to her with a tremendous sense of relief that perhaps he had never opened them himself. He parked the car in the Warehouse car park, leant over to touch her arm, and when she winced, said, 'I'm sorry. I'll just leave those boxes in the back and unpack them later. It's nothing urgent.' He smiled. Surely he wouldn't be so unconcerned if he had known what ghastly material was in the back of his car? Perhaps, Jenny thought desperately, the simplest explanation was the right one. Was Matt just storing the boxes for someone else?

'Anyway,' he went on gallantly, 'I'll walk up with you to your office.' There was no point in telling him that she hardly needed an escort to her desk. Clearly, it made him feel good to be at her arm, so she allowed him to walk beside her, his hand cupping her elbow.

Kate bustled by, hurrying out of the kitchenette. She looked pale herself, but had a busy air, and Jenny wondered why she was holding two hot cups of coffee.

'Hi, Jenny. Good morning! You're the first one to arrive this morning. And Matt, nice to see you too.' Kate beamed benevolently at them. 'Guess what, Jenny, we've got a visitor.' She turned to walk down the new corridor between her own office and Jenny's little cubicle.

'Come and say, hello, both of you. Matt, I'd like to introduce you to the man who brought Jenny and me together. He was in London last night for an awards dinner, and he thought he'd pop in this morning with a proposal for Food and Health!'

Jenny could say nothing, not even 'hi'. She was astonished. She couldn't believe that Nick had the effrontery to come back. It had been weeks since they had grappled under the bridge, and she had assumed he was as disgusted with her as she was with herself, and to see him sitting there, smirking at her in Kate's office, was to trivialise the whole wretched encounter.

Except that he wasn't smirking any more. Nick's smile had stopped halfway across his face when he saw Matthew Lavelle put his hand proprietorially on Jenny's shoulder. 'Hi,' Matt said genially. 'I have to go and unload the car. Call me in half an hour, Jenny, and let me know how you are.'

Jenny was only half aware he had gone.

Kate looked from Nick to Jenny and said quickly, 'I've been thinking for a while that we should make our own programming instead of just buying in. Go and get yourself a coffee, Jenny, then come back, and we'll discuss it.'

While she was away, Kate refused to catch Nick's eye, and shuffled the papers on her desk. When Jenny reappeared, she looked more composed, though Nick still shifted awkwardly on the skinny metal chair, and his cavalier smile seemed forced.

'OK,' Kate said with determined cheerfulness. 'Let's hear the ideas again, Nick.'

He outlined his proposals and Kate launched all three of them into a demanding discussion about programme budgets.

Eventually Nick said, 'Thanks for seeing me, Kate. I realise you were working along the same lines yourself. And I'm glad you liked the idea, Jenny. I'm sorry I couldn't persuade you last time we spoke.' Kate saw Jenny's eyes narrow.

'Why don't you see Nick out?' she said.

Jenny left the office and walked silently ahead of him to the double doors. 'You *know* your way out, of course.'

'Yes.' Neither of them referred to his previous visit. 'It was nice to talk to you again this morning, Jenny.' Nick held his hand out formally to her. Jenny did not take it. Part of her deliberately wanted to be rude. And part of her was scared of his touch.

'Goodbye, Nick.'

He nodded briefly, then turned from her and loped away with his energetic bounce. Jenny closed her eyes and waited until she knew he had walked through the big glass doors and disappeared across the car park, and only then did she acknowledge the temptation to run after him and grab his arm and start the spiral of lust and rejection all over again.

But outside the door, she noticed Matt Lavelle's car parked at an angle, less than perfectly for once, because that morning he had been so anxious to deliver her safely to her desk.

And she did run out across the yard, but to Matthew's office. He was sitting hunched grumpily over some plans. He looked up at the noise Jenny made as she came through the door, but she gave him no time to react. She skirted around his desk and threw her arms round his neck.

'Oh, Matthew.'

'Jenny! You must be better!'

Her grip tightened. 'Yes, yes, I am, Matthew, much better now.'

CHAPTER NINE

In her own office, Kate sat ruminatively over her own second coffee of the day. The meeting with Nick and Jenny had upset her.

How could she have been so obtuse? The attraction between them had been a bit of a joke among the staff at Northern TV, but Kate should have realised it had gone beyond flirtation. And to some extent this explained Jenny's sudden intense relationship with Matt. Maybe she was on the rebound.

And maybe he was what Jenny needed, if Nick had messed her around. But Kate felt there was something about Jenny which was eluding her. In the main, Jenny's work was great and, by and large, her common sense and strong ideas were perfectly matched. But sometimes there were signs of trouble. Even getting rid of the rogue phonecalls had not made Jenny feel completely secure, Kate could tell. There were times when she stared blankly at a cup of coffee, before pulling herself together. She seemed to cling too much to Matt, and rely on him in a way Kate found slightly unhealthy. Kate blamed herself for not realising that another of Jenny's problems had been a stillborn romance with Nick Malcolm. But perhaps the reason she had failed to spot Jenny's problems was because she had so many of her own.

She had still been tired that morning when she had left John's sleeping side for work. He had returned from Polly's at nearly midnight the night before, leaving Kate tossing and turning in bed in a frenzy of worry and recrimination. When he had come in, he had apologised profusely for being late. He whispered as he climbed in beside her, 'Kate, listen, love.' The use of the endearment soothed her. 'I need to talk to you.'

'OK.'

'I know this wedding thing is difficult for you. Look, this doesn't sound very romantic, but I'm a priest and I believe in Holy Matrimony. I've got to practise what I preach. I can't afford to wait too long.'

'All right, John. But give me time. Let's just say the autumn. Before Christmas. OK?'

'I'd like it to be sooner, but fine. We'll discuss the details later.' They had lain together in a knot of mutual tension before sleep came.

Throughout the next day, Kate felt drained. At one point she shouted at Chloe for not finishing the logging of a 'Floyd on Food' series. It was rare for Kate to raise her voice, and Chloe looked alarmed, which made Kate feel worse. Bullying a weak member of the team wasn't going to achieve anything, and Kate disliked herself for trying it, but sometimes Chloe's manner annoyed her, even though she knew the girl was making more effort.

By evening, Kate felt generally out of sorts. She wanted to put off going home. She had phoned Felix Smart earlier, and asked if he would like to meet for a drink. Delighted by her agreement to take part in his discussion at Edinburgh, he convened a quick meeting at the Groucho Club with the other panellists whom she could reach at short notice.

Although she was pleased to be meeting Felix, driving into the centre of London in the evening was a chore Kate did not relish. She was already late when she left the Warehouse, puzzling about the best route into town. She opened her car and flung her briefcase inside, then saw the secretary to Matt Lavelle's department emerging from the administration block. The woman, a striking, sociable redhead named Michelle, called brightly, 'Hi, Kate, how are you?'

'Fine, Michelle. I'm glad I've bumped into you.' Michelle was a well-known frequenter of the West End. 'Which is the best way to get into town?'

'I'd do the A4. It'll be busy though.'

'Will it? Oh dear. I hate driving in London. Not to mention parking!'

'Well, let me give you a lift! I'm meeting someone in Mayfair myself, but he has his own garage, so I'm OK.' I bet you are, thought Kate, looking at Michelle's designer clothes and little red car. Michelle was one of those people from a wealthy background who see their role as oiling society's wheels rather than earning a living, but her invitation was sincere. As she drove expertly into London, she chatted to Kate at length.

'Yes, I'm PA to Matt Lavelle's boss. It's quite interesting, though I'd rather work in Town. Mind you, at the moment we do feel rather important because of this exciting new channel. All very hush-hush but rather thrilling. There's an American chap due over in about a fortnight to start running it. All very glam, I must say!'

'Yes, it sounds it!'

'Absolutely. The offices are really nice, much bigger than yours. I'm in the office next door to Matt, so I tend to take an interest. Matt's nice, isn't he? We used to be an item. But it didn't work out.' Well, he doesn't have a place in Mayfair, Kate thought, then reproved herself for being uncharitable. Michelle was saying, 'Now I hear he's going with that girl who works for you.'

'Jenny? Yes.'

'I'm glad for him.' Michelle beat three male drivers to the traffic lights in front of Harrods. 'Matthew needs a nice girlfriend. He'll go far. He's got the ambition. His problem is his background. I mean, Slough! But he'll make it in the end. From what I can work out, he's already on his way.'

'Really?'

'Oh yes. There's more to Matthew Lavelle than meets the eye. He's on to a nice little number. I'm sure he's got something going, on the side. Good for him.' Michelle swooped down the underpass to emerge at Piccadilly, then with amazing good luck hit a relatively empty road and a run of green lights.

'Here we are,' she cried breezily. And within seconds of Kate struggling out of the car, Michelle had revved away.

At the club, Felix welcomed her but Kate felt he was marginally less warm than usual. Settled in an uneasy chair in a crowded corner, she waited for him to come back with the drinks. Round her, distinctive voices brayed or whispered. Other characters posed at the bar, striped by the evening sunlight shining through the narrow blinds. Less noted media people clustered in the dark green corners. There was an air of irritable self-importance about the place, as if some of the members felt they should be there because of their notoriety, yet resented anyone staring at them. Kate wasn't sure where to look. Felix came back and settled himself in an armchair at their little round table, then scooped up a generous helping of mixed salted nuts and shiny little crackers.

'You're quiet, Felix!'

'Am I?'

'Yes, you are. What have I done wrong? Here I am, actually early, and you're sitting there saying nothing. You, the media world's greatest source of knowledge! What's the problem?'

Felix leaned forward. 'Kate, I deplore that remark. But you've hit the nail on the head as usual. You remember Jeremy Woodley? . . .'

'Yes. Derek Boulder's friend. I know him . . .'

'Well, he's been flapping like a wet hen about this new cable channel. He's very worried. I just hope you're not involved.'

'In what? You mean the Chester-Lang channel?'

'Yes. The mail order thing. You must know more about it than I do, because frankly, Jeremy's been tighter than a gnat's arse . . .'

'Did you say "mail order", Felix?'

'Yes. At least that's what I've heard. Why are you looking so surprised?'

'Because I had no idea that was what Chester-Lang was into. What are they planning to mail out?'

'Christ knows. All I know is that Jeremy has definitely got all worked up about it. You know what he's like. He thinks because he's one of the old guard he can get round the ITC about anything. They have such a lovely time interpreting the rules that if you have the right approach you can get away with murder.' Kate nodded, and smiled dryly. 'But this time, Kate, even the slithery Woodley can't pull it off. And he must have been banking on one hell of a success fee, because he's getting very rattled.'

'Fascinating! But I can assure you, Felix, it's nothing to do with me.'

'Well, I wouldn't like to think you were involved in something dodgy, Kate. Not now, when you're getting your reputation back.'

'I'm not! Involved, I mean!' Kate swallowed her tomato juice and sat in the dusty, filtered sunshine from the darkened window, thinking. She would ring Daniel Chester-Lang that night, and see, with this snippet of information for leverage, if she could glean more. She wanted to know what it was that was causing so many people so much unease.

Then Felix leapt to his feet to greet the two other panellists, a man from London ITV and a woman from Discovery Channel. And minutes later Derek Boulder arrived, and sank into the chair Felix had vacated.

'Aha, cable TV,' he sighed. 'I don't really know how anyone can defend most of it.' So then Kate forgot all her other considerations for an hour, and prepared to do battle.

On the way home on the Tube, still smarting after the heated discussion, she suddenly remembered that she had left her briefcase in her car, in the car park. It was a real nuisance because her mobile phone charger, and a copy of *New Media Markets* magazine she had planned to read in bed, were all inside.

She got off the tube at Hammersmith, and caught a bus to the Warehouse. At the stop, she called Jenny on her mobile phone.

'Look, Jenny, I don't want to interrupt your evening. But Felix Smart said something strange to me tonight in the Groucho Club.'

'Oho, name-dropping!'

'What? Name-drop? Me, a friend of Greg Dyke's? Never!'

'Stop clowning, Kate. I must say you sound perkier.'

'Only because I've been sharpening my brain on that self-important pig, Derek Boulder. But I've also got some news. Apparently the Chester-Lang channel is based on some sort of mail order system.'

'What, like QVC?'

'No, I don't think so. It can't be like that. There isn't room for two shopping channels. I think there's something much weirder about this. I'm going to ring Daniel Chester-Lang tonight from the office. I don't suppose you want to meet me there, and hear what he has to say?'

Jenny paused. Tonight was supposed to be special. This was to be the first time she had stayed overnight at Matthew's, and she had never spent the whole night with a man before. Kate understood from Jenny's voice that this was a dramatic development and felt a rush of sympathy. Sex was relatively easy – after all, some people reduced that to a transaction. But sleeping with someone was far more intimate, lying there worrying about snoring or farting or dribbling, and wondering what you would look like in the morning. She remembered the first time she had stayed with John, at his cottage in the Pennines. It seemed funny to think of Jenny going through something similar. And ironic to think that tonight, for the first time ever, she didn't want to go home to John.

'I'll get there if I can, Kate. But . . .'

'Jenny, really, it doesn't matter. I'll tell you what he says in the morning.'

'Thanks, Kate. That's really understanding.'

Ten minutes later, Kate sat on the top of the bus, watching the tall, stately Victorian mansions, candle-bulbs twinkling through fanlights, give way to Edwardian red brick. The bus pulled up. She could have alighted one stop earlier and taken the short cut down the canal bank, but with dusk falling, she chose to walk down from what had once been the village centre, characterised by The Narrowboat and the now derelict church.

The road to the Warehouse was well-lit, and tonight there were still a few strollers down by the canal. She even saw Mr Chandip the newsagent finally packing up and closing the shop. She was tempted to wave and call to him, as she watched from the other side of the water. She could see he was as irritable as ever, tugging plastic stands back into the premises, and shouting machine gun instructions in Gujerati to his bored and weary sons.

She hurried on to the Warehouse car park, glanced at her watch, and tried to work out what she would say when she rang New York. As far as she could tell, Daniel was doing very little work on the new channel, other than arranging the movement of his father's money. As an ex-actor and restaurateur, performance was probably in his blood, and he must have thought, momentarily, that a British TV channel was a great opportunity. But she knew from the only two phone conversations they had had, that he was more jaundiced than ever. The only good thing, he had said apologetically, was that Sonya's accident had kept his father out of his hair. Antony Chester-Lang had actually wanted Daniel to stay for longer in New York before coming to London, which was good news for Daniel, though it surprised Kate. Why would his father want to keep Daniel away?

Kate moved her swipe-card through the security lock and

punched in the number. It wasn't easy to get into the Warehouse after hours, and she still believed that when the office had been vandalised, Chloe had told Jason the code number, perhaps without realising what she was doing.

As Kate climbed the stairs she slowed down. She realised that unlike the usual hush of evening in dormant office blocks, this had the feel of the working day. She was unsure why, until she pushed open the glass doors, and saw Debbie and Chloe at their desks. Her first reaction was one of immense delight that they were working late, swiftly followed by concern.

'Hi,' she said. She saw Debbie's face, looking back at her in shock. Chloe was sitting at her desk as normal, but she was typing furiously into her computer. Then, suddenly and jerkily, she turned, pressed 'eject' and almost wrenched a cassette out of her video and flung it on a pile in the corner. Chloe had her headphones jammed on. Her eyes were huge. Then she cracked open another black plastic cover, tugged the video out, and flung it into the machine, turning back to the computer to make notes as the opening titles of another cookery programme flickered onto the screen.

'What's going on?' Kate asked sharply.

Chloe peeled off her headphones, then stood up and shouted, 'Hi, Kate! Debbie thought we should put in some extra work. And so did I, after you bawled me out today. Look, I've done all those programmes in a few hours. Isn't that great?' She laughed in a high pitched way Kate had never heard before. Her face was flushed, and even as she talked her arms and legs were moving, jigging on the spot.

'Can't stop now, Kate,' she giggled stupidly. 'Must get more of these shows logged. Or shall I make you a coffee? We could have coffee, couldn't we, Debbie? That'll keep us going. Or do you want tea, Kate? We've got lemon tea and herbal tea and peppermint tea. All sorts of tea. And there's two types of coffee as well. We've got decaff, haven't we, Debbie? Then you can help us Kate, we've got so much to do. Kate, why don't you have some tea, or some coffee, we've got . . .'

Horrified by the thought of hearing the list chanted again, Kate moved forward.

'Chloe. Chloe! Stop it, for Christ's sake. What's wrong with you?'

'Me? Nothing's wrong, nothing at all. I'm just working hard, conscientiously, doing the right things to be a good researcher. I want to be good, Kate, I'm going to make it in TV. . .'

'Don't,' Debbie said, warningly.

'Chloe, are you pissed?'

Although the girl couldn't move from the spot, Chloe twisted and shook.

'Oh, God, it's drugs, isn't it? What are we going to do? I know nothing about it.' Kate turned to Debbie. 'I don't suppose you know anything about this do you?'

'No, course not, Kate! I don't do drugs. She was a bit excitable when we first came back up here at half past six, like. But then it came on really badly. I've just been sitting there, watching her get worse and worse.'

Chloe seemed to be slowing up. She was still conscious but so pale and fragile she looked almost transparent.

'God knows what we should do with you. But right now, we'd better call an ambulance.' Chloe looked at Kate in terror. 'No,' she said. 'I'm not going to hospital. I'm not going there. You can't make me, you mustn't ring an ambulance, please, no, please, please . . .' Her voice began to rise.

'All right, all right,' Kate said desperately. Behind her she heard the glass doors open. 'Oh, Jenny, thank goodness.'

'My conscience got the better of me so I got a cab here. What's going on?'

'Chloe's high on something.' Chloe trembled in front of them, trying to stop her hands dancing on the desk top.

'Is she responsible for that mess?' Jenny nodded towards the pile of fractured cassette boxes hurled into the corner.

'Yes.'

Jenny looked at the shaking girl. 'I should say she's been on speed, Kate, that's all. And she's either taken bad stuff or too much of it. She's winding down now. She's in a state. But she isn't going to die on us. She's just going to be shattered and drained.'

'But what do we do now?'

'Well, we'd better get her into bed and make sure she's warm and gets plenty to drink. But she'll need watching overnight, even when she gets home.'

It was rapidly looking like there was only one solution. Kate realised she couldn't dump Chloe on Jenny, not tonight. And anyway, if Kate herself was really into caring management, this was the time to show it.

'If you lot'll help me get her downstairs, and into the car, she can come and stay with me and John.'

Jenny's grateful look and Debbie's gasp of relief were rewards in themselves. As she drove the dazed Chloe round to the house, Kate reflected that one of the many good things about John Maple was that he tended to be unfazed by extremes of human behaviour. He might be a little annoyed at having Chloe unloaded on him, but he was obliged to be a Good Samaritan. He merely raised his eyebrows when Kate told him what she had done.

'I've got another mattress under a sheet upstairs,' he said. 'I dusted it down this morning to see if it might do for when Andrew comes to stay. I'll put it in the spare room. Mind you, Kate, I hope we're only putting her up for the night, not adopting her.'

It was on the tip of Kate's tongue to say that adoption might be the best she could offer, when surprise at John's tone stopped her. For someone anticipating late fatherhood he sounded remarkably disillusioned about kids. But she pursued the thought no further because of the sound of groaning from the living room. Chloe was struggling to sit up.

'Where the fuck am I?' she said thickly to Kate, then blinked. 'Oh God, Kate, sorry.'

'You're at my house. How are you?'

In answer Chloe retched and looked in panic for directions to the bathroom. Kate pushed her into the kitchen just in time for her to vomit in the sink. Gagging herself, Kate steadied the shuddering girl, and guided her back to the living room.

'Can I have a drink?' Chloe said feebly. Kate brought her a mug of water. Chloe looked awful, white and shivery, but she was conscious, and she no longer had that terrifying transparent tinge.

'You'd better tell me what you took, Chloe. I know nothing about drugs, but I do know when some irresponsible little moron is threatening everyone's work!'

'I swear to God, Kate, I didn't take anything.'

'Oh, for Christ's sake.' Kate turned away from Chloe in disgust.

Chloe followed her eyes and saw John, still wearing his clerical collar.

'What the fuck's he doing here?'

'He lives here. And so do I, most of the time. And so do you, for tonight. Now *tell me*!'

'Kate.' John came forward warningly. 'Chloe? It is Chloe, isn't it?' He had done a lot of voluntary work with the homeless, and when Kate had met him, he had been a part-time helper at a shelter for drug addicts in Camden. It was one of the things his wife had liked least about him.

Chloe stared at him. 'Chloe, if you can bring yourself to tell us what it was you took, we might be able to make you feel better, faster.'

'Jenny says it was speed,' Kate said angrily. She appreciated John's kindly approach most of the time, but at this moment she wanted to wring Chloe's slender white neck.

'It seems to have been a bit intense for that,' John said musingly. He was crouched beside Chloe now, looking at her face to face as she slumped on the sofa. 'Was it speed, Chloe?'

'I've just told you. I haven't taken anything.' The girl suddenly sat up and pulled herself round so her knees were on a level with John's head. 'Listen to me. Kate won't believe me but I swear to you, cross my heart and hope to die, that I don't do drugs any more.'

Chloe shook her head vigorously until she realised it ached more when she did that. 'Look, we left work quite early, just after Kate went into London. But then Debbie suggested that we come back tonight and finish a load of logging, so that Kate would be pleased. I thought it was a good idea. Kate had been angry with me this morning for going slowly.'

Kate nodded, slightly mollified.

'It was quite a nice evening, so we walked down to The Narrowboat first so Debbie could get her wages. When we were there, I had a couple of glasses of wine, because Debbie got them on the house. Oh, and a G & T.'

'All that!' Kate said.

'Oh, come off it, Kate, it's not much really. And I tell you something, I wouldn't drink anything if I was taking speed. I'm not that stupid. Why double up on resources?'

John smiled. That rang true. 'But you must know yourself that you were high?' he suggested mildly.

'Yeah.' Chloe looked at him as if she was waking up. 'I've done speed, I know what it's like. And it *is* like that, but not so . . .'

'Intense?' John supplied.

'Right. You go up, then you come down. But that was a fucking roller-coaster. No, I told you, the only things I had were the drinks, and a packet of crisps.' Kate could bear witness to the crisps, having cleared the vomit from the sink.

'Are you sure I can stay here?' Chloe said, suddenly rather pathetically.

'Yes, of course. That's what I said.' Kate sounded marginally less annoyed.

'Then can I go to sleep now, guys?' asked Chloe, with the self-centredness of the young. Kate, calmer now, realised they would be unlikely to get any more information out of her. She said tersely, 'There's a mattress for you upstairs in the little bedroom. It's nearer the toilet. I suggest you sleep there.' Chloe mumbled assent and struggled to her feet.

That night, Chloe slept like a log and was still comatose when Kate left for work the next morning. Kate put Debbie on to finishing Chloe's work, and found that Debbie was even slower, which made Kate feel guilty and annoyed with herself. More well-disposed to Chloe, when Kate came back to John's house in the evening, she found to her surprise and pleasure that Chloe had made them a pleasant, if limited, meal of reheated packet lasagne. Kate put no pressure on the girl to go, and it seemed inevitable Chloe should stay on with them for a day or two at least, until she found somewhere else to live, somewhere as far as possible from the appalling Jason.

Kate worried that he might turn up, crazed again, at the office, but he did not appear, and he failed to make any enquiries about Chloe's whereabouts. When Chloe went back to her flat, accompanied by John, to pick up her things, it looked as if the boyfriend hadn't been back for a week. Chloe didn't move out of John's house until the following Saturday, when she had found a room in a house rented by three cheery-looking temps.

In the meantime, she and John seemed to get on surprisingly

well. Chloe worked each night until nine, at a steady pace, as if to prove she could do it. On two nights she visited friends. But the other nights she came back to the house, and talked. She made Kate laugh with her anecdotes about working for an independent TV production company which had a nice line dubbing Swedish gay tapes for a seedy little shop in Old Compton Street, but Kate's laugh hid disquiet. It seemed wrong that someone young, wanting a start in TV, should have to do it that way.

Kate had known from Chloe's CV that she was better educated than she seemed. But it was only now that Kate realised much of Chloe's resentment was the result of qualifications which led nowhere, and a lower middle class background which in no way prepared her for the intellectual and social snobbery of the media world. It reminded Kate fleetingly of Michelle's remarks about Matthew Lavelle. Slough! Michelle had said in contempt. Kate felt sickened. Media was becoming more and more unashamedly the preserve of those bred into it. Broadcasters subsidised their children to work for years with no pay, and encouraged them to gain a foothold working for their own friends, with no compunction. At a time when media was mushrooming the pressure and the prejudice were worse than ever.

On the day Chloe left, she presented Kate with a huge bunch of flowers. She had been unobtrusive in many ways, yet her presence had always been there, the sound of her knock on the door always imminent. And that had given Kate an excuse not to talk very deeply to John.

Kate had also failed to have much of a conversation with Daniel Chester-Lang. She couldn't reach him, and he did not return her calls. She began to wonder if he had finally decided to throw his lot in with his father and no longer needed her as either moral support or a spy. It was just as well, she thought, because work was hotting up on Food and Health. They had now bought nearly enough programmes to fill the first few months' schedule, and the new logos were looking great.

A week later, Kate lay in bed sleepless at her lover's side. She was wondering whether or not to tell him that she had been to the doctor's that morning for her first lot of twenty-one-day progesterone blood tests. His even breathing assured her he was asleep. But she could not rest, for thinking about the test results.

'We may need two or even three goes to be sure,' the doctor had told her. Now, Kate listened to the sounds of the house. A board creaked. Somewhere, perhaps down by the river, someone shouted, and the rip in the silence made by the noise went on long after the noise itself had finished.

Then Kate heard the other sound. It was her cellphone, bleating plaintively in her handbag at the bottom of the bed. It was so long since she had heard it ring out she lay there for five or six seconds before leaping out of bed. For a moment she wondered if it might be the tinny voice, with its sick message. But then she told herself not to be ridiculous.

'Hi,' she said, forgetting her number in her shock.

'Kate? It's Matt.'

'Who?'

'Matthew Lavelle. It's an emergency. Can you get to work, please? There's been an accident at the Warehouse. No-one's hurt, but there's a lot of damage. Your offices have been completely flooded.'

'Flooded?'

'Yeah. The water tanks have burst. Can you get here right away?'

'Sure. This sounds nasty.'

'It is. Most of your work's been ruined.'

CHAPTER TEN

In the Warehouse car park Matt Lavelle could be seen talking animatedly to a group of men in suits and hard hats whom Kate thought must be insurance assessors. From the outside, the building looked exactly the same as usual. But in the courtyard there was a fire engine and a mass of fat tangled worms crawling across the cosmetic cobbles. Jenny was there too, arms folded across her chest.

'What are they for?' Kate asked Jenny, pointing at the hoses.

'They're pumping the water back into the canal.'

'So what happened?' Kate asked.

'Matt says it looks as if the big old cast iron storage tanks in the loft have burst.'

'How badly is our office damaged compared to the others?'

'It's the worst hit, Matt says. Some rooms on the ground floor aren't damaged at all, but in our section the whole place is drenched. I think the computers have had it, and the tapes are ruined. Plus the paperwork. And of course the carpets are beyond repair. God, it's creepy here at this time of night, isn't it?'

'Yes. Mind you, it can be creepy in full sunlight. Once I saw . . .' Kate was interrupted by Matt, who strode over to them. 'Hi, Kate. I'm sorry, there's no way you can go in yet. The water's damaged the old flooring, and it could be dangerous. I hope I haven't called you out for nothing.'

Matthew's air of busy competence was irritatingly dismissive. Kate was sure that it was the Warehouse's duty to replace their damaged equipment. But she had no idea where they could go, the next morning, to work.

'Matthew?' she called tensely, but he was hurrying away for another discussion with the insurance people.

'God, I'm freezing,' Jenny said. 'There's something about this building which really gets to me.'

'Too much history?'

'Yeah. Let's find somewhere warmer to wait. What about the new wing?' Jenny nodded towards the transmission block, still unfinished inside. 'We should have a look, Kate. It's pretty smart. Perhaps they'll rehouse us in here?'

Jenny walked across the yard to the new wing, the extension of Matthew's stable block HQ. She was about to use the code and swipe-card, but the door opened when she pushed it.

'Is all the electricity switched off?' Kate suggested.

'I suppose it must be. There's just the emergency lighting on. We'll have to walk round inside to keep warm. Come on.'

Kate followed her into the building, where they stood in the entrance looking out at the firemen. Jenny looked at her quizzically. 'Kate, out there you were going to say something else. About it being creepy here. And I agree with you! But then you dried up.'

'Yes.'

'Well go on, tell me what you were talking about. Or did you just mean the mad phone caller?'

'No. I don't know what made me think of it. Unless it was being down here, by the canal.' She stopped.

'Oh go on, Kate!'

'Well, this goes back months, Jenny. To that freak heatwave in April . . .'

With embarrassment at her own gullibility, Kate told Jenny how she had seen the ghost girl on the canal bank all those weeks ago. She did not see Jenny's face, half-turned away from her in the gloom. 'Afterwards I thought I must have imagined it. But it really worried me.'

'No, Kate, listen, if you were hallucinating, I was too. Because I've seen her as well. I'm sure I have.'

'You have?'

'Yes! I know exactly who you mean, she's really strange, isn't she? You can't be sure if she's real? She just seems to appear. And she's really thin?'

'With stringy hair in a knot on top, like a Victorian?'

'Yes! And she had a long, narrow black dress on, though it was pouring with rain.'

'No, it was white, and red hot sun, when I saw her. But you're right. The dress was long and narrow.'

'And she seemed to appear and disappear, just between here and the bridge!'

'Exactly! I couldn't see as far as the bridge, because I was standing outside Chandip's, looking back up the towpath on the other side. But she did seem to be running down from there. And Jenny, she looked so desperate. That was what horrified me. I couldn't see her face, but she was stooped a little, and her arm was at her breast like this.' Kate gave her impression of the stumbling ghost.

'And when I saw her, she seemed almost to be floating through the rain. It has to be the same woman.'

'But who is she?'

'I don't know . . . a tramp or vagrant?'

'Where does she come from?'

'I thought she just melted in and out of the canal bank. It was raining so hard . . .'

'And I felt she merged into the buildings. It was the way she walked, moving from side to side, almost snakily, because she was so thin . . .'

'And though we call her a girl, we don't know about that either. I mean, perhaps she was any age. A sort of bag lady without bags!'

They stood in their separate thoughts. Then Jenny said suddenly, 'Kate, there's something else. I haven't told anyone. The weird phone calls are bad enough, but one Sunday, while you were in France, I was working late. For several reasons.' Jenny still didn't want to tell Kate how she had lost the draft contract for 'Cook of the North'. ' . . . And I know this sounds mad, but when I came back into the office after having a drink with Matt, I saw . . .'

'Yes?'

'I saw Laurence's mug, the pig mug that's still in the kitchen and used by everyone now, well it was on his desk. And Kate, it had coffee in it.'

'You're joking!'

'No, I'm not. It was really creepy.'

Kate said nothing. She could see Jenny was shaking, badly. The ghost girl was one thing. But hot coffee, in a mug on a desk, had to be the other woman's imagination overworking. How sure could Kate be that Jenny really had seen the thin girl? The phone calls too had been directed at Jenny. Only the fact Kate had had a phone call herself, reassured her those were really happening too. Unless . . . but Kate stopped herself thinking anything more paranoid. The idea that Jenny might be making the calls herself was absurd. Jenny was saying, 'Now I've told you, Kate, I just feel stupid. It is stupid, isn't it?'

'Of course it is. Look, anyone could have made a coffee and left it there. They probably have cleaners in on a Sunday. You should ask Matt.'

'No. No, I don't want to do that, Kate. I don't want him to think I'm going mad . . .'

The phrase hung in the air like the water vapour rising from the fat hoses. Jenny's voice rose with unnatural bravado. 'Oh, come on, Kate, we shouldn't be stuck here, waiting. We should have a nosey round!' Bracing herself to be cheerful, Jenny led the way up the darkened staircase, and on to the landing into the master control area. Matthew had told her where the machines would stand to pump the Food and Health channel out to the cable systems all over Britain.

'Now let's look over here. This must be the new office for the Chester-Lang channel. Matt was very wary of letting me see this.' Jenny crept up to an internal wall, with a glass window into another office area. 'Hey, no wonder. Look Kate, it's like Versailles compared to our place.'

Kate crept up behind Jenny and peered in. Chester-Lang's new office was palatial. Immediately in front of them was his secretary's smaller ante-room, but even that had a fake Victorian fireplace, a new deep scarlet fitted carpet, and racks of mahogany shelves.

'Cool!' Jenny laughed. 'Pretty smart, hey? Pity this wasn't flooded.'

'That's not a very kind thing to say!'

'No, but it makes me feel better. God, it looks as if he's got half a rainforest in there. Come on, Kate, let's try and get in.'

Jenny pushed the door casually. It slid sideways. 'Christ, of course, the electrics aren't working. Look, Kate, it's open.'

'I can see that. But that doesn't mean we should go in. '

'Why not? Perhaps you could ask for us to be relocated in here, permanently? Oh, come on, let's see just how fabulous it is.' Jenny padded silently inside. Kate was just behind her, and for reassurance she asked herself what anyone could say if they were found here? Nothing, probably. They were just looking. Then Jenny stopped short and Kate bumped into her back.

But Jenny was rigid. And her hand was over her mouth but the sounds that came from it were muffled and incoherent.

'What is it, Jenny?' Kate said, pushing past.

Hanging on a rack at the far side of Daniel Chester-Lang's new office were rows of long narrow fluttering diaphanous night-dresses. And underneath were piles of white boxes. For a moment Kate too gasped, until she realised.

'It's all right, Jenny. Really. It's only clothes. Nothing more. What did you think? Another ghost?'

'Oh Kate, let's get out of here. I can't bear it.'

'Hey, I want another look at this. I can't work out what it's for . . .'

Jenny grabbed her arm. 'I can.'

'What?'

'Kate, we need to talk. Let's get out of this horrible office.' Jenny grabbed Kate's arm and started to pull her out of the rooms, back through the secretary's section, and through the door. Then she pushed Kate bodily through the corridor and down the stairs, till they clattered back into the foyer, and out into the cold misty vapour-filled air of the dark courtyard.

They were standing, with Jenny clutching Kate's arm, when Matthew Lavelle came pounding over, every inch the man in charge at the scene.

'There you are!' he said importantly. Kate turned round to look at Jenny who had been standing behind her. She seemed unnaturally docile, hands clasped in front of her, head bowed slightly. Kate hadn't realised how thin she had become. Her face had a worn, old-young expression.

'Well, girls,' Matthew said, 'we'd all better get home. They've cleared up the worst of it, though I guess the fire brigade boys will be around for a few more hours. I'm sorry I dragged you out, Kate, but at least you know what's happened. If you get back here at about nine o'clock in the morning, we can discuss whether or not you need to be relocated.'

'Kate?' As if in panic, Jenny pulled on her arm. 'Let's meet for breakfast. Can you pick me up at eight?'

'Well, yes, if you want.'

'That's a nice idea, Jenny,' said Matt approvingly. 'But we can all get some sleep now. I'll see you in the morning, Kate.'

Kate watched them go, Matt guiding Jenny like a child. The image, of a strong muscular father figure leading a thin and shaky Jenny through the courtyard, his protective arm round her shoulders so she could not even turn back, worried Kate as much as Jenny's confusion over the boxes in Chester-Lang's future office. Sexy nighties! Perhaps that was what it was all about. Tacky, but not that threatening. So why had Jenny been so disturbed? Again, Kate felt the worm of doubt . . .

Half an hour later, she arrived home to find John was awake. It was two o'clock. 'Go back to sleep,' she said to him as she pulled her jeans off. 'I'm going to see if a cup of hot milk will calm me down.' In answer, he sat up in bed and tugged her over to him, Barbour and all.

'How bad is it?' he asked.

'Pretty bad, but not a catastrophe.'

'Will the flood ruin the project?'

'No. Or at least, I'm not going to let it!'

'That's my Kate!'

'What's with all this affection, then?' Even now, Kate felt John's touch like hot water on her tired skin.

'I do love you, Kate. I admired the way you went out earlier without so much as a backward glance. And the way you've come back tonight, all taut with determination. Not that I don't want to loosen you up!'

'What? Now? A man of your age?'

'Definitely. We've hardly made love since Chloe left, and it's been nice but, well, you know . . .' Kate smiled. She knew. Sex lately had been fine and they had gone to sleep smiling afterwards, but it had been more perfunctory than usual.

But tonight, at this weird hour, the usual considerations dissolved as he smiled and pulled her into bed. He began to kiss her as she took each garment off, starting with her all-purpose baggy jumper, and working down to her socks. As he did, he asked her more about the flood, and she answered him in between gasps. She was surprised to feel more suddenly and urgently aroused. Perhaps it was a need to exorcise the anxieties of the night. But afterwards, lying naked in his arms, with one sock hanging off the end of her foot, her body flushed and relaxed, it all still haunted her.

They were both shattered at seven when the clock woke them, but Kate steeled herself to get up, drink black coffee, and drive around to pick up Jenny. Kate saw her in the distance as if noticing her for the first time. Jenny was now painfully thin, Kate thought, her stick-like legs in black leggings mushrooming into off-white trainers at one end, and into an unflattering bloated anorak at the other. Even her hair had lost its sheen, and her pretty face as it came into focus when the car drove up was pinched and patchy.

Kate leaned over and opened the door. 'Hi,' she said cheerfully. But Jenny blinked back at her miserably.

'Where do you want to go for breakfast?' Kate asked.

'Anywhere but the office,' Jenny said bleakly.

Kate drove silently back into Twickenham and a coffee shop by the river. She tried to be jolly, ordering croissants and coffee, but whereas Jenny would normally have asked for a cappuccino, with white flimsy cream on top and a dusting of chocolate, this time she just ordered black espresso, and merely played with the croissant.

'Come on,' Kate said when they were organised. 'You asked me to come and see you for breakfast. What's this all about?'

Slowly Jenny began to explain. She talked Kate through her first evening with Matt, and their passionless sex. And she described how she had tripped over and disturbed the boxes by the bed, with their secret cache of lingerie.

'The same boxes we saw last night?' Kate asked.

'Yeah.'

'Jenny, this is weird.'

'It gets worse. I saw Matt again, the Sunday you were in France and . . .' Jenny paused. ' . . . And Matthew was so kind, and I was on my own and feeling pretty bleak. I decided there couldn't be anything sinister about him, because he seemed so normal and cheerful. And anyway, he really *wooed* me. Then, about a fortnight ago, I saw some boxes again . . .'

Jenny tried to describe what she had found the second time. The disgust on her face made it clearer than her words. Kate pressed her.

'But what was it, Jenny?'

'It was for . . . sado-masochism I suppose is what you'd call it. I always thought of it as slightly comical before. You know, suburban housewives playing at Miss Whiplash, whatever turns you on as a consenting adult. But this was vile. It was about real suffering. You can't tell me those women in those pictures enjoyed it. They were exploited at best, victimised at worst. I felt sick. The next day Matt delivered the boxes here.' She shook her head. 'I tried not to think about it. I was sure they would turn out to be props, or something he didn't know about himself.'

'Well, he may not have known exactly what was in the second lot.'

'Perhaps not . . .'

'Have you talked to him at all?'

'No. It's not that sort of relationship. It's, well, not very open. I'm scared of, you know, rocking the boat.' Jenny put her head in her hands. But while she was waiting for Jenny to go on, Kate was thinking. If what Jenny said was true, the Chester-Lang channel was clearly based on mailing out sexy clothes. The negligées, hanging up and catching the tiny breeze wafting through that office, were innocent proof of that. But if what Jenny had seen in the boxes was part of the same system, it wasn't just sexy clothes, but kinky sex aids. Daniel Chester-Lang had mentioned two consultants for the channel. One was Jeremy Woodley, certainly. Could the other one be Matthew Lavelle?

When Jenny said nothing more, Kate said, 'Look, soft porn channels are legal. Mail order for sexy clothes would probably be legal too, a sort of sexy shopping channel. It might not ooze integrity, but it needn't be illicit. But from what you've said about this stuff, it sounds very suspicious indeed.'

'I know. I've been thinking about it. They must have ordered those . . . those things, as samples. They'll probably sell the ordinary stuff on the programmes, and keep the really weird stuff under the TV counter, if you know what I mean. Maybe it will be some sort of secret code. You know, using credit cards.'

'Yuk. I'm going to get advice from Joan Thompson, and maybe Charlie Mansfield in New York as well. I'm sure if the cable operators knew what Chester-Lang was planning, they'd throw it out anyway. Particularly if some of the stuff they are considering is as vile as you say.'

'It is!'

'So let me talk to our own shareholders and get their advice. If this is true, they may not want anything more to do with Chester-Lang anyway.'

Kate sat thinking, and stirred her own coffee so the spun creamy topping disappeared into the murkier brown liquid underneath, ruining the cappuccino effect. But she was preoccupied. Then she caught sight of the time on the watch strapped round Jenny's flat bony wrist.

'God, look at the time! We need to get back now. We've got our own problems to consider too.'

'Yeah, but I can't stop thinking about that . . . stuff.'

'Put it out of your mind for the next few hours, Jenny. We've got a lot to do. Please. Don't let this get in the way of our own project.'

But Jenny stayed deep in thought as they drove back to the Warehouse. Suddenly she said, 'You didn't like Matthew anyway, did you?' Kate tried not to react too sharply, and took her time about turning left up to the A4.

'Well . . .' she began, unsure what to say. Kate felt she had been so conspicuously wrong about so many people that she felt she had no right to pass an opinion. And she didn't want to interfere in Jenny's love life either. But Jenny was waiting in almost aggressive silence for her answer.

'I think I made the mistake of seeing Matt as just a nice young man, but not very bright, to tell you the truth. It seems to me now . . .' – Kate paused and remembered her conversation with Michelle – ' . . . that Matthew is actually very ambitious and clever. So I suppose that I don't so much dislike him, as feel annoyed with myself for misreading him.' And was he really so bad? She remembered Matt's genuine discomfort when Laurence's body had been discovered. She had sympathised with him, then. Surely he wasn't a complete monster?

'I was thinking about my bag,' Jenny said half to herself, in a dreary exhausted voice.

'Your bag?'

'Yeah. It seems so reasonable, doesn't it, not to drop your bag in the hallway. So you put it all tidily in the bedroom. And the next thing you know, you're becoming a different person. And look at me, Kate!'

Kate felt her eyebrows rising. Again she said nothing. But she was trying to remember how Jenny looked when she met her off the train at Euston all those weeks ago. Jenny had had glowing skin, long glossy hair, a well-rounded figure and strode confidently down the station platform. And Kate had prided herself on how she was going to give this vibrant young woman the opportunity of a lifetime!

Now, at Kate's side was a scrawny example of wretchedness. She could see that Jenny was too thin, hair like a Brillo pad, skin blotched with uneven applications of false tan, one over the other. But worse was the expression of strained resignation on her face. Kate wasn't sure that Jenny had the nerve to tackle Matthew about the boxes. Something about her had been sapped by this relationship. The Jenny she knew was sliding away from her, stressed by mad phone calls, hallucinating over half-filled coffee cups, disappearing without trace into a relationship with a man who seemed to be taking her over.

Kate glanced away from her to realise that she had taken the wrong turn out of Twickenham.

'Damn,' she said, 'I've gone the wrong way. We're going towards Teddington.'

'We'll have to turn,' Jenny said lifelessly. Then she sat up in the passenger seat. 'Hey, Kate, look over there. It's Debbie!'

'So it is. D'you think she needs a lift?'

'I don't know. I can't think what she'd be doing here. Hang on, Kate, she's with someone.'

Kate was attempting a three-point turn without knocking down someone's garden wall. As she heaved on the steering wheel, she saw Debbie out of the corner of her eye, with a tall moon-faced man.

'Who do you suppose that is?' she said.

'Well, it's unlikely to be a lover,' Jenny replied with a touch of her old sharpness. Within minutes Kate had turned the car round, and was back on course.

'Funny, seeing Debbie.'

'Actually, I remember now, she asked for some time off this morning. The dentist's, I think. I'm not surprised she has trouble with her teeth. Have you seen the drawer of her desk? Stuffed with chocolate wrappers!'

'But at least she won't be waiting for us, on the office doorstep, looking shocked. Chloe might be there before us, and that won't do. We'd better hurry.'

Jenny sat in silence as Kate drove back to the office, then she groaned to see Matthew already in the car park. But whatever Kate's suspicions, she still had to deal with him as normal that morning, and she hailed him as he walked across the courtyard, despite the crisis still managing to appear stunningly well groomed. If anything, it added to his look of total control. There was no doubt Matt Lavelle dominated the scene. He seemed somehow larger than life.

'Hi, Matt.'

'I think you should go up to your office, Kate. The contract cleaners have been in, and I'll send Michelle over shortly to help you make an inventory of what's damaged. It's safe now, but not very pleasant up there. Then if you could possibly take your team off somewhere else for today . . . ?'

'We'll go to my partner's house.'

'Yeah, that would be great, thanks.' Matt beamed at her in relief, and for a moment Kate too felt his charm. Sighing, Kate motioned to Jenny to go in, and they picked their way up the stairs. When they pushed open the glass doors, for a moment their office looked normal. It was only when Kate refocused that she realised everything was a deeper shade, soaked through with water. The carpet that remained was no longer beige but a deeper brown. The chairs seemed to dig further into it, and the desks had a sheen where the contract cleaners, working from six that morning, had wiped them but been unable to get rid of the final layer of moisture. The sheer volume of water that had cascaded down had bent some of the tinnier shelves. In the trays, the swatches of paper hardly dribbled. They were just heavy and grey with blotted water. She had expected to hear dripping, but there was none. The water had settled now, and a sort of truce had been declared with no drops, no puddles, just total capitulation of anything that could sop up any liquid.

'God,' said Jenny, in awe.

It was also sickeningly warm. The odd fetid smell, plus the tiredness and strain, made Kate feel ill. Without thinking she sat on a wet chair and felt the water seep through her jeans, warm, not cold, but like blood.

As they stood there in the dank atmosphere the mood was pierced by the buoyant tone of the phone.

'Business as usual,' Jenny smiled, picking it up. Then she paused. 'Ugh!' she said, and slammed the phone down.

'That bloody pest again?'

'Yep. First time since we changed the numbers. Shit, Kate . . .'

'Jenny, he could get the number from anywhere. Even Directory Enquiries. We're running a TV channel. We can't be incommunicado. Look, if you're really upset, we'll get the police on to it . . .'

'Oh, no Kate, we can't do that. I mean, it's just some idiot, obviously.'

'We should try getting it traced again . . .'

But just as Kate was about to try, Matt swung through the doors, startling them.

'What is it?' Kate turned.

Matthew was standing, just looking at them. Instead of seeming in control, he was leaning over, one arm on the desk, paler than Kate had ever seen him under the varnish-like patina of his perfect skin.

'Matt? Have you been up to the plant room? How badly damaged are the tanks?' she asked.

In response, Matthew grasped the table, then lowered himself onto a wet chair, oblivious to the sheen of damp. He was clearly upset, and the sudden change from man of action to bewildered looking boy hit Kate forcefully.

'Tell us,' Jenny said, approaching him to put her hand reluctantly on his heaving shoulders. He looked genuinely shocked and distressed. He put his hand on hers gratefully, and Jenny didn't take it away.

'There are the tanks, right, and there's a bloody big hole in both of them. It does look like vandalism. That would have been bad enough.' He stopped again, shaking his head. 'Christ, I'm sorry. I can't help it. I'll get my act together in a minute. Listen, there's a door at the back of the tanks. There would have been no need to go through it. But the assessors wanted to see everything. I knew there was a little cubbyhole behind there where we used to keep tools, things like that. And it leads down to the old fire escape, you know the stairs I mean.'

Kate nodded again. 'So . . . ?' she said.

'Oh God, in the room it was vile. Some tramp's been living there. We had no idea. It's full of, well, half-eaten food, and old rags. God, it's foul.' Matt took great gasping breaths, as if talking had helped clear his lungs.

'Oh, horrible,' Kate said. 'God, what a shock.'

Matt heaved in another breath.

'So this tramp may have damaged the tanks. Perhaps accidentally?' Kate asked.

'Maybe. I don't know.'

'And where is he now?' Jenny asked.

'God knows. Only . . .'

'Only what?'

'I'm not sure it was a he.'

'What?' Kate jumped up from her wet chair, feeling the sticky uncomfortable dampness through her jeans. 'A woman?'

'Oh Christ, I don't know,' Matt said wearily. He had stopped gulping now, and looked exhausted, and more lined than Kate had ever imagined his tanned skin could be.

'All I know is that I thought I saw female clothes. A pair of track suit trousers. Small trainers. Some sort of shirt thing. Most of it was filthy rags, anyway, like a burrow. I'll have to get the cleaners to come back. But they ain't going to like this one little bit. I hope they've got masks and more rubber gloves.'

He eased himself out of the wet chair. 'Sorry about that,' he said bleakly. 'Bit pathetic, really. I need to keep moving.'

'Don't worry.' Kate felt far more sympathy for Matthew when he wasn't being a super-efficient manager. His distress at what he had seen seemed at odds with his cold-blooded involvement in the

Chester-Langs' obscene project. He couldn't be completely insensitive, Kate thought. She watched him go.

And she thought for a minute about the tramp. Had the same thought occurred to Jenny? Was the vagrant squatting at the top of their building, the same weird woman she and Jenny had seen on the canal bank? Kate glanced back at her friend. Jenny was kicking at a soaked piece of carpet, thoughtfully. But Kate guessed that Jenny's thoughts were all about Matthew Lavelle.

A few minutes later, downstairs in reception, Kate rounded up Debbie and Chloe, who had just arrived, to go back to John's house. They had been sitting huddled together. Chloe looked wretched, and Debbie was clucking over her as if she was glad of the responsibility.

'What's the news?' Debbie asked Kate, with an interested air. Kate told them about the state of the office, and how they would leave the Warehouse that day, and go and work from John's.

'And were the tanks smashed?' Debbie asked with subdued excitement.

'Yes. But it looks as if the insurance people have worked out who did it.'

'They have?'

'Yes. It seems to have been some sort of vagrant, who was squatting in the plant room. The mess is ghastly, apparently.'

Chloe slumped forward. Kate was unsure whether her reaction was relief, or disgust.

'Yer what?' Debbie said, her large blank face stretched and her mouth open in a gape.

'There's been some sort of tramp living in the plant room,' Kate repeated tiredly.

'Bloody hell,' Debbie had lost her thrilled air. She looked rather sick herself, and sat down by Chloe.

'I know,' Kate sympathised. 'It's much nastier when you realise someone has been there, squirreled away like that, all the time we've been working. But it's cordoned off now. Come on, we need to get back to my house. We'll camp there this morning, and I've got some tapes I took home last week, which we can work on.' John had finally bought a TV and video which stood alone in the corner of his front room. 'By the way, Debbie, we saw you this morning. In Teddington.'

'Did you?' Debbie looked puzzled. 'Oh, yes, I was going to the dentist. One of my neighbours offered to refer me. It's hard to get registered, and I need a decent dentist.' She nodded seriously at Kate, her head bobbing inside the thick grey duffel coat she always wore when it was less than baking hot. 'I've had rotten toothache. Too many sticky buns again.'

'We should put you on a healthy eating programme when the channel starts, and chart your progress. The viewers could watch you get fit. You could be the channel mascot!'

'Not on your nelly,' said Debbie. 'God, me doing aerobics? You'd need to get the floors strengthened.' The plump girl laughed, and Kate joined in, her cheerfulness a relief after the strain of the morning.

It didn't take Kate long to get everyone organised and on their way to John's house. When they got there, Kate left the girls with Jenny in the front room, sorting out who would watch what. She perched in the half decorated kitchen, on a bar stool in the corner next to the sink, clutching John's cordless phone. Of course she needed to keep her shareholders informed about this latest problem.

She tried ringing Joan Thompson but her secretary said that she was in Atlanta, the same way as other people might be in the canteen or out at lunch. At noon, Kate rang Charlie Mansfield in New York. She was immediately put through to him, but his secretary wasn't quite as loud and friendly as usual.

'Gee, you've been hard to get hold of since you changed all your numbers,' she said reprovingly. 'Here's Mr Mansfield for you.'

'Ah, Kate,' Charlie rasped. His impatience crackled down the line at her. 'I've rung your office already this morning. Spoke to some office manager guy. Hey, it's a flood now, is it? Christ!'

Kate listened to the implied criticism. Charlie had never reproached her before.

'It seems to be one damn thing after another,' Mansfield growled.

'We've had our problems. But it's under control.'

'Oh yeah? Well, Tony Chester-Lang called me at six o'clock this morning, my time. Six a.m.! Jeeze. He demanded that I speak to you first thing. Absolutely first thing. He says that he's been out of it for a month because his wife's been ill, but now he's back on the case, and it's chaos.'

'Charlie . . .'

'He say he finds you impossible to talk to, and that I should call you and find out what was going on. He tells me Food and Health is a mess.'

'That's rubbish . . .'

'Well, some guy who's consulting for him . . . Jerry something . . . ?'

'Jeremy Woodley?'

'Yeah, he's informed Tony that most of the Brits in cable have grave doubts about the channel. He's got another pal, Derry . . . ?'

'Derek Boulder.'

'Right. He says you were involved in a discussion about cable TV at some club recently and were so aggressive you alienated everyone. And he met you at some big TV festival in the south of France – God knows what you were doing there – and you made a complete fool of yourself taking your clothes off. Sounds crazy, I know. But there's no smoke without fire. It's not looking good for you, Kate.'

'But this is all crap, Charlie. It's just second-rate gossip.'

'Oh yeah? What about the kid who died? Tony told me that he killed himself, which is not the way you sold it to me. And they say another of your staff is on drugs and tried to wreck the office. Plus the fact that the channel logos which cost over fifty grand, went missing. I wasn't aware of all this. It sounds like things are a mess, a real mess.'

Kate felt cold and weak.

'Have you spoken to Joan?' she said quietly.

'Not yet. She's coming through New York Friday. We're meeting then, to discuss all this.'

'Charlie, you have to believe me, things have been difficult, but the channel is absolutely on target.'

'Yeah?' She could hear a slight upward inflection in Charlie's voice. He wanted her to vindicate herself. There were some bosses who liked you to cock things up, who wanted an excuse to pounce. Charlie Mansfield wasn't like that, thank God. But like a lot of powerful men he respected strength and Kate had to curb her tendency to be open about her weaknesses. Don't wheedle, Kate told herself. Have confidence. Don't placate!

'Look, Charlie,' she said, with authority in her voice. 'This is all poisonous eyewash. I know why Chester-Lang wants me out of the picture. He doesn't give a stuff about Food and Health, and if you listen to him, you'll damage this business. He's got his own agenda and I know what's on it.' She took a deep breath. 'If Joan is with you in Manhattan on Friday, let me be there too. I don't care whether the company pays or not. I'll get my own flight. You can't stop me coming over at my own expense, and believe me, whatever you've heard, our team is strong enough and well-briefed enough to cope without me for two days. You've always seemed fair. Let me come to your office, and justify myself.'

She could hear Charlie wanting to believe her, but struggling. After all, he was on the directors' boards with Tony Chester-Lang, they had transatlantic acquaintances in common. They knew men who were captains of industry – golf-playing, power-wielding men who gave donations to political parties, lunched in the House of Lords, and travelled on Concorde. Who was she, by comparison?

'OK,' he said. 'But if you can't deliver, Kate, you're out. Fast. We still want to get this channel on the air by the Fall, and if it doesn't work out, we'll need to fire you and get someone else.'

'I've always admired your directness, Charlie.'

She made him laugh, and the sound was a little friendlier.

'Be here Friday. And Kate?'

'Yes?' She kept the hope out of her voice.

'Don't spend your own money. My company will pay the fare. Business class.'

'Right,' she said. 'Thanks.' And she put the phone down before he could change his mind.

CHAPTER ELEVEN

It was evening in New York when Kate landed at JFK. She had been wide awake on the flight, preparing. Things were in reasonable shape at the office. Jenny was still obviously confused and worried about Matt, but Kate could only hope she would tackle him, in her own time. But on the operational side of things, Jenny was coping quite well, preparing the team to be re-housed in the Warehouse. She was planning to teach Debbie and Chloe to use the scheduling computer, as well as working with the freelance presentation producers who would compile the advertising breaks and links between the programmes so there would be one 'look' for the channel.

Kate had found every scrap of paper she could dry out, to prove how much work had been done successfully in acquiring programmes. Fortunately much of the evidence was already sitting in the tape library, in the form of actual programme cassettes, ready to go. The jewel in the crown was the award winning, highly-rated 'Cook of the North'. That alone should convince Charlie of their competence, and she had other programme ideas to put to him.

Kate had tried to phone Daniel Chester-Lang to tell him she was coming to the States. She wanted to see him, to tell him face-to-face what she believed was really going on, and to find out what he knew. But Daniel did not answer the phone, or respond to the messages she left. However Kate had a good memory. She knew there was another way she might be able to make contact with him, although she wasn't sure about the ethics of using it. She put the possibility to the back of her mind.

On the plane, to clarify her thoughts, she had written out an account of how Jenny had found the boxes in Matt's flat, and how they had reappeared in the office planned for Daniel. If she could prove Tony Chester-Lang was planning to pander to perversion, it might undermine any relationship between him and Charlie Mansfield. But the link would be difficult to demonstrate. A channel supplying black lace nighties, or even split-crotch panties, might be acceptable to Charlie. He might not like it, but his business sense would probably overrule any other misgivings. She would need to demonstrate that Tony Chester-Lang was really into dealing in dirt, to sabotage the business contact between the two shareholders.

Yet there were little nuggets of hope – Charlie's secretary had called the day before, in her old loud and cheerful way, to say that Charlie's office was booking Kate into the Algonquin Hotel, where Joan Thompson always stayed. But the tension meant Kate felt little pleasure at the thought of staying at one of New York's most famous hotels.

She waited impatiently to clear the brisk, intimidating US vetting system, unperturbed by the sharp voices and heavy, deliberately casual officers, or the surprisingly low-ceilinged, harshly-lit airport. The bleakness of the queue for yellow cabs hardly touched her. The hunched cab driver, whose grasp of English left her yelling instructions like a demented British nanny, did not annoy her. Nor was she delighted, as she should have been, by the trip up Fifth Avenue and the lights of Times Square, or the atmospheric lobby of the hotel, with its grandfather clock and mahogany furniture. It was only when she reached her bedroom on the sixth floor and looked out of her window that she allowed herself a tiny shiver of pleasure at being in Cagney and Lacey country.

She sat on the bed, looking at the hunting prints and hearing the brass bathroom fittings rumble. Then, just to see what might happen, she tried Daniel Chester-Lang's number. There was, of course, no reply. Kate unpacked her best suit and black shirt, dark tights and shoes, and new white, crisp knickers and bra for the morning. She knew she would need to feel smart right down to the skin. She stood up, then sat down again. She wondered about food, but she didn't want any. There was only one thing on her mind.

She looked at the phone. Then she sat down heavily on the bed, and this time picked up the receiver resolutely. She dialled zero.

'Hello. How do I get through to directories?'

'Ma'am?'

Kate repeated her question.

'You dial nine-one. Where do you want?'

'Connecticut.'

'The main area code would be 1203,' he said obligingly, 'followed by 555 1212.'

'Which city?' said the tinny sounding voice at enquiries.

'I don't know the city. But it's an unusual name. I think there'll only be one entry. It's Wannawicz,' said Kate, amazed at the unhesitating clarity of her own pronunciation. She had been subconsciously rehearsing this moment on the plane for hours.

'How are you spelling that, ma'am?' Kate's mind raced back to Daniel's jokey remarks about his stepfather's name. W-a-n-n-a, he had said jokingly, like wannabe, like my mother was before she met him! She spelt out the first five letters to the metallic voice . . .

'I'll check the area directory. Just hold on please. No, I'm sorry we have no Wannawicz in this state, ma'am.'

Kate felt disproportionate disappointment as she put the phone down. It had only been a try. But tiredness mixed with a desperate desire not to have to lie on the bed and think about the interview with Charlie Mansfield made her pick the phone up again, and hold it between her chin and her shoulder while she thought. If Daniel's stepfather had died, was it possible his mother had moved to be near him?

'Do you have a Wannawicz listed?' she asked the New York City operator.

'Yes, ma'am, we do. One listing. N. Wannawicz. Here's your number.' Kate wrote the number down. It had to be right.

She dialled so fast her fingers stumbled over each other. The phone burbled, a low, flat, single ring. Its unfamiliarity let Kate feel she wasn't really making this terrible intrusion into the life of a woman who probably wanted to forget everything she had ever known about Antony Chester-Lang.

A crisp English voice said, 'Hello.'

'Mrs Wannawicz?'

'Yes, speaking.'

'Mrs Nadine Wannawicz?'

'Yes.' It was said with a flicker of irritation. 'There are no other Wannawicz's in New York.'

'Of course, I'm sorry. That's why I was able to get your number.'

'Who are you?' The sharp voice rose, but it sounded vexed, rather than alarmed or intrigued.

'Mrs Wannawicz, I'm sorry to bother you, but I've been trying to get hold of your son, Daniel Chester-Lang, for several weeks now.'

'And you are . . .'

'My name is Kate Wilkinson. I work in the cable TV business in the UK. I met Daniel in France. I'm in New York because of problems I have, owing to Daniel and his father. I really need to get hold of him.'

There was a lengthy pause. Then Nadine Wannawicz said, 'He's out of town.' The voice was extremely calm and sensible, but also wary and unrevealing.

'Mrs Wannawicz, has Daniel talked to you about the TV ventures we're involved in, in London?'

There was another, more fractional silence. 'Yes,' said the other woman brusquely.

'If Daniel isn't there, I wonder, could you help?'

'Me?'

'Yes. Look, I'm really sorry to do this, but I desperately need to talk to someone.'

There was a silence. Then Nadine Wannawicz said, with a less steady but still sensible tone of voice, 'I'm not prepared to talk about my son's concerns.'

'I understand that, Mrs Wannawicz. I really do. Believe me, I don't want to cause trouble between Daniel and his father. But I need to talk to him. I'm not sure he realises what his father is really doing.'

'And what is that?'

'It's something very risky, and could be very damaging, to Daniel and to other people, like me. I've tried to phone Daniel but he hasn't returned my calls. I don't know if he even understands what is going on in London. If he won't see me, I need to talk to you.'

She was aching with suspense when Nadine Wannawicz suddenly said, 'Why don't you come over?' Kate waited to let the terse words sink in. She hadn't expected such a positive response, particularly one disguised by the neat but rather hostile tone. Her own voice became clipped in reply.

'I will. Anywhere. Now.'

Nadine Wannawicz repeated her address again, then put down the phone without another goodbye. When Kate replaced her own receiver on the rest, she realised her hands were wet with sweat.

She washed and changed into clean jeans and a jumper and took the elevator downstairs to the lobby where one of the bellboys, all of sixty years old, hailed her a cab.

As the cab swung along, she took in the lights on Broadway, the noise and bustle of sudden lively streets interlocking with silent black facades, no apparent reason for the gaudiness of some and the shadows of others. In the darker areas tall Edwardian buildings with frilly stonework on solid brick squares gave the city a sort of thirties look, like an unblitzed and unfamiliar provincial Britain. But often when she squinted and looked up at the skyline she could see the stencilled blue outline of the narrow, graceful Chrysler building and the chunkier outline of the Empire State, as points of reference. She could smell the warm hint of burning rubber and spicy food and steam, different from the dank, fried smell of London. And the buildings by night were blacker and flatter, with none of London's white eighteenth century curves or bulging bays.

Kate had been to New York in the seventies, as part of a lavish package holiday to the States with her husband. Theirs had been a marriage measured by the things they did rather than the things they felt. Looking back, she seemed two-dimensional then, as if there was really no more to her than the flat grinning girl in the joyless photos she still kept in a box, somewhere in her bedsit.

As the cab criss-crossed one way and then the other, Kate tried to work out where she was going, envisaging Manhattan as a huge tongue licking out to the Atlantic, but she soon lost her bearings, and sat back, allowing nervousness to wash over her.

The cab drew up outside a terraced house with steps up to the front door and railings, which Kate guessed must be one of the fabled brownstone houses. It was warmer than in England. As she emerged from the cab, the front door of the house opened, and the figure of a woman was silhouetted.

'Welcome to Brooklyn Heights,' said the same crisp voice.

Inside the narrow hall, Kate could see what Nadine Wannawicz looked like, and for a moment she had the strangest sensation of seeing one face superimposed upon another. It was Daniel Chester-Lang all over again, but the face was wider and the hair was longer and thicker, with broad ashen stripes.

His mother must have been in her early sixties, though she had the figure and unlined face of a woman thirty years younger. But she was still old. 'What makes a face look its age?' Kate thought fleetingly. Is it the thickening round the jaw, or the droop of the mouth? Or something undefined, like pain? Whatever it was about Nadine some sort of strain seemed to exaggerate it. Her chin jutted slightly, and her eyes were wary. Under her arm was a little dog, the sort of pale curly poodle creature Kate disliked. It blinked at Kate with the same assessing expression as its mistress, and Kate instantly associated it with the passé glamour of the fifties night club singer. For a moment Kate wondered how she could possibly have thought she might like Nadine Wannawicz. But then the woman said in the same sharp voice, 'Follow me.'

Kate followed her into a sitting-room with high ceilings, a stripped pine floor and two huge comfortable sofas. 'Sit down,' said Nadine peremptorily. 'Would you like a glass of Chardonnay?'

'I would!' Kate tried smiling. The woman did not smile back, but the angle of her jaw dropped a little.

'Are these houses Victorian?' Kate enquired, to break the silence. 'I expected everything in New York to be either very modern or nineteen twenties-ish. You know, Damon Runyon.'

'Oh, New York was a big place a hundred years ago. These were the first sort-of middle-class houses, you know. I liked this one because it reminds me of Fulham. The high ceilings are a sign of history. Do sit down.'

Nadine Wannawicz had a cut-glass English accent but a deep, slightly husky voice. Years ago, Kate surmised, she had developed it that way to sound sexy. Now it sounded slightly dated, but not unpleasant. They paused, looking at each other. Then Nadine disappeared, and came back with the wine. She said, 'The reason Daniel hasn't been returning your calls is quite simple. He's been wrapped up in his own affairs, and then he needed to go to France again. He probably told you about his partner, Johnnie Pelot, didn't he?'

Kate nodded.

'Johnnie died a few weeks ago. He had been weakened by the virus even though he seemed to have recovered. But we didn't know that he had already contracted lung cancer.'

'Oh, no! I didn't realise. I'm so sorry!'

'Quite.'

'But why didn't Daniel tell me Johnnie was ill?'

'Oh dear.' Nadine seemed pained at Kate's lack of understanding. 'You know, it's not like that. Dan tried to pretend it was just flu for a month. When Johnnie was dying, Dan was really in denial, in fact, they both were. And for at least a week after Johnnie's death, Dan stayed in the house, unable to face anyone. He had convinced himself Johnnie would be the one AIDS case to live. People do that, especially with high profile illness. They hate to think of themselves as just another statistic, and the press is always detailing miracle cures. It helps, until the last breath.'

'God, how terrible.'

'Yes. But Daniel has grieved very intensively, which may be best. And he's a young man. There'll be other lovers.'

Kate said nothing, wondering at her pragmatism.

'I daresay you think that sounds cold. Perhaps it is. But I thought my life was over when my first marriage collapsed. And then my second husband came along. I saw him as a rescuer at first. It was later I learnt to love him. Daniel will come through in the same way.'

'I don't know much about bereavement.' Kate sipped her wine. This unexpected dipping into emotion reminded her of her own private fears, but her own concern was with starting a life, not the end of one. It was depressing and debilitating, her constant concern about conceiving. But she tried to imagine how she would feel if John died, and knew it would be far, far worse.

'I've been a widow for twelve years,' Nadine said flatly. 'You always blame the dead for leaving you. It's the ultimate infidelity.'

'So where does Johnnie's death leave Daniel?'

'In debt to his father.' Nadine raised her eyebrows expressively. 'Tony gave Daniel some money last year when Johnnie first fell ill. I tried to advise Dan not to take it, but short of selling the house there was nothing I could do. I didn't realise Daniel had actually got Tony's cash until it was too late. I knew then that Tony would extort some sort of . . . payment from Dan.'

'What made you think that?'

In answer, Nadine Wannawicz got up and put her passive little dog into its basket. Then she lit a cigarette and walked around the room in front of Kate before sitting down again.

'What do you want to know about Tony?' she asked.

'As much as you can tell me.'

Nadine smiled grimly. 'You start.'

'Really?'

'Go on.'

So Kate talked briefly about the rumours surrounding the new Chester-Lang TV project, and how she and Jenny had stumbled on just what it was Chester-Lang was planning to mail out to the subscribers to his cable TV channel. When Kate came to the description of the vicious sex aids neatly stacked in the new offices, like the samples of books or freebie products scattered liberally around more ordinary premises, Nadine interrupted.

'I haven't spoken about this to anyone very much,' Nadine said, in her cool, sharp way. 'Not because of shame or discretion, but because it doesn't matter. But that's why I left Tony.'

'Sorry?'

'He was a sadist.'

'You mean a bully?'

'No.' Nadine sounded almost contemptuous. 'No, he was a sadist in the real sense. He liked to hurt me, physically. He beat me, even when I was pregnant. I only saw him once between leaving him, and meeting Gregor. He promised me he would never hurt me again. He seemed genuinely contrite. But a leopard can't change its spots.' Her voice was still calm, but her shoulders shook.

'You mean, he indulges in this stuff himself?'

'Yes. It wasn't so . . . commercially available when we were young. But there were one or two places. Tony met me in a club in London. It was a cabaret club, all very "naice" of course, like everything in the fifties, but after hours, things happened. A lot of men had been in the Forces then you know, not just World War Two, but

Suez and Korea. They had seen and done things they could never talk about like we do now, but needs had arisen and places were started to satisfy them. The swinging sixties grew out of the fifties you know.' She seemed lost in thought for a moment. Kate waited.

'I wasn't involved, because I knew which side my bread was buttered on. In those days, there were bad girls and good girls and no women. Tony took several of the girls out. I wasn't the only one, but I was the one who had pretensions to being good. Only because I was calculating, you know. I just said no, for longest. One or two of the other girls told me what he did to them, but I thought they were either lying, or that it happened because they were trashy and deserved it. How stupid and snobbish I was! After I married Tony, I found out the hard way.' She laughed dryly at her own dismal pun. Kate looked at her face. She was no longer concentrating on Kate, but was looking through her to some other life. She was like Kate in the cab, thinking about coming to New York in the past. Kate broke the silence.

'Your ex-husband seems to be a bastard in a lot of ways, Mrs Wannawicz. He's more than happy to ensnare your son in something that could ruin him, and he's done a bloody good job of rubbishing me to my shareholders.'

'It isn't a lot of ways. It's all the same way. Tony likes to hurt people.'

'Yes. Yes, I see.'

'What are you going to do, Miss Wilkinson?'

'I really don't know.'

'And how on earth can I help you? Of course I'd like Daniel to give Tony a kick in the teeth, but he's still his father, and Daniel is in debt to him. I'll talk to Dan, and to anyone else you might like. But what is anything I say, about a marriage forty years ago, going to prove?'

'It proves that Antony Chester-Lang is a vicious pervert.'

'So? Hundreds of these establishment men have their little predilections. Tony is clever. You've admitted that it's entirely possible that he will market frilly nighties, and the fact he's a sadist will remain his own business. I'm afraid you can't do much with the snippets of information I've given you.' Nadine paused. 'What do you make of his latest wife being so badly hurt?'

'Sonya?' Kate had never questioned what she had been told. 'She was attacked by a burglar, wasn't she?'

'Was she?'

Kate sat and sipped her wine, wondering. Daniel had told her that his father actually discouraged him coming over to Britain, in a way that surprised him. And Daniel had told her that he and Sonya had got on well. Perhaps Antony Chester-Lang was worried about what would be said if they got together.

'If Sonya was beaten by Tony, and brought charges, like I should have done . . .' Nadine said quietly.

'But you didn't.'

'I had a baby, and in those days no-one would have believed me, or cared. But it's different now.' Nadine shrugged again, and suddenly looked tired. Kate, high on the exhaustion of jet-lag and the over-stimulus of all this new information, felt like going on, but saw her hostess's shoulders sag.

'Mrs Wannawicz, you've been very kind. And you've helped me understand. I don't think it's likely, but *if* Tony Chester-Lang's second wife could be persuaded to talk . . .'

'Second wife? Whatever made you think Sonya was his second wife?'

'Isn't she?'

'No, not at all. I was his second wife.'

'Then what happened to the first?'

Nadine looked at her levelly. 'She died. Quite a coincidence, really. She was beaten up and left for dead, by a burglar. It sounds to me as if Mrs Chester-Lang the Third is lucky to be alive!'

In the cab on the way back Kate sat, bemused. What Nadine had actually confirmed was that Chester-Lang was a vicious man who liked to see others suffer, physically and mentally, especially if he could engineer it. The certainty strengthened Kate's sense of self-preservation. She would not let the man's insidious ability to dominate extend to her. She could tell Charlie she was sure Chester-Lang was going to market sinister sex gadgets, but in the end she had no proof except a pile of boxes. It would be better to concentrate on rebutting the allegations against herself. There was plenty of evidence to prove she was doing a good job. She sat back in the cab, watching the city that never sleeps and feeling some of its confidence and energy buoying her up.

Under her door when she arrived back at her room was a message. Joan Thompson would meet her for breakfast in the Oak Room at eight thirty. Things were starting to improve. Kate lay in bed, willing sleep to come. When it did, it was not deeply satisfying, but it was better than she hoped, and when she woke in the morning it was without a headache or anything more than the stiffness of tiredness.

She met Joan at her breakfast table in the oak-panelled room.

'Dorothy Parker used to eat here,' Joan said without any niceties as Kate took her seat. 'Remember Dorothy Parker? "One more drink and I'll be under the host." Pity she gave in to the pressure in the end.' Joan smiled.

'You're damn right,' Kate said. 'But I'm not giving up!' She noticed that the other woman, as usual, looked as bright and well-rested as if she had been at home in Crouch End. And Joan was not the sort to beat around the bush.

'Well, Kate, I'm glad you're not whining into your English Breakfast Tea. I leave the country for a week, and all the worms come out of the woodwork. I hear from Charlie that Chester-Lang has been after your head on a plate. I'm glad you had the sense to get on a plane and try and sort this out. I gather you were angry too. Ha! That was a good move. Charlie expected you to collapse in tears. Have an English muffin.' She liberally buttered the spongy circle on the plate in front of her.

'I was furious, Joan. We've had our problems, but who hasn't, and I've got a brilliant senior producer, and two good researchers. There can't be an available cookery programme in Britain which we haven't looked at, and we've bought enough material, with sensible repeat options and good licence periods, to be able to schedule the first three months. The logos are great – after all, I sent each shareholder a tape, and you all approved the style – and we're on budget. So what's the problem?'

'The problem is that Tony Chester-Lang wants to hang you out to dry. And he's big enough to make Charlie listen. The question, Kate, is not what's wrong with you, but why Tony Chester-Lang has got it in for you.'

'Probably because I wouldn't use Sonya as a major fitness presenter?'

'And?'

'You're right, that wouldn't be enough by itself. I think he'd like to see the failure of Food and Health altogether, and it may be that getting at me is just a way of damaging the whole thing. Sabotaging our channel would mean that he might be able to sneak his own into the slots we couldn't fill!'

As she spoke off the cuff, Kate realised the truth in what she said. If Food and Health was sold to all the cable companies, but collapsed at the last minute, then Chester-Lang might think his own channel would be grabbed gratefully, without too much scrutiny, to take its place. Succinctly Kate outlined to Joan what she thought Chester-Lang's own TV channel was to be. Joan hooted with laughter, which Kate found both disconcerting and reassuring.

'Anyway,' Joan said after another bite of muffin, 'there's no way any of the cable companies would take that sort of crap.'

'I don't know, Joan. If Jeremy Woodley managed to get him a licence from the ITC, and the really suspect stuff was done under the counter, why not? Sexy underwear isn't criminal. And the other material could pull in vast amounts of money. It would be much more efficient than his magazine chain was. He could corner the market in kinky clothing for the whole UK. And he'd have a network for pornographic paraphernalia second to none. After all, if none of it appeared on screen, but was a by-product that went straight to the consumer, what could the regulators do?'

'Interesting point! It's a very clever idea. There's plenty of soft porn on the air, but none of it associated with home shopping. And nothing under the counter.'

'And once you send out the innocent sexy nightie, a little booklet advertising more exotic accessories could be included in the package to the buyer. Chester-Lang could actually form a whole empire in no time.'

'I hear his son is coming over from the States to run this.'

'Yes. But Daniel isn't what you'd expect. I've met him, and I suspect he would hate the whole idea. That is, if he even knows about it yet. I think his father likes having him under his thumb. Chester-Lang is a very complex and unpleasant man.'

'Correct. But Charlie Mansfield isn't, thank God. If we're going to get to this meeting with him we'd better put a move on.'

In the stretch limo on the way to Charlie's glossy pink building in lower Manhattan, Kate filled Joan in on the background to Chester-Lang's allegations, including the story about how her stockings fell down in Cannes, much to Joan's amusement.

'We can rebut everything else, Kate. But Charlie's a hell of a prude. That might help us when it comes to nailing Chester-Lang. But we could lose the game because of your hold-ups!' She laughed hugely.

But the meeting, largely thanks to Joan, went remarkably well. After a rather edgy start, Kate suddenly saw the chance to make a pre-emptive strike, and she launched into her idea to produce new original programmes for the channel, rather than merely buying older material from elsewhere. Easily distracted from unpleasantness, Charlie pounced on this idea. From then on, it was a question of controlling his enthusiasm. After an hour's discussion about the programme and the fascinating question of who would present it – 'I don't think Princess Di has a demonstrable interest in cooking, Charlie' – it was actually Kate who directed him back to the question of Antony Chester-Lang. Kate described what Joan could not help calling the chain-mail channel, despite Kate's attempts to keep the matter serious. She was rewarded by Charlie's obvious disgust.

'But Tony wouldn't be involved in something like that!'

'I happen to know his family. I met the son, who is going to run the channel, at MIP. And I met Daniel's mother last night.'

'Last night?'

'Yes. She lives in New York. She told me about Tony Chester-Lang's . . . er . . . preferences. He's deeply involved in procuring this stuff, himself.'

'But Tony knows how important it is for cable TV to have credibility in the UK! I've been to cricket matches with Tony, for Chrissake.'

'I may not be right. And if I am, you may not think it matters . . .'

'Of course it matters! If this guy is really a weirdo, selling weirdo stuff, we wouldn't want anything to do with him. But it takes more than chit-chat, Kate. We need a clear steer on this.'

Kate nodded and said nothing more. She realised from Joan's warning glance that if she became any more vehement she might risk losing Charlie's burgeoning sympathy.

'Hhmph . . .' he said eventually. 'And what about this business of you making a fool of yourself in France.'

It was at that point that Joan stood up.

'God, Charlie,' she said. 'I'm having hellish trouble with my stockings.' In exactly the same way as Kate had at Cannes, Joan stood up, stepped out of her shoes and wriggled her stockings off.

'Jeez, Joan, what in God's name . . .'

'I'm taking them off, Charlie. That's exactly what Kate did in France, in 80 degrees, when they started to unpeel. Now, if you're going to condemn her for indiscretion, you can condemn me too.'

'Oh, my God. Well, I guess you have me there, the two of you. Why did this guy take so much exception to that?'

'Either because he's not as broadminded as you are, Charlie,' Joan said shrewdly, 'or because he's interested in maligning Kate. He's got truly competitive interests here, Charlie, and we don't know how many people he's giving backhanders to. But from Mediaworld's point of view, I have to say that if what Kate says is only half true, we'll want him off the board.'

'OK, OK, Joan. Point taken. Jeez, you had me worried with those darn hose!' He laughed to show what a liberal, new guy he was!

Then just as they were leaving, he said, 'Kate, one thing. You've done well, but your balance has been wrong.'

'Sorry?'

'The mix. In your office. Young people work best with older people. Get someone in with a bit of maturity. It doesn't matter what the role is. Just get that element in there.'

'Sorry?'

'An older person. It helps.'

Later, in the cab to the airport Kate reflected on what he had said. There was a great deal of perceptiveness in it. Despite his American hail-fellow-well-met amiability, Charlie Mansfield was pretty sharp. And as she thought about it, Kate allowed herself to relax and contemplate how the tide had turned in twenty-four hours. She now felt absolutely on top. There was no doubt she had put an excellent case for the structure of Food and Health, and for her own stewardship. Joan Thompson had backed her and clearly Charlie was going to give her longer to prove her worth. It was the best feeling she had had for a long time.

She dozed as soon as the plane was airborne. But for some bizarre reason, her dream was less assured and she saw Laurence Smith, as clearly as if he were alive. He was sitting at his desk, drinking out of his silly mug, the one with the pig in Y-fronts. He was wearing his rather endearing, enthusiastic smile, looking openly at Kate, the way he did when she had given him the job.

He said in the dream, as he said at the time, 'I'm very grateful for this chance and I won't let you down.' All recruits said things like that and she had taken the phrase for granted. But now, his words made the flesh crinkle at the back of her neck. She shivered in her sleep, and said, 'Laurence, it's me who let you down.'

Yet his death was now months ago. Why was he there, in her subconscious? Her new found faith in her own management, the blossoming of confidence stimulated by Joan and Charlie, reassured her that she had chosen a good solid worker in Laurence. She felt jabs of guilt, for even suspecting that he had been unstable or deceitful. The plane rocked slightly with some Atlantic turbulence and Kate jolted upright, disoriented. When the cabin officer passed, she ordered a whisky, and sat, thoughts streaming around her in the grey false dawn of the plane, like a vapour trail.

Jenny had cleared Laurence's desk. Yet she had said that the silly mug had reappeared. The mug, standing on the drip mat on the empty desk, with the hot coffee inside it and the steam rising slowly, had alarmed Jenny more than any knives or blood or gunshots could have done. Real terror was the ordinary, the domestic, only slightly out-of-kilter. That was the way madness lay. Big fears required big action and dramatic, cathartic solutions. The appearance of a mug of hot coffee on a dead boy's desk, something hardly even remarkable, was much more insidiously undermining, and much more frightening. Had someone just made the coffee, and coincidentally put the mug on Laurence's desk? Or had it been some tasteless joke? The fact that common sense dictated there could be no huge witch-hunt or interrogation made the fear induced by the incident even more insidious.

Who had done it? And who made the calls? And who was the thin woman? Kate remembered Jenny's stick-like legs poking out from under her anorak. And the servile way she had kow-towed to Matthew after the flood. Jenny wasn't herself, that was certainly true. Suspicion touched Kate like the glacial grey cold feel of the plane's interior wall as it held her in an icy egg and sped through the freezing clouds. Jenny? Clearly, Jenny was ambivalent about Matt. Was that because of deeper, more destructive confusion? Kate remembered Jenny's brittle resentment in the first few weeks they worked together. Perhaps that hadn't gone away. Perhaps Jenny had just started to channel her bitterness differently. But if Jenny was involved in this slow, aimless destabilisation of the office, then why – in the comradeship they shared after the flood – had Jenny revealed Matt's involvement with Chester-Lang? Unless she was playing two games, involving two projects . . . with a good job for herself as the prize in either of them. It was a misgiving Kate tried to quell but which she knew would haunt her.

She managed to sleep properly in the last two hours of the red-eye flight. When they landed at Heathrow it was Saturday morning. Kate desperately needed to dispel the awful distorted fears that had been born in the half night of the flight. She called at the bedsit to drop her luggage, planning to go on to John's for the great long renewing sleep she owed herself.

The door swung open. Kate rarely received any post at the bedsit, but there was a thin, brown letter on the carpet. She ripped it open, snagging her nail on the brown paper fold in her urgency.

'We have been trying to reach you. Your tests have proved inconclusive,' it read. 'Please telephone for an appointment.' She sat on the bed and looked at the letter. Was it bad or good news? She didn't know. Instead of going to John's she stripped off and lay on the bed in her own attic room, watching the light from the dormer windows soften on the opposite wall. She heard Polly's children calling out as they played next door, and wallowed in her own jealousy and anger. What did it matter if everything was all right now with Charlie Mansfield and the Food and Health Channel? Who gave a bugger? The researchers and

Jenny and all their neuroses didn't matter a stuff.

At that moment Kate would have handed the victory over to Antony Chester-Lang with a whoop of joy, and told him to get on with his own vile business in perfect peace, if she could only have withdrawn from the fight into the cocoon of her own pregnancy.

In the house next door, Polly looked at the remains of the Saturday late breakfast she had served her son. She felt weak with relief. Without prompting, he had eaten the yolk of his egg, and some of the soft pink fresh bacon she had filleted exhaustively of fat and rind. He had taken a bite from the centre of a thick brown piece of toast, though she noticed he had scraped the butter off. Still, it all probably added up to as much as two hundred and fifty calories.

Polly took her son's plate and scraped the leftover food into the organic waste bin she had started, in one of those strange rational moments one can have in a continuing crisis. If Richard wasn't going to eat his food, she had decided, she couldn't waste it and would make compost and put it on the garden. She remembered the times when whole untouched meals had gone into the bin. Now, tears filled her eyes with a smarting sensation. It really did look as if Richard might be on his way to being better.

What had the doctor said? 'Be realistic. Yes, anorexia can kill, but only one in ten fails to make it.' But how much overwhelming effort from the families of the other nine did it take, to make sure the figure wasn't two, or three, or more in ten?

Polly had read all the theory and thought it through for herself. Perhaps in earlier centuries these people had been the saints and martyrs. At a time when 'teenagers' did not exist, had Joan of Arc and Bernadette of Lourdes and so many others been people whose willpower found its outlet in control of their eating? The lack of nourishment and ensuing visions might be no less a sign of spirituality for being caused by lack of food.

It was a theory John Maple had tentatively suggested in the darker weeks, earlier that summer. She liked to mull it over, cherishing it, secretly rejecting the more common concept that the stress of modern living led to the neuroses of today's young. What could have been more stressful than fighting in the First World War at sixteen, like Richard's great-grandfather? Or living as an adolescent in the blitz in Leeds, like his own grandmother? What earthly reason could there be for her son to be the one in this family to nearly kill himself with a self-imposed self-created illness, so that psychiatrists looked at her dolefully and talked about stress? Her anger bubbled again, and she consciously stilled her shaking hands where the remains of the egg waggled on the greasy plate.

What upset her most was her own stupidity. She just hadn't realised that boys could have anorexia. She knew that part of her urge for another baby was to get it right with a boy this time. But it was a stupid, indulgent idea. She had confided the hope to only one other person, John Maple's fiancée, the woman next door.

It made Polly sad that they had never talked again, yet she was also relieved. She knew she had allowed herself to mislead Kate, to let Kate believe that her life was some sort of domestic idyll.

Yet surely it was odd, in the circumstances, that Kate knew nothing about Richard? Surely John would have told her? Polly hadn't really thought about Kate's reactions. But now, she started to muse. Her conversation with Kate had been strangely one-sided. One would have thought, given the connection, that Kate would have been keen to talk about John. It was the first time that Polly had met a potential second wife who failed to show any interest in the first.

Leaning against her kitchen counter, looking at the food mixer and remembering the daiquiris and her opening remarks to Kate, Polly was struck by an amazing thought. Perhaps Kate didn't *know* . . . not just about Richard, but about everything!

But that was ridiculous. John would have told her, of course. Wouldn't he? Or perhaps he hadn't. Perhaps he had assumed that she, Polly, had told Kate herself? That might explain a great deal. Polly was a perceptive woman, and somewhere towards the end of their conversation she had sensed Kate's developing hostility and had been unable to place it. But if Kate didn't know about the connection, and just thought that Polly was some interfering, over-familiar parishioner, well of course she would retreat!

Polly was tempted to call John Maple straight away, but fond as she was of him, there was a reserve about John. She needed a go-between.

Polly went into the sitting room, and thumbed through her

address book. The phone rang out, and a light, northern, cheery voice answered. Polly said 'Hi! I'm so glad I've caught you. I think I might have committed rather a social gaffe, and that you can help me get out of it.'

'Me? Just say the word, Auntie Polly,' said Andrew Maple.

CHAPTER TWELVE

While Kate was in New York, Jenny supervised the team's work, first at John Maple's house for a day, and then back at the Warehouse.

'We ought to get out of here and back to the office,' Debbie had announced with surprising force. Since the flood, and during Kate's absence, the plump girl had slowly started being more assertive, and to her own discomfort, Jenny was surprised to find herself resenting Debbie's interference. Jenny blamed herself for lack of understanding, and silently accused herself of jealousy and insecurity. That in turn, she knew, made her crosser with the flawed and irritating Chloe, whom she could domineer in turn. Since the drug incident Chloe had been both more docile and more tearful, easily undermined and surprisingly ready to accede to Debbie's rather bossy requests. Her animosity to Jenny still lingered, but it was a slyer, less open kind of revolt.

Yet between them, and with Chloe pulling more weight than Jenny knew she gave her credit for, they managed to plough through quite a section of routine work, and on the Thursday evening, back at the Warehouse, Jenny announced that the last job they would do would be to finish logging the cutting notes for the Keith Floyd shows they had bought. They were all, she thought, showing signs of strain.

'Come on, Chloe,' Debbie said smartly. 'You've still got another series to log. You started the first one. You know perfectly well the notes are in your top drawer. You can find them if you look properly.'

'I can't. I don't know where they are. I did them then they disappeared.'

Hearing the new note of tetchy panic in Chloe's voice, Jenny looked up sharply.

'Oh, for goodness' sake, Chloe! We need to get that series finished before Kate gets back. What's stopping you?'

Chloe looked almost tearful.

'I'm sorry, Jenny. I just can't find my notes.'

'They must be in your drawer.' Jenny suddenly felt a surge of vexation. First Chloe had been truculent and difficult. Now, she was acting like a wet rag. Jenny leapt up from her desk, strode across the office, and pulled open Chloe's drawer. It was empty.

'They're not here. You must have put them somewhere else by mistake.'

Chloe's voice trembled. 'But they're not in my desk. And they're not in your desk. And they're not in Debbie's desk.' Her eyes flickered involuntarily to Laurence's. The desk seemed to gawp back at them, now stripped of his computer and his files, and pushed to one side. Jenny stared at it, and then back at Chloe. What was the girl trying to say?

Suddenly, on an impulse, Jenny got up and strode over to the desk. She looked at it, and the others looked at her. Then, feeling stupidly melodramatic, she pulled open the top drawer and plunged her hand inside, only to pull it out as if she had been bitten.

And in a sense she had. Little shards of pottery still punctured her skin as she pulled her hand back shaking it violently. As she did, tiny red dots of blood oozed from the punctures. In her fist were Chloe's notes, all right. But on top were the smashed remains of Laurence's pig mug.

Jenny was aware of Chloe and Debbie both screaming, but the panic had the exact opposite effect on her. This was rampant hysteria, and she was going to stop it now, get a grip on them all, and tackle whatever it was that was infecting this awful building with its petty poltergeists.

'It's nothing,' she yelled back at the others. 'It's just a few scratches.' The blood pouring from her hand looked terrible but she knew it was only a surface wound. 'It's only a mug, for Christ's sake,' she screamed back at the two girls. 'Just a mug, and some monster who's trying to scare us.'

As she said it, she knew it was true. But who might that monster turn out to be? Jenny pulled the drawer wide open. The pig's face looked back at her. The broken mug was shattered on one side as if whoever had done it had plunged it with such crazed force into the drawer, that one side was shattered in hundreds of pieces, while the other was broken in just two places so the pig's face, intact, smiled up at Jenny. It looked so crude and naff, Jenny thought, that suddenly she felt like smiling back. The monster, she thought, is mad. Mad in the sense of crazed, erratic, unpredictable, dangerous – but also pathetic. Like I was becoming, Jenny thought. Whoever did this was crazed from the inside out, while she had let outside things get in. But not any more. The tyranny of objects was over.

The next morning, a newly forceful Jenny stood in Matt Lavelle's kitchen before going to work.

'No eggs in the fridge again, Matt. I thought we bought half a dozen last weekend.'

'Did we?' Matt countered lightly.

'Yes. So where have they gone? I haven't eaten any? Did you eat them?'

'Possibly. I like eggs.'

'I know. But that many?'

Jenny stepped back and let the fridge door bang shut. She could see Matt in her mind's eye, spooning powder from a black tub into a glass of milk each morning.

'Matt,' she said slowly. 'Do you put eggs in that new drink you take each morning?'

'Oh yeah, that will be it.'

'But that means you're eating an egg every day. What about your cholesterol level?'

'It's OK. It's just egg whites. Nothing to get worked up about, Jenny.'

She paused. 'That drink, Matt? Is it steroids?'

'Jenny! Calm down! I'm just trying out a little supplement, that's all. It's actually made a difference already. And I'm not going to get hooked, so stop quizzing me. I can't stand being nagged.'

But it was a one-way street. The night before, Matt had tutted at her confession that she had missed the gym session the morning of the flood, and lectured her on keeping up her routine. Exercise was god, and there was an unwritten rule that Matt should set the pace and that she should not question him, about anything. She had lain in bed beside his relaxed brown torso, listening to his even breathing, and realised that she had been soothed to passivity by this anodyne relationship which drifted on effortlessly, because she never spoke her mind. And it had been so easy. After all, the only thing Matt asked of her was that she keep fit.

But Jenny calculated that this simple request meant ten hours a week at the gym, another five exercising at home, plus a constant analysis of diet and appearance which was as wearying as the exercise itself. She couldn't remember the last time they had watched TV without him astride his exercise bike, gone out to eat without her calorie counter book, or had sex without admiring themselves. The obsessional nature of their life had struck her, and she resolved to face him, about this, and about the boxes.

Until that moment she had tried every way to persuade herself that the issue of the kinky clothes didn't matter. And with Kate away in New York, there had been no-one to prompt her to tackle him. But now she wanted to face up to it, before Kate got back. Something had changed in Jenny in the last twenty four hours. Finding the smashed mug in Laurence's desk, as if it had been there to scare her, had hardened her. Things at the Warehouse were careering out of control. She had to start now to sort things out, and whether they were connected or not, the first item to be straightened out was her debilitating relationship with Matthew Lavelle. That too, she realised, had been all about external things. Will the real Jenny, she said fiercely to herself, please stand up?

On Saturdays, she and Matt broke their routine, and had a late breakfast. She decided that would be the moment.

So while Kate was sleeping off her transatlantic flight, Jenny sat with her orange juice, watching her lover and seeing for the first time the increased ribbing of the muscles on Matt's brown arms. She thought he looked like a dinosaur with his small head and new shaved hairstyle, emphasising the huge bulging body. The morning light hinted at reflected sun through the high north-facing window, and hit the steel of Matthew's units with a dull, whitish glare. It was bright, but it was not real sunlight. Suddenly to Jenny everything in the room looked false. What am I doing here? she thought.

'Matthew . . .'

He turned to grin at her.

'Matthew, I need to talk to you.' She was shaking.

'Do you? You're not going to rabbit on about my food supplement again, are you?' He smiled again indulgently. He believed everything could be normalised with his smile, both his obsessive body building and the way he was transporting that disgusting material for the Chester-Langs, she thought. She was shaking now.

'I've been a fool, Matthew. I'm sorry. But I've let you take over my life, and I want it back. You can kill yourself with drugs for all I care. I've had enough.'

'Hey, sweetheart, hang on . . .'

'Look, I was lonely and susceptible and you were . . . kind, and I bought into all this fitness crap. But that's what it is. Crap. I'm packing it all in. It's gone too far. Christ, look at me.' She looked down at her own skinny, mottled, dyed-brown legs, like Twiglets poking stiffly from under her loose nightie. Her heart was racing in a way that alarmed her and made her aware of how skinny her chest had become. She swallowed, to slow herself down. There was no point in raving at him for the next few seconds. She wanted what she had to say to be clear.

'And talking of the body beautiful, Matthew, I ought to tell you that I know the truth about what was in those white boxes you were delivering to work.'

'Do you?'

'Yes. I kicked one over by accident. And then, the next time, I looked in one for myself.'

He stood up suddenly, and she tensed. But the sound she was hearing was not anger but laughter.

'Hey, Jenny, calm down. Why are you uptight about it? So the Chester-Langs are involved in something a bit kinky? That's not our fault, is it? I've been making quite a bit on the side helping them set up. Listen, this will make you feel better . . .'

'What?'

'I've nearly got enough saved to put money into a house.'

'Sorry . . . ?'

'A house, Jenny! I'm on the mailing lists now of quite a few estate agencies between Wimbledon and Kingston.'

'Matt, how can you talk about buying a house when I'm trying to tell you that I'm appalled by what you're doing?'

'Look, all I'm doing is collecting the samples and storing them discreetly. Tony Chester-Lang's got a deal with a couple of suppliers, and we needed somewhere to put the goods. OK, so it's a bit more risky than your average sexy nightie, but what's the problem?'

'Problem? Have you seen what's in the boxes? What about the whip and the mask, and the studs? And those vile magazines?'

'Yeah, well I suppose they are a bit OTT.'

'OTT? Matthew, they're despicable. Haven't you thought about what you're doing?'

'Of course I have. Tony is paying me an extra thirty per cent bonus to help him organise this. He reckons the ratings will be huge for a sexy shopping channel, especially if there's a hint of something a little more risky. It's a brilliant scam.'

'A brilliant scam? What else has he got on offer? Kiddy porn? A nice line in Alsatians? Can't you see this is the height of sleaze?'

'Oh, come on, Jenny. Whatever turns you on . . .'

'Do you mean that? Do you honestly think that for every sadistic bastard out there, there's a complementary masochist shouting "Beat me, beat me"? Have you seen the pictures of those women, the strain on their faces? Those terrible forced smiles, like grins on skulls?'

'Jenny, that's not up to us . . .'

'Not up to us? Of course it is. You're despicable, Matthew.'

He looked after her, genuinely perplexed. Then she stopped and turned to him.

'Was Chloe's boyfriend part of this?'

'Who, Jason?'

'You know who I mean.'

'Well, yes, actually, he was. Only because we needed someone to pick up some stuff from the continent which came into Heathrow.'

'You mean obscene stuff?'

'Well, perhaps not as bad as that. But not the sort of thing you'd want Customs gawping at. I wanted Laurence Smith to pick it up. He looked like the last person to be receiving kinky goods. But obviously Laurence must have subcontracted the work to that stupid cretin Jason.'

'You mean Laurence was in on this?'

'Well, not exactly. I mean, he didn't know what was in the boxes.'

'But you had him lined up to receive deliveries? Because he was too damn nice and too conscientious to say no?'

'Well, sort of. Except that it wasn't me that started it.'

'So who was it?'

'Jenny, I don't know. Laurence knew about it, and offered to help. He didn't know what we were actually collecting, but he'd been tipped off.'

'What a fool you are, Matthew.' Jenny's voice was cold because her views were crystallising. She suspected that, despite his ambition, Matthew did not have the nous to run a major enterprise like the Chester-Lang channel. And with her disgust with him also came relief. However venal he might be, Matthew had neither the malice nor the imagination to conduct a campaign of terror against four women in an office. Someone else was doing that, and she was sure it was linked to Laurence Smith. Now Matt had revealed that Laurence was involved, even unwittingly, on the fringes of the Chester-Lang channel, Jenny was beginning to see a bigger, but unfocused, picture.

'So who else is in on this, Matt?'

'I told you, I don't know. Don't blame me! Tony's got someone I haven't met yet, setting up the mail order side at the Warehouse. That's the person who's in charge.'

So Matthew was somebody's stooge. Jenny was really calm now, and detached and repelled, almost outside of herself. Matthew felt the level assessment of her gaze and despite himself, he dropped his eyes.

'Matt, how could you be involved with something like this? Can't you see how awful it is?'

'Oh, come on, Jenny,' he mumbled.

'Everything about you is superficial, Matt. And I loathe what you're doing with Chester-Lang. I wouldn't buy a house with that money if you were the last man on earth.'

Jenny turned her back on him and went into the bedroom. She stuffed her clothes into the capacious duffel bag, slung on a thick cotton sweater and leggings, flung the bag over her shoulder and walked down the passageway to the front door as if someone else's legs were carrying her away.

Two minutes later, breathless with running, she was standing on the pavement, and she raised her face to catch the summer sun. Despite the drone of traffic and the hot gritty litter of the dusty street, for the first time in weeks she gulped the city air, filling her lungs with the greasy, sweaty smell. It felt far less polluted out here than in the air-conditioned cleanliness of Matthew Lavelle's flat, and far more alive than the creepy sterility of the Warehouse TV Centre.

Kate woke in the late afternoon with that sense of nausea which sometimes accompanies heavy irregular bouts of sleep. It was true that travelling east from the States was far worse than going the other way. The energy with which she had set out to tackle Nadine Wannawicz after an eight hour flight amazed her, looking back. Now, she was too drained to get out of bed. Her mouth felt as if it had been attacked by tiny wall-to-wall carpet fitters, while her stomach was still on the turbulent jumbo jet. When she crawled out from under the duvet and washed she felt marginally better, but venturing outside on to the fire escape, the bright sunshine cut into her like a knife blade into butter.

It didn't take too long to drive to John's. She had the duty-free whisky as a peace offering, but even so, she was aware of a feeling of unease. So, *this* progesterone test was inconclusive. But say next month they told her she was fine? Wouldn't everything be OK? Should she make an issue of it now?

She parked outside the house and walked up the steps of the tiny front garden with an air of gloom. She put her key in the lock and walked into the hall. To her surprise and dismay, she disturbed John and a woman in deep conversation, sitting on the horsehair sofa.

John leapt up. 'Kate,' he said.

He pulled her through the open door into the living room where Polly sat, a large glass of wine in her hand. For one ghastly moment Kate wondered if Polly and John were about to tell her something she might dread hearing. But John still had hold of her hand.

'It's my fault, Kate.' He hated saying it. 'I've been an absolute prat. I left Polly to do the explaining, which wasn't fair, because with her usual tact, she had left it up to me!'

'What on earth are you talking about?'

Polly turned to her. 'Oh, for goodness' sake, John, don't make a meal of it. It's no big deal, Kate. Let me introduce myself to you all over again. I'm John's sister-in-law. My children are John's nieces and nephew.'

'Sorry?' Kate sat heavily beside her on the sofa. Was she still in the half life of daytime sleep? Polly repeated herself.

'John is my brother-in-law, Kate.'

Kate sat, stunned. 'Give me a moment, you two. This is on top of jet lag! I need to take this in. What does it mean?'

'Nigel is John's wife's brother. I mean, John's ex-wife's brother!'

'What? Really? But John, why on earth didn't you tell me . . . ?' Kate looked up at him.

'I thought Polly had told you. And I didn't want to talk about it. I'm sorry, Kate.'

'So the picture in your living room, Polly? The one where your husband looked so familiar . . . ?'

'Exactly. Family resemblance! You've never seen Nigel. But you have seen his sister's son, Andrew Maple, who is the image of his uncle.'

'Oh, no!'

'Yes, Nigel and his sister are still really close. She lives up in Harrogate now, of course, but we all used to live in the north. Nige and I have always seen a lot of Andrew, along with his mum, but not so much of John until we heard he'd moved down here. But I'd always liked John, and I wasn't so convinced all the blame was on his side. That's why I started going to St Mark's.'

Kate started to laugh, though the sound was dry. She remembered the crazy hum of Polly's huge food mixer and how she had misheard what Polly had said. And it all boiled down to more bloody happy families! She looked at John, who was shifting from foot to foot, truly uncomfortable.

'So is that why you spent so much time with Polly?' Kate breathed.

John looked more awkward, but for a different reason. 'Well . . .' he said, and looked to his sister-in-law for help.

'Not entirely, Kate,' said Polly. 'I'm afraid I misled you slightly when you came for that drink. One of the reasons I wanted to meet up with John again was because I needed help. We've had a great deal of difficulty with our eldest son, Richard, the seventeen year old. He's hopefully coming through it now, but he's had anorexia.' She swallowed painfully.

'Oh, God, I'm so sorry,' Kate said, taking the glass John was holding for her.

'Don't be sorry for me, Kate. It's Richard who's really been in hell. I'm just beginning to accept that it isn't totally my fault. But John has been great. That's why he's been seeing so much of us.'

'I see!' Kate said lamely, and raised her glass to her lips, only to put it down again as the doorbell rang.

'I'll get it,' John said, leaving the room in a hurry. The two women looked at each other, each silently aware of his painful embarrassment. Then a thought struck Kate. 'John mentioned the bedsit to me when I was looking for a place to stay. Did he get the address from you?'

'Yes! I told him the place next door was for rent. Poor John. He's a wonderful man, but a mass of pride really, isn't he?'

Kate found herself nodding in surprised agreement, then jumped up at the sound of a familiar voice. She could hear Jenny talking to John in the hallway. Suddenly, more mind-blowing than any confusion about Polly, she thought about Jenny and her suspicions on the plane.

She stood up and called out, 'Jenny! What are you doing here?'

'Welcome back from New York, Kate. John's just let me in. I'm here to scrounge some company. I've said goodbye to Mr Schwarzenegger and I'm staying with you two for some supper, whether you like it or not.'

'You've split with Matthew?'

'Yep.' Jenny looked unsteadily at Kate, locking her eyes, and Kate felt a sudden, enormous, almost physical sense of relief.

'Oh, Jenny,' she said, and put her arms round her, to comfort herself more than to comfort Jenny, who shrugged her off affectionately.

'Hey, come off it, Kate, I'm a northerner. We only kiss children and old ladies. On second thoughts, though, you do look a bit wrinkly!'

Her attempt to be funny turned Kate inside out. Poor Jenny . . .

'You must have a drink . . .'

'Too right! In fact, I'll start now with a large glass of wine and half a ton of crisps, please. Hey, have I stumbled on a party?'

Jenny dumped her bag with complete abandon in the middle of the floor. Kate remembered with a shiver Jenny's description of the way Matt had started to take her over. She caught Jenny's eye. For the first time in weeks the two women looked properly at each other.

'Jenny, I've thought some terrible things . . .'

'Shut up, Kate, I know. I don't blame you. But I'm fine now . . .'

'Are you two OK?' John asked, hovering.

'Great,' Jenny said. 'And I'd love a drink.'

'Well, let's open another bottle. A party's a good idea. Jenny, meet Polly, a close relative of John's. And my neighbour. And listen to this!' The story of the misunderstanding now seemed a funny, light-hearted way to glaze over Jenny's awful pallor, and clearly shaky self-control. As if it were just a funny story, Kate told Jenny about her re-introduction to Polly. And in the recounting, the story seemed to become just a daft anecdote of a family cock-up. Polly followed on with other stories while they drank.

'Oh, John, d'you remember when Nigel and I first met and came over to you and your wife for tea? I was so awkward, Kate, that when Nigel told me his sister had made the cakes we were eating, I said, "Oh, they're lovely, they taste like real ones!" '

Jenny roared with laughter that was only half forced, and even John started to smile.

'And do you remember, John, how furious I was with you when you missed Richard's christening? John, our family star, was supposed to be officiating and at the last minute we had to get the curate because John was ill. He was too heroic to tell us till the day before, although he looked like a hamster and could hardly walk. But that curate was unused to babies and nearly dropped Richard in the font!'

John had stood up during this anecdote, and he walked over to the window. Kate knew he hated talking about all this, but for once she wasn't going to acquiesce to his sensitivity. 'I bet you never wanted to speak to him again after that.'

'Correct!' Polly laughed. Then she fell silent, and Kate knew she was thinking about Richard.

'My son has been ill,' Polly said to Jenny. 'He has anorexia.' Kate felt an almost physical pain for her, having to explain this freshly to every new person. Jenny's eyes widened. 'A *boy*?'

'Yes. I know it's rare.'

'God, how awful for you. And there's absolutely nothing you can do once they're down that road, is there?'

'Nothing. But he seems to be getting over it now.'

'Well done you! How did you manage that?'

Polly looked at Jenny gratefully. 'I don't really know that I did anything . . .'

'Yes, you did, Polly,' John said.

'Well, there's no way what I did would have worked if Richard hadn't wanted it to. But what I did was ask him to eat his little sister's leftovers. I wouldn't make him a meal for himself. And I stopped trying to persuade him to eat his own dinners. But I'd say, "Oh, look, Sarah's left her egg. What a waste." And he could somehow eat that because it wasn't his food. That's how we started. Now, he'll almost eat a meal of his own. But it's taken nearly three horrible years to get to this stage, and at the end of the day, it was only because he wanted to come out of it, and I gave him a way to do it without losing his pride.'

'God, how amazing. We should have a whole section on the channel about food disorders, Kate.'

'Well, if you want any help . . .' Polly said. 'Oh gosh, look at the time! Nigel will be wondering where I am. I told him I'd only be an hour.'

'I'll walk back with you,' John said quickly. 'Kate and Jenny will want to talk work.'

And some, Kate thought as she watched John and Polly leave, then settled down to tell Jenny all about New York, including her own stupid speculation about Jenny herself. And in return, slowly then in a rush of relief, Jenny told Kate about the broken mug, and how it had somehow, against all the odds, broken the spell and forced her back to reality.

* * *

Walking back through the drowsy Saturday town, John said, 'Polly, listen. Could I ask you a favour?'

'John, after you've been such a fantastic support to me, I can deny you nothing. It's not my body you're after, I take it?'

He laughed, but not wholeheartedly. 'I'm serious, Poll. Look, I want to ask you, well, not to discuss, you know, the past, with Kate.'

Polly turned on him. 'Now come on, John! That's a bit of a tall order. And it makes you sound as if you can't trust me to be objective.'

'No, honestly, Polly, it's not that I'm frightened of Kate knowing the truth about what happened between me and my wife. She virtually knows that already. It's something else . . .'

'What?'

'I . . . I don't want to talk about it. It's something I've got to tell Kate about, and I don't want you letting the cat out of the bag first, without realising it.'

'What on earth are you talking about, John?'

'Polly, just do as I ask, will you? Don't talk about those times to Kate. Not till I talk to her first.'

'OK, vicar. If you say so.'

He could tell she was aggrieved. But he was playing for time. Please, God, give me the strength I need to get this over with, he prayed, as they walked in pained silence, watching the Canada geese squabble for chunks of bread along the tide-line of the river.

For the next hour, Kate and Jenny sat on the dusty floor of the still unplastered dining room, and Kate filled Jenny in on the events of her trip. And Jenny told Kate how things had finally ended with Matt. Then they sat, thinking.

After a moment Jenny said, 'Nice woman, that Polly,' licking at the crumbs of cheese crisps at the bottom of the dish. 'Awful about her son.'

'You handled that well, Jenny. It's a difficult subject.'

'Yeah.' Jenny licked her finger for salt. It's odd, but I could feel myself slowly becoming as obsessive as Polly's son, about my body. It was becoming a symbol of how much better I was than everybody else. In Matt's case it's worse. He's obsessed with his own body, but can't see the dignity in anyone else's. Unless it's an exhibition specimen, of course. That's probably why he can't see the evil in what Chester-Lang is doing.'

'Yes. I know what you mean. Even Joan thought it was funny, at first. But you saw the pictures. That would be enough to convince you.'

'Yeah. Gross. And Matt is in it up to his bull-like neck. But for all his drive, and his ability to do a great job looking after buildings, Matt hasn't got the organisational ability to run the back-up for the whole thing. And from what you say, the Chester-Lang son, Daniel, was just a front anyway. There's someone else involved, I'm sure.'

Kate shivered slightly. 'God knows who.'

Jenny pondered. 'Matt doesn't! It must be someone who sees themself as a sort of administrative person. It will be the mail order side of the channel which will need real work.'

'Maybe it won't happen, if enough people have enough misgivings.'

'You mean cable operators?'

'Yes, principally. But if they're all geared up to take Food and Health, and we cock up, then perhaps the Chester-Lang channel will slide into our place. Or at least, perhaps that's what he hopes. We've got nearly a hundred per cent of cable operators keen to take us, thanks to Joan Thompson's influence. But if we fall off the air, there will be a hole to fill. And Chester-Lang will be there, waiting!'

'God, Kate, that's frightening.'

'Yes. He wants us to fail.'

'Do you think that could be behind all these weird things that have happened?'

'You mean the phone calls, the mug, that sort of thing?'

'Yeah. It's so clever, isn't it, Kate? Cleverer than actually burning the place down or knocking us over the head with a mallet or something. It's the sinister moving of little, domestic things. Mugs. Phone calls. Notes. None of them big enough in themselves to make a fuss about. But all corrosive, adding to the insecurity. Nothing would be more unsurprising to our middle-aged male masters than a gang of women having to give up because of neurotic worries.'

'But who could do it?'

'Anyone. Matt, except he hasn't got the imagination. Michelle, maybe? What about Chester-Lang's wife? How ill is she, really? Could she be creeping around?'

'Oh come on, it's hardly likely. But if it is someone acting deliberately we can stop it by changing our own office dynamics. Charlie Mansfield did make one good point. He said that perhaps we needed one older, more stable person when it came to researchers. I've just been thinking . . .'

'Go for it!'

'Go for what?'

'What you're thinking!'

'How do you know what I'm leading up to?'

'Because it's obvious.'

'What, asking Polly to join us as a researcher?'

'Yeah. Why not? I like her, you like her, she knows as much about the subject as anyone, and she'd be a great balance to Chloe and Debbie.'

'She told me she was looking for a job. Though she also said she was thinking of having another baby. But I think I'll ask her.'

'Why not? She might just say yes.'

'Mmmmm . . .'

'But while you're thinking about it, what's for supper? I'm staying whether you ask me or not.'

'We're having an Indian takeaway.'

'Yum!! Let me order a huge prawn curry and nan bread to go with it!'

When Jenny got back to her own grimy flat late that night, there was a scribbled message one of the girls had taken from Matt, asking her to ring him. She felt the tears smart in her eyes when she remembered the good moments . . . his kindness in The Narrowboat that first Sunday, and his occasional guileless, beaming smile. Despite her anger, she knew there was nothing actually evil about him. But she also knew that what he could get away with, he would. And she turned her back on the note.

At John's house, Kate lay and hugged him in dark silence, both of them cradling their own separate worries. When he sensed she was sleeping lightly, he got up and walked to the window.

If he didn't tell Kate about what was worrying him, then Polly might. He had hated asking her to keep silent, but he dreaded Kate finding out. Three months ago, the suspicion had entered his mind and he had dismissed it. But as time had gone on, he had begun to wonder more and more. And if what he feared was true, how would Kate react?

Until now, John had seen any assessment of his failings as a matter for him and his God. Even his divorce, at the end of the day, he had seen as a broken contract between him and Christ, rather than between him and his wife. But then, he had never really seen his marriage as a relationship between equals, he admitted to himself, and he ached at his own arrogance. He was paying for it now.

John was not used to insecurity. All sorts of other dilemmas, yes, but this sickening fear was new for him. He prayed as he stood looking out: *please God, don't let her leave me.* This was the first time Kate had had the right to be disappointed in him. He crawled back into bed, scared to touch her in case she woke.

The morning was hot and grey. Kate still felt shattered, as if she had misplaced most of her body. Her head seemed to be on a long stalk some way to one side of her shoulders, and a breakfast of bacon and eggs while John was at church did not seem to help. She hadn't been to the Warehouse since the team had moved back in, and she decided to go and have a look while it was quiet, to fill in time as much as anything.

Kate drove on autopilot. The sun was disappointingly sultry and for the first time, as she parked, a slightly rotten smell from the canal seemed to pervade the car when she opened the door. It was almost completely windless, so she could hear the buzz from the Chandips' shop and the drone of traffic on the A4. The jet lag nausea seemed to want to come back, she could sense it knocking somewhere round her temples. Head down into her jacket collar and hands in her pockets despite the heat, Kate trudged towards the glass doors. Out of the corner of her eye, she realised that there was something blocking her way, and she looked up to see a large yellow skip in front of the building. Two men in overalls were coming out, both with plastic gloves which gave their hands a dull, rather sinister shine. One said to the other, 'We need more black bags, Sid, because there's more stuff at the back. Gawd, it's disgusting.'

'Yeah,' said the other. Kate stopped by the skip. 'Hi,' she said. 'Is it all right to use the first floor?'

'What? Oh yes, love, the first floor is fine. Our problem's up in the loft.'

'Oh yes, where the tramp has been squatting?'

'Tramp!' said the other man derisively.

'It wasn't a tramp, sweetheart,' said Sid, with the greedy eye contact of someone who wants to shock. 'It was a *woman!*'

His attitude irritated Kate. She was aware of the British male's practical gallantry which demanded that women were somehow nicer than men, as if their sole role was to calm and civilise brutish males, and she disliked it. It also gave them the right to be doubly vindictive when women slipped from the pedestal.

'So are women tramps worse?' she asked dangerously. The other man, who seemed more objective, was lighting a cigarette, still wearing his plastic gloves. He passed the matches to Sid. 'It don't usually make a difference, love. We've cleared up squatters all over. But this!'

'What was so bad about it?' Kate was genuinely curious now, and aware of a creeping sensation of fear.

'It was filthy. She's used it as a toilet too, which you don't usually find. And there were clothes, clothes everywhere in bundles. And food. Vermin had got into the back of the loft, because she was hoarding bits of food there.'

'Bleeding disgustin',' Sid growled. 'Not like the usual.'

'What do you mean?' Kate's voice sounded small and cold.

'Well, now, most squatters keep the place, like, sorted out in their own way. But this was, well, like a nest. Someone really weird was up there. All the mess was in together, food, shit, rubbish. Only one thing was separate. Look . . .' He plunged his hand into the skip, and Kate waited mesmerised. Then he pulled out a large thin white plastic bag, like the sort which contained dry cleaning. 'In here,' he said, groping inside in a way that made Kate feel disgusted without knowing why. He pulled out his arm, and in his huge glistening hand he held a flourish of what looked like filthy but flimsy lingerie. He waved the fluttering nylon at Kate.

'Now, where the fuck, if you'll excuse my French, would a squatter get stuff like this?' For him the question was rhetorical. But Kate knew the answer. 'Oh God,' she said, staring at the skimpy nighties in the man's big fist.

'Weird,' said the man.

'Bleedin' weird!' agreed Sid. 'Ain't seen nothin' like it. Anyway, love, you go on up. Don't mind us, we've got more of this garbage to get out yet.'

Kate backed away from them, unable to take her eyes off the skip. Her back hit the glass doors of Reception and she burrowed her hands in her bag for her security card. Inside, insulated from the heat and the smell, she leaned against the wall and waited for the nausea to subside.

Somehow, the ghost girl had got hold of some of Chester-Lang's supplies of sexy underwear. But nothing had ever looked less erotic to Kate. She walked slowly and thoughtfully up the stairs towards her own office. Presumably the girl had stolen the stuff, which must mean she had access throughout the Warehouse. The idea that someone might have been prowling through the offices at night filled her with flesh-creeping disgust. And more to the point, she thought suddenly, where was the ghost girl now?

Kate opened the office door and jumped. Sitting at her desk was Chloe.

'Kate,' she said defensively.

'Chloe! What are you doing here?'

'Oh, just, you know, trying to get things sorted. How was New York?'

'Fine.' Kate looked at Chloe coolly. It was entirely possible the girl was really trying to do extra work. 'What exactly are you trying to tidy?'

Chloe reddened. 'It's my logging sheets. I wanted to – well, check them.'

'Check them?' Kate said sharply. 'Why?'

'Oh, just to go through to make sure they were all still here.'

'And why shouldn't they be?'

'Well, you know, with the flood . . .'

Kate remembered what Jenny had told her about the broken mug. Someone had smashed it and put it into Laurence's desk, and from

212

what Jenny had said, Chloe had virtually led them to it. And she had access to the office which meant she could come in at any time to meddle. Kate suddenly wanted Chloe off the premises. She could not be sure, but seeing the girl here on her own on a Sunday morning, when she was not known for her dedication to work, made Kate shiver. Kate turned away and went into her own office for a token ten minutes. Then she emerged and said, 'As everything here seems to be in order, I'm going to go home now, Chloe. Perhaps you'd better come down with me, so we can leave at the same time. I don't want you working too hard.'

It had been more of an order than a suggestion.

'Let's go,' Kate said.

They walked downstairs together. Sid and his mate had disappeared from beside the skip, and though Chloe's glance hovered in that direction, Kate said nothing about it.

Chloe broke the silence. 'Kate?' She stood on one leg, her arms folded and a slow blush of confusion started to spread over her cheeks.

'What is it, Chloe?'

The girl was still silent, her upper teeth chewing at her lip.

'Oh, it's nothing.'

'What do you mean, Chloe? What is it?'

The two of them stood in the steamy heat, eyeing each other. Then Chloe looked down at the file she was carrying. She had drawn her name on the front like a schoolgirl: Chloe Carr, with the o made into a smiley face and flowers doodled around the capital Cs. Underneath she had written, months ago when she first started at the job, a list of everyone who worked on Food and Health, like a TV programme's credit list. There were more flowers doodled round Debbie's name, and little sketches of a stick man next to Laurence's. It seemed to Kate to be unbearably naive and touching and at odds with the drugs and the insecurity which bedevilled Chloe's life.

'Chloe, what is it?' Kate said more gently.

The girl looked back at her, trying to make eye contact but with every muscle in her face implying avoidance.

'Nothing, Kate, really. I was just going to ask you about New York.'

You weren't, Kate thought. But something about Chloe's nervous, almost pleading glance stopped her pressing the girl. The dull lemony sunlight seemed to be seeping into both of them and Kate could feel half-moons of sweat welling under her arms. Even while she waited, Chloe's glance shifted.

'I'm off then, Kate,' she said suddenly, and turned and almost ran out of the courtyard towards the dark towpath and the walk up to the main road. Kate watched her go. She was troubled by Chloe's evasiveness, but knew that however hard she had pressed, the girl would have said nothing more. She slowly walked towards her car, unlocked the door, and sat down in the cage of heat. The sun was full-on to the windscreen as she manoeuvred down the lane. She still felt shattered, but somehow overwound. It occurred to her that if she took a bottle of wine home, it might encourage John to talk about Polly and the past, and herself to sleep, though not at the same time!

Kate parked outside Chandip's all-purpose newsagents, and went in to the dark warren between racks of greetings cards.

'I'll take a Californian Chardonnay,' she said, thinking of Nadine Wannawicz. The silent woman in the deep green sari behind the counter turned to get it. As if at the sound of Kate's voice, Mr Chandip came bustling out.

'Aha,' he said gleefully. 'On Sunday too! How are you after your disaster at the building?'

'Oh, not so bad now, Mr Chandip. I think we'll be back to normal this week.'

'Jolly good! What a lot of problems you've been having, ever since that poor boy drowned! I don't know . . .' He seemed to be gearing up for the usual tirade. 'You know, Miss Wilkinson, I often wonder about that night. The row. Your young people! I suppose it should be expected, but even so I . . .' he stopped and looked over Kate's shoulder. Behind her, Sid from the skip was looming, a big, grumpy looking white worker in a set of overalls. Kate noted his close shaved head and tattoos, and how Mr Chandip instantly forgot her, and slid into an obsequious pose.

'Yes, sir?' he was saying.

Kate took her wine, and slipped passed Sid without acknowledging him and out on to the pavement where the bright metallic light hit her in the face. She blinked and turned full circle to go to the car.

And as she swivelled, she saw her again. This time, the sun was drooping behind the Warehouse and as always that side of the towpath was unnaturally dark. Her back was to Kate, yet Kate was absolutely sure the ghost girl knew she was there. The certainty made the flesh ripple involuntarily down Kate's spine. The sensation was pure fear.

They stood, locked together across the water, Kate staring at the girl's back, and the girl's back, unmoving, challenging Kate to shout out, yet arrogant in its immobility.

But Kate could not speak. She could only stare. The long slinky white dress over the elongated body was just the same. The hair was flowing down this time but now there was no sense of desperation, more a sense of deliberate provocation.

With an unmistakable gesture, the ghost girl twisted a hand behind her back. And with a quick, vicious jab in the air, she thrust two long thin fingers up at Kate. Then she turned and started to run along the bank.

CHAPTER THIRTEEN

Kate tried to convince herself, driving home, that the vagrant was obviously mad. Why would the girl pick on her, other than because she was there? But Kate was still scared. Twice, her sweaty palms slipped on the steering wheel and the second time, the car lurched across the white line, nearly into an oncoming bus, the only other vehicle on the midday Sunday street. Kate pulled it back, then had to stop and wipe her shaking hands on her jeans. She put her head down and took deep breaths. It was jet lag still, she told herself. Anyway, no ghost girl was going to kill her!

When she got home, John was back from church. She thrust the wine at him, then rushed upstairs to wash her hands, furiously scouring more than sweat from them. When she came downstairs John was looking at her anxiously.

'You looked awful when you came in,' he said.

'It's not surprising.'

'Hey, what's up?'

She pulled him towards her. And then, sitting on the horrid horsehair sofa, she told him all about the ghost girl, right from the beginning, and he held her as she talked.

'It must be awful to know she's still around, Kate. You need to get that chap of Jenny's to check the loft again.'

'Too right. Mind you, he's not turning out to be exactly the Rock of Gibraltar, is he?'

She realised how little she had told John about her trip to New York, or Jenny's revelations, or her fears for the channel. She had told him some of it, in unconnected bits, but somehow there had never been the time to go through it all clearly. And she had always been concerned that he might not want to listen. After all, John had his own professional worries, and she wasn't part of that. But now,

217

her deepest fears came bubbling out. And going through the whole sequence with him, she felt there was a pattern she couldn't pin down. It made her feel sick with inconclusive anxiety.

John said gravely, 'You've got too much on your plate.'

'I think maybe I have, at the moment. I seem to have had nothing but hassle and anxiety since that bloody flood. Or is it the flight? Christ, I don't know!'

'Shut your eyes. Relax.'

'Oh John, you are so good to me!' He kissed her gently on her forehead. 'You know,' she went on, 'what I want most today is a lovely, normal lazy day, with no more crises.'

So you won't want to hear what I ought to tell you, John thought. Yet he couldn't let this go on . . .

'Kate . . .' he whispered, 'listen . . .'

'Oh, I know. You feel really bad about the way you handled things with Polly. Well, forget it. Most of the time, you're too good for me, so a little misjudgement on your part isn't going to do much more than reassure me you're human!'

John breathed out, and said nothing. His own internal voice told him to be grateful. He had been given the time to think, which he had prayed for. He would tell her what he had really meant to say, of course, but he would pick his moment. This way, he could put it off and feel sensitive rather than cowardly.

They polished off two bottles of wine in the end, and lost themselves in silly films on the telly, and the afternoon went by in a mindless haze.

At the Warehouse, Monday and Tuesday passed with no sight of the ghost girl, and word spread through the Warehouse that the loft of the building was now squeaky clean. She was obviously not back there and Kate tried to forget about it, helped by the fact that all of a sudden, they were all much busier. The need for a third researcher became acute.

It took two weeks to sort out Polly's admission to the team. Kate was surprised how pleased Polly was at the offer of casual work. And once she joined, the office changed. Chloe seemed both more enthusiastic and more capable with Polly's motherly eye on her and Debbie was freed up to become less administrative and more creative. Kate suspected that Debbie missed being at the organisational heart of things and there was some mild territorial friction between her and Polly, but it was soon resolved. It was a better balance, Kate thought with satisfaction, overall.

For Jenny too it was a time of preoccupation with work, which meant that her personal life faded more into the background. She was determined to ignore Matt's phone calls.

And the ambience had changed. The Warehouse suddenly had a workaday feel, with an atmosphere of imminent operation. The old sense of four women rattling round in a hot, empty building had gone. New people were coming on board to run the editing and transmission suites, filling the car park and the offices, investing the place with a new reality. A couple of freelance tape-editors had moved into the new technical block, and the transmission suite was now into broadcast tests. They all moaned about the smell of the canal and the dark side of the building, but their complaints were like the whinges of any office group, and the sense of something sinister at the Warehouse lessened every day.

And the other tests which happened were Kate's personal ones. Once again, the twenty-one-day progesterone blood test was taken, and despatched to the hospital, and the bland note duly arrived asking her to go to the surgery for the results. Kate felt stupidly hopeful, although she knew that even if they told her she was still ovulating, there was still a long way to go before actually getting pregnant. On a grey day in mid-July, to her surprise and discomfort, Kate bumped into Polly outside their local doctor's surgery, at half past eight in the morning.

'Polly! Fancy seeing you here!'

'Yes, I have to come here each month. I get a high protein drink for Richard on prescription.'

'Oh. Of course.'

'Actually, I might as well tell you the truth. I'm not just here for that. Do you remember me saying I wanted another baby?'

Kate waited.

'Well, there's no chance. That's why I took the job. I reckon I'm in the menopause.'

'What? You?'

'Yeah, earthmother incarnate. But I've missed two periods, and

I'm definitely not pregnant. I'm having some sort of tests here, to see if I'm "in the change".'

'Snap!'

'You too?'

'Well, they're actually testing me to see if I'm still fertile. You know, I can't believe I'm standing out here, casually chatting about this! It's been my own deep secret for months. Only Jenny knows, and we only talked once. I'm glad I bumped into you. Look, why don't we meet for lunch? To swap notes.'

'Lunch with the boss! That would be lovely. Where?'

'There's a pub called The Narrowboat just down from the Warehouse. How about a quick sandwich at one o'clock?'

'Excellent, Kate.'

The doctor was beaming when Kate walked in. 'I shan't beat around the bush. Your test gave every indication that this month you produced a perfectly healthy ovum.'

Kate smiled. She felt light-headed, and unsure she was taking it all in.

'But in this case, there *is* something else.'

'What?'

'Don't panic! It's just that it would be unforgivable of me to waste resources on you, if your partner is the one with the problem.'

'John? But I've told you, he has a son.'

'That's why I didn't insist earlier. But now we know you're fertile, then we really should test him. Male fertility can diminish as well as female fertility, you know. If, for example, your partner was ever involved in a radiation accident . . . ?'

'Hardly. He's a vicar.'

'Fair enough. But what about undiagnosed, serious diabetes? Or a very serious attack of orchitis . . . ?'

'What?'

'Mumps.'

'But it's hardly likely, is it?'

'Well, about one in a hundred men who get mumps get the infection in the testicles. And then one in ten of these poor chaps become infertile.' He paused. 'And of course, there are venereal infections.'

'I see.'

'The odds are against it, but the test is standard practice. Mind you, the news is really very good. As long as you're producing eggs, the possibilities are so much better! We can try and repair damage to your tubes, if that's the problem. And even if we can't, there's always the test-tube method. Cheer up! Now, you can go back to work with a spring in your step!'

But that was hardly how Kate dragged herself through the morning. She knew John would be happy to go ahead with a sperm test, but she was sure the problem must lie with her own reproductive system. If it was to be a case of endless operations, or the gut-wrenching anxiety of trying for a 'test-tube baby', how would they cope?

The irony of it made her feel sick as she sat in a cab on the way back to the Warehouse, after a successful if slightly hazy morning with the designers. It was John who had awakened her interest in having a baby. If it turned out that she had a physical problem with her system and nothing could be done, he at least had his son. She would have no child, and all the guilt.

Polly was waiting for her at the table at The Narrowboat, with a slightly disgruntled look. Before Kate could launch into her news, the other woman said, 'Look who's behind the bar.' Kate looked up. Debbie Allen was pulling a pint.

'Debbie? Why's that?'

'Apparently the landlord called her this morning and asked her to fill in. I gather from Chloe that it's part of her tenancy arrangement. She's supposed to help out if they're stuck.' Polly said nothing more, but Kate felt her disapproval.

'Well, they might as well all earn as much extra cash as they can now, Polly. It's going to get very hectic in the next couple of months. We're still on target for an October launch.'

'Yes, of course. And it's nothing to do with me. It's just that . . .' Polly stopped in mid-sentence. Debbie had come out from behind the bar, tray in hand, and was looming over their table.

'Hello there, Kate. I hope this is OK. Hi again, Polly. Can I get you a drink, waitress service?' She smiled engagingly at them. She could really be quite attractive, in a rather unusual way, Kate thought for the first time. Her big, round face seemed to wake up when she smiled, which wasn't often, Kate realised. She had a strong jawline, and her small eyes could have been made much more attractive with some mascara. It was a pity about her bulky body, swathed right up to the ears in floppy roll neck sweaters. But that was fashion amongst the student class, Kate thought in amusement.

'I'll have a lime and soda,' she said. 'Thanks, Debbie.'

'And I'll have a white wine.' Polly smiled at the girl more indulgently now. She was already speaking about something else as Debbie moved away.

'Lime and soda, Kate? Do I take this to mean you don't need alcoholic support to help you cope with this morning's news?'

'Absolutely not! According to the doctors, I'm still in working condition!'

'Great! So what's the next step? Going at it like rabbits? John is quite sexy, I suppose. He certainly looks a lot better than he used to. When he and Janice were breaking up he used to look like death warmed up . . .'

'Well, I'm glad I've made a difference!'

Kate's pleasure at Polly's stray remark was pathetically obvious. It made Polly rethink her promise to John.

'You do, definitely. John is better in every way. He won't tell you, because he feels guilty. But his marriage was hell at the end. He looked really ill. Nothing serious, of course, but he used to keep working until he was ready to drop.'

'You said a few weeks ago that he was so ill once that he couldn't do a christening. You said he looked like a hamster and couldn't walk.'

'That's right! Of course, Andrew was at that age when they're always bringing all sorts of illnesses home from school. Chicken pox, measles . . .'

'Mumps?' Kate asked, her heart pounding.

'Goodness, yes. In fact, I think it was mumps John had when Richard was christened . . .'

'I'm really sorry I'm taking so long,' Debbie called over from the bar. 'I needed to change the optic for the lime . . .'

'Polly, I can't drink it.' Kate was already standing up. 'Please forgive me. I'll explain later.'

'Kate, what is it? You look terrible. What have I said?'

The bastard, Kate thought. 'I'll have to go. Tell Jenny I'll call her this afternoon. I've . . . I've just remembered something . . .'

She was backing away from them, leaving Polly upright in her chair, and Debbie frozen in surprise. The younger woman's arm was stretched up as she reached for the optic, and as Kate blundered backwards she saw Debbie's droopy grey jumper with the thick elasticated wristbands falling back to reveal a grey arm.

Kate said nothing more but scrambled out of the door. Her conscious mind was thinking how crazily she was behaving, blundering around like this, looking stupid in front of Debbie. But she had to get to John, to confront him after the way she had bottled up her fears.

It's *you*, her frenzied imagination was screaming at him. I've tortured myself with this, and all along, it's been *you*! She was racing along to the cab rank, desperate to face him. In her hurt she wasn't sure which emotion was winning, fury or despair. She was sure that most of all what she wanted was to rage at the man who had put her through all this torment. But when she got into the false soothing dark of the taxi, and the driver asked her where to, she gave him the address of the bedsit, and went home by herself.

In the private hospital ward where Sonya Chester-Lang was still recuperating, the sound of the traffic outside was muted to a thick, consistent buzz through the double-glazed window. Then, like the faraway call of an animal, a car horn sounded. Hearing it, Sonya turned her head away from daytime TV and looked towards the glass. Her life was so routine that even a car horn seemed like an unscheduled intrusion.

She had been in hospital for three months. Of course, she had been physically better for a long time now, but it was no wonder she didn't want to go back, everyone said, after what the burglars had done to her.

Of course, there had been no burglars. And Tony knew she knew, and that thrilled him. He enjoyed it most when they both played a part in front of the many doctors of different disciplines whom he had brought in, she in terror, he with complete and satisfying confidence. She had even done it with the tame policeman who had questioned her gently, a few weeks afterwards. The officer had asked Tony to leave the room, and Tony had done so in the absolute certainty that she would not give him away. So she had repeated all the things she had heard Tony say, and her indifference and lethargy had stopped the man pressing her. She neither knew nor cared if he believed her.

Sometimes, lying there exhausted by the effort of being alive, she wondered why she hadn't told someone the truth. But she was just too tired to face the fuss, too frightened of being alone, and resigned to the slow suicide of life with her husband. Her life was there for him to play with and the future was a dark inevitable tunnel which sucked her closer every day. Only the hospital had been her refuge and she felt that if she could lie here, day after day without moving, time would stand still and she would not have to go home.

Three months was a long time to convalesce. But if you had no friends, no commitments, no life outside to pick up . . . and plenty of money, well, why not stay here as long as possible? Tony came to see her, regularly but never predictably, so she was always on edge in case he would pounce. People like the nurses told her how marvellous he was, how he spared no money for titbits and treats for her. But Sonya felt like a piglet he was slowly and voluptuously fattening up for the slaughter.

The car horn died away. Then to her astonishment the phone rang.

'Mrs Lang.' It used to annoy Sonya when people shortened her name but things like that amused her now.

'Mmm.'

'Mr Lang is here for you. Ooops, sorry, Mr Chester-Lang.'

Sonya felt the usual sick-wave of nausea her husband's visits provoked. She lay absolutely still holding the phone to her ear. Then she said, 'Fine.'

'I'm just a temp on reception. Do I send him up to see the sister on your floor?'

'No. He knows the way.' She put the phone down. The effort of speaking had left her drained. She lay stock still, apprehensively watching the door, listening for Tony's heavy commanding footsteps in the corridor, waiting for the inevitable fuss of flowers or magazines that turned his visits into events, with nurses bustling around him to take his burdens and compliment him on his devotion.

But this time there were no authoritative steps, and the door opened without the usual unheard fanfare. And it was a long thin blond figure who tentatively followed.

'Danny!' Sonya sat bolt upright, pulling her peach lace negligée over her flabby chest in her first acknowledgement of her own body since the attack.

'Sonya, darling. Howareyu?' Daniel Chester-Lang sank on to her bed, ignoring the large visitor's chair, his light body hardly denting the fluffy bedspread.

'Oh, Dan . . .' Sonya could say nothing. She had forgotten how to speak to anyone except health professionals and her husband. Other than Tony, this was the first visitor she had had for three months.

'When I rang I was told you wouldn't see anyone.'

'That's not true . . .'

'Shhh, sweetheart, I thought they might be wrong. But I've tried to see you twice and been told you weren't awake.'

'What? Danny, I can't sleep . . .'

'I know, honey. It's OK.'

They sat looking at each other. Then he leant forward and kissed her cheek and Sonya sat there with her eyes closed, marvelling at the tiny, warm, wet sensation on her face. Real and gentle affection. Her long clawlike fingers rose and felt the place where Daniel had brushed his lips.

He said, 'The new girl downstairs thought it was fine to let me in this time, because of the name! She's probably been told only to admit Mr Chester-Lang.' He started to giggle, and Sonya joined in like a startled schoolgirl, an impression shattered when her other long arm snaked out from under the covers, its fresh fat lying in folds along the bleak ridge of bone. Her hand, still skeletal, grabbed Daniel's.

'Danny . . .' Sonya's voice was husky now, and he saw the tears in her eyes. 'Danny, I don't know what he told you, but it wasn't burglars . . .'

'Sonya, darling! I know. I understand.' Daniel Chester-Lang shuffled up the bed and took his stepmother's shaking shoulders in his arms. 'I really do understand. It was him, wasn't it?'

Mutely Sonya nodded. It seemed odd that Daniel knew, but no

odder than the fact that it had happened in the first place.

'Sonya, wait until you hear what I have to tell you. I just can't apologise enough for not coming to you earlier. I was supposed to come over in June, but with . . . everything that has happened, my arrival was put back to August. You see, my life has been hell too.'

He told her about Johnnie's death, and from there the rest of it flowed from him, including the whole background to his latest job working for his father. Johnnie's death had put off his dreaded start-date, but not for too long.

'But he didn't tell me you would be running the TV channel, Daniel.'

'Of course not. If you'd known, we might have got together, and maybe even started to enjoy ourselves!'

The thought delighted Sonya. She put her claws to her mouth and laughed behind it like a girlish flirt.

'Sonya, what I'm going to tell you is upsetting. But it's really important to me that you at least consider helping me.'

'Danny, you know I would . . .'

'I may be asking too much, Sonya. Listen.'

Slowly, he told her about how his mother had invited him for Sunday lunch, British style, a week or so after his return from France. He expected Sonya to pout, as she had always done in the past, at the mention of Nadine, but this time she just lay, her brown eyes in the pale brown skin fixed on his face. Even as he was talking, he could see a faint pink line rising in colour along her new, loose jawline from some sort of stitching. The bastard must have really gone for her, he thought.

Nadine's lunch had been arranged so she could tell him the truth about his father. Tony Chester-Lang had subjected his mother to continual sexual and physical abuse for three years. One day, when Daniel was three months old, Nadine had gone shopping in the West End, her only allowed recreation. In Harrods, Nadine had met one of the girls she had known at the nightclub where she had worked, who had been lucky enough to land a rich elderly businessman. The other girl had said speculatively, 'Tony Chester-Lang! So you actually married him! Well, he's older now, of course. Perhaps it's not so dangerous?'

'What do you mean?'

'Well, they've all got their funny little ways, haven't they? I mean, Godfrey likes me in a French maid's outfit, bending over with a duster. And there's the spanking, quite fun at first, but it can get boring, can't it? But let's face it, dear, that's why they end up with girls like us, not English virgins plucked straight from the Home Farm!'

'What are you getting at?'

'Well, Tony Chester-Lang! I mean, I had a nasty bruise, and that was just after he patted my bottom! Godfrey knows him from the club. There was quite a lot of gossip about his first wife, you know. Some story about the house being broken into and she was found beaten up, raped and dead? Godfrey says some of the boys did wonder . . .' This was in the days before forensic testing. The other girl had looked at Nadine from under her round fur hat, her coated eyelashes as sharp and vicious as black park railings.

Nadine had left Harrods, and caught a cab home. She had taken one expensive suitcase, the baby, and fifty pounds from her husband's bureau. Then she had caught a cab to Earl's Court and the cheapest respectable hotel she could find.

'So you see Sonya, it's not just you,' Daniel whispered, to finish.

But if he had thought that this knowledge would reassure Sonya, he was wrong. She looked back at him, silent and even hurt, as if her one last tiny shred of self-respect had gone. If she had been the only woman to provoke this reaction in Tony, then at least she would have been unique. But if she was just the latest . . .

'Sonya.' Daniel's face was coming closer. 'Please. Press charges against him. Mom would support you. Please.'

Sonya felt her head sinking through the pillow. I am nothing, she thought. Nothing. It was actually easier to be nothing than to be in pain. Though Daniel's face was inches from hers, she could choose not to see him. She closed her eyes.

The bedroom door swung open to announce the arrival of the sister on the ward. A superficially jolly woman, she was irritated by the lethargy of the wealthy Sonya Chester-Lang. It pleased her to assume first name terms with the wrecked creature in the bed, and to harbour secret and rather titillating suspicions about the real nature of her injuries. Money wasn't everything, sister thought with satisfaction.

'Goodness,' she boomed. 'Have we been allowed a visitor? I wish I'd known, dear, I'd have helped you tidy yourself up. Goodness me, look at your hair! Hubby wouldn't like to see that, would he? Let's just put a brush through it, shall we? Now, sitting on the bed is not allowed, young man, so if you'll just move over I'll give Sonya a hand. Here's the hairbrush and I'll just bring the mirror over.'

'No!' screamed Sonya.

For the next half-hour she said nothing, but lay, her large bony hand lifeless in Daniel's. When he eventually left she was still staring at the wall opposite with unseeing eyes, and perfectly coiffed hair.

'It *was* mumps,' John said quietly.

'Oh, God!'

'I've been going over and over it for a few months now. It was a really bad attack. And yes, my groin swelled up too.'

Kate was sitting on the horsehair sofa, cradling her coffee cup. John had his back to the window.

'Then why the hell didn't you tell me?' Kate had spent two hours alone at the bedsit. She had cried until her eyes were as puffy as lychees, and at first she had raged and roared too, hearing her own sobs and shouted blasphemy as if she were listening to a mad woman raving nearby. Then she had lain in an iron tension, completely still, furious with John for misleading her. Finally, she had stood up and made a cup of tea. Then she had sat on her bed and drunk it. She realised that sometime, perhaps two or three months before, she had started to consider that there might never be a baby. She wondered, looking back, if she had ever truly expected to have an actual child. After years without a partner, after considering herself unlikely ever to give birth since the hurt and disappointment of her miscarriage, she found the idea of being childless strangely familiar, like a manageable ache returning after searing pain.

John was saying, 'I was very ill. But my wife was furious with me. She said I had let the infection get out of control by not going to the doctors. That was true. I wanted to suffer, at the time. I felt my life was too snug, too easy. I really can't remember whether or not the doctor told me I could be sterile. You see, it didn't matter then. My wife wanted another child, desperately. She was haunting the doctors. But I couldn't even . . .' he stopped, his face distorted and his body tense with the remembered shame. 'We never had sex. I couldn't do it, even though she wanted me to. I was a terrible mess, Kate. Afterwards, I put it all out of my mind.'

'You put it out of your mind?'

'Kate, I'm so sorry.'

She stood up, and walked away from him through the dining area to look out of what was to be the French window at the back.

'Like I told you, I've been going for tests for two months, John. I wanted to be sure before I committed to marrying you. But you were the opposite. You pressured me *before* you were sure, so I'd be trapped.'

'No, Kate, that isn't true. I haven't pressed you for a date for the wedding for months now. And I was so afraid . . .'

'Afraid! You, afraid! What of? Not being perfect? If we'd ever talked about your first marriage in any detail, the mumps attack would have been mentioned ages ago, and I would have been warned!'

'I did torture myself, Kate. And I asked Polly not to talk to you, because I knew I should tell you myself. But I just couldn't. Dear God, I feel such appalling guilt.'

'Oh, I know that. All your sins are huge ones, aren't they John? They're things that you sort out with God, aren't they? They're far too important and interesting to be aired just by talking to me!'

'That's a cruel thing to say, Kate.'

'But it's true, isn't it? Your wife has a great deal of my sympathy!'

For several moments she stood looking out. The clouds were blowing over, and the hot afternoon sun was trying to burn through. In the darkest corner of John's garden, the last of the unopened pink roses seemed to be almost leaning forward, straining for the light.

He said, 'All the things you say are true. But I wanted everything to be absolutely right, Kate. I suggested a baby because I thought that would make things perfect. I know you think I'm an arrogant bastard, and possibly you're right, but everything I wanted, I wanted for love of you. Now, I feel desolate. Absolutely desolate.'

At last he had appealed to her. Kate knew she was crying again, but this time in pity for him.

'I've let you down, Kate. I'm going to have to live with that. And I'm not sure I can.'

They stood, with silence like a wedge of cotton wool between them, muffling their responses to each other. She thought he held out his hand to her, but she did not turn round to find out. Minutes passed.

'I know that now you have every right . . .' – he repeated it – ' every right, to despise me. And I know you're still young enough to meet someone else, and have children.'

'Oh yes? Which biological planet are you on?'

'But you could . . .'

'Oh, for God's sake, what d'you think I am? Some sort of broody hen? I took up with you because I loved you, not to get impregnated. It was your idea to have a baby, remember.'

'I know. But if you want to leave me, I'll understand.'

'Well, that's big of you! Oh for God's sake, John, you sound like something out of Jane Austen!' She turned round to face him. 'Do you really think my love for you is so damn feeble? Of course it isn't! You may find this surprising but I'm equally good at loving and forgiving as you! Coming to terms with that will be punishment enough for a self-righteous bastard like you!'

If she had ever wanted reassurance that John Maple really loved and needed her, the sudden relaxation of his body as he held her said it. They stood together, feeling the warmth through the window, and for a moment she thought that he was crying too. When the phone rang, they both physically jumped.

'Bloody hell! I bet that's Jenny. I just ran out of the pub, then to the bedsit for a couple of hours, and I never called her to tell her I wouldn't be in. What's the time?'

'Four thirty.'

'She'll be wondering what's going on.' Kate picked up the phone to hear Jenny's anxious voice.

'Kate? It's me. Listen, we've got a shareholder alert!'

'Oh no. What?'

'Charlie Mansfield's in town. He's been over to see Ajit Dalvi from Cox, and Adam Singer from Flextech. He sounded like he was breathing fire when he phoned.'

'Right, I'll get back to the office right now. I wonder why he's

been to see those two? They're pretty high-powered directors.'
Charlie was certainly mixing with movers and shakers.

'You didn't tell him I . . .'

'That you weren't there? No, I didn't. I said we'd be delighted
to see him, and that we had a lot to show him.'

'Well done, Jenny. I've got the car at home so I'll be with you
in twenty minutes.'

Kate drove against the prevailing traffic like a maniac, her sore
eyes behind sunglasses. At five o'clock Charlie Mansfield was
sitting in her office, a smile of satisfaction on his face.

'It's looking good, Kate,' he said, and just stopped himself from
leaning forward and patting her on the knee. 'Nice bunch you've
got working here, although these offices give me the shivers. Still,
that Jenny girl seems to know what she's doing, the young kids seem
keen, and the older woman . . . Polly?'

'Polly.'

'Yeah, whatever her name is, she's an asset too. Now, listen, Kate,
I've been talking to a couple of major players in the industry. The
story on the streets is that Tony Chester-Lang is out to get his
channel carried instead of ours. At board level, this is going to mean
quite a fight, I'm tellin' you. But on your level, it means something
worse.' He laughed. 'I talked to Joan this morning. It ain't going
to be easy, Kate.'

'What isn't?'

'Getting this show on the road a month early. We want Food and
Health to be on screen by September 1st.'

'*What?*'

'Aw, c'mon, you can do it.'

'My God.' She paused, doing rapid calculations. 'Yes, it's
possible. I'll speed up the work on the continuity designs, and ditch
doing Felix's panel at Edinburgh.' She was thinking aloud.

'Hell, no, you can't do that. I mean, you can't give up doing that
Edinboro Festival thing. You told me you would be in the slot
Michael Grade took a few years ago. Shit, Kate, this is just the sort
of exposure we need! Can't your team cope for one day without
you?'

'Well, of course they can, but . . .'

'There you are then. Anyway, that's the thing that Boulder guy said you were too aggressive for, wasn't it? I think you'd better go, and carve the bastard up! Don't worry. I'll make sure there's enough in your expenses to cover the flight. Get there and back in a day.'

'Well, if you think I should, that will make things a lot easier.'

'And that's not the only bit of your budget I'm going to increase. We think you need an extra twenty five per cent to make these new programmes. Those guys this afternoon convinced me production is the way forward. Go for it, Kate.'

'Thanks.' She smiled back at him feeling confidence flowing between them. A few minutes later she called the team into the main office, to break the news of the new deadline. They took it with a great deal more assurance than Kate herself felt.

Afterwards as she and Jenny, each in a slight state of shock, left the office together and walked across the courtyard to the car park, they were hailed by Matthew Lavelle. He had his hands deep in his jacket pockets and looked uncomfortable, particularly in front of Jenny.

'Hi. Listen, we've been sorting out some of the stuff which came to light after the flood. We should have done it earlier, but it's been so busy. Kate, there are a couple of things you'd better see.'

'Fine.' Kate said briskly. 'Jenny will come too.'

Matt was leading them across to his office. 'It's that bloody squatter woman's stuff. There were a whole lot of papers squirreled away up there. Most of the other things they found were just garbage, disgusting stuff, but the cleaners advised me to keep any documents we found. So I kept one bin-bag of papers. Then I forgot about them until we had a clear out. A lot of the things were really filthy, but Michelle got some rubber gloves and we went through the top layer a few hours ago. There's even more underneath, but I think you should see this first.'

They went in and up the stairs. Matt's own room was, as always, strenuously neat. But a pile of soiled and ripped papers lay in isolation in the centre of his floor. There were bags, wrapping, newspapers, some meaningless order forms and old catalogues, and the remains of what looked like cardboard boxes. Matt nudged them gingerly with his foot, and the pile separated to reveal, to Kate's surprise, a slightly less soiled copy of a book. It was Sonya Chester-Lang's 'How to Diet to Perfection!' Matt looked up anxiously at

Kate and Jenny as his foot poked at something else.

Jenny went, 'Oh God,' and her hand flew to her lips. Kate sensed rather than saw her shock, because she was too astonished to lift her eyes from the pile of paper.

There, torn neatly in half, but unmistakably legible, was her original draft contract for the 'Cook of the North' series.

CHAPTER FOURTEEN

Back in their own offices Jenny explained.

'I've been a real fool, Kate. But I couldn't tell you that I'd mislaid the draft and the notes!'

'Why not? I'm not an ogre!'

'No, no, of course not. But it was early days. We've all made so much progress since then, but in the beginning I desperately wanted to prove myself. And I was terrified of letting you down. I couldn't face telling you I'd lost the stuff.'

'Jenny! Oh, for goodness' sake. So you asked Nick to help you.' Kate raised her eyebrow.

'It wasn't like that, Kate! I had no idea he was the new Head of Programme Sales.'

'Well, console yourself with the fact that Nick's a consummate professional. He wouldn't help you out without knowing what he was doing, and if he felt he ought to give you a helping hand on your first big deal, then you should accept that gracefully!'

'Yes. Yes, you're right. But it led to Nick and I meeting again, and . . . oh well, you can guess.'

Kate nodded.

'God, Kate, I felt so disgusting afterwards. I was so ashamed. Don't get me wrong, Nick didn't help me just to get sex. To be honest, if he'd turned up I'd probably have had sex with him anyway. He has . . . had . . . that effect on me. Crazy.'

'Well, not totally,' said Kate, thinking of the effect John had on her.

'But that was when I saw the weird girl, Kate, after Nick and I . . . well, yuk, you don't want to know the details. But how weird to think that she took the draft. God, you don't think she was spying on us, all along . . .'

'That's what worries me, Jenny. Perhaps someone put her up to it?'

'Like who?'

'Like the same person who has been phoning us, moving mugs around and surreptitiously losing or damaging material from this office since the beginning?'

'Oh, my God.'

'We're going to have to be shit-hot on security for the next two weeks, until the launch. And the end of August will be the worst, because that's when Charlie insists I have to go to Edinburgh. We'll be working all weekend, so you'll have to look after things.'

'I can do that, Kate. This time, I know I can.'

Stress levels rose for the next fortnight. There was a great deal of practical work to do, and on top of that, Kate wasn't happy until everyone else had left the premises each night and she could lock up. Often Jenny worked with her, and sometimes Polly stayed too. 'Nigel doesn't know what's hit him,' she murmured.

Kate also made sure all the office team stayed and worked together as much as possible, and that outsiders, including Matthew, hardly ventured over the threshold. Every day, with a sort of manic determination, she checked and re-checked the programme cassettes waiting in the library area, the tapes of the channel design waiting in the new transmission machines, and the list on the computer.

A few days later Kate had a serious conversation with Joan Thompson, who warned her to keep away from Daniel Chester-Lang.

'We're still none the wiser,' Joan had said. 'But I gather he's not properly ensconced in the UK yet. Some sort of family trouble. I've heard rumours that his partner died of AIDS. The whole project seems to be delayed. But according to Jeremy Woodley, they're still going ahead, and Woodley believes he's persuaded the ITC to support them.' Kate said nothing more to Joan about what she knew. If the Chester-Lang channel went ahead, under the guise of being a sleazy but acceptable home shopping service, there was nothing they could do except be dissociated from it, and hope the competition wouldn't hurt. Kate thought it pointless to talk to Joan about the other problems in the office. She was unsure herself whether or not the inept attempts at sabotage were anything to do with Chester-Lang. Now his project was officially delayed there would be little benefit for him in trying to oust Food and Health in order to get his own channel into its place on cable systems. Even if Food and Health were to fail, there just wouldn't be time for Chester-Lang to be up and running by the beginning of September. Not for the first time Kate admired Charlie Mansfield's shrewdness.

Kate's team worked through the last Saturday in August, until the evening, on what turned out to be a very busy day. For the last week at least, there had been a strict routine to the work. Polly had manned the computer. Debbie had worked over in the edit suite, her head encased in headphones and her eyes on the screens. Chloe had worked between Debbie and the main office, and Jenny had constantly logged and scripted.

Kate called a halt at seven fifty-five that night. A quick check down the list confirmed that almost everything had been done.

'Right,' she said cheerily. 'We are absolutely on target for September 1st. I suggest that everyone comes in tomorrow, goes through any last minute task, and clears up their own personal desk area. Then we'll have a dry run when I get back on Monday.'

'Great,' Chloe breathed.

'Now, two final jobs for tonight. Jenny, will you and Chloe go over to transmission and do a last check that the tapes are all there and ready for Monday? And Polly and Debbie, will you stack the next tranche of tapes on the shelves? If we put them in order, it'll minimise the chance of trouble.'

Kate watched them all leave to start their jobs, then sat thinking. OK, so for the last two weeks, there had been no phone calls, no disappearing mugs or missing files, but the hiatus was making her nervous. Ironically it was probably because she was deep into that thought that she did not immediately hear the crash, only the noise afterwards of spilt tapes clattering down the stairs, and Jenny's outraged yowl of pain. Kate slammed the phone down and rushed outside. Jenny was sitting on the stairs rubbing her foot. 'Jeez, I think I've broken my ankle,' she said. Chloe was trying to pick up the tapes and replace them in the right plastic boxes. Debbie was at the foot of the stairs already stuffing more tapes back into cases, while Polly was unlacing Jenny's trainer. It was clear after a quick examination that whilst Jenny's ankle wasn't broken, she couldn't walk.

'I'll take you home in the car,' Kate insisted. 'Jenny, your ankle is really swollen. Listen,' she said to the others, 'this couldn't have happened at a worse time. I'm in Edinburgh tomorrow, and now Jenny's out of action with just a few days to go. But I know you three will cope.' One look at Polly's pale face and anxiously blinking eyes confirmed her fears. 'Polly?' Kate asked worriedly.

'But Kate, I can't be here tomorrow. You know that. Sarah Louise is in a swimming gala, and Nigel has to take Laura to her archery lessons. I asked Jenny about it and she said it would be fine.'

Oh God, Kate thought. From the bottom of the stairs, Debbie said helpfully, 'Don't worry, Kate, there's me and Chloe. We'll come in tomorrow and make the final checks, and see that all these tapes are back in place.'

With some grunts and groans, Jenny was installed in Kate's car, and Kate gave the others strict instructions about locking up, before starting the ignition.

Jenny was very quiet as they drove through the warm summery dusk to her flat.

'Will you be OK?' Kate asked.

'Yeah. Actually, it isn't as bad as I thought. It's just a sprain. In fact, it was the shock as much as anything which upset me. I was just going down the stairs with my second pile of tapes, when it happened.'

'I've always thought those stairs were slippery. We need to ask Matthew to get them carpeted.'

'I don't know about that, Kate.'

'Sorry?'

'I don't know about getting the stars carpeted. You see, I don't think I stumbled at all.'

'What do you mean?'

'I don't think I slipped. I think I might have been pushed.'

Kate pulled up sharply at the lights. 'Are you sure, Jenny?'

'Oh, God, I don't know. I thought I was sure. But now I can't say for certain. I think I felt a hand in the small of my back. But maybe it was a twinge of cramp.'

Kate saw the scene in her mind's eye. They had all been in the office, and she had sent Jenny and Chloe off to stack first. Although the others had caught up with them, Jenny and Chloe must have been closest together.

'That's a frightening accusation, Jenny.'

'Yeah. Forget it. It must have been my imagination.'

'I hope so.'

Back in the office, Chloe had stayed at her desk to print out the latest schedule sheet, and Debbie told Polly to follow her with the next pile of tapes. Polly walked behind the younger woman across the yard to the transmission block, and up the stairs to the Food and Health suite.

'We'll put them here,' said Debbie, and began stacking her tapes along a waist level shelf.

'Hang on,' said Polly. 'That's not right, Debbie. If you do that, they'll be out of sequence. We ought to put them on the top shelf.'

'That's pretty awkward.'

'Look, I'll go and get us something to stand on. But you're not that small, Debbie. You could try reaching up.' Creeping along the dark corridor, her feet noiseless on the thick carpet, Polly experienced a moment of sheer disorientation. What on earth was she doing here, prowling round at night, while she had a family waiting for her at home? She turned noiselessly back, only to see Debbie stretching to reach up to replace the tapes on the top shelf. She had no idea that Polly was standing behind her, staring.

A week earlier, Sonya Chester-Lang had been pushed into the wheelchair and made to sit up like a naughty child by the grinning sister. Then she was pushed like a toy in a doll's pram down the corridor to the lift. She was wearing a shapeless, ugly green dress Tony had bought for her in Harrods. It was a size sixteen, which made Sonya laugh in a way that had embarrassed the young nurses who were trying to dress her.

As the chair was pushed over the thick soundless carpet, behind her she could hear Tony fussing and calling out. He had two huge bouquets ostentatiously on his arm, one from him, one from his secretary and the Filipino couple who kept house for them. Sonya wondered if he meant her to think that the flowers symbolised her isolation. Despite their abundance, they represented the only people in the world who had thought about her – three of them because Tony had told them to.

But Tony could not hurt her now. She had two defences. The most effective was her belief that she was a non-person. And the other, which crept increasingly into her thoughts, was that whatever Tony did or said, she had found him out, and both his son and his ex-wife knew.

They went down in the lift and then there was the endless fuss and commotion of saying goodbye. Tony, she knew, had enjoyed the cross between luxury and stark steel functionalism of the private hospital. There was something about the lush soft furnishings alongside the clinical scalpel and kidney dish which excited him. A nurse had been engaged to stay at their home. With this hint of the institutional, her husband could still catch the thrilling flash of cutting blades in the bedroom, even if they were only the scissors for the last tiny dressings Sonya still needed. But it was the atmosphere he would enjoy. And perhaps the nurse would be some sort of accomplice for him. That would be novel, Sonya thought.

He loaded her into the car with maximum commotion, and waved graciously to the members of staff deputed to see them off, in strict relation to the bills they had paid. As soon as his driver pulled away he snapped at Sonya, 'You might have said thank you.' He was working himself up to punish her, she thought dully, and said nothing but turned to look vacantly out of the window at the season she had missed. Summer had been and almost gone, and she had lain in bed and been senseless to all of it.

At the house, the new nurse and the secretary were on the step, alerted by Tony's mobile phone to stand there looking like retainers. Then it was up the newly-installed ramp, into the house and more manhandling into the new escalating chair that took her to her room. She was allowed to droop on to the bed and to feel the nurse undress her while Tony looked on greedily, supposedly a proprietorial and loving husband. But Sonya knew why he watched her body. The very fact that she had put on gross ripples of fat in the least attractive places, and that she never washed herself or combed her hair, excited him even more. She was abject, and he loved it.

When the nurse had gone for her break, ostensibly to leave them alone 'for a nice little chat to help you settle in', he pulled down his trousers and fell on her. She was wearing only the white silky nightie that the nurse had pulled over her head as she sat, legs apart and arms flapping, like a stringless puppet on the side of the huge divan. The nightdress had been loose and flowing when she had left home. Now it was tight, cutting into her arms like wire, leaving red circles within seconds. Tony pulled it up roughly with his hand to reveal her sparse, dry pubic hair and swelling belly. He was so excited he came almost before he was in her, but she was neither dry with fear nor wet with desire and his big, smooth penis pushed into her numb vagina, thrust convulsively and emptied itself while she felt nothing but the discomfort of his huge, heavy, smelly body. As he rolled off her he slapped her, almost conversationally, on the face, as if he had meant to do it before but had forgotten.

Sonya couldn't help laughing inside when she caught sight of herself in the smoked glass mirrors. What a fat disgusting bitch she had become. And he had splatted into her with more desperate urgency and speed than she had ever experienced before, despite all that wasted effort. She was still laughing when the nurse came running upstairs, to give her just a little something to calm her down.

He did the same thing each day for a week. And each time, he manhandled a little more. Each time took him longer to satisfy himself, and each time he became angrier. She never said anything, but her complete passive acceptance of her fate, and his failure to arouse her fear, infuriated him. I am nothing, she thought, as the pain stung her again and again. He was desperate now to see Sonya flinch, yet each time he hit her she merely looked at him in dumb amusement, her lip curled. By the end of that week, he was beginning to realise that unless he went further, he could cause her no real inner pain.

On the Saturday, the nurse took the afternoon off. He asked her to be particularly kind before she left, and dress Sonya in a pair of ridiculous baby doll pyjamas in blue chiffon. Her now fat white legs stuck out from the silly frill like uncooked potatoes.

'Silly cow,' he said, advancing on her. Did he really think she cared how silly she looked? In fury, he hit her so hard that this time she had to shut her eyes, but not for long. When she opened them, he appeared to be advancing on her with some sort of dildo. She didn't even brace herself for the searing agony. Enraged and still engorged, her husband withdrew whatever he had used, and his penis protruding as usual from the hideous maroon dressing-gown, he flung her over on her stomach and started to ram her from behind. Sonya minded this least. She didn't have to see him and her back was strong enough to take the thrusts. She could hear him rearing and grunting like a bull, the obscenities and insults he yelled at her as always spurring him on. She realised that, looking sideways, she could see herself in the mirrors again. Her own blank eyes looked back and she could just catch sight of his furious twisted face. How long this time? she thought, and turned away.

The fact that she moved at all forced him to greater efforts. She could hear him raving. Then suddenly the regularity of it stopped. He was making a strange, uncontrolled gurgling noise and seemed to be sliding down her back. In fact, his sudden uncontrolled weight bearing down alarmed her more than his blows. She felt as if she was about to be crushed and suffocated by the huge lard-like mass of his gross torso.

Then his body suddenly tipped away from her and she rolled around, flexing her shoulders at the unexpected freedom. Testing her unused limbs, she crawled awkwardly out from under his huge stomach, and tentatively swung her shaking legs around on the bed. Tony was doubled over behind her. His penis had shrunk to a silly, crumpled little bud and for a moment that was all she looked at. As she watched he fell slowly and heavily to the floor and clutched at his chest.

She heard him say, 'Oh God.' Then he seemed unable to speak, crawling on one arm back towards her on the bed, the other arm clutching the dressing-gown against his chest. He was trying to say something to her, nodding his big head in the direction of the phone.

He's having a heart attack, Sonya thought with interest. She watched him crawl in agony on the floor, gulping as if he was about to roar with pain, but unable to get the sound out of his large fleshy lips. She was fascinated to see that they already seemed to be turning a purply colour.

Then she tutted to herself. She crawled with watery limbs down the bed, then shuffled off it and half-crawled across the bedroom floor. The carpet seemed to stretch for acres. She took a moment to look back at the shuddering maroon mound on the floor. Tony's eyes caught hers beseechingly, and he groaned incoherently. His wife looked back blankly. Then she waddled crablike, out on to the landing, and shut the door properly behind her.

At eleven o'clock that night the live-in nurse came back after a lovely evening with some friends in Guildford. She was singing softly as she let herself in, and started to walk up the large curving staircase. She stopped abruptly when she saw Sonya, immobile, sitting at the top of the stairs, wearing only the top of her baby doll pyjamas. The nurse pulled her up, not unkindly, and felt Sonya's stone cold limbs. 'Oh dear, how long have you been here? Has no-one seen you? You're frozen! This isn't very good, dear. What on earth's the matter? We'd better get you into bed.' Clumsily, thanks to a few glasses of Riesling, and encumbered by the weight of Sonya on her arm, she pushed open the bedroom door. Then she saw what was inside, and to Sonya's surprise, the nurse began to scream hysterically.

Kate did not leave for Edinburgh until Sunday morning, and she drove herself to Heathrow. John had been preoccupied with St Mark's that morning, but he had kissed her and wished her good luck with the speech. Now the time had come, Kate dreaded the idea of publicly sparring with Derek Boulder.

It was a beautiful day and she had a window seat on the plane, so she could see Britain laid out like a relief map beneath her. It looked so much emptier than she had realised, with rolling fells and the occasional bright mirror of water. It reminded her of when she and John had met at Northern TV, and for the first time in a few weeks she thought about how far their relationship had come. Since the mumps disclosure, things had changed. Of course there had been bad days and good days, but overall, Kate no longer believed that she was lucky to have John, but was slowly beginning to see that they were lucky to have each other.

Looking back, she felt as if, in the past, she had thought she needed to be on her best behaviour with him. This had led to times of compatible bliss, but also to times when her unspoken frustrations had boiled over. But since their last discussion, life had become somehow both more everyday, and easier. We're like a real couple now, she thought happily, we're through the learner stage. Then she sat watching the Pennines unfold like crumpled brown paper under the plane.

Her nervousness about the panel discussion increased on the taxi journey through Edinburgh, but Felix greeted her with his usual bonhomie in the hotel foyer and ushered her to the restaurant where Derek was already holding court over a pre-panel lunch. Despite her nerves at such a prestigious event, Kate warmed to her theme and was beginning to almost look forward to tackling him in front of an audience, when a bellboy appeared with a note. Derek looked at it in genuine surprise, and hurriedly left them.

'I wonder what that was about?' murmured Felix.

Through the restaurant door, Kate saw Derek in agitated conversation with a gesticulating Jeremy Woodley. Her voice petered out, and the rest of the group followed her eyeline. The two men were in fraught conversation, until they became aware they could be seen. Then Woodley laid what could only be seen as a warning hand on Boulder's arm, and they stopped. Boulder walked purposefully back to the table, and stood looking down at them from his great height without speaking.

'What's the problem, Derek?' Felix asked.

'Something really rather tragic. I don't know if anyone here knew him well, but apparently Antony Chester-Lang is dead.'

'What?' Kate gasped. 'How did it happen?'

'Heart attack last night, Jeremy tells me. Chester-Lang's poor wife is a little bit out of it, to say the least, so she was too traumatised to call an ambulance. The poor chap seems to have died at home, in terrible circumstances.'

From then on Kate knew she was talking on autopilot, even when she took her seat on the dais in front of an audience of over two hundred TV professionals. Her brain was trying to claw back time to think through the implications of Tony Chester-Lang's death. It would surely mean the end of his channel, she thought with a guilty rush of relief. The debate lurched and bumped through its starting speeches but as it grew more heated, Derek Boulder seemed to have lost his nerve. He conceded several points to her, and the fact that she knew she was right did not mean that she enjoyed seeing him give in without a fight. Neither did the audience. Felix, in the chair, was clearly cross that the discussion had gone soft. Boulder's speech just tailed off. When Kate rounded on him with a further attack it had all the satisfaction of punching a cuddly toy.

She cast her eyes over the people assembled to listen. Most now looked glazed, though some had an attitude of interest, whether genuine or practised she didn't know. It was tempting just to fix on one friendly face, but she made herself look from side to side, her eyes like searchlights roving through the audience to try and assess what the mood really was.

Halfway down the aisle, at one side, she saw someone who looked familiar. For a moment she couldn't quite place him. She heard her own voice faltering in the middle of quite a complex point about the proportion of production to repeats. Fortunately the woman from the Discovery Channel weighed in to reinforce her point, and Kate was able to look again. The man was concentrating hard, and he scribbled a note on a small jotter on his knee. Placing him seemed of pre-eminent importance. Then the familiar features of his face clicked into place, and another face slid over his, like one exposure of a camera against another.

But it was ridiculous. While Derek droned on making some long-winded point about the right of man to watch subsidised sports, Kate nudged the woman from Discovery and said, 'See that chap four rows back, with the wiry black hair? The one who's taking notes? Who's he?'

'Oh, that's whatsisname. Big independent producer. Makes a lot of stuff for Channels Four and Five . . .'

'Are you sure?'

'Certainly am. I can't afford him. Works out of Teddington, since Pearson sold up.'

Kate sat back, baffled. It was only when the muffled noise of a mobile phone ringing was heard coming from somewhere on the platform that she came back to earth. For a moment she looked as startled as everyone else until she realised that the ring was actually pealing from under her own chair.

'Goodness, a ringing handbag!' Felix attempted to joke. 'You'd better answer it, Kate.'

Kate grabbed her bag and left the dais to go to one side. She knew half the audience was still watching her and with a terrible attempt to be both brisk and courteous she said, 'Yes' into the phone, a look of fury on her face.

'Kate?' It was Polly's voice. 'I know no-one is supposed to ring you, but . . .'

'Absolutely. It was a complete oversight on my part to leave the phone switched on.'

'Thank God you did. Kate, you've got to come back, now.'

'What?'

'Kate, please. I came into the office after all this afternoon, and it's completely vandalised again. But that isn't all.'

'Oh, no.' Kate felt the hall spinning. She had to keep calm, with at least fifty pairs of eyes on her, and a distraught Polly at the end of the phone. 'OK, Polly, I'll leave the debate now. I'll call you again in five minutes.'

Trying to act like an unshakeable executive, Kate mounted the platform and, ignoring protocol, made her excuses to a furious Felix. As she raced down the aisle, half aware of the astonished faces on either side, she could hear Felix saying, 'Well, I'm so sorry everyone, but Kate Wilkinson has been called away, quite literally. Now, let's move on . . .'

Outside, with shaking hands, Kate called Polly at the office again but there was no reply. It took her ten minutes of pure frustration to catch a cab, then she tried again. This time, Polly answered. Her voice was trembling.

'Polly, this is Kate. Tell me clearly what's happened. And where are the girls?'

'They're not here, Kate. I can't find anyone. I called Jenny first, and there's no reply from her flat. The office is in a state. It's the tapes, Kate. They're all over the place.'

'Has someone broken in? Are the girls safe?'

'I just don't know. All I know is they aren't here.'

'Polly, you should call Matthew Lavelle out. I'll be there in two-and-a-half hours, which isn't much use to you.' Kate was trying desperately to think what else she could do to help.

'Polly,' she said suddenly, cutting across the other woman's nervy chatter. 'Call John too. You shouldn't be there on your own. And try Jenny again. Even with her ankle, she should be able to get down there in an emergency.'

The phone was popping now, and Polly's voice was fading in and out. Kate heard her say, in a frantic version of her usual stream of consciousness, 'I had this awful feeling something would go wrong, so I got the neighbours to ferry the children around. I really wanted to go into the office because I was desperately worried after last night . . .'

'After last night? Why?' Jenny hadn't confided her suspicions about her fall to anyone else. Perhaps Polly had seen something? Her friend's thin voice, wavering through the atmosphere, rose and fell indistinctly, so Kate could only make out half of what she was saying. But it confirmed her fears.

' . . . there have been times when I felt quite frightened. And then last night I saw her arm . . .' Polly's voice died away, and the cellphone suddenly packed in.

So Polly had seen something? Could it have been an arm extended, pushing Jenny in the small of the back? Kate leapt out of the taxi at Edinburgh airport, and ran to the Shuttle desk. She pushed past two waiting businessmen and demanded a seat on the next plane to Heathrow. The attendant looked her up and down, and remarked that if she hurried through, there was space on the three-fifteen, which was running late.

Twenty minutes later, Kate was airborne again, and on her way home.

CHAPTER FIFTEEN

On the plane, there was a phone service and Kate used it to call John. There was no reply, merely the click and drone of the new answer machine he had installed. She left him a message which she knew was garbled. 'John, it's me. I'm on my way home. Someone's broken into the Warehouse again. If you get a chance this afternoon, can you get over there?'

Kate was beginning to get the tell-tale trembling in her legs and dry fluffy mouth which meant she was panicking. She had visions of Jason coming back on the scene, madder than ever. She called Polly again, and there was no reply, which added to her fears.

This time she was in an aisle seat, and she was standing ready to leave before the seat-belt sign was switched off, getting a stern look from the cabin staff. But Kate pushed past the families and businessmen to be one of the first people to run up the walkway, along the corridor and out into the Arrivals hall.

The queue for taxis seemed endless, but the traffic was reasonably light, and in the twenty five minutes it took to get to Brentford, Kate tried phoning the office, Jenny's flat, and John's house, all with no luck. The cab dropped her in the Warehouse car park. For a moment the stillness baffled her. She had imagined police cars, and Matthew Lavelle and his boss, arms akimbo in the yard, plus a general commotion. But there was nothing.

Kate ran over to the reception doors, which slid open in response to her security card. For a second, inside the foyer, Kate wondered if she had imagined the whole thing. There was an air of Sunday torpor, and no sign of an intrusion. But the impression was fleeting, and she was bounding up the stairs before she really thought about it. She crashed through the doors into the Food and Health offices, and a silent scene of destruction met her. Tapes and boxes were strewn everywhere. A computer had been flung on its side. Papers and stationery littered the floor, and Kate felt her feet crunch on spilt staples. But that was the only sound, and it was the dead quiet which was most alarming.

'Polly!' she shouted, to break the silence. She raced through, into the offices beyond. There in her own little section, sat Jenny. 'Where's everyone?' Kate shouted. 'What's caused all this mess?'

'Kate listen . . .'

'What do you mean, listen? Where are the others? We need to get the police.'

'That was what I thought to start with. But hold on. You need to look at this.'

'Jenny, I don't understand . . .'

'Neither did I till I thought about it. Listen, Kate, I reckon there's a link between Chloe and that creepy cow who was squatting in the loft. I've suspected Chloe for a while. I think she pushed me last night. I know I felt someone's arm in my back. I felt better this afternoon, but this morning I just lay there and thought about that ghost girl. And when I got here, half an hour ago, I went straight over to the admin block and up to the cupboard next to Matt's office. It wasn't locked. I got the bag of stuff out.' Jenny pushed at a pile of papers spilling from a black bin-bag at her foot. 'Look, it's the rest of the garbage they found. Not only was there the contract, but there was this . . .' She poked at a couple of food bags, one still holding a rock solid croissant. 'And this, Kate.' With her toe, Jenny dislodged a couple of large grey tape boxes.

'Oh God, the original logos!'

'Yep. And at the bottom of the bin-liner there was even more crap that Matt and Michelle never got to. Half of my files are in there too. So when I got over here, I was almost expecting something. I think Chloe did this, Kate. In fact, I think she and the ghost girl must be into drugs together. It would explain why they've been trying to destabilise us. Perhaps Chester-Lang put them up to it, and they use the money for dope. And what about this?'

Gingerly, Jenny reached into the plastic bag and took out another clear refuse bag. In it were the remains of a smashed mug, the handle poking up through the plastic. It was particularly pathetic.

'Kate, it's the companion mug to Laurence Smith's. Look, it's a pig, in knickers.' Kate looked again at the silly, cheery picture on the side of the mug.

'So where has Debbie gone? And what does Polly think?'

'What do you mean? Polly's not here today.'

'Yes, she is. Or she was. Haven't you seen her?'

'No. I've been here an hour . . .'

'Christ, where is she? I thought maybe you'd let her go home! She called me in Edinburgh a couple of hours ago, and asked me to come back. That's why I'm here.'

'Oh, my God! She wouldn't have just gone home without seeing anyone, would she?'

'So where is she?'

'How the hell would I know?'

'Oh God, Jenny, there's something very nasty happening here.'

Jenny closed her eyes. It seemed that for some reason, the scene of sexual passion between her and Nick Malcolm by the canal was playing through her mind. She shook her head fiercely, but the scene wouldn't go away. In her mind, she slunk away shamefully from the bridge, pulling her skirt down, into the wind. And there, ahead of her, was the ghost girl, shimmying through the rain, and suddenly disappearing ahead of her into the bank of the canal.

Jenny shouted. 'It's that girl. She's still here! I know she is. I reckon she's got another squat.' Jenny leapt up on her damaged foot and sat down again, swearing.

'What? What do you mean, Jenny?'

'*I reckon she's got another squat.* On the canal bank. She's got a second nest, up in those impenetrable bushes. Perhaps she did trash the office, Kate, and the others have gone to sort her out . . . Kate? Kate!'

Kate was looking down at the disgusting pile of rubbish, the cracked fragments of mug and the strewn papers. All of a sudden, a thousand little images rejigged in her mind like the discarded frames from a film on the cutting room floor, all meant to lead to one scene, but capable in a different edit of adding up to a totally different picture.

'Jenny, you know about eating disorders, don't you?'

'Well, not as much as Polly.'

'But often it's linked to much worse psychiatric problems, isn't it?'

'Yes, I suppose so.'

Kate re-edited the discarded shots in her mind, and a new and frightening story grew like a horror film out of ordinary, normal vignettes.

'Jenny, I think Polly worked it out. How could I have been so bloody stupid? I think you're right about another squat. Chloe and the ghost girl aren't in league. Can't you see? It must be her!'

Kate was already running out of the office, forgetting Jenny's injured ankle. Jenny was hobbling behind her shouting, 'Who, Kate?'

Kate hurtled down the stairs, and out through the glass doors into the slimy buttery warmth of the hottest day of the year. As she ran, she glimpsed Matt Lavelle's sports car drawing into the car park. Whether he was there because he couldn't stay away from work, or because he had finally listened to a desperate recorded message from Polly, she neither knew nor cared.

Kate began to run up the towpath, her feet hitting the dry ground so hard her calves hurt and her chest tightened. The sound of her own shoes reminded her of that ghastly shuffling, all those months ago, when she had first seen the ghost girl. If she had only investigated properly then, instead of being so wrapped up in her own body . . . She felt now as if she had been working with people and not really looking at them. Polly had been there just a few weeks, and she had seen the truth, while Kate, who had set herself up as the great manager, had been unable even to see the obvious. Kate knew she was shouting now herself.

'Polly! Polly, it's all right. I'm coming!' Oh God, she thought, if anything had happened to Polly . . .

'Polly!' Kate was screaming into the bushes. 'Polly!' Then a little further up the bank, Kate saw it. It had been brilliantly constructed. What looked like a mound of old cardboard boxes, blown between the undergrowth and the bridge, moved slightly despite the fact it was the hottest, most windless day of the year.

'I'm coming!' Kate screamed, and began to beat her way through the bristly, thorny, dust-filled spikes of the fierce little bushes. She felt the thorns sticking into her skirt and the scratches on her legs and arms but she kept going, through vicious urban brambles which had grown like barbed wire, undisturbed for decades. Crazily, salty sweat dripping in her eyes, she clawed her way through and with her bleeding hands began to pull at the dry but squidgy, smelly cardboard. And then suddenly it gave. Kate had a last mad thought of Sleeping Beauty in the brambles, as the final piece of corrugated cardboard fell away down the bank, and like exposed mice in a hole, she saw the stiff, filthy faces. A cloud of dust from the dry earth underneath was raised and billowed around them, scouring their eyes and mouths.

Then the ghost girl rose up in front of her like a screeching witch, her long scraggly hair pouring over her face, which was ghastly white, caked with panstick make-up, and a blood red flower of lipstick blossoming across it. The eyes, blackened with mascara, held Kate's for half a second before, with a scream, she turned and started to pull and claw herself out of the burrow, and up the brickwork along the bridge.

It was a Victorian cast-iron railway bridge, with great bolted plates of metal holding the tracks in place. Because of the construction there was a clear ledge along it, and the girl, in her fouled flowing peach dress, one of the Chester-Lang specials, began to clamber along until she was spreadeagled above the canal. But Kate had fallen back, and Polly, her arms still tied with some fragments of thin, sharp lace, was staggering out of the hole, half crying. As Polly moved, she kicked before her the sharp, pointed iron file which, Kate knew, looking through eyes stinging and blinded by the dust, had been used to smash the water tanks.

Jenny had come stumbling along behind her.

'Stop them,' Kate screamed down to her. But it was too late. When Kate looked up there were two female figures on the ledge. The second was balanced with one arm locked round the bottom of the ironwork, her other arm stretched out in an agony of supplication to the ghost girl on the knife edge ahead of her.

The ghost girl looked back, directly at Kate. And the ghastly white face started to smile.

Kate was transfixed by the face. It was a round, moonlike face, but why had she never noticed how *bonily* round it was, a plain-Jane face with little piggy eyes, but with stretched skin and no spare flesh? It was the same face as the man in the audience at the debate that day, the man who'd been walking through Teddington with his daughter. And she remembered the optic in the pub, and the same arm reaching up . . .

Kate screamed, 'For Christ's sake, Debbie, please!' and as if on cue, the ghost girl leapt out in a graceful arc, and plummeted into the green slime of the canal. And before they could even turn to take this in, the other body followed it, as Chloe threw herself in the stinking water after her friend.

In the crazed splashing that followed Kate realised that both Matthew Lavelle and Jenny had also plunged in. There was a huge, frenzied mess going on in the middle of the canal, till Jenny pulled back, her head covered in oily slime, and trod water. Matt submerged twice, then forced himself up, his huge shoulders pumping through the water, and in the middle of this, a knot of limbs tangled as Chloe and Debbie fought. Then in all the splashing confusion there was suddenly quiet. The water sealed over, and the two girls were gone. Kate was aware that Polly was next to her, shouting, and that the other noise she could hear was her own screams. Then Matt reared, shaking his head like a dog, breathing huge gulps of air, and duck-dived down, followed by Jenny.

A few seconds later he came up holding Chloe, and Jenny, gasping and crying out, followed him, holding what looked like a bundle of wet peach cloth. Matt held one girl up, and with his other huge arm he pulled on the bundle Jenny was supporting until Debbie's deadly face appeared, and it became clear he was holding the two girls up. Jenny swam behind him as he laboured to the bank. A crowd of four or five had already gathered, and several people were there to haul all four of them on to the side. Debbie was unconscious, but Chloe lay and groaned on the bank. One of the bystanders was already trying the kiss of life on them and Debbie suddenly hit out with her leg, alive, and then lay, concussed but breathing.

Kate found she was clinging to Polly. 'An ambulance?'

'A chap at the back with a cellphone has called for one.'

'Thank God.'

Jenny and Matt sat side by side on the bank, breathing in huge gasps, unable to speak. Behind them Kate glimpsed someone else.

'John!'

There was a woman with John whom Kate barely recognised. She was smartly dressed, in her fifties, with well-groomed dark hair and wearing a neat suit. The cracked doll from the funeral had been miraculously repaired. Joyce Smith looked as if she might survive, driven to live by a need to find out what had really happened to her son. Polly was already at her side.

'Joyce,' Polly was saying quietly. 'I'm glad you came. I wasn't sure when I rang you. It was only a hunch, but I just thought . . .'

The woman looked at her grimly. 'Thanks. If it's true, it will help put my mind at rest.'

'You don't mind being here?'

'I'm beyond that sort of pain. And anyway, I wanted to come.'

Then like everyone else, her eyes turned to the drama on the bank, where the ambulance crew were pulling the unconscious Debbie on to the stretcher.

Joyce Smith started forward. 'Yes,' she said. 'My God.'

Polly's arm went out to stop her, and Kate watched in horror as the woman raised her arm to point, her face white and her fingers shaking.

'That's her,' she said hoarsely.

'Debbie? Yes, the ghost girl,' said Kate, still mesmerised.

'No, that's *her*,' Laurence's mother shouted out. 'Now will everyone believe me? The girl on the stretcher, the one in pink. That's her . . . my son's girlfriend.'

While John took Joyce Smith home to his house with a promise that she could wait there for the other women, Polly and Kate went in Polly's car to the hospital. They waited in the Sunday hush of the casualty department, along with a cricket accident and a drunk, the sunlight green through the upper windows and the smell of antiseptic cleaner and septic humanity deadening their reactions. Polly was astonishingly calm, as if being bound and threatened was to be expected in the crazed half-world of mental illness.

'I can't believe it,' Kate said quietly.

'I think you can, Kate, if you put it together.' Polly shook her head. 'I'm the one who should have realised earlier, with all my so-called experience. But it was only last night, when she reached up to put some cassettes on the shelf, and I saw that brutally thin arm, that I put two and two together. Yet it was so obvious. Whatever the weather she wore those grey or black droopy clothes, and chiffon scarves up to the neck. It's often the jawline which gives it away, but in Debbie's case she had such a wide face she looked big even though she was so thin. But of course, her eating disorder must have been controlled. There was far more wrong with Debbie than anorexia. I tell you, Kate, she makes Richard look like a walking miracle!'

'But why didn't we spot it?'

'Because she was crafty. We thought we saw her eat, but we didn't. Oh yes, there were always crumbs, and bits of food around. But the bulk of it must have been stored up in the nests she seemed to build for herself. It's classic disturbed behaviour.'

'Like planting the shards of Laurence's mug. Perhaps she meant to cut herself with them, but Jenny got there first,' Kate murmured.

'Yes. I heard about that from Chloe. But when I saw her arms, I was ninety per cent sure.'

'I saw her arm too, that day at the pub when we met for lunch. But I was so obsessed with myself . . .'

'Don't blame yourself, Kate. Debbie was very, very clever.'

'Did Chloe know, d'you think?'

'I'm sure she suspected. But in a way, I think she almost tried to cover up for her. There was a sort of camaraderie between them, though I think that was more Chloe's kindness than anything. And bravery too.'

'God, yes. She's quite something, isn't she?'

'Yes, she is. Chloe Carr is going to go a long way, Kate. But you know, that's thanks to you.'

Kate felt the tears and cried softly into her torn and dirty blouse until she was called behind the screen for her cuts to be treated. As the antiseptic stung her scratches she had a sudden sense that this slight burning pain went nowhere near soothing or cleansing her deeper, dirtier wounds. I've been a fool, she thought bitterly.

'Kate,' Polly said softly, 'don't be too upset. You're a good boss. Really.'

'Getting in a state like this?'

'Yes! Can't you see? That's why!'

*

It transpired that Joyce Smith had met Debbie once, in her role as glamour girl, just two days before Laurence's death. Laurence had been thrilled to introduce her to his mum, but his romantic link with her seemed to have gone no further than the gift of the silly mug, which Debbie had hoarded in her nest. When Joyce and Debbie met, the girl's only conversation had been to ask whether Joyce Smith could store some boxes for her.

Joyce had thought Debbie odd. And she had not liked the effect she had on poor moonstruck Laurence, who was both thrilled to be with her, but also in awe of her. Joyce had not even been told her name, and Debbie had been treated as visiting royalty. Joyce had hoped the attachment went both ways and that the girl Laurence had brought home would be distraught at his death.

'The night he died, he didn't tell me where he was going, but he seemed really worried. I think he knew what was going on by then, and didn't like it, and went to meet her.'

'I wonder why Debbie let Laurence see her in her true light?' Kate mused.

'Power again,' Jenny said quietly, still nursing her foot. 'Laurence would have been a perfect foil for the Chester-Langs. Matthew has to take some of the responsibility for that. He earmarked Laurence as an ideal runner for the other channel – quiet, conventional, ambitious. Debbie must have wanted him on board, too. So she tried to impress him. But it didn't work, because unlike some people, Laurence did have a sense of decency.'

'You mean, unlike Matt? But Jenny, think of what he did this afternoon!'

'Yeah. But think of the other things he did, too.'

'But would you consider going out with him again Jenny?'

'I don't know, Kate. I really don't know.'

A few days later, Chloe Carr discharged herself from hospital and insisted on coming back to work. In the comforting formality of the office, Kate asked, 'How much did you know, Chloe?'

'I knew she was weird, but I never realised how weird. Or how thin! But we all knew she was really determined. As soon as Matt Lavelle started secret recruiting she said she'd bypass him because he was no-one, and that she'd got family contacts, and would go straight to the top. I know now that she phoned Mr Chester-Lang, on her bloody cellphone. You never knew she had one, did you, Kate? She used to show off about it to the rest of us all the time.' So it was Debbie who rang the office on her untraceable mobile, with the strange asexual voice and the horrible giggle. 'I didn't work it out for ages, but she was the mad caller, Kate. You can dial by pressing one button, which explains why she picked Jenny's number time and again, and you can be so quick you can almost phone while you're walking from one room to the other, then ring off before anyone realises! Anyway I think she went to see Mr Chester-Lang, as well as phone him. She phoned him all the time. Though I don't know why he took a fancy to her.'

Kate suspected, but raised her eyebrow and said nothing.

Chloe went on, 'Probably Debbie just blagged her way in. She went on and on about it, when we were in that foul burrow of hers. She said Mr Chester-Lang was the only person who really believed in her. She'd convinced him that with her access to everything at the Warehouse, and her secretarial skills, she could run the mail order side of his business.'

'And when she heard he was dead . . .'

'Curtains to the big career!'

'But why did she work so hard on wrecking things for us? And in such a spasmodic way?'

'She needed to hedge her bets. You see, she wanted to be a producer like her dad, and that's what her plan was in Food and Health. But she was soon shown up. Remember the day you shouted at me about logging? Well, the next day you put her on to it and she was even slower, wasn't she! She couldn't hack it, Kate. That was why she needed the Chester-Lang job because it was about organising systems, not creating something. Anyway, it suited him to have her sabotage us.'

'But why did she pick on Polly?'

'She had it in for Jenny first. She tried to make trouble between me and Jenny too, like putting cigarette ash in my lovely ashtray so Jenny would think I'd been smoking. But it was worse with Polly. Polly had started to guess, I think. On Sunday when I came into the office, Debbie was already trashing it. I tried to stop her but she was crazy. Then she took me back up to the loft. She always wore one of those silky things under the big baggy jumpers, and she could look quite sexy in that stuff, though she was always a bit whiffy, you know.'

'I didn't realise. I suppose I never got that close to her. In any sense.'

'Well, you were the boss. Why should you?'

Kate shuddered with guilt but said nothing. Chloe went on. 'We heard Polly come in unexpectedly and we waited, but Polly wouldn't go away. So Debbie went down to get her.' Chloe shook now, with the memory. 'She grabbed Polly and tied her wrists, and said she was taking her to see her own office as she called it. So I went with them. I couldn't leave Polly. And, God, it was vile. Debbie'd made another nest in the bushes, stuffed with garbage. It was then I realised how mental she was! But the pressure on her was huge, Kate. After all her father was . . .'

'That TV producer Jenny and I saw that day, in Teddington . . .'

'Correct. She tried to pretend it was someone else, but she'd already shown off to me about her connections. Pathetic really.'

'Yet she tried to blame you for so many things, Chloe. And what about the drugs she put in your drink that night?'

Chloe put her head on one side to think. She looked much younger, but also wiser, without her make-up, in the hard sunlight.

'Come on, Chloe.' Kate insisted. 'You were never that fond of her. And you really did suspect her, didn't you? That was what you were trying to tell me that Sunday morning . . .'

'Yep. But I couldn't do it, when it came to it. Drop her in it, I mean. She was my first real colleague. We'd both been through hell to get proper paid work in TV. It meant everything to both of us. In a way, I could understand her. You see . . .'

'Yes?'

'It really was a job to die for, Kate.'

In the next few days Kate made a decision that the best thing for all of them would still be to get the channel launched as fast as possible. When she pushed the button in the transmission suite on day one, only a week later than planned, she knew that she had made the right decision.

Kate had invited Joyce Smith to see the channel launch. She knew it was an odd thing to do, but she felt compelled to do it, and Joyce was genuinely appreciative. Kate was almost sure Debbie and Laurence had argued on the canal bank, and that he had backed off from her and missed his footing. Kate thought back to what Mr Chandip had said, that Sunday morning when she had been so desperate to get away from him. 'Your young people. The row . . .' She had thought he was making a generic point about the West. But perhaps he had meant *your* young people . . . her employees at the Warehouse. And perhaps the row was a specific argument between two of them.

Debbie was not from Manchester at all, but was the youngest child of a successful south London family. John had taken Kate and Polly to see her parents in their big house in Putney the following weekend. Agonised, her mother had said, 'What did we do wrong?' just as Polly had done. The pain and the silence had ached. You probably did nothing wrong at all, Kate had thought, and it gave her some comfort when she contemplated her own childless future.

At home, one Saturday a few weeks later, as the first autumn clouds gathered and a few stray leaves fell, she and John lay on the bed together. It had been a while since they had made love. And there had been so much to say about other people for the last few weeks, they had said a great deal less about themselves.

'Kate, there's something I want to tell you.'

'Mmm?'

'I went to the doctor's last week.'

'Yes?'

Kate sat up on the bed and crossed her legs, looking back at him quizzically. 'What for?'

'I gave them a sperm sample.'

'What? Without my help? That's almost infidelity.'

He laughed with her, but noticed her fingers were pleating the bedspread.

'And?' she said.

'You were right. There's no possibility of me ever fathering a child.'

She sat and looked at him. So now they knew for certain. She hadn't asked John to check out her suspicions. But because he had, she felt a conflicting mixture of emotions. She realised to her surprise, that relief was one of them.

'And how do you feel, John?'

'As a matter of fact, bloody awful. I didn't think it would matter to me, except that I was letting you down. But actually, and this is ridiculous at my age, I feel a bit . . . incomplete.'

'John!' Kate could sense his tension. Yet it was so much easier to love someone who suffered too. For a while they lay there.

'So there's no need for us to get married!' he suddenly said. 'We shouldn't, just because it would suit me.'

Kate wriggled into the crook of his arm.

'Well, maybe we will. Sometime, when everything's right for both of us. To suit ourselves.'

'That would be good, Kate.'

'Mmmm. Of course, before then, I need to find out if you really *are* incomplete. But I don't think so.' She rolled her eyes at him as her hand went down his body. He laughed as he turned towards her.

'I don't want a baby,' she whispered. 'I want you.'

'Will right now do?'

'Oh, yes, yes please.'

Afterwards, she said, 'Things feel better, now. Not just with you, though that's the main thing. But at work too. Although . . .' she stopped.

'What?'

'I've just remembered. It may be a Saturday but Joan Thompson invited Jenny out to lunch today. I wonder why?'

Jenny was wondering the same thing, as she sat in the American Bar of the Savoy, waiting for Joan and feeling overawed. But she had other things on her mind too. The night before Matt Lavelle had asked her to join him at The Narrowboat.

'Listen, Jenny,' he had said. 'I realise now how bloody stupid I was. But I'm not a bad bloke. Just a thoughtless one.'

'But you took Chester-Lang's money, Matt. And you knew what he was up to.'

'But he told me the ITC approved! And anyway, it was Jason who caused all the trouble over the money.'

'Oh, yes. Jason. What happened to him?'

'Oh, he buggered off weeks before. He got more cash out of Chester-Lang, and off he went. He and Debbie had palled up together, I realise. I guess he was the real boyfriend. Talking of which . . . there's something I want to ask you.'

'What?'

'Would you consider giving it a go again?'

She remembered his kindness, the little things he had done which had made her so fond of him before. And his bravery on the canal bank.

'God, Matt, I . . . well, let me get through the weekend, and think. Can I phone you on Monday?'

'Great, Jenny. I'll look forward to it. Now, would you like another red wine? I'm having a pint of Guinness.'

She had laughed. And she had been seriously tempted, not just by the claret. But now she was into something much headier.

'Hello, Jenny,' Joan Thompson said in her usual brisk fashion. 'Don't get up. I'll have a dry sherry,' she said briskly to the waiter, waving him away. And after minimal niceties, Joan launched into what she had come to say.

'Jenny, we have a proposition for you. We're starting up another channel after Christmas. It's an arts and entertainment diary. It has huge sponsorship potential. I'd like to talk to you about a senior programming role.'

'Me?'

'Yes, you.'

'But Joan, what about Food and Heath? It's only just on the air.'

'Exactly! Quite right! And very good it is too. But within a year you'd be fed up with being Kate's sidekick. This new channel is a very complex proposition.'

'Well yes, it sounds fascinating. But what about Kate?'

'She knows better than anyone that cable is fast growing and you have to grab chances. And I have to grab talent.'

'But we've worked so well together . . .'

'Kate also knows that in management the first thing you learn is that people are there to work for you, not love you, and the second thing is that people move on. She could lose you to something far less compatible in a year or two. You mustn't worry about Kate.'

'But what sort of role would I have?'

'You'll be number two to the Managing Director, but in a much bigger structure. I was very impressed with what you did on Food and Health, but the real impetus came from the man we've appointed as MD. He speaks very highly of you and has expressed a desire to work with you again. Ah, here he is.'

Jenny lifted up her eyes from her glass. Coming through the arch was Nick Malcolm.

In the refuge of the ladies' loo two minutes later, Jenny looked at her own stretched face in the mirror. There was no doubt that at the sight of Nick, the old electric shock had gone through her. And it was great to imagine really working alongside him again, actually seeing a whole project through.

But where would that leave Matt? He really wasn't such a bad bloke; he had saved two lives, after all. And he seemed to need her.

Oh God, Jenny thought, what should I do? Does nothing ever have a proper ending? She looked at her new, plumper face in the mirror, and went out to make her decision.

At the same time John and Kate went for a long walk in the late afternoon, early autumn sunshine. For the first time in weeks, Kate found herself on the canal bank. Like everyone else, she did not want to walk on the dark, sinister Warehouse side with its feeling of a dank Victorian past. Even now, she felt the building itself had been part of the insidious suspicion and fear which had slowly poisoned the office. She and John stopped to buy a paper at Mr Chandip's, intending to stroll down the path opposite Kate's office.

As she exchanged her usual pleasantries with Mr Chandip, Kate heard a booming noise outside.

'What's that?' she asked the newsagent.

'Oh, it's very good, very good, about time too. They are demolishing the building behind us. It's a warehouse like yours was, but never done up. It will make such a difference now.'

'I suppose it will,' Kate said thoughtfully. John was waiting for her outside the shop.

'Look,' he said.

As the dirty two-storey building behind them collapsed in a cracking sound of collapsing masonry and bouncing plaster, the afternoon sun, for the first time in a century, was able to reach the whole of the north side of the Warehouse. And as Kate watched, the dark shadows where the ghost girl had nestled were flooded with sun, and dispelled forever.